The Fifth Horseman

by Freida Kilmari

Content Guidance

Violence: This book contains scenes of graphic violence and deals with this both physically and emotionally.

Profanity: This book contains excess profanity from all characters.

Sexual Situations: This book contains explicit sex, including MM, FF, and MMF scenarios.

Dark Themes: This book deals with flashbacks, nightmares, and other PTSD symptoms that some may find uncomfortable. It also tackles gender identity issues.

*To all the oddballs, misfits, and not-fitting-iners.
This one's for you.*

PROLOGUE

In the year 2089, the Shifter, Fae, and Vampire communities banded together to expose themselves to the outside world, bringing about a new era of unstable human-supernatural alliance.

Now, after a hundred years of having no control over the supernatural community, of tentative peace and suffered silence, humans are fighting back, to rid the world of magic, and to bring back the old world of mortality.

With the world on the brink of magical war, the Four Horsemen of the Apocalypse are struggling to keep the balance they've maintained over the last two millennia. But with four supernatural communities tearing each other apart, and with the humans gearing up for a war against magic, they're going to need more than their usual team to handle this mess. They're going to need the Fifth Horseman of the Apocalypse: the Horseman of Magic.

Chapter One

Gray light shatters my blurry vision, but all I can see are shapes as voices grate my eardrums. I can't make out any particular words, but a lilting sound flows its way toward me, a singing voice so beautiful in its cadence, I'm having a hard time focusing on anything else. Though there are other voices in the room, I can't stop my curiosity wandering around that lilt.

Where am I?

Who am I?

What's going on?

"Her eyes are opening . . ."

"She's practically awake, but she's still really weak."

"We're going to continue using this language, then?"

"It's only polite."

A thud startles my eyes open the final few centimeters, and four faces I haven't seen before meet my bewildered gaze. But now that I think about it, whose faces have I seen before? My memory . . . It's all a giant blur. And the harder I try to clear the picture, the blurrier it gets. I only remember a coppery smell, the feeling of drowning, and an ache in my feet.

Why?

"Miss, please don't be frightened." A woman's face vomes into view, framed by beautifully blond hair—impossibly blond, actually, like the color of the sun chose her head out of billions of others to shine its radiance—that seems to trail all the way to the floor in two long braids. Save for the few strands of hair straying around her face, everything is perfectly in place, from the dimple on her left cheek to the deep green of her eyes and the feather earring hanging from her left ear.

"W-Who are . . . you?" My voice sounds so strange, as though it belongs to someone else and I'm stuck in a stranger's body.

"Name's Con, short for Connie." She grabs the pillow and maneuvers it into a more comfortable position. "Reckon you can sit up, hon?"

I nod, not wanting to hear my strange voice again.

She gently grips my elbow and half lifts me into a sitting position.

The other three faces—all male—sit patiently in the room, which I now recognize as some sort of bedroom, though it's like none I've ever seen before. The light filtering through the wall of crystalline window on my right is patchy from the forest dwelling just outside, while the room itself is covered in plush rugs and lounge chairs in all sorts of bright colors—some of which I've never seen before. From turquoise greens to burnt orange-yellows, it reminds me of peace. Of calm tranquility.

"Where am I?"

One of the men steps forward. His stubble just grazes the

edges of his face, but he's an otherwise large man, towering well over six feet and carrying nothing but muscle. "You're safe."

"Where. Am. I?" The edge to my voice has a bite to it, and I can feel frustration showing on my face.

"Our home. We call it *Sheruta*. It's a realm separate from Earth."

"Okaaay." Clearly, I've gone insane. That or this is just some elaborate dream my stupid brain is concocting while I'm deep in a coma somewhere.

"No, sweet thing." Another one of the guys steps forward, and my eyes latch on to bright red swept-back hair sitting on top Asian skin, glinting in the sun. "You're not dreaming."

Did he just . . . read my mind?

"Yup." He smells like a bonfire in winter, and his hair's dirty bright red continues to flicker in the light, as though it were indeed a flame of its own.

A shiver escapes my body. That's right, I'm cold.

He looks to the muscular man from before. "Get a fire going."

I look down his slim form and chuckle at his t-shirt, which reads: YOU'RE ONLY A 10 ON THE PH SCALE BECAUSE YOU'RE BASIC.

While Muscle Man places some chopped logs from a wire basket into a fireplace at the other end of the room, the red-haired man sits by my bedside with a smile. "Name's Nine. It's nice to finally meet you, sweet thing."

I look to the only other man in the room, who sits in the shadows on the other side of my bed, as pale as death and almost translucent. "And you are . . . ?"

He steps forward, surprise etching his face as his black hair falls around his eyes in wafting waves of dark beauty that frame perfectly angular cheekbones, a chisled jaw, and a snake-bite piercing both sides of his lower lip. "You are able to see me?" As the light catches his features, that translucence turns into an opacity of ungodly beautiful skin.

Is it weird? To like a guy's skin? Probably.

I realize then that I've been staring and haven't even bothered to answer his question. "Well," I start, "yeah. You're standing right there."

A smile reaches ear to ear, his raised eyebrows settling back down, and he leans forward to touch my forehead. "My name is Dea, and I was the one who reclaimed your life, little angel."

That smile is perfect, angling his jaw in all its chiseled lines and perfectly placed shadows, but his rugged hair and piercings gives him a messy, rockstar kind of look. I didn't know they make men like him. He's so beautiful it almost hurts to look. But what's most enchanting is his eyes; they circle in a swirling galaxy, whose pinnacle of golden starlight rests in the very center, where most people's pupils sit.

Nine chuckles. "You're distracting her, bro."

I can feel the blood rush to my cheeks. Damn telepath. I look at a smiling Dea, suddenly remembering what he just said. "Y-You saved m-me? How? When? Wh—?"

"That's enough," Connie butts in. "She needs to rest." She stands and ushers everyone out of the room, a dark look in her eyes that says she means business. "C'mon. Scat!"

Everyone practically runs out of the room, but Muscle Man still tends to the fire, slowly poking it and stoking the small flames into a roaring inferno. He gets up to leave once finished, not saying a word but following everyone else nonetheless.

"Wait!"

He stops at the doorframe and turns around with a scowl on his rough features.

Wonder what a smile would look like on that perfect face?

"Your name? What's your name?"

"What does it matter?"

"I just . . ." Fuck, I don't even know. Why do I want to know his name? "Would like to know your name." I look away and try turning over, only to meet a stabbing pain that has me whimpering before I can hold my tongue.

He sighs, and I hear his heavy footfalls getting closer before he gently helps turn me onto my side and places the pillows into a better position before leaving and clicking the door shut.

What a strange man.

Chapter Two

"The path to vengeance is fraught with fear, darkness, and ice-cold despair." That saying echoes in the background of what I think is my new reality, what I think I have to suffer through for the rest of eternity.

The darkening alleyway leers against the setting sun as my head spins back and forth. I pull my hand away from the sharp pain, and it comes back bloody.

Shit. I've smashed my head on the concrete wall.

"Still think you can take me, hunter?"

The man standing in front of me wobbles on unsteady legs, his pale complexion only getting paler as the sun sets on the safety of daylight. His fangs glint in the orange glow, and if I were someone who found that kind of darkness beautiful, I would reach out and touch them.

"Yeah, I'm pretty confident." I shrug, not wanting to move my head too much. "You're just a turned Vampire. I've taken down born ones of your kind."

His face blanches. "Liar! No one can take down a highborn Vampire! They're the strongest creatures on Earth."

"A little egotistical there, aren't you?"

I love watching them freak when they realize what a mistake they've made by not running. I love the looks of horror etched on their faces before I turn my magigun on them.

And just like every other time I've taken down a turned Vampire, this one holds his hands up in surrender before I pull the trigger.

His scream makes me smile—a satisfying echo to match the beauty of his darkness.

I shove some magicuffs on him, immobilizing his Vampire strength—the only form of magic a turned Vampire has—and drag him to his feet.

"C'mon, big guy, work with me here."

He doesn't help, of course, because he's unconscious, but I hope some kind of goddess or deity takes pity on me having to drag his slumped body to my car and grants me temporary superstrength.

But alas, no such stupid prayers are answered because if there are gods or deities, I wouldn't be stuck in this shitfest of a life.

A few hours after I fell asleep—or, at least, I presume that's the case, since night has fallen by the time I wake—my stomach rumbles with a ravenous hunger as I fight off the sweat-soaked nightmare.

Shit. What was that? It felt so . . . real.

Another grumble of my stomach has me remembering reality.

Food! That's right, I haven't eaten in a while.

A knock sounds at the door before someone twists the handle.

Shit. Someone's coming in.

Fear wells for a reason I'm not too sure of. I'm in a strange place, surrounded by people I don't know, that is apparently not Earth . . .

I look around, frantic, searching for anything to use as a weapon, and only find a pair of tweezers on the nightstand. I grab them and aim toward the door as it swings open, preparing to throw if necessary.

"Whoa there, sweet thing," Nine says as he steps through the now-open door. "It's just me. Nine? Put the deadly tweezers down," he says through a chuckle.

He comes in carrying a tray of something steaming hot in a bowl, with some brown crusty stuff on a plate beside it, and a cup of something that smells like roasted heaven.

"Here." He hands me the tray once I sit up, and he cracks a smile. "No need to try to injure us, we're just trying to help." He gives me a smirk, as if my tweezers weren't even going to put a dent in this man—which they probably weren't—and I melt slightly at the sight of his smile lighting up that red hair.

"Sorry." Taking a large sniff, my belly rumbles once more, louder this time. "What is it?"

"Soup? It's just chicken soup. You're not vegetarian, are you?"

"Chicken soup . . . Right." I look at his confused face and let out a pained laugh of my own, my injuries getting in the way of me really enjoying the ridiculous moment of not knowing whether I'm vegetarian. "No, not vegetarian. I don't think."

"You don't think?" His amused smirk seems to make his hair a brighter shade of red, and it hypnotizes me for a long moment. "Shouldn't that be something you know?"

"S-S-S-Sorry," I stammer, "my memory . . . It's not remembering anything."

"Anything at all?" Concern etches across his features—genuine concern—a surprising change from his earlier smirking.

I just shake my head and put a piece of the brown crusty stuff into the soup—bread, of course it's bread—and take a bite. Taking a sip of the coffee, I exhale in relief as I remember the taste and smell of liquid life. Goddess, I need more of this amazing stuff.

What is wrong with me?

"I see." He leans forward, places a gentle hand on my forehead, and closes his eyes. He takes a deep breath and seems to concentrate, so I just continue to eat my soup while he sits there for a few minutes, continuously taking deep breaths now and then. Finally, after an awkward five minutes with his hand practically glued to my forehead, he opens his eyes. "Your memories, they've been damaged, it seems. I can't get a single read on them."

"Read? You can read my memories?"

"Yeah, along with other things. I can read your mind and look into your dreams. It's part of my gift."

"That's nuts. Cool, but nuts." I practically inhale the rest of the soup and wipe the bowl clean with the last chunk of bread as my belly rumbles a loud thanks.

The interesting room catches my eye once again. It's so colorful: The fireplace sits across from the bed and roars a gentle mix of green and orange flames, occasionally letting out a crack or pop as the dark wood splinters and burns. The rest of the room is full of turquoise-and-orange-shaded colors—a beautiful mixture of dawn and dusk. I raise my head and look over at the fancy closet to my right: sequins layer the side I can see, with white double doors and tassels hanging off the handles.

"Whose room is this?"

Nine chuckles and turns to look around. "Seems it's yours. The house is a little mysterious. It's magical, so it kind of has a mind of its own."

Mine?

Yes.

"Whoa. What was that?" I cough and splutter for a moment before catching my breath. "Did you just . . . ?"

"Speak into your mind? Yeah."

I see. Interesting. "Can the others do it?"

"No. We all have different gifts." He takes back the tray and places it on the nightstand next to a crystal lamp that seems to change color every few minutes. A hand lays gently on my left leg as he looks at me.

"So . . . err . . . What's going on? Who am I? What am I doing he—?"

He holds out a flat hand midair to stop my questions. "We'll answer your questions. Promise. But after you've recovered. You were . . . in an accident."

"Dea said he saved my life?"

Chuckling, Nine says, "Yeah, he's always had a flare for the dramatics, that one. But he's right in a backward sort of way. You'll get used to him."

The memory of Dea's smile flashes across my mind, but I push it away when I remember that Nine can probably see it.

Damn, that's gonna take some getting used to. I sigh. Time to see the damage, I guess.

My legs feel okay, and it doesn't hurt when Nine places his hand on the left one. I can wiggle my toes just fine, and my arms seem to be whole and functioning. Limbs are intact. My head pounds, but I can turn my neck without too much of a headache. But my chest . . . I can't really move it. Every time I inhale, my lungs rattle and a searing pain shoots through my left side.

I need to see the damage.

"Can I take a bath or a shower . . . or something?"

"Oh, of course. Your bathroom is just through there." He

points to a door on the other side of the room, to the left of the now-raoring fireplace. "And the other door"—he points to a door on the right side of the fireplace—"is your study."

I nod slowly, not really understanding how all of this is mine. Do I have to pay rent?

"I'll get Con to help you bathe. Is that okay?"

I give another slow nod, not really sure what else to say, as I still puzzle over how any of this belongs to me.

This room is mine. How? Nine said something about a magical house. Maybe I've just been assigned these rooms to recover in? Maybe they'll send me home soon.

But now that I think about it, where is home?

I remember everything about the world: the countries; magic (Fae spells, Witch elements and charms, various Vampire gifts, and all the other random types of magic in the lower supernaturals); the different species (Vampire, human, Shifter, Fae, Witch, etc.); how to use a plasmascreen and all kinds of magical technology; history. But none of my personal specifics. It's as though my life has been erased—no memories of family, friends, what kind of food I like, what types of coffee there are . . . None of it exists for me anymore.

What do I even look like?

Connie arrives with a couple of towels just as that question flits across my mind, and she offers a gentle smile that breaks me out of my downward spiral into panic. "Bath?"

"Yes. Thank you. Sorry for troubling you."

"No trouble at all, hon." She goes to the bathroom door and swings it open on silent hinges.

What I can see of the room beyond takes my breath away. Well, I don't really remember any other bathrooms right now, but given the spa-shaped pool in the center of the floor and all the crystals and bright colors dancing over the semitranslucent tiles, I'm going to go out on a limb and assume this isn't standard.

But who knows, maybe it is?

She fills the pool—bath?—with steaming water from an array of taps on the side, and the room steams up as the tiles turn a bright blue crystal color, losing their translucent quality.

She adds various types of salts, crushed crystals, and a liquid that bubbles when placed under the running taps—bubble bath, of course—before turning around to me.

"Want help getting out of bed?" She comes over to the bed, hands at the ready to ease me up.

"No, I got it." I inch my way to standing and let the hem of my nightgown slide along the floor. It hurts like hell to put one foot in front of the other, and breathing through it is fucking hell on earth.

"Do I have many injuries?"

"Just two. One to your head, which we've stitched up, and the main wound to your chest, which is healing slowly with the aid of Dea's magic."

That explains the headache and chest pain.

I crawl my way forward toward the now-steamy bathroom and try to pull off my nightgown in the process, but I wince the moment my arms move above my head.

"Here," Connie says, "let me." She undoes a clasp at the back of the gown, then slides it down my body with ease.

"Thanks."

I cover my breasts, which are only just visible above the giant bandage wrapping my chest.

"Oh, would you prefer I waited outside?"

That's the question, isn't it? I would prefer that, yes, but I doubt I can bathe on my own, and I really need to feel clean.

It's amazing the dilemmas you find yourself in when

waking up battered and bruised in a foreign world surrounded by magical weirdos.

"Ermmm, no. It's okay."

She lowers me gently into the bath, which sits into the floor in all its golden grandeur, and then brushes a comb through my hair that hangs in clumps down to the middle of my back—something about that seems wrong, though, but I can't quite place why.

I resist the urge to cover my whole body with the bubbles surrounding me, not wanting to seem prudish, but my cheeks burn a bright shade of red every time I feel her eyes rest on me.

Goddess, this is so awkward.

"So," I begin, trying to start some kind of conversation that isn't focused on my nakedness, "what kind of gifts do you have?"

She coughs in surprise.

Oops. Maybe I'm not supposed to know about that? "Sorry, Nine said you all had different gifts when I asked." Fiddling with my thumbs, I add, "Just curious."

"Ah." She stays silent for a while longer, and I don't think she's going to answer. But then I hear her take in a deep breath. "My skills are more practical and battle-focused. I'm a good archer, I can hit any target from any distance so long as I can see it, and I never run out of stamina, no matter how little I've eaten or how long I've been fighting."

"Wow!" So she's basically a warrior badass? A really beautiful warrior. "That's amazing."

She giggles, and I watch in awe as her blond hair sways with the movement, a perfect contrast to her reddening cheeks and dimpling smile.

She applies some shampoo to my hair and lathers it in. "I

guess it's pretty cool. Sometimes I kinda wish I had more passive gifts. Ones that make me a little more feminine." She sighs.

"Eh. Screw being feminine. You're fucking badass. Roll with it." Somehow, that sounds more like me—a voice that a deep part of my consciousness recognizes.

This time, Connie lets out a loud laugh that echoes across the room. Even her laugh is damn beautiful. A hint of jealously creeps up my spine, but mostly I'm just awed and fascinated. This woman is incredible. As beautiful as she is deadly.

"What about the others?"

"Dea and Arrie?"

Arrie? "So that's his name! The fucker refused to tell me anything."

She snorts as she helps me sit up a little more to rinse out the shampoo. "Yeah, he's a bit of a brooder, but you'll get used to each other . . . Eventually."

"Doubtful. He's an ass."

"He's the most powerful warrior among us. Don't piss him off."

"Even better than you?"

She pauses for a moment, as if considering my question. "In hand-to-hand combat? Yes. I haven't once beaten him without cheating."

Fuck. Maybe I'll consider my words more carefully when speaking to him. Given that I'm already injured, I don't want to have another accident.

She rinses the shampoo out and works the conditioner into the ends.

Maybe she'll know what's going on? "Sorry, but I really want to know what's going on. I'm being really calm, all things considered, and I'm pretty sure I should be freaking out."

"Yeah, we were talking about that while you were sleeping. You're probably still in shock. This is a strange place to wake up in after losing all your memories. But honestly, we don't know that much about you either."

"Oh." Really?

I can't hide the disappointment, it seems, because she stops lathering my hair for a moment to look me straight in the eyes. "Chin up. It'll get easier. And you'll remember things over time."

"Really?"

"Yeah. That's what Nine thinks. But hush. Enough about that. Tell me, do you like popcorn?"

I laugh but quickly wince as it constricts my chest. "Don't remember," I groan, rubbing my chest. "Sorry."

"Well, let's try it out. Movie night? We're watching CHURCH BELLS AND DOORKNOBS?"

That rings a bell in the back of my head somewhere. "I think I've seen that, but I can't remember."

"Well, Dea and Arrie hate it, but it's one of mine and Nine's favorites, and it's our turn to pick this week." She rinses out the conditioner and begins scrubbing my body with a soft kind of soap; luckily for my dignity, she doesn't wash anywhere private, just the other important bits.

"Sure. Why not? Might need some help walking more than a few paces, though. It's kinda hard to breathe."

"I'll help. Don't worry." She stands and grabs a towel. "Now, let's get you all dried off and wearing something better than that nightgown."

"Ugh. Finally."

Connie helps me towel-dry and then goes to the closet to see what she can find that won't irritate my injuries. She pulls out item after item—none of which I recognize—until she finally finds a nice baggy dress and leggings that will match and leave my chest free from tight-fitting clothes.

I stand in front of the mirror in the bedroom and take in my reflection.

I have long pink hair that lightens the farther down it goes and frames my Japanese features. My chest is wrapped in waterproof bandages that have small flecks of dark red in a semicircle along my left side. But what really takes me by surprise is the skull tattoo across my collarbone in a long triangle that reaches all the way to my shoulders and down to my cleavage.

"Interesting tattoo," Connie mentions as she comes up behind me.

"Thanks. It's pretty."

"You have another one on your back. It's a lion in splashes of bright color."

"Really?" I try to turn around to get a good look but wince and quickly give up when a sharp pain radiates out from my left side.

"Yeah. It's cool-looking."

I turn around to face the clothes she's picked out and laid on the bed. "Err . . . where did all these clothes come from?"

"They're yours . . . from wherever you came from. Though we will add to it when you're better, otherwise we won't be able to . . . Never mind. That'll just start too many questions. Movie time!"

They're mine? But . . . I don't recognize any of them.

She helps me into the clothes in silence—with the noticeable absence of a bra, I might add—and styles my hair so that it's dry and sitting well with none of the weird bed-head kinks it's prone to.

How do I know that?

Gah! This memory thing is confusing.

"C'mon!" She grabs my hand and leads me slowly out the door. I get the feeling she would have dragged me down the hallway running if I could move any faster than a damn snail.

The hallway outside my rooms is decorated with beautiful paintings, some of the guys and Connie in various historical periods, others of people I don't recognize, and sometimes the odd decorative piece. But what I do notice is the beautifully open-plan space the hallway is; each room coming off of it is separated by a set of double doors, with some rooms only having an archway opening. Every room I can see into has a different feel, from music rooms with heavy drapes and dark décor to lounges with bright open spaces and pops of color.

Connie leads me down a large winding double staircase that really is like a fairy-tale dream come true, with the golden patterns on the railings and a plush cream-white carpet that has my bare feet feeling like I'm walking on clouds.

"What kind of place is this?"

Connie laughs but shrugs. "It's a pretty impressive house, isn't it?"

I just nod, not really knowing what else to say.

Have I died and woken up in some weird kind of heaven?

Chapter Three

To the right of the downstairs and around a corner is another large archway, but this one leads to a chef-style kitchen with warm cream-and-grass-green colors threading throughout cream-white worktops and a stove larger than me.

"She's alivvvve!" Nine sings as soon as he sees me from his seat at the kitchen table. He throws his hands in the air and waves them around like some silly child.

"He's gonna be a handful," I mumble to myself.

Connie laughes beside me, guiding me into a chair. "Yeah, he's a special kind of crazy."

"I heard that!" Nine is sitting in the chair next to me, placing a gentle hand on my knee while scowling at Connie. "You doing okay, Sweetie?"

"Sweetie? I see you've upgraded my nickname."

"Well, if we knew your actual name, I'd call you that."

My name? I haven't even thought about it. What is my name?

My echoing silence seems to answer their unspoken

question, and Dea steps away from making a cup of tea with fancy fresh leaves and asks, "So you remember nothing at all?"

I shake my head, trying not to let the tears fall as I struggle to take a deep breath. Why can't I remember anything?

"It doesn't matter." Connie opens a glass sliding door that leads to a giant set of stairs curling into a darkening pit that descends below ground level.

Where does that lead?

Is this where they kill me and bury my body?

Nine helps me to my feet with another gorgeous laugh.

Does he ever stop laughing?

"Don't worry, it's just the theater. We're not about to take you to some secret basement to murder you. So you can stop those silly thoughts right now." He jabs me in the arm and helps me descend the stairs.

The darkness is stifling, but somehow, I can still see where I'm going, as though the darkness has no effect on me.

Nine notices. "You can see in the dark?"

"I guess . . ."

"Interesting."

"Or totally freakish."

Arrie follows us all silently, his gaze boring a hole in my back as I feel every shift in his vision as he apparently takes me in. The whole thing puts me on so sharp an edge I almost can't breathe.

Light brightens the way the moment we step through the door at the base of the stairs, and a giant room with plush chairs, sofas, and beds takes up the space. They all face the same way, and I realize that Connie was being serious—this is a theater.

They have a freaking theater in their basement?! With

beds?

"Yes, we do." Nine sits me on the couch in the centermost area of the room, facing the wall-length screen in front of us. "Hold on." He presses a button on the side of the sofa, and a circular platform rises from the ground, lifting us into the air.

"Fae magic." It reminds me of the smell of alcohol and a glowing room as an image of faceless bodies dancing in pulsing lights flashes across my mind.

"Yeah. It manipulates the air beneath the floating surface and thickens it so everything above it floats as high as you need. Just push this button to determine the height." He holds out a controller he plucked from the side of the sofa with a few basic buttons, but he points to the arrows. "Take it."

"Okaaaay." Instant unease shoots through me, though I'm not sure why. My hands shake, but I clench them tight enough to slow the tremor to a tremble.

Stop being so stupid.

Taking a deep breath, I hit the down button, and the platform lowers. "Ah, I see."

I experiment with the buttons until I get the height that I think is right while someone puts the movie on. To my left, the other three are cuddled on a corner sofa on another platform just below us, Dea with his arm around Connie's waist while she rests on his shoulder, and Arrie curling up between her legs.

Are all three of them together? Like, together together?

I look at Nine, hoping he'll answer, but he's busy arranging the cushions into their plumpest forms with the utmost concentration.

"Come here." He gestures for me to lie on the cushions, and I realize he's probably trying to make things as comfortable as possible for me, given my stupid injuries that seem to plague my every other bloody thought.

That's super sweet. I can't help but smile at him as I lay down on the bed of pillows.

"Just know"—he sits on the other side of the sofa, giving me a fair bit of space—"I'd totally cuddle you, but since you're still injured, I don't want to hurt you." He looks a little sad about that. Disappointed, almost. And the distant look in his eyes makes me feel a bit guilty. He probably usually joins the others.

Wait, why do I feel guilty about that?

"Come here." I mimic the tone he used earlier with a beckoning finger and lift my legs to lay them in his lap as I entwine my arm under his outstretched hand. "Better?"

He nods as a wide grin spreads across his face. "Much."

We fall into companionable silence as a movie with high-speed car chases and loud gun fights plays on the large screen, each scene clicking a fragment of memory into place for me.

I have seen this before, at the local theater, when I was a teenager with some friends . . . I think. The smell of popcorn brings a memory back . . .

"Taytay . . . C'mon!" A boy with rainbow hair and bright pink jeans ushers me forward, grabbing the Coke from the counter. "I don't wanna miss that hunk of a man on the big screeeeen."

I roll my eyes. I'm used to his antics but still find them funny. "Okay. Okay."

"You cannot deny his gorgeousness!" he sings as steps into the elevator, and I step in beside him. "Even your little virgin ass can appreciate those eyes."

"G, stop being a little ho. You know I'm not fuckin' blind."

He holds his hands up in surrender (while still holding the Coke) and smiles.

"How long is the movie again?"

He gives me a look I know to mean he isn't impressed with the question, but he answers anyway. "Two hours. Then you may get back to whatever stupid romance book you're currently drooling over."

"Great!" I hop on the spot and steal a piece of popcorn, before reveling in the salted caramel taste that echoes across my senses.

I've trailed off from the movie toward the end, too busy sorting through these new snippets of memory to bother concentrating.

What are they?

Who is the friend?

Where was I in that memory?

"Errr . . . Sweetie?"

I snap out of my thoughts and realize the sofa is back on the ground, and I'm lying here, staring up at the crystallized ceiling, as the others stand around me. "Yeah?"

"You dazed out on us there. You okay?" Connie kneels beside me, a look of concern plastered across her face.

"Yeah, sorry. It's nothing."

I stand up and walk out of the theater—crawling is more like it—and head up the stairs, but it isn't long before I have to stop to catch my breath halfway up as I clutch at my chest and wheeze like I've swallowed a dog's chew toy. Every breath rattles. When will my lungs finally collapse? I'm bloody surprised I made it this far.

Arrie sighs and grumbles as he comes up behind me, scoops me into his arms, and carries me the rest of the way to my room in silence. My face brushes against his chest as he takes me up every stair and down every corridor, his strong arms wrapping under my back and legs as he silently carries me to my rooms. "There," he says once we reach my door.

"Would have taken you double the time."

"Would not." I cross my arms and turn my back to him, opening the door and stepping inside.

"So you're not injured and you didn't nearly die recently, then?"

"Nope. Not at all."

"Well, then you'll be okay to go on a run with me in the morning?"

Ugh. No fucking way. I can barely walk. "Fine. Thank you for helping."

He laughs. A proper full-belly laugh, and his face lights up in a way I've never seen before, softening those usually frowning eyes into pools of ice blue I instantly want to get lost in. "God, you're stubborn."

I nod in agreement and step into my room, not even bothering to respond. My room. My new room, in my new house, with my new . . . friends? Something about this feels strange and makes my hands shake as I shiver.

Chapter Four

The shape of the woman in front of me, with her long blond hair and perfectly manicured nails, shrinks into the shape of a goat, her cute little horns protrud from the top of her tuft of white fur.

"You are cute, love. And honestly, I hate hurting animals. But you're worth twenty thousand dollars"—I shrug—"and I have rent to pay."

She lets out a bleating rally cry, and I almost cave—she is the cutest Shifter I have ever hunted.

Looking up, I stare at myself in the woman's lounge room mirror. Dark pink hair sitting at my shoulders stares back at me, alongside a look of pleasing terror, one that probably gives any surviving victims nightmares.

I shrug, not really caring. They're supes. I don't really care what happens to them. But this woman seems lovely, and she is cute, so I decide to show her mercy and stun her quickly.

In the time it takes to blink, I have my magigun in hand and fire two shots to her body and watch her go down without a single bleat.

Her body turns back to human, and I quickly shove a pair of magicuffs on her and drag her to the elevator.

"You . . ." she whispers, "are a terrible human being."

I just laugh at her. "Yeah . . . Yeah, I am."

A distant knocking wakes me up, and I shoot up in bed, making me wince in agony. "Holy fuck!" I shout-whisper into the morning light of my room. What was that dream?

Dea walks in at what I can only assume is the asscrack of dawn, as pale yellow-orange light filters its way through the window I didn't bother to cover with the heavy drapes.

He interrupted a nightmare—but this time, I got a look at the person I was. It was me. But with short pink hair rather than the long pale pink hair I have now.

"You can draw those curtains, if you would like?"

"I think I prefer them open, but thank you." The morning sun makes me smile beneath its warmth, and the moon comforted me while I slept in a way I can't explain, like how the fire warmed me when Arrie first lit it. It just feels more . . . homely. Is that weird? That I feel kinda at home despite knowing next to nothing about this place or these people?

Yup. Definitely weird.

Dea nods as he rubs his hands together and helps lift me into a standing position.

"I'm so stiff. Fuck."

"I am not surprised, Angel. You really did nearly die when I found you."

"You found me?" I let him run his hands over my forehead and down the lengths of my arms. "Why? How?"

"We will have a meeting this afternoon, and I want you there. I think it will help if you know what we are and what you are destined to become."

I didn't even think about what they are. They have gifts I have never heard of, and their magic scares me a bit, makes me uneasy in an almost instinctive way I can't control.

Dea's hands give off a green glow, and I flinch away, taking an instant step back.

"It is okay," he whispers. "I am just going to analyze your injuries. I use healing magic."

"Sorry. Not sure what came over me." I step forward toward his glowing hands and peaceful eyes, and I close my eyes as a warmth tingles its way down my arms to my fingertips.

"You seem to be healing well. The head injury should be healed after another healing bath. I reckon another two weeks of daily healing with me should have you up and running them in no time."

"Healing bath?" How long was I out if they were giving me daily treatments? "How does your magic work?"

"I am able to manipulate a person's soul and encourage it to do what I wish, including to heal." His hands still rest on my arms as he looks at me with the warmest smile. "I have been doing that daily since you got here."

"Oh. I see." I take a deep breath. "How long have I been here?"

He flinches at my question. "Eight months."

"W-W-What?"

He nods, a solemn look overtaking his usually charming features. "It took a while to nurse you back to health, Angel.

Why do his hands feel so warm and gentle?

I'm still leaning into his touch. Fuck. I flinch back and sit down to change the subject. "Could Connie help me get dressed again? I still can't really lift my arms over my head."

"I will fetch her." He nods. "In the meantime, I placed some breakfast on the bedside table." He points a delicate hand toward the nightstand closest to the door. "You should eat something. You need your strength."

I smile a quick thank-you and watch as he leaves, still smiling like an idiot minutes later. Ugh, get yourself together, girl. Clothes. You need clothes. Let's see what you like to wear.

The closet is a fascinating insight into who I am—or was?—and I eventually pick out something I like that won't irritate my chest. A pair of dark red shorts, a baggy midi-crop vest I pair with a wireless bra I find at the bottom of the pile of underwear, and a pair of tights with a cat-ear pattern on the thigh. Just need to find some shoes and . . . There! Some makeup, too.

While waiting for Connie to come help me get into my clothes, I brush my hair out, apply some smoky eyeshadow and winged liner, and try my best to do something with my hair (not trying to think too hard about how I know how to do certain things and not others).

Eight months, though. Fuck. I've been away from whatever life I had on Earth for eight months.

Fuck, fuck, fuck.

It eventually becomes too painful to keep my arms raised, so I stop.

"I can help with that." Connie walks into the room dressed in a light blue dress that reaches the floor and cinches tight at the waist, displaying the delicious curves that catch my eye and make me blush. Her hair is in her usual two braids that trail down to the floor. "Pass me the brush."

I pass it over, and she gets to work brushing everything into place, even capturing a few lose strands that refused to do anything when I tried to tame them.

She turns toward the closet. "Now for the clothes . . ."

I point to the outfit I laid on the bed earlier. "Those, please."

"Wow. You have an interesting sense of style. Let's get those tights and shorts on first, ey?"

I remove my nightgown and step into the rolled-up tights she has ready for me. After bending my body this way and that, trying to find the least painful way possible to get all of my clothes on, we finally have me dressed (even if we have to pull the midi-crop up over my legs rather than down over my head).

"Feel free to lounge or explore the house. There's nowhere you can't go. Though there are a few places that might bring you more questions than you're ready to deal with right now. Just shout if you need one of us."

"Okay." She turns to leave, but I grab her arm and yank her to a stop. "Connie . . . thank you." She's been genuinely lovely since yesterday; they all have, really.

"Stop being silly. You're more than welcome. Wouldn't want one of the guys helping you into clothes, would we?" Her smile lights up her face as her giggle echoes around the room after she leaves.

I take one last look at myself in the mirror, once again noticing my pale pink hair and the tattoo that sits on my chest, and go to the only place in my rooms I have yet to explore: the study.

The door creaks open slightly, and what lies beyond has me standing stock still at the sight. I have paid no attention to this door until this morning. But I should have. I really fucking should have.

Books. Thousands upon thousands of books lining every shelf as far as the eye can see. This entire room is larger than the basement theater, and I can't see the end, no matter how far I crane my neck. The volumes sit on dusty, dark-wood shelves that seem to fill the room in no particular order or strategy, some piling on top of one another, some sitting in neat orderly rows, and others spilling over the higgledy-piggledy shelves.

This is all for me?

I can't help it—I squeal and inhale the scent of untamable knowledge and endless adventures at the tips of my fingers. It's all for me? I don't . . . understand.

Why? How?

Those seem to be the questions I keep repeating to myself. But Dea promised he'd do some explaining this afternoon, and I don't think I'm in any immediate danger, so I may as well explore my library.

My library! Wow. What an insane thing to be thinking.

Connie bursts through the open door, blond braids whipping behind her. "You okay, hon? I heard a scream?"

"Oh, sorry. It's just . . . Look at this place! It's really mine? All of it?"

Connie looks sheepishly to the floor, an embarrassed blush setting her face on fire. "Sorry. I have good hearing. Sometimes I panic. But yeah, it's all yours. None of us have been in here yet, but wow!" She spins a 360 to get a good look at the room. "The house must really like you."

"You've not been in here?" I make my way to one shelf near the door.

"Nah, we couldn't get the door open. Seems to only respond to you. You must be a really private person."

"Hmmm. Private, cute punk-style clothes, a bookworm. I'm a strange person."

Connie laughs another one of those beautiful laughs I like hearing so much as she rests an elbow on my shoulder—not enough to cause any pain, but enough to know she's there. "I'd say interesting. You seem interesting."

"Really?"

"Yeah." She walks over to another wall of book-lined shelves. "May I?"

"Yeah, sure. Help yourself."

"Eeeek! Thank you, thank you, thank you."

"No library in the house?" I flip the page of the first book I pick off the nearest shelf: DRAGONS AND WHERE TO FIND THEM.

"Not one this big, no. This is fucking insane." She sits in a comfy rainbow pouf in a reading corner by the door and starts devouring the book she picked. "I wonder if you're someone who likes a bit of fun and mystery?"

"Huh? Why?"

"Because I bet there are secret doors and hidden passageways in this thing. It seems like that kinda place, you know."

A part of me can't help but wonder how the house knows that I like this kind of room, but the other part of me can't help but get a little excited at the prospect of exploring. "That would be awesome, I'm not gonna lie.

Chapter Five

We spend hours reading in the corner just beside the door, Connie on the rainbow pouf and me on the sparkly sofa (can't quite get down on the floor without feeling like a million knives are stabbing me in the chest).

Before long—when I'm halfway through my book—Nine walks in with a smile on his face. "Ah, so this is where I find . . ." He looks up and sees the room for the first time, his eyes glowing in amazement. "Fucking whoa. What did you do to deserve this kinda room, Sweetie?"

I shrug and give a noncommittal grunt, sticking my nose back in the book.

"Well, as great as this is, and as much as I want to watch you reading in that hot little outfit, Dea wants to chat with you. We all do."

The meeting. Fucking finally. I place the book back on the shelf and slowly stand up, but Nine runs to my aid and steadies me, before helping me walk out of the room. Not that I need the help by this point, but it's a sweet gesture nonetheless.

Wait, did he just call me hot? Like, sexy hot? The realization has my cheeks burning and my eyes looking anywhere other than at him, so instead my gaze lands on Connie, who stares at us with a knowing smile and raised eyebrows.

Oh, for fuck's sake.

I shake my head and hobble ahead of them, not even wanting to think about the looks they're likely giving each other.

Why are they all so damn hot?

Nine leads us into a small room down a hallway I've not explored yet, a few hallways past the kitchen. This place is like a maze; I really need to go exploring at some point or get someone to draw me a damn map. The room seems to be some kind of small, unique-looking study with a desk sitting in the center. And at that desk sits a black-haired god of a man with all the right angles it almost makes me jealous I'm not him. Dea.

Are they all amazingly beautiful in one way or another? 'Cause that's gonna get real old, real fast.

"Now we are all present," Dea starts, looking to Arrie, whose white hair stands out from the shadows in the far corner, "we can get started filling you in, Angel."

"Before we begin, Dea," Connie interrupts. "You should see her fucking library! It's insane. It's easily the biggest room in the house."

"Wait, what?" Dea turns to look at me, but I don't know how to hold his intense, stormy gaze. "Really?"

I nod, not trusting my voice to speak a coherent sentence. He continues to look at me expectantly, and I realize I need to answer him. "Finally explored my study today, but it's more of a library, really. How did you know it was a study if you've never been in there?"

"We all have one." He gestures to the room we're currently in. "This is the bottom floor of mine."

Hmmm. It's cozy and different, and I like whatever that amazing smell is. . . Smoked lavender. It permeates every drop of air around me, as though whatever makes that smell spends every waking moment in Dea's study. The desk we're sitting at is rather large, but the rest of the room is covered with overstuffed bookshelves, various maps, and weird objects I've never seen before, and piles upon piles of paperwork and unbound books litter the space.

Goddess, it really smells like heaven in here.

"Anyway." Dea snaps my attention away from his study and back to his face. "We have a lot to tell you, but we are not sure how."

Ugh. They're going to beat around the bush again? "Just spit it out. You'll never know how I'm going to take something if you don't just damn well tell me in the first place. It's not like I know where I am enough to run away, you know."

Nine laughs, and I even get a snort from Arrie and a giggle from Connie.

"Right. Okay." Dea spreads out his arms on his desk. "What do you know of the Bible? The Christian one? More specifically, the Four Horsemen of the Apocalypse?"

"That they existed. Well, according to the Bible. But religion isn't something that's overly practiced anymore, so I'm not too familiar, sorry. War, Death, Famine, and Conquest, though, right?"

Dea raises an eyebrow in question.

I shrug one of my shoulders and wince. "Went to church when I was little with Grannie." I rub soothing circles over my sore chest. "Clearly, it didn't stick. Wait . . ." How do I know that?

The image of my grandma sticks in my mind: her kind smile, her pink-gray hair that she kept in a rainbow of colors over the years, and her short, stocky frame that was never far from me when we walked anywhere.

Connie rubs a hand over my shoulder, trying to comfort my poor mind back into reality. "Things will come back to you over time, and often they'll be triggered. Try not to stress over it; let it all come back naturally."

Dea gives me a sympathetic look before continuing. "Well, they exist. And have for around two thousand years. They balance out the world and try to . . . keep the peace."

I can't help it—I snort my surprise. "Peace? That's what you call the state of the current world?"

I mean, seriously? What are these idiots smoking? The Vampires are months away from an attack on the Supernatural Council (otherwise known as the SC—the human government that deals with the supernatural) for restricting blood supplies—again—and the Witches still haven't come out of hiding; not to mention the Fae causing all kinds of issues in sex trafficking and human manipulation. And that doesn't account for the fact that humans are now growing complacent about magic, hating the side effects on society its presence has caused.

Arrie's giant frame enters my peripheral vision with a face like thunder that has me shrinking in my chair. "It could be worse."

"Errr . . . sure." His attitude rubs me the wrong way, and rather than continue shrinking, frustration edges my mind into retaliation. "The magical community could be heading toward war. Oh wait, they are." I fold my arms across my chest, not really sure why this line of conversation bothers me so much. "They should have just stayed in hiding."

Do I really mean that? Is that how I feel? Felt?

Dea's incredulous expression gazes at me, but he continues. "We are a group of magical beings as old as time. Ones that you have heard of. Apparently." I do not miss the scorned sarcasm in his tone.

"Wait a minute." The pieces are coming together faster than my mind can process. He asked about the Four Horsemen . . . "You're really the . . . Four Horsemen? That's what you're trying to tell me?" That's not possible. The magical community's mainly non-human, but ancient myth? No. There's always science to the magic. In fact, a lot of people resent the use of the term magic because it isn't factually accurate. Magic is just science we don't understand yet, after all.

Dea stares at me, waiting patiently for me to react. Probably for me to break down. Well, he's not going to get that. It seems Arrie was right: I am stubborn, and I seem to be getting some of my personality back, though I'm not sure I quite like the person I was. Am. Whatever.

He gestures to himself. "Death." Then points to the others in turn, starting with Arrie. "War." He moves on to Connie and says, "Conquest," and then points to Nine. "Famine."

Well, that explains their weird names.

Dea gets up and points to an old painting above his desk that depicts a traditional picture of the Four Horsemen in all their colors, with Death being a glassy translucent color. "We were all human once, until we died and were chosen by an old magic when our seals were broken." He points to each of their artistic depictions in turn. "And we woke up here, in this house, and have been trying to keep Earth peaceful over the years. Ending wars, pacifying political conflict, helping end world hunger . . . That sort of thing."

"So, you're not the cause of those things?"

"No," they all say in unison, each with a scowl upon their beautiful faces.

Seems that might have been an insensitive question.

Dea continues, however—without explaining why I was wrong—with his story. "We each have our own set of unique gifts. We have been alive for millennia, Angel, and not once have we come across the situation we have presently found ourselves in." He looks straight at me with a blank expression, one he's most likely forcing upon his face to hide his real emotions regarding what he's about to say. "There were seven seals, lost to history now, but only four were broken. Until recently. Now the fifth seal has been broken. And Fate has chosen a Fifth Horseman. You."

Nothing. My mind conjures nothing. No anger, no sadness, no confusion, nothing. I'm the Fifth Horseman, hey? So I get cool powers and get to live with my own personal library in a house full of hot and sexy people? Okay. I'm currently failing to see the downside.

But . . . why me?

"We don't know why we're chosen." Nine responds to my internal question with a smirk. "Sometimes it becomes clearer over time, as it might for you as you regain your memories." He steps out of the shadows from behind me. "But the magic will only wait so long before choosing someone, and it only has the recently deceased to choose from."

My mind gets stuck on that word. "D-Deceased?"

Connie looks at me with a guilty expression. "You didn't almost die. You did die. Dea was called to your location and whisked you back here."

So wrong place, wrong time, then? I see. Why am I not

freaking out? I should definitely be freaking out. They could kill me any second they choose. I should most definitely be scared. At the least a little apprehensious.

"We're not going to kill you, Sweetie. You really need to relax about that."

"It's instinctive!" I snap and instantly regret it with a wince the moment I see his pained expression. "Sorry."

I get up and walk out the door in silence, leaving all four of them in the wake of my semi-calm exit. The only reason I don't run is because I fear what I might do to my already damaged chest.

The library (my library—eek!) is the only place I can go without being interrupted, since they can't seem to get in without me, and its gracious walls and comforting tomes of wonder greet me upon arrival.

"The Fifth Horseman? Fuck!" I just want to learn who I am and go back to whatever life I have. "Is that too much to ask for?" If I didn't value books so much, I would probably give in to the urge to throw things around right about now.

"Calm down, girl. This is probably still just a dream." I will probably go to sleep and wake up in my normal life again tomorrow. Whatever kind of life that is.

There are four main magical communities in the world, three of which came out of the supernatural closet a hundred years ago: Vampires, Shifters, and Fae. The other community is the Witches, but they haven't come out of hiding with the others. (Salem issues.)

And now I learn the Four Horsemen of the fucking Apocalypse are the real masterminds behind the world, the leaders keeping everything together (and currently failing).

But me, the Fifth Horseman?

Fuck no.

I take the book I was reading earlier and sit back down on the sparkly couch to finish it, absorbing myself into a world of words and sentences that take the very fabric of life right out from under my feet, along with all its craziness, and sweep me away on a dream-filled adventure. I read every word on every page and every sentence of every chapter until my eyes can't hold themselves open a moment longer, and then I doze off with thoughts of dragons and a book resting gently on my face from where it slid from my grasp.

Chapter Six

"Angel?" A loud rapping knock jolts me awake. "Angel!"

Only one person calls me that: Dea. And it seems he's knocking rather loudly on the library door.

"What?" I half shout back as I get up to swing the door open, rubbing the stiffness out of my sore chest muscles. "What is it?"

Rubbing the haze of sleep from my eyes, I step into the doorway and am met by Dea's dark swirling eyes and bare chest, with his slacks hanging low on his hips and sweat glistening across every inch of his delicious skin.

Was he just working out?

"I wanted to know if you were okay."

"Is that all? You woke me up for that? Fucking christ, Dea, you scared the shit outta me."

"Oh," he says with a smile. He watches me stare at his tattoo—all golden swirls and stars on his left shoulder that trail down his chest to sit at the yummy V marking a descent lower than my eyes are allowed to go—with a bemused look on his face. "Enjoying the distraction?"

Most definitely. "Yeah . . ." I shake my mind out of the gutter it dragged itself into and force my eyes upward—not that staring at his handsome face with those dark swirling eyes that look like mini galaxies capturing my attention every time I glance at them makes me feel any less hot.

"Can I see it?"

"See what?" I ask with a squeak as I feel the heat rush to my cheeks. Eesh, I really need to deal with this sudden onslaught of heat rushing to places it has no business being.

He gives me a knowing smirk. "Your library," he says with a laugh.

Oh, of course he meant that. "Sure." I step out of his way and invite him in.

He steps into the room with a look of awe and jealousy, and I briefly wonder what the big deal is. Don't they all get rooms that suit them? Seems not.

"This is . . . astounding." He runs his fingers along the spines of various books as he examines the shelves. "What books do you keep in here?"

"No idea. There are fiction ones on your left and some nonfiction magic textbooks on the shelves over there." I point to the ones in the corner where Connie and I sat earlier. "I've not really explored much farther."

"Well, let us go, then." He pulls me to his front, propping my feet on top of his as he grabs my waist with a firm hand spread over my lower abdomen. I can feel the smile taunting his lips when he whispers in my ear, "Hold your breath there, Angel."

I take a deep breath, and we speed past a few rows of shelves faster than humanly possible, until he slows down enough for us to see what's in each section. We speed past nonfiction guides to the realms (plural?), more fiction books of every genre imaginable, and into a section that holds a few artifacts and maps. The place is incredible, and I really want to explore it in greater detail at some point.

Eventually, we stop at the back of the library, where a small desk sits with a laptop resting on top. My study, I presume.

"Ah, here it is."

He looks at the things surrounding the desk: more fiction books and magical guides sit behind on a set of overfilled shelves, every nook and cranny filled with some kind of book, stack of papers, or object. The plasmascreen laptop lies on the desk, ready for use whenever I need it; and a music dock sits on the edge of the desk with some kind of old iPod or something in the cradle.

"Seems you like music, books, and a place to collect your thoughts," he says as he hands me a black leather-bound journal he scavenged from the top drawer of the desk.

"Seems so." Flicking through the blank journal pages, I sigh. No clues as to who I am in here.

I sit in the chair, noticing how this is the one section of the library that isn't bright and colorful; instead, it's filled with deep browns and the scent of age-old knowledge.

Opening the top drawer, I find a translucent stone full of swirling mist I can just about see through that draws me to its gaze, and I turn it over and over in my hand, wondering what it is. Dea didn't pick it up, so clearly it isn't particularly unusual.

Maybe Dea would know?

I look up and see him sifting through the songs on the music device, frowning every now and then, but mostly in his own world of curiosity—probably trying to figure me out.

Wish I had the answers to his questions.

The golden swirling irises of those galaxy eyes of his scroll up and down as he pilfers through the playlists I assume are on there, and a smile catches his features on fire for a moment. Not a smirk or a teasing grin, but a genuine, heartfelt smile that highlights his angular face in a way that softens some of the hardened edges and makes his eyes seem a little darker.

Goddess, he's . . . I don't even have the words. His pale skin that seems more solid and less translucent today with the strange golden tattoo swirling down his torso stands out in the dark, brown-toned room, but the black choppy hair that falls from his head in short tufts and sits just at the crook of his dancing eyes frames his face in a way that brings out those gorgeous angles. And fuck, those lip piercings add an extra edge to his look, and I find myself wondering what kissing him would feel like. How I could roll my tongue over those piercings and feel them dig into my lips as I—

A small pop brings my eyes back to the desk, and a book sits in front of the plasmascreen that wasn't there a moment ago. What the—?

Dea grabs it and laughs, reading the title out loud. "PLEASURE ISLAND: AN EROTICA ADVENTURE NOVEL." He gives me a look I can't decipher, but there is definitely a hint of amusement behind those eyes. "Really?"

"Wait . . . What?"

He looks down at my hand still wrapped around the strange stone and lets out a laugh—a full belly-deep laugh that has him bending over slightly. "It is a Seeing Stone. It provides what you need by reading your emotions and thoughts. It seems you need some alone time." He raises his brows in a questioning gaze and bursts out laughing once more.

Well, him standing there half naked doesn't exactly fucking help. "Give me that!" I snatch the book away with a wince and quickly sit back down, rubbing a hand over my chest. "I don't even know what shelf this fucking belongs on." I groan under my breath. "Great."

"On a more serious note, Angel, if you need any questions answered, just think them in your mind and hold that stone, and it will do its best to give you the information you seek. Seems yours arrives in book form. Which makes sense."

"Oh." That is actually rather awesome. All these questions I have, I can get answers to them? Just like that?

"But unless you would like any help with that"—he gestures to the book still in my hands—"I am going to leave you to read it in peace."

"No. That's not . . . I don't intend to actually read it."

"Uh-huh. Sure. Well, you are immortal now. You have all the time in the world to experience life and live a little."

A memory shoots across my mind.

Live a little . . .

That phrase . . . It reminds me of someone. Someone I care about? Someone trying to persuade me to loosen up and live a bit more freely. But I couldn't—wouldn't.

"C'mon, Tay, live a little. He clearly likes you. Just go dance with him." It's the same boy from before, only this time, he has glow-in-the-dark blue hair.

We are in some kind of club, and this mysterious friend of mine is trying to get me to dance with a green-haired Fae eyeing me across the dance floor.

"But," I start, "I don't want to."

My friend sighs and turns me around. "Some day, Tay, you're gonna have to just take the plunge and get to know someone—anyone."

I sigh and turn back around, ignoring the stares I'm getting from the Fae man.

My eyes gaze out of focus as my mind reels with barely there memories and feelings of a past I have all but forgotten.

When I come to, Dea is kneeling at my side, rubbing my arm and trying his best to smile. "Are you okay? What did you remember?"

"Nothing important. But that phrase, 'live a little,' triggered some kind of memory. Similar one to the theater. But all I recall is the scent of alcohol and a glowing room. And someone important to me. It's all so . . . hazy." Before I can stop it, a tear escapes and falls in a singular lonely path down my cheek.

Dea raises a hand to wipe it away and lingers there a moment, resting my head in his palm. "If you ever want to talk . . . all you have to do is ask."

A coughing sound comes from somewhere nearby, and I look up to see Nine leaning over the desk, looking at us suspiciously but with amusement flaring in his eyes. And something else . . . something like a fiery heat. As though the sight of us makes him . . .

Oh. Oh no.

The last couple of days flood back to me in a rush of hot memories: the snuggling on the sofa, bathing with Connie, Arrie carrying me to my room like some kind of bride on her wedding day, and now this. No, no, no.

I can't seriously be attracted to all of these people after only two days!

Nine coughs again.

"Shit! Get out of my head, Nine!"

He smiles at me and sits on my other side, his sight caught

by the book still sat on the desk.

For fuck's sake.

"What's this, Sweetie? Some nighttime reading?"

Dea chuckles, and I just know this is going to get out of hand. "It is what popped up when she held her Seeing Stone. Turns out hers gives her books."

Nine tries, he really does, to hold in his laughter, but the redder his face gets, the more hilarious he seems to find it, until he bursts out laughing and crashes to the floor, holding his sides as they probably split with laughter.

Dea stands and turns toward us. "Seems our little Angel is all flustered and having other problems right now that do not concern us. We should probably leave her be so she can read her . . . informative book." He winks at me—he actually winks at me—and walks around to Nine, who he helps up off the floor with a single hand.

Nine reaches over to me, whispering a gentle caress in my mind. *Or you could just fuck one of us and get it out of your system.*

"What? Don't be absurd!" Despite my best efforts at an honest refusal, my mind has other ideas, as the sudden urge to grab them both and shove my tongue down their throats swerves its way across my mind.

And by the look of Nine's embarrassed yet smiling face, he also got a frontrow seat to that little imaginative movie sliding across my mind.

"Just leave already! I have questions I want answered."

Dea and Nine both raise their hands in mock surrender, with matching sly smiles, and back out of the study area. I have no idea if they stay in the library or not, but they are at least out of my hair. For now.

Silence fills the air, and I can finally hear myself think. The Fifth Horseman, 'ey? Well, I could get really cool powers, live in a magical house, and have some new friends, but I bet it probably comes with some kind of catch, like saving the world in one of those hero-type books.

I roll my eyes as I place the wanton book on a nearby shelf of romantic fiction. What kind of questions do I have? What ones seem most important? Ah, I know.

I pick up the Seeing Stone and think about Dea, Arrie, Connie, and Nine, about the fact that they're the Four Horsemen, that they have magic, and wonder how old they are and where they come from. What are their origins?

A giant tome of well over a thousand pages lands with a thud on the desk. It is old, leather bound, and has thick parchment pages with bits of paper and corners sticking out at odd angles here and there. The cover is mostly blank—only some faded letters remain around the painted seal on the front.

Opening the first page, I gawk at the intricacy of the interior design—it's like something out of a movie. There are all kinds of deep colors decorating the frames of each page, with diagrams, illustrations, and curly titles littering the pages with ease. But the language isn't English.

I scowl at the Seeing Stone still sitting in my palm. "Fucking really? You're giving me the answers in a foreign language?"

Of course it is. What do I do now? Can I translate it? Do I know this language? Do any of the others?

Pop! Another book landed on the desk: GUIDE TO MODERN TRANSLATIONAL MAGIC. Aha! Perfect. Wonder if there's some kind of magic-enhanced technology that'll help? Since I'm pretty sure I don't have any magic yet, and even if I do, this probably won't be it. Seems silly for a Horseman of the Apocalypse, even for me.

The contents page lists everything from Translational Abilities of the Fae, to Shifter Species and their Animal Languages, and to—bingo!—Translational Technology. Page 457.

From rare stones to enchanted glasses to various spells and potions, there are hundreds of ways to translate various types of languages, but all of this requires magic to be used by the person doing the translating. I am looking for a more passive approach.

Ah. There! translational bookscreens and their many uses. That's what I need. A translational bookscreen. Wonder if we have any in the house?

Grabbing the Seeing Stone, I ask, but nothing happens. Seems the answer isn't in the library—or available to me, anyway.

My stomach growls, interrupting my thoughts. I probably need to eat something, so I call it a day and go in search of food (and a translational bookscreen).

It takes me nearly an hour to get out of the library and find the kitchen from yesterday (my injuries and apparent shitty sense of direction being the main cause), but I find it empty.

Hmm, that's weird. It's usually filled with the team at this time, or at least, the last couple of days it has been.

Straining my ears, I pick up laughter coming from outside and head into the darkened night of the garden to an unusual scene. They have a bonfire going and are roasting s'mores and laughing with each other. Even Arrie.

Dea and Nine cuddle on one log placed as a makeshift bench while Connie and Arrie cuddle on another.

It is a beautiful sight in its own way, but if I go over there, I'll be intruding. So instead, I head in the opposite direction and sit at the edge of the forest, looking at them with wonder and longing. I'm not cold, as the fire's warmth reaches all the way over here, but a different kind of chill creeps up my spine. They're good together, all of them, in a way that seems almost natural.

You can join us, you know.

Nine! Fucking christ, you scared the shit out of me.

Sorry.

I'm okay. But thanks.

Why not?

I don't know how to answer that, but somehow, joining you is intrusive. You have a wonderful balance between the four of you, one you've spent thousands of years forming. I don't want to ruin it.

You wouldn't be. You'd be adding to it. But I won't force you.

Thank you.

I watch as Arrie lifts Connie into his lap and sends a trail of kisses up her neck. When he reaches her lips, she melts into him as her arms wrap around his neck. I probably should look away, give them their moment, but it's interesting and beautiful to watch. The way the team interact is . . . unique. I get the feeling they are all together somehow, but not like how normal couples do things.

Please join us.

Why?

Because you complete us.

I stop fiddling with the grass at my feet and stand up, sighing, aiming to go over there, but something stops me dead in my tracks. Something a little like fear. If I go over there, will they stop laughing? Will their smiles vanish?

"Sweetie!" Nine calls out the moment I step into view. "There you are. Come join us." He gestures for me to sit next to him. "We've just roasted s'mores, want one?"

Well, there's no going back now, is there?

I'm not even sure if I like s'mores, and the frustration of that fact crawls its way permanently into my mind.

Will I ever know who I am?

I shake my head. "No thanks."

Nine falls silent as the others continue to talk and debate what team they prefer and what players are better in some kind of magical sport they all watch. Connie is still sitting in Arrie's lap, but they've stopped their interacting, which confirms my suspicions that having me here is interrupting them.

"You know, you can always just try the food and see what you like now. You don't have to remain the same person forever. Live it up and try new things, see what kind of person you become. You've just been handed a giant reset button. Use it." Nine pats my knee.

Everyone falls into silence. My frustration and bad mood must have affected him, given that he can sense my emotions and thoughts.

Guilt edges its way into my mind.

"Sorry," I mutter. "Got a book as an answer to a question, but it's in a language I can't even read, and now I'm just frustrated. Could really use a translational bookscreen." I groan under my breath slightly, but everyone just sits here and listens with understanding; even Arrie doesn't poke fun or make a shitty comment.

A gentle smile graces Dea's face as he watches me. "There's one in my study. You're welcome to borrow it."

"Just show her how to use the house's magic properly," Arrie grumbles between a mouthful of marshmallow. I give him a questioning look, but he just grunts. "You can request things from the house, and it'll just give them to you. So long as you know what you want and it's a simple request."

Fuck, damn! This is the best house I have ever heard of in my life (not that I remember many right now, but you get the point).

Nine laughs. "That it is, Sweetie. That it is." He grabs a plate and starts piling a piece of food onto it from every container they have littered on the grass. "Here. See what you like. Enjoy."

I grab some random triangle thing with seeds on top and take a tentative bite. Mmmm. That tastes good. "What if I have an allergy to something or, like, an intolerance?" I'm a tad worried about puking my guts up in front of these people. (Friends?) It really isn't a good first impression.

Dea chuckles under his breath, blushing with hidden laughter. "Sorry," he says, holding out a hand in surrender. "I do not mean to laugh." He looks over at me with a serious expression. "We are immortal, Angel. We cannot die from allergic reactions, or from anything, really. Well, we can if we are killed in the right way."

"Right way?"

"Here we go," Connie says, still with her arms wrapped around Arrie's neck. "Way to scare her, Dea."

"I'm not scared. Just curious."

Nine smiles and gives me a pat on the shoulder. "She's really not," he says in a way that has me thinking he's a little impressed.

Dea shrugs, giving Connie a shit-eating grin I recognize as an 'I told you so' smile. "If someone deals a fatal blow after burning our seals, it can kill us instantly. No chance of reviving or anything."

"That's . . . intense."

"Now she's scared." Nine places his hand back on my knee, probably trying to comfort me, but it just confuses me further.

Is he being flirty? Just friendly? Is he embarrassed by my stupid dirty thoughts earlier? Ah, goddess, why did I have to remind myself of that? What if he finds me weird? What if they hate me? What if me finding them all stupidly hot is somehow weird?

Oh my goddess, I'm stuck with them for eternity!

"You're spiraling, Sweetie. Over something seriously silly." Nine leans down to whisper something in my ear, tucking a strand of hair behind it. His other hand hasn't moved from my knee either. "I'm just being nice, probably a little flirty, and no, there's literally nothing your mind can conjure up that will embarrass me. Much."

No one else hear him, given his quiet voice and close proximity to me, but Connie lets out a giggle, throwing me a raised eyebrow, and I'm suddenly reminded that she has great hearing. She heard my shriek when I first entered the library. (Then again, who didn't hear that?) Guess that's one of her gifts.

Nine looks at me and watches as my mind spirals once more. Does Connie think I'm weird? What if she has a thing going with Nine?

"Oh my god, just stop!"

He yelled. He actually just yelled at me. I've never heard Nine speak above a gentle lilt the entire past three days. It actually makes me put my food down and stare at him incredulously.

"Sorry." He pinches the bridge of his nose. "I've not had to deal with a mortal thought process for a long time. It's a little frustrating. Literally none of us care. We're all immortal."

He raises his eyebrows in a way that I guess is supposed to mean something, but I'm drawing a blank.

"Ugh. You know what, I promise to come back to this conversation when we don't have other people listening in like we're the latest soap opera. Because that's not going to help and will only have you freaking out more."

I look around and see Connie smiling, Dea resting an amused face on his hand while his legs still entwine with Nine's, and Arrie looking utterly baffled. I nod at Nine and take another bite of the seeded triangle.

"So," I start, looking back at Dea, "nothing else can kill us?"

"No. We can be injured and fall into unconsciousness while our bodies heal, but nothing can actually kill us."

"I see."

Nine points to my food, encouraging me to try something else.

I take a forkful of noodles in some kind of sauce and shove them into my mouth, trying to give Nine what I know will be a gross but hopefully kind of funny grin.

His face is a picture. He looks a little shocked, and Dea looks almost disgusted, but they all laugh at my stupid antics anyway.

"They're good," I say once I swallow the last bite. "What are they?"

"Peking duck chow mein." Connie grabs a second helping of it. "My favorite."

"I can see why. It's kind of saucy and substance-y all at the same time."

Looking at my towering plate, I ask myself what's next. I pick up a crispy golden ball and dip it into the accompanying red sauce Nine pointed out goes with it. When I take the first bite, a small moan escapes my lips before I can compose myself. That's delicious! Like, I can easily eat that sauce all day.

By the time I open my eyes to the world again, they're all staring at me with surprised smiles.

Have I done something wrong?

Nine bursts out laughing the hardest from beside me, his fist slamming onto the ground from the outburst. "Just so you know"—he looks to everyone in turn (excluding me)—"you're all thinking the same thing right now."

Arrie grumbles something I can't hear, Dea just chuckles and gives Connie an interesting glare, while Connie goes bright red. What are they all thinking?

Honestly, my lack of good social judgment is starting to bother me. I get the feeling I didn't used to be like this, and it's only because I'm missing most of my memories that it's an issue. So far, the only ones that have come back to me are the ones in church with Grannie and a few with my mysterious friend, and honestly, they aren't much help.

"I'm going to eat this in my room, if that's okay?"

Not waiting for an answer, I grab my plate and glass of water and run into the house. Well, technically I hobble, since I can still barely walk, much less run, but in my imagination, I definitely run.

At least no one stops me.

I briefly hear Connie yelling at Nine about being inappropriate at the dinner table (even though they aren't at the table, which makes me smile despite everything) and making me feel uncomfortable, but my mind blocks it out, and before long, I can barely hear them as I get farther through the house and closer to my bedroom.

Chapter Seven

I spend the next day holed up in my rooms, with Connie and Dea having arrived earlier that morning to assist my healing. Turns out a healing bath is just a bath full of Dea's healing magic, which he swamps over my body, encasing me in a glowing green bubble for an hour.

Last night scared me, and more nightmares and flashbacks have put my mind on the edge of panic. I know I'm being silly, but it scares me nonetheless. I don't understand all the looks and other aspects of social interaction, as though I'm a toddler who doesn't understand how to share her toys yet.

I'm stuck with them for eternity. What if they hate me? What if they find me strange or annoying or too innocent now I've lost my damn memories?

Bloody fuck! I can't do this. I can't be the Fifth Horseman. I can't wield super cool magic or strength. I can't be beautiful and badass like Connie or calm and intelligent like Nine. I'm just little old me. And I'm not even sure who that is right now!

My lungs heave large gasps of air as I fail to breathe. In,

out. In, out. C'mon, you can do it. But I can't. I can't catch my breath at all, as though oxygen has stopped doing its job, and my hands shake so badly I can't grip the glass of water on the nightstand. Sweat pours in rivulets down my forehead. Man is it hot in there. Why is it so hot?

"Sweetie . . . ?"

Nine barges in through the door, takes one look at my current pacing, unbreathing state, and charges into action. He takes a blanket from the bed and wraps me tight—despite my protests that I'm too warm—and helps me pick up the glass of water, presses it to my lips, and tells me to keep breathing as best I can.

"You're gonna be fine. Promise." He goes into the bathroom, and I hear the distinct sound of water running. "Just running you a bath."

"W-W-W-W-Why?"

"Because you're having a panic attack, and I need you to calm down before we chat."

A panic attack? Is that what this is? I can think clearly, and I know my body is overreacting, but it's like I have no control over what it does.

Why can't I stop shaking?

Why am I so irrationally scared?

Am I going to die?

Nine grabs me by the hand and helps me into the tub— still fully clothed in my pajamas, I might add—and starts rubbing circles on my shoulders.

"Relax, Sweetie. It's okay. You're going to be fine."

His voice lilts from my left ear to my right, and I realize that it's the same voice that woke me up that first day. The one singing the interesting song.

"Nobody expects anything from you, nor do we want you

to be like us." He slides a leg either side of me from behind in the bath, each trouser leg having been rolled up at some point, and applies more pressure into his circling fingers, massaging the knots out of my shoulders. "I wish I could fight like Connie or Arrie, but if I even try to punch them in the face, I break my hand while their faces remains as perfect as ever. It's infuriating. Trust me. You're not the only one who wishes you were as badass as those two."

"Really?"

"Uh-huh." He leans down to my ear and whispers, "I'm sorry I scared you yesterday. I didn't realize social interaction was hard for you right now. I should have, but I just didn't think about it." He gently places his lips to the tip of my temple and gives me a light kiss, the warmth sending fireflies tingling throughout my body. "I'm sorry, Sweetie."

"I can breathe. I think."

The pressure that had welled up in my chest is lifting, and my hands aren't as shaky anymore. But goddess am I tired. And hungry. Really fucking hungry.

"We'll get you something to eat in a moment. Promise. But we really need to chat."

"Okaaaay." My suspicions rise, but I remain as calm as possible. I'm sure it's just about yesterday.

Correct. It is about yesterday. Listen, we're immortal, meaning things are different for us. We don't do relationships or love. He sounds a little disappointed by that, and part of me hurts for him. *And we've been around since early humanity. It doesn't matter to any of us who you find attractive. I promise. And no one is going to think you're weird. Or annoying.*

Really? But . . . but what if—?

Nope. There are no what ifs. We have all found each other attractive in some way or another at some point in history. We've appeared in all different kinds of styles and appearances over the years and have been stuck with each other for hundreds of years. But love? Relationships? They're hard for the Horsemen to have and maintain. There aren't any other truly immortal beings, so we've just mostly avoided it.

None of you have ever been in love? That's . . . insane. Doesn't that get kind of lonely?

Oh, well . . . errm . . .

Just spit it out.

Haha, okay, then. We've all slept with each other over the years at some point. It's just easier, I guess. And having flings with people is fine. But, as a general rule, we just don't let people develop feelings for us, because it's been a long time—and I mean a really long time—since any of us felt anything more than friendship with anyone. Any more makes everything harder for us.

They're likely all worried that if one of them falls in love with the other, it will break up the group.

That's not—

Save it. I get it, Nine. I do. But not loving just because you're afraid of the consequences is wrong. No one should have to live like that.

I shake the thought from my head and return to something else he mentioned.

They've all slept together? Like, even the guys? I mean, Connie I get, she's stunning and beautiful, and why not? But—

Nine chuckles. *Told you, we're immortal. Silly things like sexuality and monogamy aren't really our thing.*

Silly things? Wow. Way to shit on the ideas of an entire race there, buddy.

It doesn't work if you're immortal. Trust me on that one. None of us could ever be enough for each other—sexually speaking—for hundreds of years. A life that long isn't meant to be lived with that many social restrictions. Plus, we were around before sexuality was even a thing.

Makes sense, actually. So you're all in a weird, non-love relationship that you've been in for two millennia? I have just intruded on the world's weirdest relationship.

You're not intruding, and we're all just friends. Just stop feeling ashamed of your thoughts just because you're trying to fit into something that doesn't even exist here. You can find as many or as few of us as attractive as you want. We won't think you're strange. Believe me, we've seen it all over the years.

I bet. That doesn't bother me half as much as I thought it would.

"Why did you say all that in my head?"

"Privacy. Con has very good hearing and would have listened in because she's a nosy little shit. No one can hear me in someone else's head."

"Ah, I see."

"Let's go get some food. Arrie's making brownies, I think."

Arrie, cooking? The thought of him in an apron has me laughing so loudly my chest pangs in pain, and I hiss.

"You okay? Need me to fetch Dea?" Nine wraps his arm around me in an instant, worry etching his features.

"No, no. It's okay. Just need to stretch and eat some brownies."

"Okay." Nine leads me out of the bedroom with a smile and down the stairs, going slowly and carefully to avoid hurting my already injured body. "Seems you like food."

"And books. And have some strong opinions about magic. Oh, and I had a Christian grannie that I hated and loved at the same time."

Nine laughs while grabbing my hand and leading me into the kitchen.

The delicious smell of something sweet and delectable

hits my nostrils, and I nearly cave with hunger. "What is that smell?" I sniff the air for a few seconds, reveling in the sweet aroma.

"Brownies," Arrie grumbles from the kitchen counter. He stands at the stove in black slacks, a loose black tee, and a white fluffy apron as he glides a knife through a tray of brown he's cutting into squares.

I stifle a chuckle at the sight but am more focused on the brownies, which smells of heaven.

"Arrie." Dea enters the room. "I need to borrow you for a moment."

Dea gives me a wave and another body-melting smile before grabbing Arrie by the arm and yanking him out of the kitchen, leaving me alone with Nine.

"Arrie likes to cook, even though the house will provide whatever food you ask."

"Why?" I take a seat at the kitchen table, eagerly awaiting my next foodie treat. If the house can provide whatever food you want it to, I don't think I'll ever cook.

"It's calming."

He brings over a plate and gestures for me to dig in.

A single bite into one of the squares has me letting a small moan slip free, and I flush bright red. That's what made them all uncomfortable yesterday. I don't get it, bu—

Oh, right. I'm such an idiot. It sounds sexual. Of course that makes them uncomfortable. They're all together (kind of).

"Sorry," I grumble between bites.

"It's fine. I'm glad you like them."

"Like them? They're the best things I've ever tasted!"

Nine smiles at me and grabs a brownie for himself. "You haven't eaten much yet. That you remember."

"Then I'll just have to stick around to eat more food." I grin at him, hoping it will make him smile again.

It works!

"How're you feeling today?" He looks a little uncomfortable, but I'm not sure why.

"Uhhh, not bad. Dea and Connie gave me another healing bath this morning."

I blush slightly, remembering what Nine said about them all having slept together at some point. Images of Arrie with Dea and Nine flash across my mind, but I shake them from my head. Does that mean even the guys have slept with each other? Part of me really wants to ask, but even I know that's inappropriate.

Those images do not do those men justice, trust me. And yes. Even us guys. Though Arrie does prefer women.

Get a grip, girl. Yes, it's slightly strange, but it makes sense. They're immortal, relationships with mortals are hard work if you're going to live forever. That'll just end in heartbreak, so what's the point? Everyone needs . . . attention. Even the Four Horsemen of the Apocalypse, it seems.

Nine doesn't interrupt my mind babble while I get my head around it, which I appreciate.

Wait a minute. "Are Vampires not immortal?"

"No, they're not. They do live a few hundred years and age slower than humans, but they're mortal. Like everyone else."

"Other than you—us. Other than us." Wow. That's insane. I'm immortal. I am going to live forever.

"Yes, other than us." He grumbles something under his breath and then shakes his head. "Wonder what you liked to eat when you were human? You know, some people say that senses can trigger memories. Like the taste of a particular food, the smell of a certain place . . ."

"Makes sense," I say between mouthfuls of my third brownie. "In the theater, I had a small flashback when I smelled the popcorn. It reminded me of the nachos I had when I saw that movie the first time."

"It seems your mind is having trouble remembering details of your life. If you like . . ." Nine looks to the ground, a flush reddening his cheeks. "We can cook you as much food as you like—all different types—and see if any of it triggers anything." He flushes redder—even his ears turn a bright shade of scarlet—and I can't help but smile at him.

"I'd like that. Thank you."

He relaxes and divides the last few brownies equally between us. "So what kind of powers do you want? You know, if you could choose?"

What kind of powers do I want? "I think I'd like to be badass, like Connie and Arrie, but maybe in a less violent way. I don't really know. Violence doesn't feel right to me."

"It never feels right." He looks a little dazed and distant, as though he's remembering some horrific detail.

"I think I have night vision," I say to bring him back to the present. "I could see in the corridor that leads to the theater." I point to the door to the right of us, the one we went through the other day.

"Ah! So maybe a ninja-type. Stealth and throwing daggers."

He mimics throwing daggers at me, and I feign an overactive death, making the gurgling noises and all. Goddess, we are both super lame.

"Want to come on a walk with me tomorrow morning? Arrie usually goes for a run, and Dea'll probably make you go along when you've recovered, but walking will help bring your strength up."

"Sure." That actually sounds lovely. "I don't know the first thing about this house or . . . realm. Would be nice to see it."

"Sure thing. Dawn, tomorrow. I'll come and get you."

Dawn? Like, first crack of light, dawn?

Ugggghhhh. Why?

Chapter Eight

"You going to actually talk to me?" A handsome blond-haired man sits across from me in the restaurant. "Or are we going to continue this farce of you deciding to hate me?"

"Are you going to apologize for ditching me afer my mom and dad died?"

"No." He folds his arms over his chest. "I was doing the best I could."

"Then, no." I shrug, not really caring about his feelings.

"We do these dinners every month, and every month since you were old enough to hate me, we've done them in silence." He growls low under his breath. "You're nineteen years old now, it's time you learned to grow up."

I blanch at his words. "Well, you'll be happy to know I have a job."

"Really?" He looks at me with a soft smile. "You gonna tell me about it?"

"I got accepted by the Hunter Society for the SC."

His golden tan face pales as he chokes on the mouthful of wine he's trying to swallow. "You . . . what?"

"I'm going to help the SC bring down rogue and criminal supernaturals."

"If this is about vengeance . . ."

"Don't even try to play that card." I give him a stern look, hoping it will stop him from asking questions.

"Fine."

"Heeeey." I hear a rough grumble somewhere in the distance, perturbing my dreams. "It's time to get up, Sweetie."

My eyes peel open, the remnants of that dream playing over and over in my mind as Nine's shadowy face comes into view. He's grown a bit of stubble since that first day I met them all, but it suits him. The rough, tousle-haired look makes him look like he just rolled out of bed this gorgeous from the beginning.

"Time for our walk. Get up. Get dressed."

"Oh, right." I wince as I sit up, and Nine helps me up off the bed.

The closet only really holds nicer clothes, and I'm struggling to find slacks or any kind of loose loungewear or workout gear, but right at the bottom of a pile of underwear, I find a pair of light brown slacks and a loose vest top. Looks like I'm going braless. Again. They just hurt too much, and most of my chest is wrapped in bandages anyway. But damn, I can't wait to not feel naked.

I carry the clothes to the bathroom, telling Nine to wait in the bedroom a moment. After cleaning my teeth, running a brush through my hair—which I can now just about do—I bend to lift my pants up and yelp as the action pulls at my rib muscles.

You okay in there?

"Don't suppose Connie is up yet, is she? Could really use

some help getting dressed."

Nine sighs before he turns the doorknob and walks in.

I stand there, stark naked except for the bandages covering my upper torso—not quite covering all of my breasts—with no panties on, let alone having managed to pull up my trousers. "What do you think you're doing?" I shriek.

"Helping." He walks right up to me, not staring or doing anything too weird, and pulls up my trousers for me and grabs my vest.

Yes, I am going commando. (You have no idea how hard bending over with a stab wound to your chest is, so I only want to do it once.)

"Arms up." He rolls the vest top up to lift it over my head.

I wince the moment my elbows are above shoulders and shove my arms back down to my sides in a grimace.

"Wow. This is nuts." Nine puzzles over the problem for a moment, looking me up and down like I'm some sort of new toy he needs to figure out, before he unzipps his fancy top and reveals a completely bare chest beneath.

"What are you doing?" I shriek for the second time that morning.

Nine looks at my panicked face and laughs. "Relax, I'm just giving you my top. It's a zip up, so it'll be easier to get on."

"But what about you?"

"You know, you might find it hard to believe, but after two thousand years, this is not my only top." He unzips it the rest of the way, and I stand there speechless. I don't think I'll ever get over seeing these men topless. Every inch of his torso catches my eye—not a bit of fat in sight.

But he ate brownies!

Lots of working out, Sweetie. He winks as I blush at the fact that he heard my inner crushing.

"R-R-Right. Of course." I stretch my arms outward in a signal for him to help me into his top.

We walk a few doors down the hallway, probably heading to his rooms so he can put another t-shirt on, but I'm still mesmerized by this walking piece of popsicile in front of me.

Why, thank you very much. I do try. Though keeping up with Arrie is pointless.

Pretty sure they can both crush me like a grape. "Grapes! I like grapes."

Nine laughs once more and says, "Having you around is going to be the most fun I've had in ages. I can tell." There's a slight skip to his step after that.

We stop outside a door identical to mine just a few meters down the hallway but on the opposite wall.

"I'll be just a minute."

I wait outside, and in a couple of minutes, he returns.

What does his room look like?

Nine comes back outside with a new t-shirt on—a regular, less fancy one this time that has the phrase HANGING OUT written underneath a lost game of hangman. "Okay. Ready."

Wondering what my room looks like already, Sweetie?

"I, err . . . No." Smooth. Real smooth.

Nine laughs. "It's okay. Everyone has a room that suits them perfectly, so it's natural to be curious."

"Really?"

"Yeah, that's why everyone was so impressed by your library. You're already awesome enough of a person to know what you want and who you are."

"That's ridiculous. I don't even know my name." Even I hear the bitterness in my voice and wince at the impact it has on the conversation. "Sorry."

"It's okay. You're allowed to be angry and frustrated."

We walk through the kitchen and out the back door into a garden, the likes of which I'm blown away by. Almost literally, as a gust of wind nearly sweeps me off my fragile feet, but Nine steadies me.

"Careful there."

I didn't really see much of it the other night, just the edges of the forest and the bonfire.

"Thanks."

The garden is larger than anything I've ever seen before—probably even bigger than my library. The forest is to our left, the trees multicolored, from greens to purples to oranges. They all blur into a rainbow of colors that sparkles in the morning sunlight so brightly it's almost hard to look at.

Just outside the door and to the right sits a patch of burned grass from the bonfire, and I smile at the memory of seeing everyone together. They are all soooo cute.

We've been called many things over the years, but cute is a first.

We both laugh as Nine leads me onto a path that winds through the flowers and fields in front of us; a few well-placed fallen logs and vine trails make for a more natural look. This place is clearly managed, but it's so beautiful.

"We keep all kinds of creatures on the grounds. For potion ingredients and things."

"Really? Like what?"

"Well, unicorns, for example, were hunted to extinction hundreds of years ago, but we have a small herd in the forest. Their horns contain magical dust, similar to pixie dust."

I nod my understanding.

"People wanted the high, and they were hunted for it. But they're also useful in all kinds of confusion potions, some protection charms, and a whole host of other things."

Makes sense. "What other creatures?"

"We keep a flock of pixies in the flower garden. They tend to the flowers, some of which act as more ingredients, and the pixies provide us with a monthly supply of dust in exchange for a free home."

My eyebrows raise in question. They're using pixies to get high?

"Again, for magical ingredients. But pixie-dust highs are rather fun."

I give him another incredulous look.

He just laughs and continues on through a small field of grass and . . . horses. They have horses! My face lights up, and I can't help but smile.

"You like horses?"

"I think so. They have a specific meaning, but I'm not really sure what."

"Well, they're ours. We all have a horse. I'll take you out to the paddocks sometime. They're an unusual kind of horse."

"Well, if the Horseman of Famine is saying something is unusual, that must mean it's pretty fucking strange."

"Yup." He looks ahead to the sunrise and gives a deep sigh. "Listen, I know this has been a strange adjustment for you, but if you have any questions, now is a good time to ask."

"Yeah, it hasn't been easy. I guess being the Fifth Horseman isn't what bothers me, and I don't think the fact of being immortal has sunk in yet, you know. I just want to know who I am. Who I was. Did I leave family behind? What about friends, my job, my life? Did I have a pet?"

Nine reaches over and puts an arm around my shoulders, and I feel myself melt into it slightly. "I know. We all felt the same way. But we had our memories, so we knew what we were leaving behind. Most of us had a life, a family. It wasn't easy. Be we forged a new identity, became something more than what we were when we were merely human. In a way, not having those memories might be a blessing." He looks sad, but in a peaceful sort of way, as though the memory of his former life still holds pain, but he's at peace with those memories.

"I don't think I'll ever be at peace until I know. Someday, I'm going to have to find out. But for now, I have some questions. Actually, I have a lot of questions."

"I bet." He coughs and points to some pixies in the distance, flapping around some flowers. They have all kinds of colors painted throughout their wings, and their green bodies are no bigger than my forearm. "Ask away."

Where to start . . . ? "Where are we?"

"Way to start easy." He chuckles and gestures to the environment. "This is a realm separate from Earth. We call it *Sheruta*. The house is magical, as you've probably seen." He gestures behind him, and I get my first look at the house from the outside.

I stop walking, taking stock of the . . . house. "You call that a house? It's like ten mansions melded together and had a monster baby." Seriously, the thing is stupid huge. It looks around five times the size of the White House, and that's being stingy. Various windows line the house in no particular strategy or order; it doesn't really have a structure, as though they've added building blocks to it over time. Which, I guess they have. Their needs grew over time, meaning the house probably provided for them.

"That's correct. It's a little excessive, but we like to think it's Fate's apology for lumping us with this life."

"You don't like being immortal, do you?"

I bet that's why they sleep together and try to live it up as best they can, to make the most of a shitty situation.

"It's hard being this isolated. We can't really be friends with mortals because they just die, and hundreds of years of watching our friends die gets too painful to continue."

That's . . . Damn, that's hard.

"But you have each other, though. That's a . . . friendship that'll last forever." I hesitated. Why did I hesitate? Guess it's because I don't believe Nine when he says none of them have ever fallen in love with each other. We look for love, it's a part of being human—even for mythical beings; if all they have is each other, then they've probably fallen in love a long time ago, and they're just denying it to themselves.

Nine gives me a sheepish look, and I can tell he's reading my mind but also giving me space by not answering my unspoken thoughts.

"Yes. I couldn't imagine going through this life alone, without them." He turns back around to me and asks, "Next question?"

"Is it just the house here in this realm?"

"No. There's a town with residents, shops, and all kinds of things to the west, the beach with an ocean to the east, and all kinds of creatures roaming the mountains in the north. It's not as big as Earth, but we're not totally alone here."

Shops? There are shops? "I can go shopping?"

He groans as he wipes a hand over his face. "You're just like Dea. He loves shopping, too."

Laughter erupts from behind us, and I whip around, trying to calm my beating heart into submission.

"Relax. It's just Warro, our gardener. He lives in the town but works here." Nine puts another hand on my shoulder, the gesture growing more comfortable the more often he does it.

"Ah. Sorry about that."

"No worries, dear." He has a straw hat with a large brim

shadowing his tan features and dark eyes.

"We'll let you get on, Warro."

Warro tips his hat to him, saying, "As you wish, sir."

He walks away as we continue toward the forest. "So, err . . . Does he know what you all are? Is he human? You guys have servants?"

"Stop. One question at a time. We have people to help manage the house and its grounds because the house is not, apparently, self-cleaning. And yes, we've asked hundreds of times. It never happens. So we employ the locals, who all know who we are and what we do but don't tend to get involved with us past that. We have around fifteen staff members on board, so don't freak out if you come across any of them. They're not allowed to enter our private rooms, except for the washing, and a few of the other rooms around the house, but they wander around freely other than that."

"I see. Makes sense."

"Oh, one more thing." He holds up a hand, as if mentally stopping himself. "House rule: don't fuck the staff."

I stop still and choke on my own saliva. "Why is that a house rule?"

Nine looks at my bright red face and laughs. "Because Con did that once, and it didn't end well. So, we made it a rule."

"Ah. So what happened?" I wag my eyebrows at him, kinda excited for some normal gossip.

"I'll let Con tell you herself. It's a funny story, but it's maybe a little unfair to the human staff member, hence why we don't allow it."

Oh. "Any other rules I should know about?"

"Clean up after yourself." He lists them off one by one on his fingers. "Help out around the house, don't bring guests round—ever—and don't fuck the staff. That's about it, really. We make them up as we go to make our lives easier."

No bringing anyone around? Ever? What if I make a friend and want to invite them over? Is that not okay? I know they said it will be easier if I don't make any friends, but I just don't want that. Everyone is really nice and super hot, but I don't want to live without interacting with others. How am I supposed to help protect the world if I know nothing of its people?

The ache in my chest is starting to get a little painful, and I can feel myself starting to wheeze.

"Let's stop for a bit, let you catch your breath." He gestures to a log just outside the tree line. "Sorry, I wasn't sure how far you could walk, so I just set out for a regular hour."

I wave my hand in dismissal. "Don't worry about it. I want to get back to normal, and I can only do that through exercise. Should probably work on eating right while I'm at it." I sigh. I really enjoyed those brownies.

"Well, then, we'll go on regular morning walks until you're well enough to start running. Then Arrie and you will run. I know Dea has a training plan for your fitness when you're all healed. So that'll help."

"He does? Do I get no say in this?"

"You're a Horseman. Until we know your gifts and what type of Horseman you are, we need to just work on everything, including your fighting skills, general fitness, and see if you can use any kind of magic. Things like that."

"No," I growl.

"No?"

"You heard right. No. I'll decide when I'm ready, what I want to work on, and what I'll be doing with my now-immortal life." I stand up, a new sense of determination coursing through me. "C'mon. I want to hurry and get back so I can yell at Dea."

Nine laughs a little but gets up and starts walking. We walk through the forest—along a trail that leads back to the house—in total silence, other than my occasional wheezy breathing and Nine's worried face that speaks loudly enough it's practically a physical noise. He's worrying I'm walking too fast, but I just need to let Dea know that it isn't okay to boss me around. I don't want him designing a training plan without even consulting me. Or asking if that's okay.

It's my life. It might now be immortal and belong to the Horsemen of the Apocalypse, but it's still mine.

The forest is beautiful, honestly, it is, but I'm too frustrated and angry to enjoy it. We reach the house in about twenty minutes and find the rest of them sitting around the table eating breakfast and laughing.

Connie stops what she's eating and looks at me, worry etching at her features.

"Dea!" Nine calls from behind me. "Sweetie's here to yell at you over something that I, for once, agree with." His bright red hair ruffles under the laugh he lets slip from his otherwise blank façade.

You're on my side, Nine?

Yep. He really needs to learn to talk to people before making plans. It's rude.

"You're right, it is rude," I say out loud so Dea can hear. "Dea?"

He looks up at me and gulps. "Yes?"

"What made you think it was okay to dictate what I do with my new life? You think that just because I'm not millennia old like you guys, I can't design my own training plan? That just because I've lost my memories I'm somehow less of a person?" I can feel my voice rising with each sentence, and Dea's face is reddening with each flinch of my words.

"No, I . . . It is my job to look out for us all. That includes you, now."

"Well, you can stop. I don't want someone ruling my life. I'm my own person—a woman from the twenty-second century—and I don't like people dictating what I do and when I do it. You have an idea? Fine. Run it by me. Ask me if I'd like to do that. Otherwise, keep your stupid male supremacy away from me."

"I-I am sorry. We will look at it together."

"No, we won't." I look toward the floor. "Look, I know it may seem stupid to you, but I don't even know who I am right now. I'd like to at least be able to become my own person, on my own terms. The last thing I need is someone telling me what to do with my whoever-the-fuck-I-am self."

Dea sighs, gets up, and brings his sexy, tight-chested, t-shirted self next to me.

Goddess, staying mad at him is hard.

"You are right. It was rude and inconsiderate. We have never had someone around like you before. And we did not lose our memories when we changed, so that is new, too. It is hard on us all. We can see how much this is bothering you— Nine even gets a direct link to your pain—but there is very little we can do about it, and that bothers us." He gestures to everyone in the room.

That's why they're being nice to me? Because they feel bad this is my new life?

Nine steps forward and joins us, putting a hand on my shoulder and the other around Dea's waist. "No. That's not it at all. We're nice to you because we're actually quite nice people, and we're trying our best to make you feel at home in this new world that you've just been shoved into. We've had millennia to get to know each other, and there's nothing we don't know about each other, but you're new. We don't know you. Meaning, interacting with you isn't like our normal interactions with each other. It's new for us, so please just give us time."

Guilt wells at Nine's words, and despite my spiraling thoughts that maybe I overreacted, Nine doesn't contest them.

"I'd like to take a look at that training plan with you tomorrow morning." I look at Dea and blanch at his smile. He isn't even angry with me. Goddess, it's hard to stay mad at this a-hole.

"Of course, Angel. Whenever you are ready."

Dea leans down and runs a hand from the top of my shoulder to the tip of my wrist and stops there. My whole body tingles under his touch, as though every crevice of his fingers has found every inch of my skin and set it on fire.

I want him to go further. I can feel the anticipation as my body tries to hold itself on the edge of a cliff, waiting for his next move just as I wait for my next breath. The rest of the world around us stops.

Nine's eyes glaze over for a moment, then flicker back to their usual golden brown.

Dea looks at me with smiling eyes, that mischievous glint shining in them once again. He lets his hand wander into my palm, his short nails lightly drawing circles over the sensitive parts, before grabbing it with his own. "Now, Angel, please try not to yell at us when we mess up. We are only . . . the Four Horsemen, after all."

A snicker of laughter escapes my lips, and he sighes in contentment. "That is better. Hearing you laugh is a much-desired improvement upon hearing you yell." He brings my hand up to his mouth and presses his lips gently against the knuckles.

I can feel his warmth spreading throughout my hand, and the heat of his gaze on my face sends a shiver of desire through my body, but something else comes with it, something darker.

The world shadows for a moment, leaving only Dea and me in the wake of the darkness, and something slithers over my bare arms and down to our entwined hands.

Dea jumps away, Nine right by his shoulder.

When my eyes focus on the world around me once again, I can see a shadowy mist forming at my fingertips, curling into a ball of energy connecting to every part of me. It wants something. I'm just not sure what.

"What is that?" I squeak.

"Magic," Nine says in wonder. "You're the first Horseman to have actual magic."

Panic broaches the surface of my mind, sending my hands into a shaking fury. What do I do with it? Can it hurt someone?

Nine is the one who answers. "It can't hurt us. Well, it could injure us, but we can't die. Stop panicking and start welling down those emotions. It was your desire that fueled it—I'm assuming—so stop thinking with your dick and start thinking with your mind."

"I don't have a dick, Nine!"

Connie chuckles from behind us. "It's just an expression. Stop thinking with your vagina and start using your head."

Right. I look at everyone in the room, roll my eyes, and turn around. As embarrassing as this is, I need to control this new magic, and that will be easier if I'm not staring at them.

Calmness. Tranquillity. Peace. C'mon, you can be

peaceful. Think of the gardens, of the calmness of the forest, or the tranquility of the horses.

I breathe in through my mouth and out through my nose, attempting to calm my body into being normal again.

The darkness trickles back over my arms, back to wherever it came from, before disappearing completely.

Turning back around, I ask, "What was that?"

Dea steps forward, a smile twisting his features. "Magic. One we have not seen in hundreds—thousands—of years. It is Angel magic."

Chapter Nine

Angel magic. I have Angel magic. And it's black, which is a bit disappointing. I haven't asked what Angel magic is or how it functions or why it is black, and instead I simply sit and eat breakfast in silence, listening to their bustling conversation echo around me, lulling me into forgetting how much of a freak I've just become in the space of five minutes.

Grabbing the nearest newspaper—one Connie has just finished with—I open the first page and scan the upcoming headlines: VAMP ATTACK SERIAL IN MIDWEST US; INTERNATIONAL FAE PROSTITUTION RING UNCOVERED; PIXIE DUST FARMS UNVEIL CRUEL TREATMENT.

The list goes on and on the more pages I turn, and with each new headline, I have to hold back a gasp at some new unspoken horror.

On page forty-six, however, a headline catches my eye that sends all the others tumbling into dust: VAMPIRES VS THE SC. An article succeeds it, describing how the SC has lowered the Vampires' blood supply—again. (Humans donate to the program, the SC control the supply, and Vampires get daily rations.) But if the SC continues lowering those rations, it'll cause havoc. How long will the Vampires continue to starve for the sake of peace? How much longer until they fight back?

Breakfast is an assortment of rolls, cheeses, pastries, and other insanely tasty treats. I eat what little I can, but between the world's troubling affairs and the whole Angel magic thing, my stomach's doing somersaults the entire hour.

Finally, everyone leaves, and it's just me and Nine left at the table.

"If there's anything you need?"

I sigh. "Thanks, but I think I'm just going to spend some time by myself for a while. Maybe explore the house a bit."

He smiles and leaves me to my peace—whatever kind of peace I'm going to get, given the circumstances. But I wasn't joking when I said I need to explore the house a bit. This place is like a maze. Will probably take months to learn all of its nooks and secrets.

I start by going right at the staircase that I usually turn left at to get to the kitchen. It leads me down a smaller-than-average (not that it's small by normal standards—I think) corridor and peek inside many of the rooms, but most are just storage closets, cleaning closets, a washroom, and a few guest rooms.

"Hello, Miss, can I help you?"

I jump out of my skin for a second before turning back around and seeing a petite Fae woman handling a load of laundry, and guessing from the dark, gothic clothes in the basket, I assume the garments are Dea's.

"No. Sorry. Just nosing around. This place is like a maze."

"Ha, that it is, love. Well, down here"—she gestures to the corridor we're in—"are all the servants' quarters. We have rooms we can bunk in if need be, though most of us don't bother, as we live nearby. But we have cleaning supplies, laundry rooms, and all sorts down here."

"Ah, I see. So that's why none of the team comes down here." I roll my eyes. They don't even do their own washing. Eesh.

"It's nothing like that." She looks to the floor. "We're well paid, and it creates honest work for the *Sheruta* citizens; plus, when the Horsemen are really busy, they barely have time to eat, much less keep this mammoth of a house clean."

I sigh, giving in to the fact that I will just have to go along with it. "I guess you're right. But it wouldn't kill them to make things easier on you." I reach my hands out. "Here, let me help with that."

She has one hand on her back and winces when she moves.

"Have you asked if Dea could look at your back?"

Her face flames bright red. "Gods, no!" she squeaks. "We don't talk to them."

I giggle. "They're not gods, you know. You can say hi. They don't bite."

"Maybe not your hands, they don't . . ." she says. I look at her in horror for a moment, but she waves her arm at me in dismissal. "Was just joking, Miss."

"Please, call me . . ." I look away for a moment and collect myself, lest I fall into tears at this poor woman's feet. Will I ever have a name to my barely there identity? "Errr, in fact, never mind." I grab the washing basket from the lady. "What's your name?"

"Missandre, Miss."

"Well, Missandre, you just show me where to go, and I'll pop this in there for you. And I'll ask Dea to look at your back."

She gushes a humble smile at me.

"And next time, feel free to come to me with any issues. I'll help you deal with them."

"You're too kind, Miss."

She directs me to the laundry room I passed earlier, and I help her put all the clothes into the magically enhanced machines that wash, dry, and fold it all for you.

"I'm going to continue exploring, but if you need anything, come find me."

She nods and gushes another thank-you before I leave her to her work.

"They really need to take better care of their staff here," I mumble to myself as I continue down the myriad of staff hallways that leads to a wide-open foyer decorated in beautiful Morrocan mosaic tiles. In the center stands a fountain with a statue of a woman, and upon closer inspection I realize it's Connie—those telltale long braids seem to be a trademark for her.

Has she always been this beautiful?

Shaking the question away, I walk through one of many corridors beyond, and this one takes me into a black marble circular room with four shiny marble doors—each one a different color.

Which to choose?

The red speaks to me the most, so I go to that door, only to find it locked. Hmmm . . . Interesting.

It's like being stuck down a rabbit hole in here.

Those are our weaponry rooms. You'll need magical permission to get into each one. We'll need to build you one soon, too.

Weaponry rooms? That's fucking epic!

I now understand the significance of the colors: red for

Nine, black for Dea, light blue for Arrie, and purple for Connie.

Goddess, these people are fucking nuts. Amazing, but nuts.

I spend all afternoon searching various hideaways and holes stashed all over the ground floor—hundreds of different rooms, all with various purposes—until I'm well and truly lost.

I end upin a small corridor of empty rooms, and I can't remember which way I came in or which way is backward.

Errr, Nine? Can you hear me from over here?

I'm tempted to stay quiet and see what you'll do, but even I'm not that cruel. What's up?

You don't already know?

I'm not constantly in your head, especially with how far away you are right now. Where the fuck are you, Sweetie?

I have no clue. I'm kinda lost.

I know he's laughing right now, but I'm really starting to panic. I hate being lost.

Hold up, let me just look through your eyes a sec.

I feel a slight uncomfortable presence in my mind, like someone's there with me but isn't.

Turn around and look down the next corridor for me?

I do what he says.

Ah! You're in the old east wing. There's nothing down there but empty rooms. I'll send Dea.

Thank you.

I wait all of five minutes, finding myself a comfy spot on the floor, before Dea whizzes past me and stops a few meters away.

"Got lost, Angel?"

"Just a bit." I keep my eyes on the floor. "Sorry."

"Do not be silly. It must be easy to get lost in here. I am forever saving servants when they go wandering around." He rolls his eyes when I look up, and his comment reminds me of Missandre.

"That reminds me . . . Dea, could you look at Missandre's back for me? I'm worried it's not helping her work at all."

He looks at me with a strange, puzzled expression on his face. "Of course, but she should have come to me sooner."

"They're a little scared," I say as he leads me back the way I came, and through some nearly recognizable corridors. "Of all of you."

"Really?"

"They look at you like gods, Dea. They wouldn't bother troubling you."

"Hmmm, well, we will have to change that, will we not?"

I smile to myself. Death is such a genuinely nice guy; that sounds strange, even in my head, so I don't do myself the embarrassment of saying it out loud.

Once Dea leads me back to the kitchen, I make myself a strong cup of coffee with plenty of sugar and head upstairs to read. I'm halfway through an interesting book on how to store magic in certain high-level charms—and I'm honestly rather intrigued by the prospect of potentially being able to keep smaller, less potent doses of the Horsemen's power in charmable objects—when Connie comes and gets me.

"Ready for a girly night?"

Connie and I have been arranging a girl's night for this evening that I've been looking forward to all day. Not sure what she's got planned, but it sounds like a good idea.

"Sure. Help me into my pajamas, and then we can go."

Connie helps me into my nightwear, packing a small bag of blankets and more of Arrie's brownies along the way. She drags me all the way down to the theater room, where the guys sit around the kitchen table.

"Oh, movie night?" Nine asks.

"Nope." Connie shoves open the door that leads to the dark corridor. "Not for you. Sorry, no boys allowed." She giggles as she leads us down the pitch-dark corridor and into the light beyond that signals we've reached our destination.

"Soooo," I start, "what you got planned?"

"Ohhh, it's a surprise. Well, not really, but I'm hoping you'll like it. And if not, we can just watch movies all night instead."

"We're not here to watch movies?"

She opens the door, and light seeps from within. I blanch at the room beyond. She's completely changed the layout and structure. Now the room is full of nothing but floating beds. It still has the big screen at the end, but it also has lots of floating food dancing around on various-sized plates. It's like some kind of supernatural slumber party.

"Nope. We're here to play video games and eat all the dessert we want. Figured you might want to find out what kind of things you like to do and eat, since you can't remember anything."

That's really sweet, and a part of my heart squeezes tight at her thoughtfulness. "That's . . . really thoughtful. Thank you." I can feel the prickle of tears threatening to spill, but fuck no, I won't cry over something so stupid in front of this goddess of a woman.

"C'mon! Let's hop into bed and start playing!"

I get the feeling this is one of her favorite things to do, which is a great insight into her person. She seems to not be much of a girly girl, but prefers keeping herself active and watching action movies. So she looks like a girly girl but acts more like one of the guys. She does, however, have a thing for beauty, and I really need to get some tips because I've never met someone with skin smoother than this woman's. Guess having a lifetime to figure it out sure helps.

"So," I say once she's lowered one of the beds for us to clambor on and raised us back into the air, "what we playin'?"

"Well, I wasn't sure what you'd like, so I grabbed a selection. We've got various RPGs, some shooters, a couple MMOs, and some platform adventures."

She lays them all out in front of me on the plasmascreen, and I select the one with the coolest front cover. Handing me a controller, she puts the game ANNIHILATION onto the screen. It's a multiplayer shooter, and by the way her face lights up at the loading screen, it seems I've made a good choice.

Time to see if I like it, too. The controller seems familiar, and I know the basics of what each button does, so it seems I've played video games before.

She goes through what each button does in the game anyway and sets up a practice run. "Soooo," she starts, and I internally groan. That's one of those dish the gossip *soooos*, isn't it? "What's going on between you and Dea?"

I raise my eyebrows in question, having found a good hiding spot in the game to wait out the fireball attack she's just thrown my way.

"It's not only super obvious, but we're also really in tune with each other. Plus, I heard some of your conversation with Nine, so I know he's clued you up. And that fucker, I am not nosy." She pouts in her cute little way, crossing her arms over her chest and grunting as she dies in the game. "Besides, I'm really just curious."

"I don't know. And honestly, I don't want to find out. Sex for the sake of sex just doesn't sit right with me. I'm not really too sure why, but it just doesn't. Since I have no memories right now, I have no clue whom I've previously slept with, so for all intents and purposes, I'm a complete virgin."

Coughing the sparrows away, she finally says, "Damn. Didn't peg you for the monogamous type."

"Not really sure I'd say I'm monogamous, I just want my connections with people to mean something."

She shoots me with a rocket launcher, and now I'm losing, so I playfully punch her in the arm, but it's like punching a mountain. "Ah!" I pull my hand back and wince at the red mark forming.

"Oh yeah, punching me and Arrie'll hurt like a bitch. Sorry. Nine still tries now and then with the aid of some strengthening potions."

"Noted. Would have been nice to know that before I punched you, though."

"Not half as much fun that way." She winks and loads a new game. Hopefully, I'll win this time. "And just because we're not all in love doesn't mean it means nothing to us. We all care for each other; we just don't want to complicate our already-complicated lives."

Hopping across the map, I snipe her minions down and run for where it says she is on the mini-map. "To me, it just seems like you're all scared. Do you think that if things ended badly, you'd all break up and go your separate ways and the world would be doomed? It doesn't have to be like that. You've all said it a hundred times: you're immortal. I'm sure you'd all get over it and learn to be friends again."

"And if we didn't?" She pauses the game to look me dead in the eyes. "You'd be willing to bet the world's safety on that?"

I look her up and down, noticing every inch of her curves

that peek out of her skimpy tank top and shorts. She's wearing a lacy, red bra that pokes out the top of the tank, and I swear it's the perfect color on her. They're all amazing people. They honestly are. "Yeah, I would. You're all amazing, Connie. You've sacrificed millennia of love for the world. Live a little."

She blushes a bright shade of red, and I know I've gotten my point across when a few different plates of dessert fly over. I pick a few things from each one, intending to prove my point, too. I try each of them and love them all. "What are these?"

"Custard slices, chocolate profiteroles, and raspberry muffins."

"They're all amazing!"

"Well, the house serves good cakes, but I got these from town earlier. The baker has some serious skill, and the house can't get anything from this realm, just from Earth."

"C'mon, let's play some more games." I point to an odd-looking RPG called IN THE MOMENT OF DEATH. "I wanna play this one!" I bounce slightly on the bed in excitement and gleam when I realize that reaction feels a lot more like me.

We spend all night playing various video games, stay up way past midnight, and eat more desserts than I can possibly stomach. It's an amazing night, and she's even more awesome than I originally thought.

We fall asleep in the floating bed, sharing the duvet, and for the first time since I woke up here, I feel like I really have a friend.

The next morning, we're both rather bloated and still sleepy, but we crawl out of the bed and go into the kitchen for breakfast anyway.

"Which one was your favorite?" she asks as we sit at an empty table.

"Ermmm, maybe that weird gothic RPG. It was kinda cool. The one with the girl who has cat ears."

"Ha! I love that one, too." She looks around, confused. "Where is everyone?"

Dea enters the room looking a little frustrated but mostly amused. "Well, given that it is four in the afternoon, Arrie is out in the forest getting some training in before dinner, Nine is trying to get this new piece of Fae tech to work somewhere, and I was researching something."

I gulp. "It's really four pm?"

"Uh-huh." He nods. "Guess you ladies were having too much fun to bother telling me you would miss our morning meeting, Angel." He smirks at me and looks all smug at our disheveled clothing. "You've only just woken up, 'ey?" He winks at Connie and turns to leave.

"Wait! Dea, I'm so sorry I missed our meeting this morning. I'm free whenever you are."

"It is fine, Angel. I was just teasing. I knew you were going to miss it when I asked Nine to mentally check on you this morning, and he found you cuddled up in bed, still in the theater."

He gives me a knowing look, and I know exactly what direction his thoughts have traveled in, but I don't call him out on it. Instead, I smile and let him think whatever he wants.

Ugh, I really need to stop flirting with this guy. I have no intention of sleeping with him, and I really don't want to lead him on. I'm not really hungry, so I get up and go back to my rooms.

"Could you stop flirting with her, Dea? It's really not going to happen anytime soon," I hear Connie say in the background as I leave.

I don't really know what to do at this point. Everyone is

busy, I don't feel like reading, and I have no questions I need answering right this minute. Looking out the bedroom window, the green side of the forest calls to me. I can go for a walk. I did miss walking with Nine this morning, so fitting one in now sounds like a plan. Besides, I want a chance to get to see the forest again—in a less angry mood.

With a plan in place, I get into some more appropriate clothing—sweatpants and a loose tee—and make my way out into the gardens. The winding paths that leads through the front of the gardens takes me past fairy ponds, over carefully placed fallen logs, past bright blue mushrooms and shrubs with glowing leaves, and under an afternoon sun that glares down on all the garden's splendor. It truly is a sight to behold, and the instantaneous peace that settles over my heart and mind has my thoughts lulling with ideas of ways to stay calm in this new world of uncertainty.

I know I should be freaking out, throwing some kind of tantrum or having a meltdown, but something about this place just feels like home. I belong here. A relationship, even just a friendly one, with all the Horsemen scares me, and the suddenly large expanse of my future makes me apprehensive about everything I'll see and lose along the way, but despite the insecurity, I have the potential to really exist here. I can't remember my past, and I know I've left people behind on Earth, but maybe one day, I'll go back to see what my life once was, but right here and now, this is my present, and it's time to learn what that really means.

This new power, the Angel one that presented itself yesterday, isn't normal, even for a Horseman of the Apocalypse—and that scares the shit out of me. Like, put me in a coma and make me skip a few centuries, because I can't be bothered to deal with the drama of that kind of magic terrifing. But the Horsemen of the Apocalypse have their place in this world, an important pedestal of power, and for a reason I'm sure will become clear at some point, they need me.

I reach the forest's edge, and the gentle glow of the rainbow-color leaves on this side create a haze of multicolor shadows that flit around like dancing pixies and their ever-changing wings. It really is fucking awesome.

Has it always been this way? Or has it changed at some point to someone's preference?

I log that away in my list of questions to ask either the team or the Seeing Stone. For the time being, I wander off the beaten track and weave through the trees, always keeping an eye on which way leads back to the tree line connecting to the part of the garden I know, and just let my mind wander through the maze of beauty I've found myself in.

My mind worries over so much, creates so many questions I need answers to, and wonders over the infinite possibilities of what my powers could be and the things I could do now that I have an infinite number of years to experience life. It feels good to just let my mind go, not holding it back or letting fear stop me from simply thinking.

The phrase, live a little, echoes in my mind in a voice that isn't my own or any of the people's I've come to call friends over the past few days. Whose is it? And why is it so important to me?

Grunting in the distance penetrates my peaceful mind babble. "One. Two. Three. Four," the voice repeats in some kind of ritualistic chant.

What is that?

I follow the voice and discover a topless and sweat-sheened Arrie in a small clearing running through some kind of dancelike flow of movements. They all move in to one another, from lunges to spins to jumps, they're expertly executed, and his eyes never open. Not once. It's amazing to watch; his muscles ripple under every movement, and the way his slacks hang loose on his hips has my eyes glued to him. An all-too-familiar heat rushes through me, making my core ache with a desire I'm not yet ready to quench. But there's no harm in watching (I hope).

He's tied his shoulder-length white hair up into a knot out of the way, and I get a clear look at his not-frowning face for the first time. It's aged with years of trouble. I can tell from the frown lines and shadows beneath his eyes, but his face also speaks of an experience the others don't seem to grasp so heavily. Something about this man draws me in, something dark and twisted. I want to understand his pain, to revel in that darkness with him, to understand what kind of horrors this man can inflict.

I lean against a nearby tree and watch for the rest of his repetitive routine, and with each passing round of maneuvers, the curiosity within me grows.

What kind of workout is this?

What's the purpose?

How long has he been practicing this?

A part of me knows that he probably does this every day, because inner peace seems like a big deal to him, and ritualistic habit often helps with peace.

He finally stands still in the clearing, his arms hanging loose by his sides, feet relaxing in the soft, slightly worn grass underfoot. He turns. His ice-blue eyes meet mine in a shiver as he scowls me up and down under the falling sunlight. A growl escapes his lips as his brow creases, and his mouth turns into a sneer that has my hands shaking and my body wanting to flee.

Shit. I need to get out of here.

I stand straight and turn around to walk back to the house, embarrassed, but with a lighter mind and an even lighter soul, one etched with determination. It's time to start learning who I am and what I can do.

Chapter Ten

His blood seeps into a puddle at my feet, covering my knees and bare toes as I shed a single tear. I've never cried on a job before, but this has pushed me past my moral point of comfort. I bring in criminals, rogues, people who are then prosecuted by the Supernatural Council. Not kids. Not children.

No one told me my mark is a child.

"I'm sorry."

And no one told me that this child had a cyanide pill under his tongue. One he triggered the moment he saw me.

"I'm so sorry."

I've never been responsible for anyone's death before. Imprisonment? Sure. Maybe even a broken family or two, but they should have thought of that before they commited their crimes.

But death? I'm not a killer. At least not until today.

I wake up drenched in sweat and with my face coated in a slick film of tears as my stomach roils, and I have to run to the bathroom.

"Fuck," I say through clenched teeth as I brush them with more vigor than required. "Need to get a handle on these fucking nightmares."

My meeting with Dea is in a minute, and I walk downstairs to sit in his study and wait, but I find him waiting for me. "So you don't know what I am yet?" I ask as I take my seat. "What type of Horseman I am or the skills I possess?"

Dea sinks his face into his hands and lets out a long sigh. "No, I do not. But we can assume that because you are the only one of us to really have magic that you were called upon to deal with the turbulence within the magical community and what that will later lead to."

His eyes turn stormy with the thoughts of the potential future. The potential for war among the main magical forces of the world and the human population. This is clearly something that plagues his mind frequently of late.

"Right . . . about that. What do you mean the only one to possess real magic?" I don't get it. Dea can heal. That's magic, right? And what about Nine's telepathy?

"Our abilities are based on Angel and Demon powers, and because of that, we have inherited particular types of powers, rather than magic itself. Connie, having angelic powers, and Arrie, having demonic powers, both have passive abilities that allow them greater strength and focus in battle situations; Nine's abilities, which are demonic in nature, while a type of magic, aren't active types; and I, having angelic powers, can manipulate souls and persuade them to move and change their course of action." He gestures with his hands to each of their biblical depictions in turn on the large canvas above his desk. "None of us can use spells or have any sort of active magic. You are a shiny new toy, Angel."

Angel? That cannot be a coincidence. "Is there a reason

you call me that? I didn't think anything of it before, but since my magic seems to be Angel-based, I'm now starting to wonder . . ."

"Hmmm. That is a good question. I nicknamed you that because when I found you, it was the night of Halloween, and you were dressed in a costume of the Angel of Death, which we all found highly amusing." He looks up at me with a small smile. "You looked great, by the way. Killer outfit."

"Dea, focus. Please." I can't help but smile, though; he thinks I looked good in my Halloween outfit. Wait, why does that make me giddy-happy? I don't even remember wearing the fucking outfit!

"Right, sorry." He takes a sip from his cup of tea and continues. "I am not really sure of the significance. Could just be a coincidence, and probably is, if I am honest."

He's hiding something, but if he's hiding it from me, there's probably a good reason. He's been so upfront about everything from day one. Whatever he's hiding, he isn't sure about yet.

"So we're not sure what I am, what I can do, or who I was, but we can explore more about my abilities when I'm fully healed, right?"

"Yes." A genuine smile graces his features, and my professional businesslike resolve melts as I trace the line of his jaw along his smile with my eyes. "And that should only be another week at most. For now, you just need to hold tight and try to recover as fast as possible."

"Okay. Then, can we up the healing baths to twice a day? They really help. I can breathe and move now, and I can stretch my arms above my head, meaning the wound isn't such a problem anymore. Plus, I can walk for about a half hour without getting wheezy and being in pain, so the inside seems to be healing well, too."

"Good. And yes, I can do that. I will do one bath in the morning and one in the evening. Sound good?"

"Perfect. Thanks." I pick up my plasmascreen, and bring up a timetable-like feature. "I plan to do some yoga at dawn and then spend the morning in the library doing some research."

"Okay. For now, I will do the healing baths after your morning yoga, and when you begin training, I was thinking of having you do some early physical combat training with Arrie."

"Then some study time, right? I have loads of stuff to catch up on, and it's really bugging me that I can't remember some vital details about the world." I put the cup of coffee to my mouth and sip.

"Sure. Then you will have me and Nine for the afternoon, working on your abilities and magic." He pauses then, looking up at me from the schedule. "Is that okay?"

He's trying to be considerate. That's soooo sweet, I coo in my head, but I don't want to say that out loud, so I just nod for him to continue.

"And then some weapons training with Connie in the evening."

"Ohhh, I get weapons? Oh my goddess, I could totally be a ninja with all the dark shadow magic and night vision. Can I get throwing stars? What about daggers that strap to my thigh, like in those sexy movies?"

Dea chuckles as his eyes light up a pale golden color. "We will let you and Connie decide. She is best at that kind of stuff. Arrie is pretty good, too, but we need to divide their workload somehow, and he is better at hand-to-hand combat."

I nod my understanding and bury my excitement over

what kind of weapons I'll be using. It can be anything, can't it? Completely my choice. Yay! I mentally clap my hands like a child on Christmas Day morning.

"Oh, before you go . . ." Dea rifles through a massive pile of paperwork in the top drawer until he finds something and hands it to me. It looks like a thin black pen but with two buttons on the side. "A translational bookscreen. Keep it."

"Thanks!"

I shoot out of my chair and walk to my library as fast as possible. I can't wait to be able to run again, so I can run around in my crazy, excitable moments. It feels a little withdrawn to simply walk everywhere, like it isn't really me. At least not this new, immortal me.

The rest of the day, I'm holed up in my study, using my new translational bookscreen to translate that mammoth of a book, and it's amazing! You just press a button to open the screen, which descends from the pen-like thing, and it glows a faint blue as it resizes itself to match the page underneath; the words then magically translate into the programmed language—English, in this case.

I have read half the tome by the time lunch comes and goes, where I forget all about bothering to eat, but I have learned the complete origins of the Four Horsemen:

THE FOUR HORSEMEN OF THE APOCALYPSE, ONCE HUMAN, WERE CALLED UPON BY AN ANCIENT MAGIC TO PROTECT THE WORLD FROM ITS OWN, SELF-CREATED, EVIL. A MORTAL MAN, CONCERNED ABOUT THE STATE OF THE THEN-CURRENT WORLD, WENT LOOKING FOR ANSWERS. STUMBLING ACROSS THE SEVEN SEALS IN AN OLD TOMB DEVOTED TO A GOD LONG FORGOTTEN TO THE REALM OF MAN, HE BROKE THE FIRST FOUR, BRINGING FORTH A MAGICAL FORCE SO POWERFUL, HUMANITY WOULD FOREVER LIVE IN PEACE.

THE REST OF THE SEALS, WHICH REMAINED UNBROKEN, HAVE SINCE BEEN HIDDEN BY THE MAN-MADE COURSE OF TIME. THE FOUR HORSEMEN—CONQUEST, DEATH, WAR, AND FAMINE—ARE THOUGHT TO HOLD THEIR OWN SEALS NOW, AS THE ONLY WAY TO KILL A TRULY IMMORTAL BEING THAT POWERFUL IS TO BURN THE SEAL THAT HOLDS ITS MAGICAL LIFE FORCE INTACT. DOING SO WOULD THEORETICALLY PURGE THE WORLD OF THAT HORSEMAN, CREATING AN IMBALANCE TO THE STATE OF THE WORLD AS WE KNOW IT TODAY.

JOSHUA, THE MORTAL HERO WHO BROKE THE FOUR SEALS, WAS WORSHIPPED AMONG MANKIND FOR HAVING BROUGHT AN ERA OF PEACE TO AN OTHERWISE WARRING, STARVING WORLD. LEGENDS WERE CREATED, STORIES WERE WRITTEN, AND FROM OUT OF THE ASHES, HE WAS REBORN AS THE LEGEND OF JESUS.

Wow. Jesus really broke their seals? That's . . . insane.

They're just like me, called upon to help with some state-of-the-world nonsense, and they've been doing that ever since. All right, wars break out now and then, and some countries starve during periods of poverty, but they always ebb and flow over the course of time, and that's because of them. They do that. They keep the world safe. But they won't be able to fix a world at war with magic because none of them actually have any real magic. At least, whoever broke my seal doesn't seem to think so.

Wonder who it is, and why?

No matter how many times I ask my Seeing Stone that question, no answers are given. It seems that's something I need to find the answer to myself.

Sweetie, dinner's ready if you're hungry.

Ah, food. The rumble of my lunch-starved belly penetrates the silence—it's probably best to refuel so I can come back to my questions later.

Entering the kitchen with renewed vigor, a familiar sight catches my eye—everyone in their usual spots around the dinner table, but with some kind of food I haven't tried yet.

Taking a large sniff, I recognize it in the recesses of my misted memories. "Italian."

Nine turns around, a smile on his face. "You like Italian food?"

I nod, a little unsure.

"Well, we have lasagne, garlic ciabatta, tossed salad, and a good white to wash it down with." He points to a bottle of white wine on the center placemat, and I can't help but grin.

Taking a seat, Dea asks, "Did the bookscreen work?"

"Yeah. It's an awesome piece of tech. Thanks!" I grab my plate and start loading a slice of lasagne, some of the ciabatta, and a little salad. "Been reading all day."

Connie pinches a bit of the tomato I left on the side of my plate, having discovered I don't like it much. "What were you reading?"

I gulp, unsure if they're going to be weird about the book. "The origins of the Four Horsemen."

They all put their cutlery down and stare at me, but it's Dea who speaks up. "You managed to find a book with an accurate telling of that story?"

Accurate? "I hope so . . ." Now that I think about it, how accurate is the information my Seeing Stone provides me?

"It has to be accurate, otherwise it wouldn't provide that book to you." Nine's palm rests of my thigh, which is becoming a habit at the dinner table, and each time, it sends a tingle of heat up my leg, and the smirk he always gives me tells me he damn well knows it, too. "Mine gives me website addresses to look up, and it's the same kind of deal. It only provides ones with accurate information. But sometimes, if information is scarce, the accuracy is limited to a few particular facts on any particular webpage."

Sometimes I forget how much of a nerd Nine is, but I love it. It's . . . refreshing.

Nine smiles and returns his gaze to his plate, his cheeks and ears blushing a gentle shade of scarlet. Our little resident nerd isn't used to compliments, which equally amazes and frustrates me.

Chapter Eleven

The next two days are full of note-taking, morning walks with Nine, and shutting myself indoors to finish reading that book. In the process, I learn the complete origins of the Four Horsemen and all their gifts and powers—well, the ones in the book anyway. I make hundreds of pages of notes summarizing various facts about the people I now share my eternal life with:

DEA, DEATH, CAN ACCESS THE ENERGY WITHIN SOMEONE'S SOUL AND MOVE IT OUT OF THE BODY OR PULL IT BACK IN, INCLUDING TO PERSUADE IT TO HEAL. THIS IS KNOWN AS SOUL MANIPULATION AND IS UNIQUE TO DEATH. HE CAN ALSO MAKE SOMEONE'S DEEPEST, SOUL-DEEP DESIRES CHANGE, PERSUADING THEM TO DO AS HE WISHES. HE PREFERS TO WIELD DUAL DAGGERS IN BATTLE, AS HE IS THE FASTEST OF THE HORSEMEN DUE TO HIS FAZING ABILITY, AND HE USES STEALTH-BASED SKILLS TO FIGHT. HE IS INVISIBLE TO EVERYONE BUT THE FOUR HORSEMEN UNLESS HE CHOOSES TO EXPEND ENERGY MAKING HIMSELF VISIBLE, AND EVEN THEN, HUMANS ONLY SEE HIM AS SEMI-OPAQUE.

CONNIE, CONQUEST, HAS MORE ABILITIES, BUT THESE ARE LIMITED IN THEIR USAGE. SHE HAS EXCELLENT SENSES TO HELP HER IN BATTLE, ESPECIALLY HEARING, AS WELL AS NEVER-FALTERING AIM AND STAMINA. SHE COULD BATTLE AT ONE HUNDRED PERCENT FOR WEEKS AND NEVER TIRE. SHE DOESN'T NEED TO SLEEP OR EAT MUCH BUT CHOOSES TO DO BOTH ANYWAY. SHE IS A SKILLED ARCHER, AND HER THOUSAND-YEAR-OLD BOW IS HER WEAPON OF CHOICE.

NINE, FAMINE, HAS THE ABILITY TO READ MINDS AND EMOTIONS, COMMUNICATE VIA TELEPATHY, AND ACCESS SOMEONE'S DREAMS. THIS ALLOWS HIM TO UNDERSTAND A COUNTRY OR PEOPLE'S DESIRES AND PROBLEMS, THEREFORE USING HIS GREAT INTELLECT TO FIX POLITICAL ISSUES. WHEN IN BATTLE, HE USES MAGIGUNS AND A SHORT SWORD SWORD FOR A DEADLY COMBINATION.

ARRIE, WAR, IS A SKILLED WARRIOR, WIELDING DUAL BATTLE-AXES FROM ATOP HIS WARHORSE. HE HAS A BATTLE-MODE ABILITY THAT ALLOWS HIM TO SOLELY FOCUS ON THE BATTLE AT HAND, SHUTTING OUT ALL OTHER ISSUES, AS WELL AS A STRATEGY GIFT, WHEREBY THE BEST AND EASIEST WAY TO WIN A PARTICULAR FIGHT WILL PRESENT ITSELF TO HIM.

The more I learn about them, the farther my jaw drops. They all sound amazing, and I can't wait to see them in action. It's going to take me at least a few hundred years to be anywhere near their level. Hopefully, the world won't need that anytime soon.

Footsteps interrupt my note-taking, and Dea rounds the corner, quickly followed by Nine. It's eleven in the morning, and my lunch-starved brain is dawdling and procrastinating, so they're a welcome a distraction.

Nine rounds the desk and grabs the thick leather-bound notebook I've been using for my notes and casually flips through the hundreds of pages of squiggles. "Wow, Sweetie, you've really been working hard. You practically know all our skills and abilities inside and out, probably more than any other person in the world." He hands my book back and rests a hand on my shoulder.

Dea picks up the book for inspection. "Would you like me to read it over and add some extra notes for you?" He looks at my raised eyebrows and shrugs. "You cannot learn *everything* about us from a book. Some things we never wrote down. Like the location of our seals, for example."

Of course, they probably have them hidden so no one can kill them. It's been rumored in several texts that they hold their own seals nowadays, but Dea practically just confirmed it.

"You're all so . . . fascinating. You've been around longer than any other species and have abilities I can only dream of." I can't help the niggling doubt that creeps its way into my mind—the feeling that has made a home there over the past few days.

Nine tries to interrupt my oncoming mind babble, but I hold out a hand. "I know. It's okay." I get up and put my notebook in the top drawer, closing the latest reference book I had open with a bookmark. "So what did you guys want, anyway?"

Dea smiled. "Well, we were just headed into town and thought you might like to join us. It is about time you started learning about life in this realm."

"Ohhh, yeah! Oh my goddess, tell me I can go shopping."

Nine grumbles, but Dea laughs and says, "Finally, someone who understands. Yes, we can go shopping. It is a great place to shop, trust me." He threads his arm through mine and guides me out of the library.

I can walk for about an hour now without getting too out

of breath, but I'm worried about shopping all day. Will carrying everything cause further harm?

Nine takes my other arm. "Don't worry, we're going to walk slowly, and then we'll get any stuff you buy sent to the house directly. Minimal walking and carrying. Promise."

"Okay." I blush slightly, a little embarrassed they even have to do something so stupid for me, but I wave it off when Nine tries comfort me about it.

Once more appropriate footwear has been donned—booty flats—we head out the front door (which I didn't even realize existed until now). Turning around, I stop to admire the building's front exterior. Much like the backyard, the front yard is like a fairy garden, with the house having a very Japanese feel. My Japanese ethnicity and the style of the house and the Zen style of the gardens is way too much of a coincidence, surely?

"You're right." Nine's arm wraps around my waist and gently pulls me closer. "Before you got here, the house changed to suit what it presumed was your style."

"Damn." I whistle my appreciation. "But why?"

Dea wraps an arm around my shoulders and lands a hand on Nine's neck. "I have a theory about that." They seem particularly close, even for the Horsemen, but I just give Dea a look that I hope says go on and not dish the dirt. "Well, since you are the most magical being here, we are assuming you can wield more magic than us, and therefore, you may have a stronger connection to the house."

Makes sense in a sort of fated way. Has the house been magical this entire time because it waited for me? No, that doesn't make sense. The others have magic, too, just not in the same way. Has it been existing for everyone, no matter who or what came along in the future, then? Something doesn't add up.

Turns out the town is about a half hour's walk away, which is great because I'm getting out of breath from all the walking and talking.

"Let's grab some tea before starting." Nine gives me a long, side-eyed look, and I know instantly the decision is for my benefit.

Thank fuck, because I seriously want some coffee.

Ahead of us is a cobblestoned street that reminds me a little of medieval Europe with all the red brick and gray stone each side of the street, with signposts swinging in the light, afternoon breeze.

There are a few people meandering around, all of who give us a wide berth and a small bow aimed in Dea's direction. Wait, isn't he supposed to be invisible to others? At least, that's what I've read. Maybe the book is wrong.

"I can make myself visible for a few hours at a time, but humans still see me as slightly permeable. Luckily, there are no humans in this realm."

He still has his arm around me and resting on Nine's neck, and I'm pretty sure this particular fact will garner some gossip with the locals. Ah well, who really cares? We're immortal, we'll outlive them anyway.

Wow. Never thought I would think that cold-heartedly. True, though. But does that mean I should not make an effort? I mean, people still matter. Yup. Turns out my brain needs to put more effort into being morally centered.

The café we end up at is on the corner of the first street, and the first thing I notice are the plates of desserts flying around—just like the ones from mine and Connie's gaming night. A sudden image of Connie in that bloody skimpy tee and short-short pajamas flashes across my mind, making my breath hiccup and my core ache with an unstifling need.

Nine looks at me with raised eyebrows, trying his best to stifle a laugh. "Yes, this is where Connie got those desserts for you both."

Dea grabs us a table, but Nine's still giving me a knowing look and obviously trying to hide his obvious amusement, which doesn't go unnoticed by Dea.

"What is so funny?"

"Oh, nothing. But I have a feeling our little sweet thing over here"—he wraps his arm around my shoulders and squeezes slightly—"is going to create an interesting dynamic in our lives."

Interesting, huh? Is that what he thinks I am, interesting?

A waiter comes over and takes our orders, and I ask for an extra-large coffee and some of the cream puffs I had the other night.

The café in question is an interesting mix of magical and normal. It looks like so many cafés I've been in on Earth—a few now flitter across my memory—but not. The ones I can remember are plain, boring, normal. A few have some fancy décor, a few have some interesting themes, but none are like this. There's Fae magic at work here. The plates float over to the tables, along with trays of traditional Japanese tea (another odd curiosity), rather than being brought over by the waiters, who just run around cleaning and taking orders using various types of magic. The walls are deep red and plum in color, creating a mystical vibe that, if I wasn't sitting in another realm entirely, I would have assumed was due to tourism. It certainly has that traditional magical vibe going on.

By the time I turn my attention back to the table, everyone's orders have arrived, and Nine and Dea are locked in a mental conversation—I assume so anyway, since they're giving each other raised eyebrows and gestures. I just hope they aren't talking about me.

"So . . . err, I have a question."

They both stop their silent conversation, which makes me feel a little guilty (what is the proper etiquette for interrupting conversation when you can't hear it?), and look my way with warm smiles.

"How . . . How do I buy things?" It hadn't even crossed my mind before now, but I don't actually have any money. I'm not even too sure what money is used in this place or how to earn money as a Horseman of the Apocalypse that no one even knows exists.

Dea dismisses my concerns with a wave of his hand. "We have a group fund, as it is hard to earn money when saving the world. We have various investments on Earth, which the house turns into derra, the currency used here."

Makes sense. "But don't I need to chip in? I mean, I feel kinda bad that you're doing everything for me, and I haven't been doing much." I keep my eyes on the table, nudging my cream puff and eyeing the coffee, waiting for it to cool down.

"Nah. Don't worry. Dea usually handles it for us all anyway." Nine smiles, giving Dea a fist to bump, which he does so with a roll of his eyes.

There is more going on there, more than just general intimacy between immortal friends. But broaching that topic is a no-go right now because it still confuses the fuck out of me. But at least money is one less thing to worry about.

Dea chimes in after sipping his chai latte (of course that's what he ordered). "I will give you access to the team's account in a few days, plus the house account. We use the house account for things like today, and the team account when out on jobs. The only person not allowed anywhere near money is Nine. His Famine nature drains it every time he is upset or experiencing any kind of negative emotion. In a totally magical, only-Famine way."

Giggling, I give my coffee a swirl before drinking as Nine crosses him arms and lays back, silent (for once). "Okay. Thanks." It still feels weird to have access to these people's money, but I guess I'm one of them now, and I don't really get a choice in that.

"Look, Angel." Dea grabs my hand from across the table, clearly having been filled in on my inner thoughts from Nine (who I give the stink eye). "I know this has been a rough adjustment, especially since you have no memories, but today, you can just relax. Spend however much you like. Consider it a sorry-you-are-stuck-with-us-forever-now gift."

"Okay. But if anything is too expensive, just let me know."

"Fine." Dea laughs, his face the picture of amusement.

"I get the feeling she'll freak when she sees the accounts." Nine also looks amused by my cluelessness. The fucking ass. "C'mon. Hurry up. Let's get this over with."

"Not a shopping fan?"

"Not with this one." He points to Dea with his thumb, who shrugs and feigns innocence.

But I'm excited. The thought of shopping and seeing what I like and dislike both thrills and terrifies me. I quite like Connie's beautiful dressed-up style, but I get the feeling I'm more of a quirky, gothicy kind of girl. Definitely fits with the whole tattoos and pink hair I'm currently sporting.

"C'mon, then!" I drain my cup, and, noticing they have also finished, grab them both by the hands and walk us as fast as I can out of the café. "Oh, wait a minute!"

I turn on my heels and walk back toward the small desk in the back corner. "Excuse me?"

The purple-haired, pointy-eared Fae looks me up and down with a frown. "We donnat get many visitors here on *Sheruta*, girl. Who are ya?"

"Oh, right. I'm . . ." Damn it. Still don't have a name. "That's not really important. I'm staying with them." I point to the guys in the doorway, who stand waiting for me with smiles reaching ear to ear. Nine has probably filled Dea in on my intentions. "I just wanted to thank whoever made the desserts Connie ordered the other day. They were amazing and made for a great night. Thank you." I bow slightly, lowering my head.

"Oh." The guy blushes. "No need ta thank me, deary. It's always a pleasure doin' Miss Connie's orders."

"So, you're the fantastic baker? Oh, how wonderful." I clap my hands and give him a smile. "You have quite the talent, sir. Again, thank you very much."

"It was my pleasure, Miss." He looks at me, then gives the boys a strange, questioning look and looks back at me. "If you donnat mind me askin', Miss, what's your business with the Horsemen? They donnat 'ave visitors these days."

"Oh, I'm—"

Tell him you're just visiting.

"I'm just visiting. Hanging out with Connie for a few days."

"Ah! Well, it's good to see 'em makin' friends outside of their circle again."

"Indeed. If you'll please excuse me?"

"Ah, o' course. Have a good day, Miss."

I nod, give another small bow, and exit.

Dea grabs my waist this time, with Nine's arm over my shoulder. The intimacy is nice, if I'm being honest. I know it isn't sexual or anything, but the caring nature makes me feel a little less alone.

"Sorry," Nine says. "Not ready to announce you to the world yet."

"That's okay. I should have asked. Sorry."

Dea shakes his head at me, his hair falling out of place. "Do not be sorry for what you are. We should have mentioned we were trying to keep you a secret until you are all trained up."

I nod, feeling a little . . . ashamed. Part of me, the logical part, knows they're just trying to protect me and ease me into this world gently, especially given my memory loss and strange gifts, but the other part of me can't help but worry they might be ashamed of me or trying to hide me because they know I won't fit in.

Nine whispers in my ear, "You fit in perfectly. And I get the feeling that you'll be the one to bring us all together in the end."

Bring them all together?

I give him a questioning look, but he ignores me and continues walking down the next street.

The few streets this side of town have that same medieval Europe feeling mixed with a more magical approach, and the stores are all posh and tailored, with store clerks offering to help the moment you step through their door. I don't really know how to act, so I just roll with it. It's fun pretending for a day.

"Soooo . . . I looked through my closet before coming out with you guys, and it's a little on the small side. Even for necessities."

"Well, what do you need?" Dea smirks in excitement, and I realize that he really does love shopping.

"Workout gear, running shoes, everyday outfits, underwear,

and pajamas—which I only seem to have a single pair of."

Nine smirks. "You probably weren't much of a pajama girl, but the house does only bring stuff it thinks you like, so it probably didn't bring everything."

"Right." I point to what I hope is a general clothing store. "I need general clothing, underwear, and workout stuff."

Dea grabs my wrist and pulls me into the shop while Nine laughs it up behind me.

"This is the best place for casual wear, but we actually have a special exercise clothing store here in town," Dea says.

"We probably keep it open, for fuck's sake." Nine looks at me and says, "There's a fancy underwear store around town somewhere." He winks and goes off into the men's section.

"Damn." Sighing, I sink my head into my heads. I didn't think of it like that. I just really need some damn panties and bras, since the house seems to only have brought over a handful of each. "Shoulda brought Connie along."

"She loves shopping but tends to prefer the downtime of doing it alone." Dea comes up behind me, frightening the fuck out of me. "Sorry."

"You're terrifyingly silent, you know that?"

"You are pretty light-footed yourself, Angel." He has a handful of things in his arms in all the colors of the rainbow. "Try these on." He points to a changing room at the back of the store and guides me in that direction.

Flitting behind the satin curtains, I try on the first item: a bright pink crop top with a black dead-eyed unicorn image. "Where did he find this?" I mutter to myself.

"I have my talents. Shopping happens to be something you get good at over time. Come out and show me. I want to see!" The excitement in his voice does not go unnoticed by me or Nine, it seems, who groans under his breath, having apparently rejoined Dea.

Swinging the curtain open, I show him, and the delighted grin on Dea's face makes me smile. Yup. Definitely getting this one.

We continue in this fashion for a few stores, Dea paying each clerk and ordering them to be delivered to the house, which everyone is happy to oblige. Dea seems to have a penchant for shopping, picking out various styles he thinks I'll like, from Japanese kimonos to gothic punk tees to shorts and skirts to match all kinds of outfits. I have all kinds of styles now, and even a few dresses I don't know if I'll have the opportunity to wear.

By this point, we've spent a couple hours shopping, Nine's complaining, and Dea's visibility is starting to wane, so we decide to head straight to the exercise shop and pick up yoga pants, sports bras, sweatpants, vests, and sneakers—everything I will possibly need for any kind of exercise they might throw my way. The store clerk is familiar with them both and gives us all warming smiles, even flirting with Nine a bit. Dea tends to stay out of flirtatious situations, which confuses me slightly, as I thought they're both open with their romancing.

Ah! The more I think about all that, the more confused I get, so I ignore it and continue.

Last stop of the day is underwear, and I really want to do this one alone. "Stay out here. I won't be long." I give them a don't-fucking-disobey-me glare and walk into the fancy boutique as the store's bell chimes.

"Hello, sweet pea!" A young woman comes out from behind a curtain in the back, her long blond hair flowing around her waist like a jeweled curtain. "Anything I can help you with?"

"I'm staying with the Horsemen for a while but didn't

bring much stuff with me, and now it looks like my stay will be longer than expected. I just need to stock up on some basic underwear."

Her eyebrows rise at the mention of the Horsemen, and I get the instinctive feeling she's a little jealous, given the odd glare and smile she's giving out the window at the guys, who, now that I've turned around, I notice are staring in like two kids in a toyshop window.

"Just basic stuff."

She gives me a knowing smile. "I can help. Trust me." She starts walking around the store, picking out various bras and matching panties that I think are far too fancy for everyday wear, but what do I know? I just go along with it.

"You know . . ." She gives me a smile and looks me up and down. "Nine prefers darker-laced underwear in the bedroom." Winking, she picks off some fancy black-laced underwear and adds it to growing pile.

"Oh, I'm not—"

"Please. He's rather flirtatious, that one. No one avoids him forever. You won't be the first. Or the last." Her tone turns bitter at that last note.

"So, you and Nine have . . . ?"

She giggles and waves a hand. "Yes, yes, yes, sweet pea. But nothing to worry about. Nine never sleeps with the same person twice."

Except the team.

"Our relationship isn't like that in the slightest, but thank you for the advice anyway. I'd best be on my way now. If you could charge Dea's account and have them delivered to the house, that would be great."

She looks taken aback by my statement, but she nods and takes everything behind the counter to box it all up. "Should be at the house before you get back, Miss."

"Thank you."

I rush toward the store's exit like my life depends on it, even getting a bit winded in the process, but I trip on the doorframe on my way out and nearly tumble to the floor.

"Careful there." Nine catches me before I hit the cobblestones. "Don't run if you can't walk."

"Are you okay, Angel?"

"Just fine," I say through gritted teeth.

Nine throws me a weird look, but I stare at him and say, "Stay out of my head."

Taking a deep breath, I grab both boys by the arm and head for the house, hoping to get back to my library where there are no snooty, judgmental women trying to get me to hook up with the Horsemen. I'm there to help with a possible magical war, not fuck my way through the team.

This isn't some weird fantasy romance novel.

Chapter Twelve

Boxes upon boxes of fancy clothing are on my bed when we finally make it back. The journey took almost an hour this time as I struggled and wheezed back up that hill. I'll be damn happy when I'm fully recovered.

I plan to fit in morning yoga sessions first thing tomorrow, hoping to regain some level of fitness before training really begins. Connie and Arrie look like they can sprint all day and not break a damn sweat, so working out with them will be painful if I don't prepare first.

Looking at my small closet in the corner and then back to the boxes and bags, I wonder if I truly have room for it all. Oh my goddess, a walk-in closet would be fucking awesome! Wonder if I can ask the house to adjust? Is it that simple?

Placing my hand on the wall and feeling a little ridiculous, I take a breath and mentally ask, Can I maybe get a bigger closet? Something a little more me. I like looking stylish, and having somewhere to do that each day sounds like a great idea. Love the original color scheme, though, and the general style.

I open my eyes, looking at the original closet, and let out a breath I didn't realize I've been holding. Of course it isn't that simple. That would be ridiculous.

I turn back toward the bed to unpack some of my new clothes when I hear a deep rumble from behind, shaking all the walls and floor like an earthquake.

What the—?

I turn back around to look at the cause and am astounded by the lack of a closet that's been replaced by a door to the right of my nightstand

Where did my closet go?

Opening the door, I take a nervous breath, wondering if the house really is connected to me that much. Inside is a lavish set of connected areas, each one serving a separate purpose: shoes and bags, jewelry and makeup with a large dressing table and mirror to match, everyday wear, party and evening wear, and even a section for my new workout gear.

"Whoa."

This is fucking nuts. Great, but nuts. I can just ask the house for anything I want? And it'll just expand and renovate itself to accommodate me?

Footseps thunder into the room, and the entire team tumbles through the doorway, looking ready to throw down at the first sign of an intruder.

"What the fuck?" Arrie is the first over to me, peering through the open door. "Did you just ask the house for a walk-in closet, and it gave you this?" He gives me the stink eye, and I can't help but stifle a giggle at his obvious jealousy. The Horseman of War is jealous. Of me.

What a life.

Connie walks over next, marveling at the space in the

room. "It's just like mine!"

"Really?" She has one similar? Makes sense; she is a woman. An immortal woman, but a woman nonetheless. And she always looks impeccably well-dressed. Even in pajamas, which is just ridiculous.

"Wanna help me put everything away?"

She gives me an excited smile.

I go to grab everything and take it into the closet. "I mean, you don't have to. I just thought—"

"I'd love to," she whispers. "Let me help grab some of those." She shoos the boys out with a wave of her hands and a mean look I know means business—as do they, clearly, as they scamper.

She bounces into the closet with all the boxes and bags, closes the door, and gives me a look. "So, Nine tells me you met Claudia and have been a little standoffish ever since. I just wanted to take the time to apologize for her fucking attitude."

"Claudia?"

"That shitty excuse for a woman at the fancy underwear boutique?"

I nod and start unpacking the workout gear into the otherwise empty section of the closet.

"Yeah, I know. She has this weird obsession with Nine after sleeping with him, like, three years ago, and she's been a petty bitch with me ever since, too. I try to do all my underwear shopping on Earth to avoid her."

So Nine has slept with her then? But only once. That seems . . . strange. "You shop on Earth?"

"Of course, but I feel that's not the question on your mind." She raises her eyebrows and stands with her hands on her hips. She's clearly not moving until I spill the beans. "Ask away."

"I really don't want to talk about it. I just want to learn who I am, learn about my magic, train, and be useful to you all. Nothing else matters."

"Oh, hon . . . That's not . . ."

I wave a hand at her and turn around, trying not to let the tears brimming at the edges of my eyes spill over. I really am interrupting them, aren't I? I mean, I know they've all slept with each other over the years, but it's like Connie has her own personal harem, and I'm the only other woman to live with them. Ever. And I have just interrupted them.

"Let's just get this stuff unpacked. I have more research I want to do before bed."

"Okay. But, listen, if you ever want to chat about us all and the weird kind of family we all have, it's totally okay. For us, it's as natural as breathing and goes back centuries, but for you, it's like a whole strange concept. We get that. We want you to fit in here."

I can hear the desperation in her tone. They don't want me to fit in. They need me to. Because what happens if I don't? We all have to work together, no matter what.

I'm starting to understand Nine's point of view: What happens if I don't fit in? Will I be able to stay? Will I stay living with people where I'm not wanted just for Earth?

We unpack everything other than the last couple of ribbon-tied boxes, which I assume hold the underwear. Connie grabs them and peeks inside. "Ohhhh, these are fancy. And tell me . . . who are they for?"

I roll my eyes at her antics. Everyone here is completely insane. "Me." I'm not sure I want to start seeing anyone right now, especially not any of the team.

"Whatever you say." She holds up a purple lacey bra-and-panties set to my body. "But I think you'd look super hot in this."

My cheeks flame into two burning balls of heat, and man, is it hot in here. "Really?"

What the fuck? Why would I let that slip out?

Connie looks me up and down and smiles. "Yeah." She steps closer, holds the set up to my body again, and says, "Yup. Definitely hot in this."

"T-T-Thanks. I . . ." Why can't I get a single word out? Just the thought of her seeing me in that kind of underwear makes me hot under the collar, nervous in a way I've never been before.

She goes to put them in the fancy drawers in a section I didn't know was dedicated to underwear and comes back to me and wraps her arms around my body in a tight embrace. "You're doing great."

The warmth of her body seeps into my limbs as I inhale the musky, rose-tinted scent of the perfume she wears that mingles with the mango scent of her hair. Her entire body presses close to mine as she backs us up against the nearest wall so I can lean on something to take the edge off our now-joined weight.

"Really, you're going to be fine here. Nine and Dea really like you, and I think it'll be great having a girlfriend around the house."

I snort my surprise—girlfriend?—but try to hide it with a comforting sigh.

She's taller than me, not that it's a great accomplishment given my five-foot-four frame, and my head rests lightly on her shoulder. Slowly, my arms tangle themselves around her waist as I pull her the last few inches flush against me.

We stand like that for a few moments, listening to each

other breathing, and I rejoice in some kind of nice touch that makes me feel a little less lonely.

She pulls away slightly, and a small moan of protest escapes my lips before I can stop it, and I'm pretty sure I can't be more embarrassed by this point. But she doesn't break contact; instead, she keeps her arms wrapped around the small of my back and pulls her head and chest away. Her lips are inches from mine, and I can feel the gentle caress of her breath on my face. Everything slips away from me in that moment. Nothing matters. Not the pang of loneliness I've been trying to fill with studying, not the confusion of my feelings toward the team, and not the pressure of finding my place among the Horsemen.

It's as though something pulls my head in toward hers, and I can see her leaning in, too. Oh my goddess, she's totally going to kiss me. But just as heat floods my core in a way that makes me almost want to try on that underwear for her, panic sets in.

Heart racing, I pull away. "Connie . . . I—"

She pulls back and holds up a hand. "It's okay. I didn't mean to make you feel uncomfortable. I just meant to show you that this"—she gestures to the two of us—"is okay." She smiles and unwraps both arms from my waist.

She knows? Seems I'm pretty fucking terrible at hiding my feelings, which does not bode well for the rest of the team. Do they know, too? Well, Nine knows everything, but that's okay. He generally keeps it to himself. Wait. Does he? Did he fill the rest of the team in?

"Hon, I can see you spiraling. I'm not Nine—I can't tell what you're thinking. You have to actually use words with me." She smiles that beautiful smile of hers, and I know she isn't trying to be horrible.

I look sheepishly to the floor, finding something in the large closet to look at besides her. "Is it that obvious . . . or . . . Or did Nine say something?"

"Ah. That." Connie grabs my chin in a slight pinch and forces me to meet her eyes. "Nine likes to tease people, but he never tells us what's on each other's minds unless necessary. So, no. I just . . . have been watching you."

Watching me? That sounds . . . creepy.

"Oh, fuck. That sounded creepy, didn't it?" I nod but can't help the laugh that escapes. "You're the first girl on the team besides me, and I'll admit that I'm intrigued by you. I can't help it. You try spending two millennia with those three and then have a girl come along."

"Fair enough." That actually makes a lot of sense, and the dread in the pit of my stomach starts unknotting itself.

"Tell ya what. Why don't we make a deal?" She holds out her hand to shake. "We arrange some kind of girl-chat evening once a week, and we just tell each other how we feel no matter how embarrassing it might be."

"So . . . like a girly sleepover?"

"Oh my fuck, yes. A sleepover!"

I shake her hand as firmly as possible and smile at the prospect of having someone to chat with—another woman who will likely understand some of the challenges of being here.

"So anything else you wanted to chat about? You must be worried about a lot. And confused."

"Let's have a sleepover tonight, and I'll dish all the dirt. Promise."

She lets out a girly squeal. "I'll come get you at six!"

Chapter Thirteen

It's five thirty, my sleepover with Connie starts in thirty minutes, and my nerves can't be more shot. It's just a friendly sleepover, I keep telling myself. But no matter how many times I repeat that phrase, the idea of this being a date has my nerves in a damn tumble. Connie said that it's important I feel okay with everything, so why doesn't this feel okay?

"Because you're worrying about what she'll think and forgetting that she just wants to spend time with you."

"Ah!" I jump to the other side of my bed and nearly fall off in fright.

Nine stands in the doorway, a bemused look plastered upon his smug face as he leans against the frame.

"Fucking Christ, Nine! You scared the shit out of me."

"Sorry." He puts a hand to his mouth, covering yet another laugh (that's becoming a habit, it seems), and I finally notice he's wearing swimming shorts. And nothing else.

Fucking hell. Living here is creating a whole new set of issues I never thought I would have to deal with. No tattoos like Dea and not as many muscles as Arrie, but the definition is still there in a very swimmer-like way, and is that a . . . nipple piercing? Part of me really wants to reach out and run my hands over that chest and through that wet red hair, but I stay put, lying on the other side of the bed, trying my best not to clench my thighs too obviously at the sudden need thriving there.

Nine clears his throat, and I realize I've been staring too long, and he's probably just read my mind anyway, so there's no point hiding my desire.

"You need to have some alone time. Your thoughts are worse than the rest of theirs put together." Nine laughs some more and comes to sit on the bed next to me. He bends toward me and mentally whispers, *But honestly, I kinda like it.*

I angle my head in question, hoping he'll explain.

Being in someone's head is really interesting, and although I try not to pry, it's hard. It's in my nature to read surface thoughts, and I don't like hiding myself away and pretending to be something I'm not. The problem is that usually people don't like that—Arrie especially. But with you, your surface thoughts are either panic and worry over your new situation, which is completely understandable, or wondering what it would be like to fuck one of us. It's kind of refreshing to see someone so . . . hot.

"Oh."

Your mind, that is. Sorry. It's really hard to explain. I tend to judge people based on how they think, since that's how I communicate and see.

I nod, kinda getting where he's coming from. But the one thing that sticks out—he thinks my mind is hot? I scoot closer, wanting nothing more than to reach out, but I hold back. "So, you don't think I should be nervous?"

It's not really a date anyway. I don't even know why I thought that.

Well, it is kinda like a date, but Connie's just as nervous, if that helps.

Really? She's nervous? That does make me feel a little better.

You should wear the new underwear she likes. Nine winks at me and gets off the bed.

We're not gonna sleep together, Nine.

I know. But just because you're not sleeping together or planning on being a real couple, doesn't mean you can't tease and have fun. It's kinda the whole point of living, Sweetie.

Oh my goddess, I really need to be more relaxed and chilled. It's just all this damn pressure: new friends, new house, new powers, new identity. It's . . . a lot.

I know. But hanging with us should be easy. Just go with the flow. Stop worrying so much.

Right. Okay.

I take a deep breath (well, as deep as I can without causing pain), get off the bed and go into the closet to change, choosing to take Nine's advice (not sure how good of an idea that'll be) and wear the new purple underwear, and match it with some sparkly, skull-covered pajama shorts and vest. The lace of the bra pokes over the low-cut vest, and, testing my chest and general flexibility, it seems like my wound is healing enough to wear wired bras. Fucking finally. I can see my actual cleavage in the mirror for once.

I'm going to get Dea to check on my wound tomorrow morning anyway. Haven't actually seen under the bandage myself yet, as the baths Connie's been helping with have been completely un-mirrored.

By the time I exit the closet, Nine has left, and Connie's sitting in the rocking chair in the corner. I haven't sat in it yet, but it looks comfy with all the cushions and blankets draped around it.

"Ready?" Connie stands up, wearing a matching set of pajamas to the other day, except these are pale blue and have tiny kittens on them. The Horseman of Conquest wearing pajamas with kittens on them is pretty funny, and I can't help but let a small hiccup of laughter slip at the thought.

I can't imagine these people being deadly. Well, maybe Arrie—he's pretty cold and grumbly—but I get the feeling he's got a lot on his plate, and his Horseman of War magic must make things hard for him.

Connie grabs my hand and drags me out of the door. "C'mon! This'll be fun. We're gonna eat pizza, I got Arrie to make us some of those brownies you liked, and we're just gonna listen to music and chill."

"Okay."

She leads me down a mind-boggling number of hallways and around so many corners I'm pretty sure she'll have to drop me back off at my room later.

"I have a room farthest away from everyone else because of my hearing. I never sleep otherwise."

"Do you even need to sleep?"

"Yes. But less so than the rest of you. I have more stamina, and we regenerate because of our immortality, so I only sleep once or twice a week."

"Whoa." Once or twice a week? She must be really useful on longer missions.

"You'll have cool abilities, too. Trust me. I have a good feeling about it. And Dea already thinks you're interesting; it's taking a lot for Nine not to study you like some kind of pet project." We walk down a final hallway and end up in front of a plain white door. "He's a bit of a nerd when it comes to magic."

"Really?"

"Yeah, he creates all kinds of new magical tech, various potions, and spells we use for both household things and on missions."

"What kind of missions do you guys go on exactly?"

"Hmmm. It varies."

Since she doesn't elaborate, I assume it's something she either doesn't want to really chat about tonight or something Dea prefers me not know just yet. Either way, I put the worry to the back of my mind and focus on the room that now stands in front of me as she slowly opens the door.

It's rather old fashioned, but it has a few modern touches. The high ceiling has a golden chandelier with actual candles lighting the room, and the floor-length window-wall on the far side overlooks the distant mountains to the north, and the town with its twinkling lights under the setting sun is situated not too far in between.

I really need to start looking into this realm and understanding how it works. I'll start that tomorrow.

But what's most impressive is the size of her bed. It could easily fit us all in (which is presumably why it's that big in the first place). It's a four-poster, with white silk drapes cascading down each side and a mountain of pillows arranged neatly at the head.

"Closet's through that door." She points to a door beside her bed and then to the one on the other side. "And that's the bathroom." While pointing to the double doors on the other side of the room, she says, "And that's my study and training room."

"Training room?"

"Well, my magic is more practical than the others', so my study has a desk in the corner, but it's mostly a private workout space. We do have a massive gym next to the kitchen as well."

Oh, a gym. Really? "Is there a pool here?"

She chuckles. "Yeah. One in the gym and one in the gardens." She gestures to a cute little set up of tea and pizza on a couple of poufs in the corner. "Shall we?"

"Sure." She's being more formal than usual, and I'm about to ask why when I remember what Nine said. She's nervous, too. "Err, Connie?"

"Huh?" She looks up from the pizza.

"Just be yourself and chill with me." I wink and sit on the nearest pouf, then pour myself a cup of what smells like peppermint tea.

She just laughs and takes her seat, looking a little more relaxed. "I also have other types of tea on the boudoir, if you'd like to try others."

"Oh, really?" I have become quite obsessed with the different types of tea I notice Connie drinking and am starting to feel like a Japanese cliché, what with my obvious Japanese descent to my love of tea, and how I'll be starting meditative yoga in the morning. Essh.

"Yeah. Let's get through this one first." She pours herself a cup with perfectly manicured hands. "I also have some dusted tea, if you want to really have fun."

I look at her in shock. Dusted tea, really?

"Oh my fuck, you should see your face." She snorts with laughter so hard that some tea dribbles out. "I do have dusted tea, but we won't have any today."

Oh, phew. Dusted anything is supposed to be quite bad for normal people and has severe side effects on humans. But I wonder . . . "What kind of effect does dust have on us?"

"Same as most of the magical community, but we do have to continue drinking to retain the high, since we have regenerating capabilities."

"Ah. Makes sense."

"Soooo . . . gossip. Remember. You get to unload all your problems and concerns, no matter how small, and I get all the juicy gossip in return."

"Well, Nine knows most of this stuff anyway, but sure. What do you wanna know?"

"Hmmm . . . Let's see. You obviously have a thing for Dea, which I totally get, but what about Arrie and Nine?"

"Errrm. Not really sure. Nine's really flirty, and I like the playful banter, and he looks great shirtless."

"They all do. Trust me. But not Arrie?"

"I dunno. He's a little . . . gruff with me."

"He'll melt eventually. He has a hard time handling his abilities and doesn't take change very well. But I don't really like gossiping about the others without their permission, so it's best if he tells you himself."

"That's okay." I've drained my first cup by this point and pour another while asking, "Can I ask questions, too?"

"Of course."

"It's just, you've had millennia to get to know the others. What kinds of relationships have you all had over the years? With each other, I mean. There have to be preferences, right?"

This feels weirdly easy. Like talking a good friend.

"Fair question. Feeling out of the loop a bit?"

I nod, snuggling in to listen as though she were my new favorite show.

"Okay. I'll get the obvious one out of the way. Nine and Dea have a rather sexual friendship. Dea seems to prefer men to women but has slept with both over the centuries. Because of Dea's invisibility, he finds it hard to sleep with people outside of the team."

"How so?"

"He has to concentrate to make himself visible, so it kinda ruins the vibe for him. Nine sleeps with quite a lot of people and has no preference. We all prefer magical species to humans, and Dea has never slept with a human. Nor has Arrie, I don't think."

Makes sense, since humans only partially see Dea. That would be kind of weird. I'm starting to see how the relationships work between them all.

"Arrie prefers women," Connie continues, "but Arrie and I have an . . . understanding."

I waggle my eyebrows for her to continue, which makes her giggle.

"We're both really strong and have to hold back, which is something Arrie's not great at. But with each other, sex is easier because we're pretty well-matched in strength. Also, Arrie never sleeps outside of the team."

"Ah, makes sense." Wonder why Arrie doesn't have sex with anyone outside of the team? I'm betting it has something to do with his abilities.

"We've all slept with each other at some point and will probably do so again in the future. Though we keep our relations with each other on the side. We don't really talk about them much, and we've not had group sex. I actually don't think all four of us have slept together at once before." She shrugs while in thought, as though that hasn't occurred to her before. "At least, not with more than just the two of us and other species."

"Why not? You've lived for centuries. And you're all having sex with each other anyway. What difference does it make?"

She sighs and puts her cup down. "We try to avoid anything that would cross the line of friends with benefits.

The world relies on us, and if any of our drama affected that, it could have devastating consequences."

Hmmm. There's something not quite right about that to me, but I don't bother mentioning it. Dea and Nine have something more than just sex going on, even if they won't admit it to themselves, and Arrie has other issues forcing him to be more wound up.

I wonder if . . . "Can we have children?"

"Your mind works in the strangest of ways." She smiles. "But yes, we can. I haven't, though. The guys have over the years. Especially before contraception was really a thing. Not in the last couple of centuries, though."

"Did they, you know . . . stick around?"

"Sometimes. Depends. Sometimes they didn't know, in their defense. But if they could, then they did. We have a very demanding job."

"Why have you not had any children?"

"Wow. I didn't realize you had so many questions."

"Sorry." I look to the floor, embarrassment coloring my features. "If you'd rather not answer any of my questions, you don't have to."

"Nah, it's all right. With the guys, they don't have to actually have any of their children live here. If I had a child, it would be raised here. With all of us. That would be . . ."

"A bit strange?"

She nods but looks away.

"Would you like children?"

"I dunno. What about you?"

"Not sure either. Maybe. Someday." I get up to browse her tea collection. She has over twenty different types of tea on a shelf above the boudoir behind us, all lined up perfectly in a neat little row. I browse past jasmine, rose, and caramel, and land on citrus blast. Holding it up, I ask, "This one?"

"Sure." She grabs it and starts putting the leaves in the silver pot's strainer and pours more hot water from a steaming jug that I'm not sure how stays hot.

Grabbing the pizza, I try a few slices—all different flavors—and groan when I find one I love. Pepperoni.

"Any other questions?" She smiles at me, and I get the feeling she's genuinely happy to answer them.

"Not sure." I have a ton of inappropriate ones, like what they are all like in bed, but I think better of asking. She's been generous so far.

I'm suddenly reminded of Nine's rule—don't fuck the servants—and think to ask but also don't want to intrude.

"What is it?"

I give her a look of confusion, wondering how she knew.

"It's written all over your face," she says through a smile.

"Well, Nine mentioned something but told me to ask you."

She raises her eyebrows. "What's the ass-rat been saying about me now?"

I smile. "Well, he mentioned the rule of don't have sex with the servants, and—"

"Ugh, that story." She rolls her eyes. "Okay. Okay. It's a fair one, I guess." She settles into the back of her chair and begins. "About three hundred years into living here, we began to employ servants to help keep the house clean, and I took a fancy to one of the Shifters—tortoise Shifter. His name was Manfred. He was really sweet." She sighs for a moment on a pause before continuing. "We had a summer fling, and I thought that was all he wanted, but I was wrong. Since he was around the house all the time, it was . . . different than usual."

"He fell for you, didn't he?"

She nods with downcast eyes and bright pink cheeks. "I didn't mean for it to happen. So I sent him away, made sure he had enough money for a while, and sacked him to make things easier. But he refused to leave. In the end, Dea had to have him escorted off the premises by the local army—no police back then."

Nine was right; it is a little funny. But that poor man . . .

"Well, then . . ." Connie places her hands on her knees, clearly wanting to change the topic. "Now that I've told that humiliating story, I have another question for you."

I nod while sipping my tea.

"If you're so attracted to them, especially Dea, then why not just sleep with them? Nine is actually a really loving person."

"Really?" I shake my head, feeling stupid for even asking. "I just . . . It doesn't feel right."

"What doesn't?"

"Sex for the sake of it. If I slept with one of you . . . I don't know. It just feels wrong to me. The way you live your emotional lives doesn't feel right. I can't really describe it, since I don't have any values or even a moral standing. Sorry."

"It's okay." She kneels next to me, her braids being pushed behind her in the process. "I get it." She leans over and whispers in my ear, "I heard what Nine said. And since you're taking his advice on the underwear"—she leans down, taking in my new cleavage-on-show look—"I don't mind the teasing and the games." She winks, and to prove her point, she lightly brushes her lips just below my ear, sending a shiver throughout my body.

I turn my head and want nothing more than to press my lips to hers and see if they're as smooth as they look, but instead I settle for a lingering kiss to her cheek, watching her blush slightly.

She leans back and smiles at me, clearly pleased with herself for some reason. "Let's put some music on."

"Sure."

She presses a button on a control panel in the wall that I didn't notice earlier, and a light piano tune trickles over the soundstrip running around the room's ceiling perimeter. An electric-blue strip lights up the system's soundstrip, and I sway along to the pleasant tune.

"C'mon!" She grabs my hand and places my tea back on the table. "Let's dance."

The music changes to a more upbeat pop song with a click of a button, and she gets on the bed and dances and jumps around like a teenager. Her braids fly everywhere, and her smile grows wider when she sees me laughing.

"You look ridiculous!"

"Only because you haven't joined me!" Her braids fly in the air as she jumps. "I've never done this before!"

The volume turns up via the controller in Connie's hand, and she helps me onto the bed, where I try to keep up with her antics, jumping around and dancing to the silly pop music. It's the most relaxed I've been since I got here, and maybe this friendship is something I need. Something normal. Well, normal isn't really a thing here, but normalish.

In true sleepover style, I actually sleep over in her room—which, yes, is as awkward as it sounds, but is actually kinda fun, too. We dance, talk, eat pizza, and do each other's hair—a totally girly night. She gives me some great skincare advice and even lets me borrow her special conditioner. Mango scented. Just like her. Mmmmm.

Light creeps through a crack in the curtains, and I groan. It's already dawn. Shit. I wanted to start yoga today.

Grumbling, I untangle myself from her arms, which have wrapped themselves around my waist in the middle of the night. I'm careful not to wake her, but a knock at the door makes all my efforts in vain.

"Whaaat?" Connie complains.

"Have you seen Angel? I wanted to check on her healing progress. Hoping to take off the bandages today and clear her for training."

Connie looks at me, and both of our faces flush with embarrassment. "Err. Yeah, she's in here." She gives me an apologetic look but shrugs. "Don't worry about it."

Dea opens the door and stands there smiling. It's so similar to Nine's usually smug face that I almost want to punch it.

"What do you want?" I'm tired. Grouchy. And hungry. So sue me. We stayed up late chatting last night, and although it was fun, I'm now seeing the downside.

"To check on your healing. But if you ladies are busy, I can come back later." He waggles his eyebrows at us.

Connie chucks a pillow at his face. "Stop being a rat-assed bitch!"

I get up, smiling at him, and lift my top. "Well, you wanted to check."

He stands there for a moment, a little dazed, and comes over. "I will need you to remove your top and bra. Sorry. It is important, though. If I can see how the damage has healed, then I can clear you for training."

"Well, I can do everything normally now and can exercise for short bursts." I carefully take my top and bra off, noticing both Connie's and Dea's eyes stuck like glue to my every movement.

I stand in front of them, naked from the waist up, while they stare at my chest, and I would be lying if I said I didn't feel terrified, but I'm also a little excited by the slight hint of heat in both their gazes.

"It is completely healed." Dea sounds astounded. "You have remarkable healing capabilities, Angel." He places a hand on the spot where the wound used to be and allows his magic to suffocate the area, sending a warm tingle through that side of my chest. "I will keep doing this twice a day until the inside is completely healed, but that should not take more than a couple of days. You are cleared for light training." He points a finger at Connie. "Light."

"Yes, boss." She mockingly salutes him while standing to attention. "Light."

"Training today or tomorrow, Angel?"

I shove my bra and top back on. "Today." I don't explain to them that I want to feel useful and powerful, like I belong on the team, but I get the feeling they already know.

"Okay. We will all meet for lunch in a couple hours, then Nine and I will start magic training with you in the afternoon."

We all stand here in silence for a moment, Connie and I looking at Dea, waiting for him to leave. It takes him a second to get the message, but when he does, he leaves with a chuckle.

"Ugh. Is being just friends such a big deal around here?"

Connie walks up to me, a smile lingering in her blue eyes, and grabs my hands in hers. "We're all friends."

"I meant—"

"I know. I'm just teasing, silly." But she doesn't move.

I get the feeling she's waiting for something . . . But what?

She moves her hands around to my lower back and embraces me in another hug, this time a little tighter. "We promised to always be open and just chat about things," she whispers in my ear. "So, I kinda want a kiss goodbye." She isn't looking at me, but I just know by the inflection of her voice that tries to cut off before she can finish the entire sentence that she's embarrassed.

Would it be that big of a deal? Nine said fun is fine, even if it leads nowhere. Well, Connie and I nearly kissed yesterday anyway, so I don't think it would be a big deal if things progress. She knows I don't want a friends with benefits kind of relationship. And Nine said fun and teasing is okay. He said that, right? I'm not just making that up.

Clearly, I don't decide quick enough for Conquest, because she grabs my wrists and pulls me to the bed, spins us around, and lightly throws me onto the mattress. "I'm not used to waiting for others to make a move. So, if you really don't want me to kiss you, then just say no."

Her sudden dominant nature shines through those usually gentle eyes, which are now a deeper shade of green, and I think this might be how she is with Arrie. The thought of her with any of the others has me squirming to release the tension building up at my core, and she notices, too, as a wide, predatory smile leaps across her face.

She straddles my waist, and my heart rate speeds up. Nine's words echo in my thoughts: Isn't that the whole point of living? To have fun. To take what we want. Especially from a group of friends who understands and doesn't mind either way.

Taking a deep, shaky breath, I grab her thighs and run my hands up the insides, tracing fingertips against her smooth, creamy skin and watching her shudder, hopefully showing her exactly what I want.

Her smile turns sultry, those delicious corners of her lips turning up enough to make her dimples appear, and that breathtaking beauty turns into a heat that flares her eyes a deep sea green. Leaning down and placing her hands either side of my head, she traces a finger along my jaw, making my breath hitch, before her thumb brushes across my lips, and I blow out a frustrated breath.

Is she going to kiss me or not? Goddess, I just want her to touch me.

The patience she's using and the time she's taking are killing me. I'm a bundle of nerves and heat and molten puddles, and I'm pretty sure I will have to take a cold shower after this.

She's really going to kiss me. She leans closer to my face, but then she pulls back, looking down at me with a genuinely curious smile and whispers, "You're beautiful."

I can't take my eyes off of her pink lips, wondering when they will reach mine. Impatience bubbles closer to the surface, and before I know it, the need to kiss this beautiful woman overtakes every rational thought, and I grab a fistful of her pajama top and yank her face to mine.

Our lips connect, and that tingling sensation her every touch has caused since I got here explodes throughout my body, making me want to feel every inch of her smooth skin against mine.

Her lips move slowly with mine, in tandem with my uncertainty, but that insecurity flies farther out the window as the seconds tick by, and her lips press harder against mine. I want more—more of her, of our lips together, of her breathes mingling with mine—and a frenzied urgency fills me as I crash harder into her, nipping her bottom lip open in a gasp.

She rips my hands off of her thighs and yanks them above my head, pinning me beneath her.

Her lips steel everything from me—my breath, my rationality, my worry over whether this is a good idea—and I meet her with equal fervor. Her hips shift against mine, and I can't help but respond. I wiggle my fingers free from her grip, return them to her thighs, and inch my fingers closer to the edge of her shorts, feeling her skin cool against the heat of my touch.

She groans against my mouth and breaks away, gasping for breath, and whispers, "Fuck. I've wanted to do that since our moment in your closet."

"Me . . . too," I say between heaving breaths.

Now the moment has dissipated, that worry and anxiety creep back in, and a million concerns shoot across my mind at once.

Is it weird now?

Was the kiss okay?

Does she hate me?

What will Nine and Dea think?

Oh my goddess, I have morning breath!

"Relax." She releases me from her impossibly strong grip and sits up. "I'm happy to spend the next millennia stealing nothing but kisses from you. Especially if they're like that."

Relief washes through me.

"I get that casual sex isn't your thing. Everything we do, as friends or otherwise, is completely up to you."

Suddenly, everything clicks into place. She held back because she wanted me to be sure. She wanted me to take what I want and just admit it to myself. And goddess damn it, I want her. I have no idea if I was lesbian or bisexual or something else in my human life, but in this life, this woman drives me damn crazy.

Chapter Fourteen

Lunch is an assortment of sandwich stuff; simple, but it allows me to try lots of different sandwiches and ingredients. Simple ham and cheese is sooo good, but so is egg mayo. (Have you ever had a marshmallow sandwich? They are divine. If there's a god, he definitely created marshmallow sandwiches.)

"Here, Sweetie, try a PB&J." Nine hands me a single-slice sandwich with ingredients I barely recognize.

"A what?" I ask as I take it from his hands.

"Peanut butter and jelly. It's an American thing. They're pretty tasty."

Taking a bite out of the fluffy white bread with a gooey filling, I don't have a weird immortal allergy to peanuts. But I don't, and that sandwich is the king of all sandwiches, evident by the fact that Arrie and Nine are smiling while Dea and Connie are frowning. Seems we have a PB&J battle on our hands, and I've just tipped the scale.

Making myself another half sandwich (only halves so I can have four or five different fillings), Dea coughs to get everyone's attention. "I have cleared Angel for training, but she needs to take the physical stuff easy for another couple of days."

Connie smiles.

Nine practically bounces in his seat, hands slamming down on the table. "Ohmigod, does that mean I get to watch and see what kind of magic our sweet thing has? I wonder if you'll be able to do something similar to Dea? Oh, or maybe you'll have actual power over life and death? No, that seems a bit OP, even for us . . ." He speaks for, like, thirty seconds without taking a breath.

Dea shoots Nine a look, and he snaps his mouth shut. "I have another announcement, one I have kept quiet until now because I did not want everyone freaking out." He pauses, looking a little unsure of himself.

It's a look I haven't seen on him before, and I'll admit it unsettles me enough to put mysandwhich down (I know, I'm shocked, too).

"I cannot find Angel's seal."

Silence fills the room as everyone stops eating and stares at Dea as though he's announced the end of the fucking world, then the table explodes into a flurry of questions, shouting, and flying hands all at once.

I don't get it. "What do you mean?"

Nine looks at me with worry creasing his eyes, and I know this isn't going to be good. "Remember, our seals are the only thing that can actually kill us. We all have ours hidden away, as they turned up here in this house with us. But yours—"

"Is missing," I finish for him. Fuck.

"Well," Dea starts, "not missing. Missing implies we lost it. It actually just never turned up."

But that doesn't make sense. "So, it could be around

somewhere? Right?"

Dea looks at me and grins. "Yes. And I wanted your permission to check your library. It is huge, and it could be in there somewhere."

Nine frowns. "But . . . all of ours just popped up in our faces. They weren't hidden anywhere." His fists clench and unclench as his skin turns paler.

No one seems to have any more questions, and we all sit in silence, finishing lunch, as the danger of the situation wells the tension in the room. Now and then, one of them looks at me with worry or confusion, and I just know they're thinking about my seal.

With a small tap on the table, Dea breaks the silence. "I want Con to ask around on Earth. Few people know about our seals. Ask if they have seen one. Do not mention it is Angel's or even bring her into conversation."

Connie frowns at him. "Why not send Nine? He's much better at interrogation."

Nine shakes his head. "Nope. Not happening. I want to be here for her initial training, so I know what magic she possesses."

Dea chuckles in that deep, throaty way of his. "Yes. I doubt I could get him out of the house while she is training."

"Damn straight!" Nine slaps the table and grabs the last slice of bread, most likely to make another PB&J. "Think of all the cool notes I can take, all the new groundbreaking magic she'll probably possess . . . ."

"Okay, okay." Connie raises her hands in defeat. "Looks like it's me, then. I'll leave this afternoon." She looks at me and smiles. "Try not to freak out over anything while I'm gone."

The emphasis on the word anything tells me everything

she's trying to imply: do not worry about the kiss.

The memory of her lips and the glimpse of her desire brush the edges of my mind, causing my face to heat like an inferno and Nine to choke on his sandwich.

I laugh and place a hand on his back. "Sorry. I'd say don't choke, but what's the point? It's not like it'll kill you."

Dea raises his eyebrows at me. "Did our Angel just make a joke?"

I shrug and get up to fit in some yoga before Nine and Dea probably spend the entire afternoon pissing me off. It's inevitable. They'll try to get me to use my magic, I'm not going to be able to, and I'll get frustrated with their pushy, excitable nonsense.

I just know it.

Half an hour later, yoga mat in hand, workout gear on, and hair pinned back, I'm ready to find the perfect spot. Somewhere in the sunny garden would be nice—breathing in the fresh air, overlooking the tranquility, inhaling the scent of grass and flowers and beauty . . . Somewhere relaxing.

It's time I take a leaf out of Arrie's book and aim for peace, just like his odd dance/yoga/stretch workout thing.

The sun shines brightly on the fairy garden, and I briefly wonder whether it does anything more than be sunny in this realm. Surely food would have difficulty growing? Ugh. I really need to learn more about *Sheruta* when I next get the chance.

I wander along the paths, hopping over toadstools and ducking under rose bushes, careful to avoid any fairy dens that might suck me in with their curiosity and exquisite magic. People have been known to lose their lives in those dens, forever breathing in the dust that permeates a fairy's air until they wither and rot.

I'm looking for a perfect place to relax, somewhere that overlooks the garden and brings me peace—but what in particular I'm looking for, I don't know. The curse of not really knowing yourself, I guess.

It's getting a little old and confusing, and I'm starting to feel like I'm in Wonderland. *Sheruta* is amazing, but I feel like one wrong footstep or one misplaced word will get me killed—forever doomed to look out at the beauty I can never be a part of.

Connie's words echo across my mind—I'm happy to spend the next millennia stealing nothing but kisses from you—and I smile. It doesn't matter if I want friendship, something more, or something in between because she just wants to spend time with me.

A familiar deep rumble fills my ears and splits across the ground, and my thoughts of Connie in those sexy pajama shorts all but dissipate into the depths of my subconscious. I run to follow the sound, hoping beyond hope that the house really has done what I think it has.

I reach the edge of the rainbow forest, with the horse paddock in the distance, but in front of me lies a hill I'm pretty sure didn't exist before.

Damn. The house really listens to me. On top of the hill is a small *Shinto* shrine. This one doesn't look to be used for the normal sacred purpose, but it overlooks the entire valley.

Climbing up the hill, I eventually reach the top and step inside. Cushions of all different shades of gold line one side, while the gaps in the walls all around the shrine allow me to look as far as the ocean, mountains, the local town, and back of the house. I can see everything from here. The whole of *Sheruta.*

Turns out I don't need the yoga mat after all, so I set it

down at the entrance and grab a cushion instead. I want to start with breathing exercises, to ease myself in and make sure I don't cause any further damage. I'm pretty much healed, but I know if I push too hard it could set me back weeks.

Breathing in, breathing out, all I think about is my new life. I'm supposed to be thinking about nothing, but that is unlikely given the circumstances.

I spend nearly two hours running through various stretches and poses, losing my mind down one rabbit hole and into the next. But I let it wander wherever it wants to go, allowing it to worry, cry, and laugh at the insanity of my new life, and by the time I finish, I feel calm again. Like a refreshed version of me.

Yup. Definitely doing this every morning. Especially if my life will be crazy for the next few thousand years. I mean, I guess I have a magical war to diffuse somehow.

That is not a good thought, so I shove it to the back of my mind as I head to the kitchen for another cup of coffee. That shit is the best stuff ever. I don't care how addicted that makes me. I'll take all the positive stuff I can right now.

"Ready, Angel?" Dea stands in the doorway as I stand at the kitchen counter drinking my coffee. He's shirtless—again—and that swirling gold tattoo catches my eye.

"Dea?" I involuntarily step toward him, forcing my hands to my sides so I don't touch that swirling, gorgeous body of his.

"Yes?"

"What's your tattoo about? I mean, I've never seen one like that before. That I know of."

He chuckles and reaches to grab my hand. Placing it on the top of the tattoo that swirls around his shoulder, he says, "It is actually a Shifter tattoo, and I got it after a good friend of mine died."

"Wow. I mean, er . . . I'm sorry."

He shakes his head. "Do not be. It was a long time ago. He died in battle, as a Shifter should."

Part of me wonders if this person was just a friend or something more, but I refrain from asking anything that will sound too pushy. Connie will probably know, but she doesn't like gossiping about the guys so probably won't tell me.

"Well," I start, "let's get this over with."

Dea leads the way to my room and asks me to open the library door, carefully observing me from the corner of his eye. "Nervous?"

"No shit." We enter, Nine having followed once we passed his rooms, and start searching for a good magical space. "So, we should find somewhere perfect, right?"

"I am hoping so," Dea says. "Both Arrie and Connie have training rooms in their study because their abilities are so active."

We go to my study area, hoping to find something nearby, but come up empty.

"Oh, there's an artefact room somewhere over there and a door at the end. Haven't had the chance to look in there yet."

Nine smiles, jumps to his feet from where he sits at my desk, and says, "Let's go!" He grabs my hand and drags me down aisle after aisle, occasionally stopping to ask me directions.

"Here we are." I let out a sigh, glad I don't have to continue running, and look around. There are objects on pedestals, behind locked glass doors and on various shelves, none of which I recognize. Unlike my study area, this is a lot like the rest of my library—full of color—but it has a certain old-world feel to it that the rest doesn't have.

What are all those artifacts?

We really do need to do an inventory check of this place at some point because some of those items are valuable magical artifacts that are pretty powerful.

I'm beginning to suspect what kind of Horseman I am. But rather than voice it in my head, giving Nine the answer, I keep it quiet.

The door at the back of the artifact section is locked, and I'm not really sure why. Only I can get in there, right? Why the fuck would it be locked? Stupid library of wonders. Nothing's ever simple around here. I try the handle a few more times and groan in frustration. "What now?"

Dea steps up and places a hand on my shoulder. "It probably recognizes your magical signature. The door to the library does the same thing, but it looks for you. This time, you need to send your magical signature into the door."

Oookay. Cause that doesn't sound like something out of a fairy tale at all. I'm not sure what I'm doing, but I place my hand on the door and take a deep breath, imagining my energy and life reaching out of my palm and layering itself around the door. That's what they do in all the storybooks, right?

A clunking sound snaps my eyes open, and shock takes hold of my mind.

"Whoa."

I'm not sure which one of them says it, but it makes me my breath hitch in my throat, and for a moment, I fail to remember how to breathe. The door swirls in blue, red, green, and milky-white tendrils of magic, with a spiderweb of inky blackness threading through every strand.

"Wh-what is that?"

Dea doesn't touch me, but he steps into my peripheral. "It

is your magical signature, and I think I know what you are."

"Really?"

"Yes. But let us all get inside."

I open the creaky door to find a cold, dark, stone-like room beyond. It isn't anything special.

Nine flicks a switch behind me, and the room lights up with those strange, annoying buzzy lights you find in hospitals and other corporate buildings. Safe to say, this is not my favorite room. The light is too bright, hurting my sensitive eyes, and the buzzing is like a drill in my already busy mind.

Spinning around to get a good look, I nearly trip over my own feet in shock. Weapons. Targets. Dummies. This place is a murderer's playground. There are racks of varying types of knives in the corner, matching a set of targets on the other side of the room. Dummies and swords lie in the other corner, with punching bags and weights dotted around the room at various intervals. Gray stone slabs the perimeter wall, and the floor consists of the same grubby-looking grayness. "What kind of room is this?"

Nine goes to look at the various swords and knives on display, while Dea looks in a set of drawers and then on the shelves dotting the room.

"This stuff looks used. Not brand new." Nine brings me a knife and shows me the scuff marks and scratches.

"Stun guns. Magiguns. Magic-dampening cuffs. A magic blocker," Dea lists as he rifles through various objects. "All with some kind of wear and tear." He turns to me with curious eyes. "Seems this is your stuff. From when you were human."

I stumble, and my jaw hits the floor. How is that possible? What did I do as a human? "I-I-I . . ." I don't know what to say.

"There are magic blockers in this room's walls, meaning

we can practice here and not risk burning down the library." Nine comes up behind me and wraps his arms around my waist, pulling me into him. "It's okay. It doesn't matter who you were, only who you will become."

But it does matter! How many people . . . things . . . have I killed?

"None. Because you aren't human anymore. You died and were reborn."

But-but-but—

"But nothing, Sweetie. We're not going to judge. Though I am curious. I'll admit."

"That makes two of us," Dea adds, coming to stand in front of me.

"Three." I want to know. Even if I hate it, I have to know. "So, Dea, you said you might know what I am?" Change the subject. Fuck! Please change the subject.

"Yes. I have a feeling you are the Horseman of Magic. Those colors on the door are indicative of a particular type of magic: elemental. Strong Witches possess elemental magic—"

"Right. They usually have an affinity for just one, though." This is information I already know somehow, and it makes me question who I was on Earth because knowledge of Witches is not common among humans, or anyone, really. They stayed in hiding, even after the other three main supernatural species came out of the closet.

"Uh-huh. But those black bits were the Angel magic we saw the other day."

Nine pulls back and gasps. "It kinda sounds like . . ."

"I know," Dea says.

"What! What does it sound like!?"

"Sorry, Sweetie. It looks really similar to an Angel-descended Witch."

That . . . makes a lot of sense. Thought it would freak me out, but it doesn't. Or if it does, I'm still in shock and will likely freak out later. Seems to be my thing. "So, what does that mean?"

"When an Angel's power mixes with a Witch's, a unique form of magic occurs. Witches can use the magical essence in the atmosphere given off by the leylines. Angels have power over life and death at a single touch. When mixed, they can, in rare cases, form a sort of death-wielding magic, where the Witch can use magical essence to create a literal tendril of death, killing whoever it touches."

Nine continues Dea's explanation, "Most species can mix, and their magic forms a collected kind of supernatural. The only reason they don't is because it's frowned upon to mix bloodlines by most supes, so they usually only breed with their own species."

"But what about the genetics of it all?" The main communities of magic, I have learned recently—Witches, Vampires, Shifters, and Fae—are all opposites and sit as the four main supernatural communities, keeping the balance of magic in place. How they interact is really specific and follows an annoyingly complex set of laws and inter-species rules.

"Right," Nine continues. "I did say most can mix. Not all. The four main communities can only mix in certain ways: Witches and Fae cannot breed together to form a mix, for example, and if they do breed, it forms one or the other because of how they use their magic."

I throw him a questioning look. I haven't gotten this far in my reading, and it seems I didn't know this when I was human.

Nine sighs and rubs the back of his neck. "Fae use leylines to charge their magic, then use it in all kinds of ways, but they need to stay near the leylines or regularly revisit them. On the other hand, Witches can access the magical essence given off by the leylines. It's a weaker form of magic, but it's so ingrained in Earth's atmosphere that they never run out."

"And Vampires use magic to enhance their external form." Dea grabs my shoulders, clearly trying to steady my spinning mind. "In turned Vampires, this is done in the form of super strength and speed, but in royals and highborn Vampires, this also gives way to their various abilities. On the other hand, Shifters use internal magic to change their internal environment, causing them to shift. It does give them some enhanced strength, but it is nothing compared to a Vampire."

I nod, absorbing all this information. "So, theoretically, a Vampire could breed with a Witch?"

Nine nods but looks a little put off by the idea. "Only born Vamps have the ability to breed, but yes. I'm unsure if anything like that exists, though. Vampires usually inbreed, and if they do mix up the genetics more, it's usually to create some kind of unique ability among the highborns."

Remind me not to get involved in Vampire politics. Sounds like a whole other world.

Nine claps his hands behind me, causing me to jump. "Let's get started."

"Right." Dea steps back, handing a plasmascreen to Nine. "Nine is just observing, offering his expertise in the theory of magic, but I will do the actual training."

Why is Dea always shirtless? That golden swirling tattoo is the most distracting thing I've ever witnessed. Fuck. Remind me not to have both Connie and Dea in their pajamas in the same room as me, because I'm pretty sure I'd melt into a puddle.

Nine snorts from behind me. *Tell me about it.*

I giggle at his antics as Dea looks at us with suspicion. "I want to know what kind of magic you have access to. Clearly death and elemental magic, but what else?"

"How do we find that out?"

"You need to release your magic so we can see for ourselves."

Even if I knew how to do that, wouldn't that be potentially dangerous?

"We can't die," Nine so helpfully reminds me from his spot at the only desk in the room. "So, no. No danger here."

"I don't know how to do that. Before, I was just angry or trying to show what I am, like with the door." I look to the floor, hoping not to see their looks of disappointment at my failure.

Dea steps forward, grabbing both my hands in his, and looks me straight in the eyes with those dancing galaxy eyes of his. "When we are accessing our magic to do something more active, like when I am moving a soul or Nine is delving deep into someone's mind, we are entering a deep part of our mind, a part we do not use otherwise."

Kind of like meditation, then. Okay. I can do that. Taking a deep breath, I sit on the floor with my legs crossed and my back straight. Relax. Access a part of my mind I would otherwise ignore. But what part?

I know so little about myself. There's the part of my mind that loves trying new things, that loves books, that has trouble sleeping, that is reminded of her past in horrible ways, and then there's the part of my mind that gets stuck on things and worries about everything, that unhelpfully ogles a bunch of people—friends?—I have no intention of getting involved with . . . But what part do I not access?

"You're thinking too literally, Sweetie." Nine comes up

behind me, passing the plasmascreen to Dea and places both hands on my shoulders. "Relax a little and just explore. Where does your curiosity lead when you think of your magic?"

My magic? Like when I nearly hurt Dea in the kitchen when I got mad at him? Well, that just leads me to self-loathing. How can I see in the dark? What about the door? I have all four types of elemental magic then, but that's not possible for any known Witch.

Not a Witch, I remind myself. A Horseman of the Apocalypse.

"Ugh! I just don't know." I slam my fist on the concrete floor in frustration and wince. "I'm sorry."

Dea sighs and kneels in front of me. "It is okay."

"Err, guys?" Nine stands at my side in shock. "What's that?"

"What's what?" I ask as I look to where his eyes fixate—on my fist punched into the floor. The concrete floor. I have created a dent in the concrete floor. "That . . . that was me?"

Nine smiles triumphantly "Strength. You're strong. Arrie'll freak."

Dea smiles at something I'm clearly out of the loop with while Nine makes various notes on the plasmascreen he steals back from Dea. "Nine," Dea says, "you will have to help her access her magic for the time being. We just need to see what we are dealing with. Then we can work on helping her access it herself."

Nine nods. "Sweetie," he says as he turns to my front, stepping in front of Dea, "this won't be pleasant. I need your permission to delve into your mind and search with you."

"Of course," I reply without hesitation. When did I become so trusting? Will he see the nightmares and flashbacks?

Nine gives me a puzzled look, like he heard that thought

and it's news to him.

Well, I've been trying hard to hide them.

"C'mon," Nine says as helps me into a standing position.

He grabs my hands and takes a deep breath as I let out a pained gasp. I can feel something putting pressure on my mind, like an odd weight squeezing at my emotions as it shifts around my thoughts and memories. He pauses for a moment on the hot make-out session with Connie, and then again on the way I stared at a shirtless Dea when he came to the library for the first time, and I briefly think I hear a chuckle in the distance, but before I can grasp onto that sound and decipher what it is, I'm dragged away again into distant thoughts and memories I have all but forgotten over the past week.

We sail around my mind, past so many misted sections I can only assume are memories from my human life, before stopping.

"We're here, I think," I hear Nine's voice echo across my mind in a weird, almost-cosmic way.

Here is an empty space, somewhere only bright magic permeates. In the center, on some kind of mental pedestal, sits a ball of power; I can feel its magical essence and powerful strength pulsing through the space.

Everywhere is pitch black, with rivulets of red running around in various ribbonlike streams across the space. "What are those?"

Nine remains silent, and for a moment, I think he might not even be here with me, but a quick glance to my right tells me he is. He stands there in all his usual geeky hotness and just stares at the space. "I've not seen this before."

Great. The magic expert is stuck.

Nine jabs me in the arm and looks mockingly offended. "Put your hand on that ball of power."

I do as he says, assuming he likely won't let me out of this mental space until I do, but as I touch it, relief flows through me in such bounds I can feel the tears flowing freely down my cheeks and my shaky arms reaching out to grab at something that no longer exists.

We're back in the dank training room, and Dea sits watching us with equal shock and amazement on his face.

The first thing I remember feeling is excruciating pain, as painful as it is wonderful, an odd, heady mixture that sends my body spasming to the ground in a rough heap.

"Angel!"

Screams pierce my ears, so intent on their journey into my soul that I only vaguely recognize them as mine, and I realize that pain can be felt in every inch of my body.

Opening my eyes, I see Dea in front of me, his body pressing up against mine in an effort to cuddle me, and I briefly feel Nine doing the same from behind, though I have no idea why.

What are they doing?

"We're trying to comfort you," Nine says with amusement.

"Oh," I think I try to say, not really knowing if it comes out as intended.

The pain is subsiding, though, and I can feel the pulse of magic in its place, a power threading throughout my body that I can tap into anytime I want.

"Whoa . . ." Dea steps back, propped up in the air by some kind of wind current.

My wind current. I'm doing that.

"Aha!" Nine exclaims from behind me. "Air magic. Excellent." He lets go of me, presumably to write more notes down, and I fall to the floor once more, weakness engulfing my every limb.

Exhaustion clings to every part of me, and I can barely keep my eyes open. "I just need to rest for a min . . ."

Strong arms pick me up and cradle me against a strong, bare chest. A brief glimpse of swirling gold strikes my vision as I let out a sigh of contentment. Dea. One day, Dea will be mine. But until then, I'll just bask in his radiance as he carries me to my room.

Just as that insane thought flits across my mind, I droop into the drowsiness of sleep, and emptiness suffocates me as not a single dream or nightmare plagues my mind for the first time since waking up immortal.

Chapter Fifteen

In a cruel twist of irony I don't see coming, everything hurts the next morning. I just healed from my injuries, and now I'm back to aching all over—again.

I fucking hate that stupid Horseman of Famine right now. I bet it wouldn't have hurt so much if I did it naturally. No one told me it would be quite that painful. Fucking a-holes!

"I heard that," a familiar, traitorous voice calls from the doorway as I struggle to do up my boots.

"Good." Let me make it easier for you to understand my current mood, Nine. You're a lying, pig-smelling, ungrateful, son of a—

Nine grabs my arm and pinwheels me into a bone-crushing hug, forgoing the laces that are only half tied. "I'm so glad you're okay."

I look up at him to see genuine relief in his eyes. He's really been worried? But why?

Because I like you. You're family now.

Family . . . The word sounds so unfamiliar. I try to roll it around my tongue, but it gets stuck.

"Come, let's get some breakfast."

Breakfast, it turns out, is a rather grand affair. Even for this strange, magical household. Platters of cheeses, breads, biscuits, cakes, and what can only be . . . bacon. The smell reminds me of a breakfast bar I used to visit, and I smile at the familiarity.

Pancakes, bacon, and maple syrup—best breakfast yet.

"So," Dea starts, "elemental magic, most likely all four types given the rainbow color of her Witch powers. And Angel death magic."

Nine shifts uncomfortably in his seat, like he's avoiding bringing something else up, and I suddenly remember what he said in my mental landscape thing: I've not seen this before.

He hasn't seen anything like my magical landscape, meaning I'm something different, but so far, my magic is something that already exists.

Something's not adding up.

Dea interrupts my spiraling—as the team have so lovingly taken to calling my mental chatter—but Nine stops him with a quick wave of his hand.

"Training's at one, right?" I look at Dea, who just nods and gazes a hole in my back my entire journey out the kitchen archway and up the stairs.

The familiar scent of broken pages and endless knowledge greets my nostrils, and I feel an inebriant sense of calm upon walking into my library. The longer I spend here, the more at home I feel, and that terrifies me. But for now, I take the long journey to my desk and start asking question after question about *Sheruta* and the house, about what kind of people live here and how this strange realm works.

It's the most complete I've felt in mind and soul in a long

while, as every question is answered with some kind response and I learn more than I ever thought possible in a single few hours of study.

Seems I'm pretty good at the whole studying thing, which surprises even me, but I'm less great at the whole using magic thing, which doesn't surprise me.

Half an hour until Dea and Nine are due to show up, I find myself trying to manipulate the air to create a cool breeze—but to no avail. I do manage a quick flick of the wrist to bring a book toward me, though, which is some kind of progress, I guess.

Sighing, I stand and make my way to the murderer's room (that's the only way I really catalogue what's going on with my human past right now), once again noticing how stupidly dark and dank this one room is compared to everything else I've been given by the house. It's like a literal representation of the darkness behind the colorful persona.

One day, that darkness is going come into the light.

One day, I'm not going to be me anymore.

Three knives in my left hand, four in my right, one sailing through the air for the twentieth time—and like the other nineteen times, it hits dead center.

Flashes of memory upon memory feed my naked mind—knives buried in various body parts, a hundred different types of targets, all with bullseyes stabbed dead center, and I can't help but whimper as I look over all the weapons once again. "What am I?"

Two. Three. Four. Five. Five. Six. Seven. Dead center. From every angle, from every maneuver I can think of. Not one is even an inch off the mark.

"Well, well, well . . . Seems we have a trained killer in our ranks." Arrie walks down the steps, his words making me wince. "You know, we've been a part of the supernatural community before the term community was even coined, and I'm finding it hard to believe Fate gave us someone who is so obviously trained to kill us."

"I can't kill you, Arrie, so fuck off." I don't even know what else to say to someone like him. He's so . . . Arrie.

"The magical community, I mean."

"You could just as easily kill them, you know." I pick all the knives out of the targets and return to my throwing position.

Arrie grumbles something unintelligible under his breath—something I'm pretty sure isn't English—and leaves.

One. Two. Three. Four . . . Fuck! He's right. Of course he's damn right. Why did Fate choose me? I'm clearly not the best choice here. I bet the magical community will hate me when I try to prevent a war, not to mention how many of them I've probably killed in my time as human.

Nine winces as he comes into the room, watching me throw the daggers perfectly every time. Great. Another Arrie reaction.

"What did he say to you?" Nine's fists ball into spheres of tension as he barely moves from the spot.

I don't dignify him with a response.

"What. Did. He. Say?"

I shove the memory at him, not really caring to repeat it out loud.

Nine gasps and throws himself out of the door, running to some unseen goal he has in mind.

Me? I honestly don't care what he does. I stop and look around the room for a moment, noticing Dea leaning up against a wall. "Can we just get this fucking over with?"

He nods, coming forward to meet me in the center of the room. "Concentrate on that wind element for now. Try to grasp it and move the air a little."

Since I practiced grabbing books earlier, I'm fairly certain I can manage that. And it's a great distraction from my spiraling thoughts.

Imagining I'm grabbing something nonexistent in the near distance, I try moving the air to create a ripple, but for a moment, everything remains static, as though I have no magic whatsoever.

Whoosh!

Dea's hair is suddenly askew as a gust of wind bats his face, and he makes a surprised yelping sound I didn't expect.

"Good." He moves behind me, redoing his hair and facing us both toward the targets. "Now try grabbing a knife and throwing it at the target."

My eyebrows rise in surprised excitement. I can see where he's going with this; he wants me to combine my gifts to create various skills and maneuvers. Combat maneuvers.

Excitement bubbles through me before I can even begin to question why I'm excited about something so violent. Being able to defend myself, actually having some skills to do the job I've been summoned for—even though we're not totally sure what that is yet—and being useful to the team . . . It's something I didn't realize I wanted so badly. Until now.

I throw myself into training that day. I use air magic to throw daggers at targets (much harder than doing it by hand); alter my aim trajectory to better hit my target, especially moving ones; hurl spears and swords across the room; and generally enhance the skills we know I already have (which aren't many, I admit). But it's a start.

Nine doesn't return, though, and I'm starting to get a little worried. The team makes it sound like he's obsessed with magical theory and wants to study me—I honestly don't mind, and his knowledge and expertise comes in handy—so where has he been all afternoon?

Dea and I eat dinner in silence, mostly because it's only the pair of us; Connie is still out on a mission, and Nine and Arrie are still missing from earlier. The worry grows until I can't take it anymore, and I slam my plate down so hard it cracks in two, marring the perfectly polished table.

"Where are they? I honestly can't live with knowing I'm causing problems between the team."

"Angel, this is Arrie's problem, not yours. Nine showed me what you showed him, and Arrie was . . . out of line. He of all people should know that our human pasts do not define our immortal futures."

I'm not sure what that's supposed to mean, but it isn't particularly comforting. I want to go talk to them, see if maybe I can have some semblance of a conversation with the Horseman of War.

Please don't be fighting just because of me.

I run around various hallways of the house—ones I know my way around—and listen for any hint of voices or sounds I can make out. They have to be somewhere . . .

"She doesn't belong here!"

A sickening crunch echoes down the hallway that leads to Arrie's rooms.

"She . . . was . . . chosen." Nine's voice sounds so faint, like he's failing to keep himself conscious.

I round the corner and peek through a crack in the just-open door. Arrie stands tall in the center of a surprisingly beautiful room while Nine lies crumpled on the floor at the base of the wall. The whole room is covered in flowers and indoor trees and has its very own spa-like pool in the center. Guess Arrie likes the outdoors. There's a bed low to the ground on the far side, with two floor-to-ceiling windows, like the ones in my room, that open up to the forest behind the house.

The sound of water trickling around the room and birds flitting between trees dotted in various corners makes my head swoon. It really is beautiful. He seems to value peace and relaxation, which is odd as shit given he's the Horseman of War. But maybe that's the point.

Nine's body slumps farther down the wall as his eyes hang heavy.

Oh goddess! Please, no. "Stop!" I run in, hands in the air, ready to try to do something—anything—to prevent this fight. "Please, stop."

Arrie turns to me with a snarl, fighting stance at the ready. "What do you want, Killer?" He growls that last word like it's the worst thing in the world, despite him being the Horseman of War. Something tells me he's killed his fair share over the last two millennia.

"I want you to stop fighting. You're a team. A family."

"We were."

Arrie fully turns around to look my way, and I get a full glimpse of Nine's condition—blotching bruises, cracking and splitting purple skin, and hair ruffled from where he hit the wall.

"You still are. Look, I get it. Change is hard, Arrie. And honestly, I think I'd rather still be human than here."

Nine looks at me with sad eyes, but understanding dawns behind the disappointment.

"Being immortal, alone forever, and stuck with a kind of magic I don't even understand, let alone know how to control . . . I don't want any of that."

"Then leave!"

"I can't!" I step forward, refusing to give up just because Mr. Strong and Moody is having a temper tantrum. "I can't just leave the world to die."

"Think you can stop a war, Killer?"

"Not alone, but yes, I think you'll need me. Otherwise, why would I be here?"

Arrie stops snarling and sighs. It's more of mix between a groan and a sigh, but at least it's not a snarl or a growl. He clearly understands what's going on here, but he seriously dislikes it.

"We don't have to be friends, and you have thousands of years to learn to be okay with this, but you can't hurt the people you love just because of me." My voice cracks at the end, and Nine shakes his head, as if trying to tell me in his half-conscious state that it isn't my fault. But it is. This would never have happened if I didn't turn up.

"I'll never be okay with this," Arrie growls. "You'll always just be a murderer."

Anger boils beneath the surface, a raging sea of frustration I've been tamping down ever since he found me in the training room, but something about that sentence just snaps any lasting control I have.

I sprint and reach Arrie in less time than it takes to inhale and connect my fist with his nose.

He flies backward, arms flailing as a surprised yelp escapes his usually perfect facade. He lands in a heap beside Nine, who lies there staring at me in shocked silence.

I look at my fist, whose knuckles are a bright shade of crimson red—ugh, those are gonna bruise tomorrow—and wonder who the fuck I am.

Dea's beside me in the blink of an eye, looking around the room at Nine and Arrie lying next to one of the many serenity ponds. "What happened?"

"I-I-I-I punched Arrie in the face . . . and he landed over there."

"You . . . punched him? And he actually fell backward?"

I nod, vaguely understanding that this is a big deal.

"She broke my nose," Arrie grumbles a little less murderously than before. "My nose is actually . . . broken."

Dea goes to take a look at them both, sees the stupidity of the situation, and walks straight back out again, not even bothering to heal them. "You can heal on your own!"

I help Nine up, who looks at me gratefully and directs me to his room. It takes an agonizing twenty minutes, but we make it to the room just down from my own. We walk through an open door and into a dark room with lots of computers and gadgets dotted around and a plasma wall set up in the corner where various plasmascreens are embedded into the wall.

It's very Nine. And I start to get the feeling that everyone has a room that suits them—somewhere they can relax and just be themselves. Connie has a suite that suits her beauty and chilled-out persona, Arrie has a set of rooms that suits his need for inner peace, and Nine has a room that suits his inner geek.

Wonder what Dea's room looks like?

I lay Nine on a chaise that lounges next to a corner bookcase, its black velvet a stark contrast against the white shelves and red cushions.

"I'm sorry, sweet thing."

He looks at me with guilt-ridden eyes, and I kneel next to him. "No. Don't be. It's not your fault. I should be thanking you for trying to keep the peace."

"I didn't really do very well." He sighs and sits up slightly, wincing the entire way. "Connie's usually the one to talk some sense into him. But with her gone, I thought maybe . . ."

"You could try? You could have been seriously hurt. Arrie's not the type to hold back, or so I hear." That gets a laugh out of him, and we both relax slightly. "I could probably persuade Dea to heal you if you wanted me to campaign on your behalf?"

"Persuade him, huh? And how would you do that?"

The suggestion in his tone has me blushing. "Not like that! I was going to simply ask him. I mean, you were trying to do the right thing."

"Yeah, but I should have just waited for Connie to get back. She'll only be gone a few days." Nine gruffs and scowls. "I was just so angry at him. He can't treat you like that. Any of us."

"He's right to be suspicious. I'd be lying if I said I wasn't also concerned about it." Nine raises his eyebrows in question, and I sigh. "I mean, why pick someone to stop a magical war who has clearly already picked a side? It just doesn't seem logical."

Nine looks at me with those sad eyes from earlier, clearly sensing the general tone of my thoughts. "You know, when I was human, I was kind of like a priest in my town."

I snort in disbelief. Yeah right.

"It's true."

"Really?"

He rests a hand on my arm, his thumb rubbing circles in slow, comforting movements. "I shunned anything magical, never took a wife, and died a virgin. When I came to in the house, and we learned more about what we were, I spent so long in denial. Suddenly I was this powerful magical being who was immortal? It went against everything I'd ever believed in." He takes a shuddering breath, and I raise the blanket up to his chin as his eyes start drooping. "We change when we become a Horseman. We have to be who the world needs us to be."

His eyes close, and I feel his chest rise and fall in even breaths, leaving me alone with his words of dooming wisdom.

The person the world needs me to be . . .

But who is that? And how do I become her?

Chapter Sixteen

Two days I spend my mornings doing yoga in the garden's new *Shinto* shrine, researching the Four Horsemen and *Sheruta* in the library, reading up about magical theory, and discussing with Nine how I seem to have all four elements as my magic.

Turns out *Sheruta* was created at the same time as the Horsemen—or that's the theory, at least, since they were the first ones to settle here—but eventually, more and more species discovered the portal, some of whom were shown here by members of the Horsemen, and the realm grew. The realm itself is completely self-managing, from having its own four-season cycle to various creatures, ecology, and culture. The most interesting part, in my opinion, is learning about the various ecosystems, and I want to make it my mission in the future to explore everything *Sheruta* offers, log all the various plant and animal species, and see what ones can be useful in various magical spells and potions.

Not even Nine has bothered to make a list, just mentally cataloguing the ones he's found useful over the centuries. For a science and magic expert, and resident nerd, he's rather lazy with going out in the field.

I spend my afternoons learning to use my new air magic in various ways under Dea's instruction while Nine makes notes. Once I gained access to the magic, it came naturally, and it feels good using it, both for myself and in training to help the team.

I have since perfected my aim with my air magic, and have for moving targets, too; I can use air to both throw a dagger and make its course more accurate when thrown by hand.

Dea and I are sitting down to breakfast early on the third day, waiting for the others.

"Eventually, with some field experience, you will learn to adapt your magic to specific situations and use it fluidly without placing limitations upon yourself," Dea says.

Arrie has said nothing since the incident, but I occasionally catch him watching me, and today I'm going to try to break that thick layer of ice, or at least chip at it a little. It's been awkward tiptoeing around him recently, and I'm ready to move on from that, like yesterday.

Nine and Arrie enter, both since healed from their stupid man-headed injuries, and sit at the breakfast table, as Dea asks the house to prepare a spread of toast and condiments.

Dea and Nine chat about something and laugh about old times while Arrie and I sit in silence.

"So, Arrie," I say, causing everyone to stop eating and talking and to look at me, "want to come join our training session today?"

Nine smiles at me, clearly seeing what I'm trying to do, but Dea looks at me with doubt.

"Why?" Arrie grumbles between bites.

"Well, it would be great to get some pointers from all of you, and you must have some killer knife-throwing skills, but I thought you might feel more at ease if you came and saw my magic for yourself." I pause, watching him stare at me with a blank face while he continues to chew. "I mean, I can only use air magic right now, but we've done some cool things with it, and—"

"Whatever." Arrie gets up and leaves, abandoning his plate on the table rather than washing it like usual. He grumbles something under his breath in another language as he heads back up the stairs with heavy footfalls.

"Well, that went well." I roll my eyes and sigh, dragging a hand over my face in frustration. Why won't he just quit with the stupid attitude and try to get along with me?

Nine places a comforting hand on my knee while Dea gives a gentle smile. "Just keep trying, Angel."

I nod, determination filling me, and head to my library. Research. More research. And today, I will look into Witch magic.

Wonder how Connie's doing? Is she all right? Shaking my head, I try to tell myself not to worry about her. She's the Horseman of Conquest, for fuck's sake, she'll be fine. It's silly of me to worry. But still, that niggling doubt persists in raising my hackles as I walk by shelf after shelf, brushing my fingertips along various spines and mentally cataloguing where they are.

Witch magic. Witch magic. Witch magic, I tell myself over and over, trying to focus my mind on the task at hand, but I fear it's going to be one of those days of mental disparity: Arrie is still angry with me for existing, no one has heard from Connie in a few days, I can still only use air magic, and I still have few memories of my past.

Did I have any friends?

Family?

People who cared?

Did they mourn me?

Did I cause them suffering?

I can feel my emotions spiraling down one of those familiar black holes of insanity, with questions being asked that I have no hope of getting answers to, and emotions being challenged that I have no place feeling. Maddening. That's what this life is. Utterly fucking maddening. And if I have to live another damn week in this stupid immortal body with no answers to any of my questions, I'm going to explode.

Standing up in a huff, I bang my fist on the desk, releasing a growl of frustration, and pace around the library in random directions. I'm not looking for anything, not really, but my mind needs to wander so it can find its way back to its usual maddening, if slightly okay, normality. The brief thought of being immortal and part of the Horsemen of the Apocalypse being my new normal has a laugh leaking from my lips. How ridiculous my life has become in such a short space of time.

A break. That's what I need. A damn break. I go to the nearest shelf that holds some deliverance of escapism and breathe a sigh of relief when, a few seconds later, I sit on a turquoise pouf with a fantasy book in hand. I don't even deliberate over the title, just see it's about some random female hero saving dragonkind—something so far from the troubles of my own reality—and sink into peace.

I have no idea how many hours have passed or when my training session is due to start, and that lack of timekeeping is the most blissful few hours I've spent since Connie left. But voices in the distance break my fantastical haze and bring me right back to crushing reality.

"Not sure where she is?"

"Around 'ere somewhere. This place is huge."

"It's fucking awesome, and you know it."

A familiar grumble ruptures the air around me and sticks to my ear like cheese to a grater—Arrie.

I get up and try to find where the voices are coming from—probably the study—and watch from a corner as Nine, Dea, and Arrie poke around my little nook of knowledge. Dea places my research notes on the desk—he must have finished going through, annotating them for me. A little surge of joy sparkes my insides at that; he's really taken the time to add details to their story.

I know it's silly, but they've got two millennia on me. They know everything about each other: their gifts, their personalities, their past, their worlds. I'm just supposed to know it all straightaway? I hate being out of the loop, and they're one large fucking loop.

Nine hasn't spotted me yet, or maybe he has and just doesn't want to tip the others off. Who knows? That guy is an enigma. A really hot puzzle I need to figure out. He's the nerd, the one to sit down and explain everything to me about their lives (even small parts that probably doesn't matter to them), the one who knows more about magic than the rest of us combined. Probably the rest of the world.

Arrie sits in my chair and flicks through the leather-bound book I use to make notes on them. I have a separate one for magic, *Sheruta*, and Earth, all packed into that top drawer. He flips through the pages, his general scowling expression morphing into one of surprise and dare I say it . . . admiration.

Have I impressed him with my notes?

I've found I'm naturally studious, and the more I let my mind become more active, the more I find myself being more like Nine. A nerd. But at least I have the potential to be magically badass, too.

Nine sits with Arrie, perching his ass on the end of his knee—the fact that doesn't weird me out is more bothersome than I care to admit—and flips through the pages with him.

"Ha! Look!" He points to something on the page I can't see. "Seems she has made correct assumptions about all of our gifts and how they relate to our personalities. Look, Arrie, she has your grumpiness down to a tee."

Arrie shakes him off his knee, his usual scowl plasters back across his face, and he slams the book shut.

Damn. I thought I made good progress for a moment there. Oh well, guess I'll keep trying. I have all of eternity, after all.

I step out of the stacks.

Nine looks my way, Dea sends me another one of those panty-melting smiles that makes my knees tremble, while Arrie doesn't even acknowledge my presence.

"Ready?" I walk past them head toward the area of the library that holds my training room.

They follow behind, or at least I assume they do—I can only hear Arrie's footsteps and Nine's endless chatter. Dea is as silent as ever.

Stack after stack, I take them through the shelves, never stopping to look back, and soon arrive at the training room door that only opens when I let my magic seep into it, lighting it up like some kind of magically darkening rainbow.

Would have been cool if I wasn't so pissed off that I could only access my air magic. There are three other elements . . . Why can't I fucking use them?

We all step into the dark room, and I walk over to the knives and start laying them out on the table next to the start line in front of the targets.

"You really can see in the dark, 'ey?" Nine says as he flicks the old-fashioned lights on, sending those irritating flickers of humming lights right into my eyes.

A small hiss and groan escape my lips. "Really need to change those fucking lights."

Dea walks up behind me. "Why is that, Angel?" He places a hand on either shoulder and gently rubs the tension out of them.

"Cause they're really fucking irritating. Hurts my eyes, and their damn humming hurts my ears."

"I do not hear anything, Angel."

I stop preparing the blades and turn around. "What?"

Nine comes up to us. "Yeah, I don't hear anything, either. They're just . . . lights."

"Okaaaay." At this point, I don't care. I'm already a freak, stand out even here among the Horsemen, and just really want to throw something. Preferably at someone, but I'll settle for a moving, inanimate target.

Nine grabs Dea's hand and pulls him away, shaking his head.

Breathing in, I line up the knife in my hand with the target against the far wall. Breathing out, I let go, using my air magic to zigzag it around the room before hitting the target. Okay, so I'm showing off a bit. But who cares? I'm stuck with this, so the least I can do is show off to the asshole who thinks I'm some kind of murderer.

But what if I am? Was?

My head shakes violently for a few seconds before I can regain control and stop it.

No, I don't think so either.

Picking up a sword from the area outlined in white tape off to the left, I look to Dea, who steps forward. "Ready?"

His chosen sword in hand, he merely nods.

I rush left, aiming for a spinning, behind-the-back shot, but he turns at the last second and counters.

The ring of metal on metal clashes around the room as he feints right but jabs left. I spin out of the way, using my air magic to push me a little farther than my legs can take me, but Dea is on me in a flash. His speed is something else. And I have yet to think of a good counter for it.

For now, I simply try to stay on top of it by keeping a close eye on what direction his feet are facing. I really hope he doesn't let on to that little trick.

We both stop for a moment to catch our breath, and I briefly have a terrifying thought of what it would be like to spar with Connie, given that she never runs out of energy. Damn. That must be insane.

Nine laughs a little from behind his plasmascreen. "She breaks every fifteen minutes for us. But yes, we're all a little terrified of her inability to tire."

Dea chuckles, clearly seeing where my thoughts have gone. He seems a little out of breath, and I think that maybe his ability costs a lot of energy for him to use. That is interesting.

With his shirt now noticeably absent—the cheating fucker—he stands, ready to continue. "Ready?"

I nod, taking a deep breath.

Dea moves first this time, coming in for a straight shot, which I quickly counter by leaping backward and meeting his sword midair.

Another clang of metal, and Dea is already pushing me back against the wall, his sword against my neck. I don't even have time to blink.

He's been holding back this entire time—fuck, damn him.

Dea drops his sword as mine clangs to the floor and my hands raise in surrender above my head. I let out a frustrated breath. "If I could use the other elements, I might actually be able to fight."

"Shhh." He holds a finger to my lips, gently stroking his thumb across my lower lip.

Seriously? He's shirtless, stroking my lip, and has me pinned to a wall. The golden glimmer of his tattoo distracts my eyes, though, as they wander over the spiraling shoulder. I remember him telling me it's in memory of his Shifter friend. I think it's a beautiful memento.

He told you that?

Looking over at Nine, I can see his head still stuck in the plasmascreen—he's trying to hide this conversation and that it's even taking place.

Yes. Though he didn't tell me the story. Just that it's in memory of a Shifter friend. I did ask. Not everyone has to keep things hidden, Nine. In fact, Dea's a . . . really open person.

Not with just anyone he's not.

I can sense the humor and insinuation in his tone, but I elect to ignore it because honestly? Nope. Not even going there.

I realize then that Dea still has me pinned to the wall, and I've been staring off into space for the last thirty seconds while talking to Nine. Damn. I'm trying to be as inconspicuous as Nine.

Dea looks at me with a sexy smirk on his face, and I can't help but smile like a stupid teenager with a crush. He really is beautiful. Even more so up close. Part of me wants to reach out and run my hands through his hair while seeing what it would be like to meet those delicate lips with my own. I've already made out with Connie, and I doubt adding Dea to that brief list will really matter.

But it will. And part of me knows that. Connie knows the deal and understands, and she's willing to be patient with me and build something, even if it ends up just being a close friendship. So I push Dea back, and he lets me, as I step out of the intense position.

Shaking off the feeling of need that settled and the intense desire to turn right back around and pin him to the wall, I instead look at Nine, who's no longer burying his head in that plasmascreen but staring at me with a longing look.

What does he see when he looks at me like that?

Beauty.

I blush at his almost romantic compliment and walk back to the knives.

"No." Arrie stands in the doorway, and this is the first time I've taken note of him. Honestly, I try my best to ignore him most of the time. "Spar with me." He waltzes down the room toward me, pinning me with those eyes of burning anger, and picks up a different sword from the rack—a heavier one.

Spar with the Horseman of War? I think I would rather keep his angry, moody self as my newest pet. I'm going to regret inviting him along today, aren't I?

Probably.

I hold in the laugh about to squeeze out of my throat and turn toward Arrie. "All right. Let's fucking do it." Bouncing on my toes, I mentally prepare myself for a sparring match with the Horseman of War. Pretty sure I'm about to lose. But I will do so with dignity.

Arrie stands in the center of the taped circle, sword drawn at his side, eyes closed.

Do I just go?

Yes.

Okay, then. I grip my sword tighter, tip my foot forward to charge, and run.

Arrie's sword meets mine while his eyes are still closed, and I'm momentarily shocked still.

I shake myself out of the unprotected statue position I've found myself in and use some air currents to propel me to his left and around to his back, aiming to strike from behind.

A clang of metal on metal meets my ears, so I knew he's countered it, even though it happens so fast I can barely keep track.

Fucking damn it. He's too fast. Too accurate.

Arrie turns so his back is to me and then makes his first offensive move: he spins in a quick 360 and meets my throat with the tip of his blade.

My feet dodge backward, but I'm pretty sure in a real fight I'd be dead. I use my air magic to make me weightless and flip effortlessly over his head—mentally, I'm praising myself for looking so epic, but I don't have time for the vocal ego boost right now—then spin and meet his wide blue eyes as my blade presses gently to his stomach.

"Yes!" Totally got a hit on the Horseman of War. How cool is that?

But, looking at him, I get the feeling he isn't really trying, as he stands there with those wide eyes, not even trying to retain a defensive position, and that deflates my new confidence just a little. (Okay, a lot, but who's counting?)

"That was . . . interesting," Arrie says. Not a grumble. Or a complaint. An actual sentence. Said to me.

I'll take that as a win. Score one for the Horseman of Magic.

"Indeed," Dea adds. "You used your magic intuitively and flexibly to adapt to your scenario. Well done."

Wait . . . I did? I just did the most logical thing to try to surprise Arrie. I didn't realize that's what Dea was on about yesterday.

Arrie stays silent, then breaks my mind babble by saying, "I'll train you."

I mean, Dea says that I will eventually adapt my abilities to suit my environment, but— "Wait, what?"

"I'll train you."

"For real?"

"Yes." Arrie puts the sword down and leaves without saying another word.

"Okaaaay."

Nine strolls up and shows me the plasmascreen. On the faintly blue, non-physical screen is a tally chart: one side labelled MAGIC and the other WAR. "I'd say that's two points for the Horseman of Magic."

We high-five, and I can't help but grin a stupid, girly smile at the nerd. I've really convinced Arrie that I'm okay. Well, okay enough to train. I'll work on the rest later.

CHAPTER SEVENTEEN

I spend the rest of the afternoon doing the research into Witch magic I meant to do that morning—before Arrie ruined my good mood. The research involves the history of Witches, how they didn't come out of the closet with the rest of the magical community because of the whole Salem thing, and how together with Shifters, Vampires, and Fae, they created the four pillars of magic.

That is the first time I'm hearing this reference (since it isn't triggering any further knowledge), and despite asking my Seeing Stone about it, no other books come up in my search. I don't know why, but something about that seems awfully suspicious. I mean, this damn library is huge. Why is the only mention of the four pillars in this one book? It's a pretty thin-looking book, too. Doesn't have much in it.

Can I ask the others? Maybe they've heard of the reference before? I'll bet my movie night choice that Nine'll know. The nerd knows everything. I kinda love that about him. It's hot, and I rely on him for any kind of question, (bonus, I can just ask internally if I don't want the others knowing) no matter how silly or embarrassing it is.

To dinner it is, then. It's seven pm anyway, and that usually means someone's thought of dinner. Good, because I'm starving. All this training has really increased my appetite.

The four of us sit around the table in our spots: me and Nine on the left side, Arrie opposite, and Dea at one of the heads. Connie's empty space bothers me more and more as the days go by, and I'm getting anxious enough to ask how they reckon she's doing, but it really is silly.

It's not silly to worry. She's probably fine. Dea was thinking about checking on her in a few days if she's not checked in by week's end.

Phew. I feel myself audibly exhale in relief, and Dea raises an eyebrow at me. I shake my head, trying to dissuade him from asking out loud.

Dinner is pizza. I fucking love pizza! Ohmigod, pizza and coffee. Now that is the stuff of dreams. From pepperoni, to Hawaiian, to Greek feta, to fancy mozzarella . . . I love them all.

But I need to stop gorging myself and actually ask Nine my question from earlier. "Nine?"

"Hmm?"

"Have you ever heard of the term 'the four pillars of magic'?"

Nine looks off into space for a moment before coming back and looking at me. "There was this guy . . . Dr. Oscar Walzto, I think. He released a theoretical paper on how the four largest magical communities kept the balance of power."

"Oh. That makes sense." Dr. Waltzo is the author of that paper-thin book I read. "Do you have a copy of that paper I could borrow?"

"Probably." He takes another bite of his pepperoni pizza.

"Why do you ask?"

"Well . . . I saw the reference and went to ask the Seeing Stone, and nothing. There were no references in the library."

Dea chimes in, obvious confusion etching across his face. "None at all?"

I shake my head. "Nope."

Nine and Dea share a knowing look and then glance back at me in this freaky unison thing they have going on.

"What?"

It's Nine who answers. "He's a particularly influential research doctor within the magical community. It's a little odd your library has nothing more on that reference."

Oh. Well, why doesn't his name or that term ring any bells? Maybe human me didn't really know much about magic. No, that makes little sense because I know all about Witches.

The all-too-familiar question raises its ugly head again: who was I? Nothing about the facts of who I was makes any sense. I know loads about specific things, but not a lot about the magical community as a whol—

A scream pierces the air, and we all snap to our feet and turn toward the source.

Connie.

She half stands, half crouches in the center of the kitchen as blood leaks from her mouth and multiple wounds across her torso. Her feet are bent in a way I'm pretty sure isn't natural, and tears streak down the side of her face in screeching agony.

Her usually perfect visage of beauty is a tangled mess, and worry shoots its way through my system and forces me to rush forward and place a hand on her shoulder.

As I get closer, I inhale an intoxicating scent, one of honey with a salty, metallic tang that has me hungrier than I've ever been before.

Stopping dead in my tracks, I sniff the air, drawing in as much of that sweet, sweet scent as possible as I lustfully scoop large gulpfuls of air with my lungs.

I want to be near her . . .

I lean closer, still sniffing the air, trying to gorge on that sweet, addictive scent. My hands tighten on her shoulders, and Connie winces in pain as she tries to pull away.

But I inch closer until my nose is flush against her cheek and my mouth centimeters from hers.

"Sweetie?"

I can hear Nine in the background, but his voice is a faded record, calling out but not quite reaching me.

Connie gasps when she pulls away and looks at my face, and a vision of pure terror crosses her eyes. "Ahhhh!" She scrambles to get away, but I grab her other shoulder and hold her in place.

Someone grabs my arms and yanks me backward, flying me off my feet.

I hiss and scramble, kick and punch. "Let go!" I need to get to Connie. Now. There's something about her scent that I need.

Breaking free of the grip that holds me, I run to Connie, but not before Arrie stands in front of me, a mixture of concern and confusion plastered across his face. "Stop."

He holds my arms in a viselike grip as Nine grabs me from behind, arms wraping around my waist. "Please," he whispers.

The plea in his voice breaks me out of my reverie.

Wait . . . What happened? What am I doing?

I wanted to . . .

Ohmigod. I wanted to eat her. To taste her blood and see what it's like. I needed to . . .

"Shhhhh," Nine comforts. "It's okay."

"No!" No. It isn't okay. I could have killed her. How is he saying tha—?

"We can't die, Sweetie."

Right. Even if I drained her dry, I wouldn't have killed her. Drained her of . . . blood.

Oh my goddess, I'm a V-Vam . . . ?

Dea pushes us out of the way and crouches on the floor, where Connie slides to meet him. "This might sting a little."

She nods, silent tears racking her body.

Dea gathers himself onto his knees and places a hand either side of her temples. Green light shines from his hands, healing her internal wounds, and I watch as she grimaces in pain, but the blood pouring from her mouth stops trickling and dries almost instantly, but my need to go to her and . . .

Goddess, it's so intoxicating.

"Lay down." Dea moves himself out of her way.

Arrie lets go of me and comes up beside her, laying her head on his lap as he strokes comforting hands over her head. I've never seen him so caring. It surprises me.

Dea heals the rest of Connie's wounds while she shakes from the pain, and before long, she's all healed and wrapped up in Arrie's arms like some kind of fragile princess. Even through the blood and torn clothing, she still looks beautiful.

"Hon . . ." Her eyes flutter open, and she looks at me with a mixture of friendliness and . . . fear. "Can you p-please get me some f-food?"

"Er . . . right." I jump up, happy to have something to do to help distract me from the obvious. I fill a plate with various flavors of pizza and kneel back down to hand it over. "I'll grab you a tea."

She loves tea.

"Peppermint."

"Okay, one peppermint tea coming right up." I get to work brewing her request while Arrie takes her into another room, followed by Dea.

Nine wraps an arm my waist from behind. "She'll be fine. She's just tired. She probably didn't sleep on her mission, and then she got wounded. She needs a good night's sleep is all." He remains where he is, and although I know it's slightly intimate, the comfort is warm and aids in stopping the shaking of my hands.

He doesn't seem to be afraid of me.

I stay silent while I pour the hot water into the teapot. My hands are shaking slightly, but not as badly as before.

"Hey." Nine holds the water jug over top of my hand, connecting our fingers. "It's okay." His voice brushes against my neck, and I revel in the comfort of his gentleness. He nuzzles my neck as his spare arm wraps tighter around my waist. "I promise she's fine. You're fine. We're all okay."

"Okay."

Nine won't lie to me. He and Dea have been upfront from the beginning, but Nine has been the one to fill me in and try to guide my spiraling thoughts into something that resembles tentative calmness.

"Bet she'd love to hear all about your new developments, Horseman of Magic."

He used my actual title rather than Sweetie, and it makes me melt against him as my hand drops from the jug's handle and comes to rest at my side. The way he says my title sends shivers down my body.

He wraps both arms around me in a tight embrace, and I

inhale his cherrylike scent and let it wash away my concerns.

New developments? There are a lot of them all right, but we'll figure it out. Hopefully.

"C'mon, let's get Con her tea."

"Mmmm-hmm." I can barely form functioning thoughts at the minute, let alone words. He's so . . . relaxing.

Nine grabs my waist once more and walks me down an empty corridor to the last room on the left. As the door opens, I see Dea and Arrie in a heated discussion. I can hear them, too, but I choose to ignore Arrie's words right now. They aren't particularly nice.

"Sit here." Nine gestures to a plump armchair in the corner. He grabs the tray from me, places it in Connie's shaking hands where she lies on the couch, and comes back to me. He sits next to me, scoots me up, and sits me in his lap, nuzzling a comforting face against my neck.

I expect Dea to say something. Hell, if not Dea, then Arrie. But no one says a word. We all stand and sit in silence, Dea and Arrie's heated words long since faded the moment I stepped into the room.

The room itself is a slightly bland but large lounge. A smattering of brown sofas and armchairs line two walls, a large plasma TV takes up another, and a fake window with an artificial seafront setting displays along the other. There's a small chandelier hanging from the ceiling, and in its holders at regular intervals sit candles that are all alight and glowing the room in a soft yellow blush that makes the situation seem a little less daunting than it is.

Taking a deep breath, I break the sience first "I'm sorry." Even to me, it sounds pathetic. As though sorry is going to cut it when I nearly drained Connie dry not moments ago. "I . . . er . . ."

"No," Connie says, sitting up. "Don't." She stands and walks over to me. "You're new. We don't know the extent of your powers yet. I just . . . have an innate fear of Vampires." She mumbles that last part, and I have to strain to hear it.

"R-Really?" She's scared of something? Like, actually scared? And that something is me.

"Yes." She gives me a gentle smile. "Maybe someday I'll tell you all about it, but for now, I really need to update you all and get some rest."

I nod, knowing that her understanding is about the best I'm going to get right now, and I don't even deserve that.

She turns around and sits back on the couch. "Thanks for the tea, by the way." She raises the cup to me, and I smile. "So." This time she faces Dea and Arrie. "I have no idea who broke the fifth seal or where it is."

"What?" Dea stands, dumbfounded, a look of incredulity on his face. "You were gone for days and found nothing?"

She nods. "Yup."

"I . . . I don't get it," Nine adds.

Connie laughs slightly. "Took me a while to track a few of our informants down, but everyone came back with the same thing: no one has heard anything about the seals in centuries."

"Okay." Dea sits on the couch next to her, lifting her feet in the process. "So what do you need to update us on?"

Connie looks to the rest of the team and grimaces. "The magical community are heading for war. If they aren't already, they will be soon."

We all stare at her, dumbfounded. I thought I'd have more time. To train, to practice, to learn who I was and am. My head spins, thoughts barely forming before they flutter away to make room for new ones. War. So it's finally happening, then.

Nine rests a head in the crook of my neck. *It's okay. We're in this together.*

"You don't seem very surprised by this news."

Dea shakes his head. "We are not. While you were away, we discovered what type of Horseman Angel is. Though we still know very little about her powers."

Connie grins. "Oh, c'mon . . . Don't leave me hanging!" She sits up and looks at me. "Tell me!"

She's like a kid in a candy store, and for a moment, it reminds of the all the dancing and fun we had last Friday. So much has changed since then.

"I . . ." I take another deep breath. "I am the Horseman of Magic."

A smile creeps up Connie's face, looking a little stunned, but a happy kind of pride takes over her features. "Well, well, well . . . Look who's got the potential to be the strongest now?"

Strongest? Ha! Hilarious.

She's right, Sweetie.

I pull away from Nine and look at him blankly. "Don't be ridiculous." My eyes pull toward Connie. "Both of you. I'll be an equal member of the team. Someday."

Dea smiles at that, and Arrie . . . Well, he just grumbles something in an unintelligible language under his breath that has Connie throwing him a scary-as-fuck look.

"I went to see Milila but got ran out by her pack before I could even get close. Hence"—Connie gestures to herself—"this."

Her pack? Who's Milila?

Milila runs the hyena pack in Ueno, Tokyo.

"Why were you run out, Con?" Concern etches onto Dea's features.

"No idea." She shrugs. "Never got the chance to ask."

Dea looks even more concerned from the lack of information and leans back into the couch, deep in thought.

"I need to sleep." Connie gets herself up off the couch.

Arrie crouchs down next to her. "I'll take you to bed." He scoops her up in his arms, and I watch as she rests her head on his shoulder, and it reminds of the time Arrie carried me like that back to my room.

Damn. Stop it! He clearly hates you. Now is not the time to be getting hot over some asshole who has barely said a nice word to you . . . ever.

Well, he is an attractive man with all that muscle.

Shut up, Nine! And get out of my head.

It's hard when your thoughts scream as loud as yours. He just chuckles from underneath me and wraps his arms tighter around my waist.

And for a moment, I let him wrap me up in a pretend ball of comfort, as though the world isn't at war and dependent on me to save it, as though I'm not in a house full of teammates I'm weirdly attracted to. As though I belong.

Chapter Eighteen

"Hon . . . You're . . . just wow!"

Connie stands in the doorway of my dingy training room the next day, observing my new skills, and so far, I seem to be impressing her. And I refuse to admit how like a giddy teenager that fact makes me. Nope. Nuh-uh. Not happening.

"Like what you see, Con?" Nine sits at the desk—his usual place—and has spent the entire afternoon teasing me about that kiss. Inside my mind, of course, because then no one else understands why I'm suddenly blushing after she whoops for the hundredth time when I hit the bullseye. Again.

Connie stands behind me and adjusts my position slightly, placing her hands on my hips. "This way, you'll be able to pivot more in the field when attacking moving targets. Keep your weight on your back leg."

"Oh." That seems to be the only word my brain can come up with because it's far too focused on her warm fingers clenching my hips and her breasts now pressing against my back.

Seriously? You're crushing hard, aren't you?

Shut the fuck up!

Nine chuckles in my mind. He actually mentally chuckles inside my head. The fucker.

I can feel the heat rising to my face, but Connie doesn't move. Instead, she wraps her arms around my waist in a backward hug and whispers against my neck. "I missed you."

"Me too," I whisper back. "It's good to have you back."

She seems to be back to her normal self today, but there's a part of my mind at the very back that niggles with uncertainty. Will she still feel the same way? I'm a . . . a . . . Nope. Still can't say it. Not even in my head.

Despite my mental spiraling, Nine's remained silent on the matter, and I get the feeling that Dea is ready to call a meeting soon and has purposefully asked him to keep quiet.

We'll all chat soon, Sweetie. Promise.

Well, that confirms that.

Connie peels herself away from me as Dea coughs from the doorway, having returned from grabbing bottles of water for everyone. He sneeks a questioning look at Nine, whose gaze goes blank for a minute as Dea's eyebrows shoot to the ceiling.

"Really?" Dea asks as he looks straight at me, then at Connie. "You two really kissed before you left?"

"Well," Connie answers, "it was more like a hot make-out session, but sure. Yeah." She winks at me and shrugs a shoulder.

I admittedly want to die on the spot. Magic, kill me now. This team is going to murder me with embarrassment before I can even do my job.

Dea gives me a heated look and walks on up to me in purposeful strides. "I did not know you were . . . bisexual?"

"Really? You guys do the whole labeling thing? You're like . . . what? Two thousand years old?"

Nine chuckles from behind. "She's got a point, bro. Let 'em be."

"Oh, I am not complaining." And to prove that point, he grabs my waist and yanks me against him, his dark glowing eyes turning golden for a split second before returning to their usual galaxy greatness.

Usually, I try to get out of his hold, but between Nine's affections yesterday, Connie's closeness even after the whole blood thing, and now this . . . My control is decidedly slipping through my fingers like sand.

"Dea . . . I—"

"Shhhh." He places a finger to my lips, and I have to resist the urge to kiss it; instead, I remain as motionless as possible. "It's okay." He pulls my waist tighter until I'm flush against him and can feel everything hidden from view. From his rigid, muscular torso whose defined lines I can feel beneath the thin material of his t-shirt, to the growing hardness pressing against my lower stomach. He's . . .

Fuck, damn it, he's gorgeous.

Uh-huh. Don't need to yell it, Sweetie. I know.

I'm not yelling it for your benefit, asshole.

Well, the mental picture you're conjuring is not giving that man enough credit. Trust me.

I-I-I . . .

Nine throws me a mental picture—memory?—of a mostly naked Dea propped up against a wall, still in his underwear but otherwise available for perusal.

Great, now my imagination has decided to take a road trip to the bedroom, and I'm keenly aware of both pairs of eyes boring holes in us—a little hot but mostly curious (I think)—and Nine's knowing smirk.

Breaking Dea's hold on my waist, I pull away. I have to swallow the whine of disapproval as he, too, steps backward.

"So I have a plan for this afternoon's training." He steps away farther after noticing my gaze is still stuck to his lips. "Connie, why don't you help Arrie with Angel'sphysical training plan?"

"Sure." She smiles and gives a brief wave and a wink before exiting. "Keep up the great work, hon!"

Dea spins to face me. "I want to see your Vampire powers."

I stop dead in my tracks, all the fun, sexy thoughts fly out of the mental window, and stare, slackjawed, up at him. "Wh-what?"

"You cannot avoid it forever, Angel. We need to see."

I know that. I do. But . . . . But I—

He's right. We need to understand. We don't have a lot of time. Nine throws the memory of Connie telling us the war is coming.

They're right. Of course they're right.

"Okay. How do we do that?"

"You need to gain some kind of control, and we need to understand what abilities you have. It's natural to assume your strength comes from your Vampire side, as well as your ability to see in the dark."

"But I'm not affected by sunlight. And I don't need to drink . . . To feed."

Nine steps into view beside Dea. "I have a theory on that. I think because we don't really need to eat, you don't need to feed. But if you did, you'd be more powerful. Just like we're more powerful and have more strength if we keep up a healthy diet."

"We really don't need to eat?" That is news to me. "You

guys need a handbook: BEING A HORSEMAN OF THE APOCALYPSE 101."

They both chuckle, and it breaks the tension for a moment.

"We eat because it increases our strength, and we get a bit . . . sluggish if we don't. But it won't kill us or make us lose any weight." Nine blinks as he mentions something internally to Dea, and I look around, feeling a little lost and out of the loop.

"Just tell her, Nine."

Nine grimaces. "I don't think you'll be fully up to strength unless you feed. And if we're ever in battle, you'll need to feed to access your full strength."

Hmmm . . . I wonder. "Is it possible that's the reason I can't access all of my magic? I mean, could they be affecting one another?"

Nine blinks in surprise; clearly the thought hasn't occurred to him. "Maybe. But . . ." He gives me a look I hate, one I instantly abhor.

"We'd need to test it to find out," I fill in the blank for him.

"And I don't think it'll work like that anyway. I think it'll make your magic stronger, but I don't think it's blocking it."

I nod. "Still need to work on that access, then."

"Yes. But for now," Dea says, "I want to fight you in your Vampire state."

"Vampire state? That's what you're calling it? I'm just me!" I can feel the frustration boiling beneath my skin. "I'm not some freak of nature!"

"Sorry, Angel. Of course." He picks up the nearest throwing knife and nicks his finger, drawing a single droplet of blood.

The heavy scent of liquid honey with that familiar metallic tang hits my nostrils, and my fangs descend in response. It smells . . . like the first piece of food I've been offered after months of starvation, as though I haven't eaten in years and this is the only smell suffocating my senses throughout the involuntary fast.

Mine. Looking at Dea's galaxy-swirling eyes, watching the slow drip-drip-drip of his essence staining the concrete floor, I know it instantly. He's mine.

I leap from my position, covering the two feet between us in an instant, and toss him to the ground with a grunt.

My fingers fly to his lips, where they keep his silence and bring a smirk to his face.

"So," he says, speaking from behind my fingers, "you are stronger than me now. Interesting. But you were not stronger than Arrie yesterday." He looks to Nine, who scribbles down the information. Dea doesn't move, not an inch. He just lies there and accepts his fate.

I run my fingers, still lingering on his mouth, down the side of his throat along his jugular, where I feel the pounding of his blood, and I sniff closer.

"Angel?"

I look up at him, irritated by his interruption, but curious about what he wants.

"What does it . . ." He looks sheepishly to the ground. "What does it feel like?"

I don't know how to answer that. What deoes this feel like?

Like I won't be able to continue breathing if I don't taste him. Like if I don't drain every last drop, my body will crumble into a million pieces.

"Remember," Nine says, "we're immortal. If you don't drink the blood, nothing will happen. You cannot die."

Right. Immortal. No need to feed: food or blood. But I

want to. "I feel like I'll die if I don't just . . . taste you."

But why am I so hot? I'm straddling Dea's waist and can feel every delicious inch of him beneath my jean shorts. I want more than just his blood, it seems (well, more than normal).

"She's also incredibly turned on. Which is pretty normal for a Vampire," Nine says in a formal reporting tone as he scribbles more notes onto his plasmascreen.

It is?

Yep.

"Okay," Dea whispers from beneath me, the vibration of his deep voice doing nothing to keep me calm. "Calm down." He raises his bloody finger—the cut on which has now healed—to my lips and smears what's left of the blood over my bottom lip. "Go ahead." His voice has turned raspy, a tone I haven't heard from him before, and I get the feeling this thing between us is making him as hot as me.

But that doesn't matter right now; all that matters is the scent of the honey-filled, metallic-tasting blood left on my lips like an offering on a silver platter of desire.

I dart my tongue out, just a little, to get a small taste, curiosity and need overcoming my better judgment. A small moan escapes my lips as my head tilts back and the taste coats my tongue. My fangs descend farther as the need to lick my lips clean becomes an itch I need to scratch.

Two and a half seconds.

That's how long it takes me to savor the taste of Dea's blood. That's also how long it takes for him to use the distraction to throw me off and pin me to the ground, his legs and arms pinning all my limbs as his torso restrains every inch of me he can.

I could lift him off and throw him clear across the room,

but I don't want to. I like the position he has me in. I can clearly bite him from here, getting more of that sweet life that has my center on fire, every sense heightened and every thought amplified. More. I want—need—more.

My vision blackens as the need to feed confuses every thought, overcomes every other instinct.

Calm, Sweetie. Stay calm. You're going to be fine. Come on. Come back to us.

Nine's voice in the distance of my mind pierces the darkness I've succumbed to, but it's faint, as though I were deaf and having trouble hearing him. But that doesn't make sense; my hearing is better than ever right now.

That's right. You're strong. Stronger than us. Please. Movie night's your choice tonight. Remember?

Movie night? Right. I want to watch some fantasy superhero movie with the promise of a great love story. I want to watch it with the team. My friends.

Friends. That's right. We're your friends. Your family. Come back.

Family?

I open my eyes and see Dea's worried gaze on my face loosen slightly as I start waking back to reality. For a moment there, all I could feel was the bloodlust. I would have done anything to drink him dry.

It's okay. We'll work through it with you.

I let Dea get off me and quickly jump up, feeling my fangless face rise to stand on top shaky legs. Physically, I feel better than I have since arriving here, but mentally, I'm weaker than ever.

What would have happened if Nine didn't bring me back? If I couldn't control myself?

"Don't ever do that again!" I raise a hand and slap it across Dea's face. "I could have seriously hurt you! You fucking dick!"

Dea smiles, not even reacting to me slapping him. "As the Horseman of Death, dying is not something I am afraid of, Angel."

I shake my head and storm out, seeking a place of peaceful tranquility to store all this new insanity. The *Shinto* shrine.

Chapter Nineteen

"I have a theory," Nine mumbles between bites of spaghetti. I requested Italian again, since I loved it so much last time. We all stare at him expectantly. "Sweetie, you mentioned the four pillars of magic, and I found that paper this afternoon. You can borrow it later."

I nod my thanks.

"I think, given your access to Witch and Vampire powers, that you might also have access to the other two pillars of magic: Fae and Shifter."

I stare absentmindedly into his brown eyes.

"It would make sense," he continues. "Since you're the Horseman of Magic."

"Is there any proof of that, though?" I ask, denial edging my tone.

"Of what?" Dea asks. "You being the Horseman of Magic?"

I nod.

"Well," Dea continues, "we were all summoned when our

powers were needed most. Mine to open the blocked gate to Hell, to allow souls to pass, Arrie and Con to help solve the world's conflicts and wars, and Nine to distribute provisions and aid countries in times of famine. Together, we brought about the modern world.

"So, given that Con proved the magical community is on the brink of war, and you have two of the four main communities' powers, it is a pretty safe assumption." He smiles, but this time it's sincere and not flirtatious, like he's trying to imbue a sense of self-confidence I don't have into every fiber of my mind.

Once again, I just nod. Turning to Nine, I ask, "But aren't the four pillars of magic opposite each other? So, you can't have a half Shifter, half Vampire?"

Nine smiles at me, a smile I'm beginning to realize is his wow-she's-a-nerd-too smile. I can't help it; his excitement over magical theory is addicting.

"Yes. Typically, Vampires and Shifters don't breed, and Witches and Fae don't breed because they each use magic in totally opposite ways. And even if they do breed, hybrids won't form; they will always be one or the other." He grabs another slice of garlic bread before continuing: "But you can have hybrid Witches and Vampires, or Witches and Shifters, or Fae and Vampires, or Fae and Shifters, et cetera."

"I see. But . . ." I've never heard of those kinds of hybrids before.

"The Treaty of Magical Crossbreeding prevents it. So, if there are any hybrids out there, they're likely in hiding."

"Ah. Makes sense." I look to Dea, who just smiles and silently chuckles to himself while watching us. "So, do you reckon my body could hold all four? It just sounds a little unlikely, even for a Horseman."

"Yes, it does. I guess, until your other powers come into play, we will not know."

"So we wait. Again?" I can't keep the irritation out of my voice; all this waiting and training is driving me crazy. I want to get out there, to do something useful.

Dea seems to sense the problem. "How about a group mission to Earth? To assess the problem, hunt for your seal, and see why the Shifters attacked Con?"

Earth? Me? With the rest of them? A silly grin escapes my usually stoic defenses, and I let out a little squeal. "Yes!"

"That sounds like a plan." Connie smiles and turns to the dishwasher, where she stacks the plates as we each finish. "But"—she points at me—"you must be with one of us at all times. You're not fully trained."

"Pretty sure I could throw a dagger at anyone who tried anything, or at least blow them a couple miles downwind," I grumble. There is no way she's playing the you're-not-strong-enough card on me. "Besides, I'm pretty badass myself now, you know."

"Oh yeah?" She stands behind my chair, where I'm just clearing the last of my plate. "Wanna put that to the test, little Vampire Witch?"

The fake venom in her voice lights me up, and I'm itching to go. I stand, forcing my chair to drag across the wooden floor in a squeal of wood on wood.

"Bring it on, Conquest." My arms fold over my chest.

She chuckles and shakes her head. "Maybe another time."

"After a few more centuries of training," Arrie grumbles.

His entire being pisses me off. All his grumbling, all his deep-voiced complaining . . . Argh!

Can't he just be nice or shut the hell up?

"Fuck you."

I storm through the open door to the cinema, slamming it shut behind me (which shakes the entire hallway, as I forget my strength is a little more than usual).

"Asshole."

Superhero fantasy. The cinematic world of fiction. Sweet, sweet escape. Pulling out the plasmascreen from the front of the room that connects with the large 4D screen on the wall, I select the movie and wait for the others to join.

I choose a bed this time, wanting nothing more than to snuggle under the covers in my pajamas and lose myself in another world. Up, up, up I send the bed, and watch with a smile as I realize no one is going to bother me this high in the air. A sigh of contentment escapes my lips.

I wait for the others to join me, and before long, they all stumble in, grim looks on their faces.

Not fair, Sweetie. I wanted to watch the movie with you.

The pout in Nine's voice and the sad puppy-dog look on his face makes me feel instantly guilty. For fuck's sake. I lower the bed, knowing I won't enjoy the movie if I've made someone upset by a simple choice.

Come on, then.

I can get Dea and Con to join us, if you'd like?

I do not miss the suggestion in his tone, but I shake my head. Not fair to Arrie. He's not too sweet on me at the moment, and his attitude pisses me off, but he doesn't deserve to be alone.

That's actually really sweet. Fine. Just Dea, then.

After a quick exchange of who's sitting where—and Nine getting his way—both Dea and Nine climb into bed on either side of me, Dea on my left, Nine on my right, and we raise the platform to the right height.

"Soooo," Dea starts, eyebrows raising, "that kiss with

Con . . . ?"

"Is that really what you want to talk about?"

"Yes." He stares at the screen as the intro music starts, a small smile on his face. "I guess," he starts, a more serious look taking over, "I wanted to know if it is just her you harbor affection for?"

Ohmigod, ohmigod . . . Is he really asking that right now? When Nine is here and can read my mind and Connie can hear the entire conversation? "I . . . er . . ."

No.

But how do I tell them that?

Nine looks at me strangely, clearly a little baffled by my inner predicament. *Just say so. It's not like we're monogamous or anything. We're immortal. That would be . . .*

Impossible. I'm beginning to see that. Or maybe it's just my stupid attraction to this entire fucking team. It's not like I've been attracted to anyone else since I've become a Horseman.

"No, it's not." I sigh. "But she knows that."

"Oh." Dea's smile grows.

"Now shut up and watch the movie."

"Yes, Angel."

Nine slips an arm over my shoulders, and I quickly find myself snuggling into his shoulder as though it's the most normal thing in the world, and I guess, in some ways, it is (at least in this world). Dea nudges up to me from behind and curls around my back, trapping me between the two.

Connie says to tell you that we'd make a good sandwich. Wink-wink.

Did you just mentally wink at me, Nine?

I roll my eyes, feeling the heat of Connie's suggestion penetrate my cheeks—and other, more heated areas—while I try to shut the idea down. But that stupid, crazy bitch's idea has ignited a random flame of desire (well, maybe not quite so random) as I resist the urge to kiss both men beside me. Having them both in my bed . . . at the same time . . . would be insanely hot.

And they clearly have something going on, meaning they would also enjoy being together. Just the thought of their hands running all over me has me swallowing a gasp of desire.

You need to stop with that fantasy, Sweetie, or this might turn out to be quite the show for the others.

Then get out of my head.

I can't. You draw me in. And your thoughts are really loud, too. Especially those kinds of thoughts.

"Oh," I say out loud before realizing it.

"Hmmm?" Dea asks from behind me.

"Nothing," I mumble before moving to get more comfortable. I hear Dea swallow a grumble behind me, but I ignore it while Nine laughs, and we all settle down to watch the movie.

The movie turns out to be pretty good, actually, a story about finding love across the galaxy while a universe-ending event tries to rip them apart. One day, I hope I get to find love like that.

"Ugh," Arrie grumbles, "I hate love stories."

"Well, get used to it, cause they're my favorite." I skip up the hallway, choosing to walk myself to my room this time. Since I'm no longer a fragile little thing, and I seem to have gained some ass-kicking powers, I think I can manage to walk around the house without Arrie carrying me everywhere.

Arrie grumbles something behind me as I leave, my legs practically running to my room (because I can now). Seems the blood has healed all of my internal injuries, because I'm not even out of breath. Bet it would have helped speed up the healing if we knew about it earlier.

"Mommy! Daddy!" I scream as I watch them run from the crashed doorway, where a group of men wearing all black and carrying guns rush in.

Mom bends down and grab me, shoving me into the closet at the end of the room. "Shhhh. Please stay quiet. I need you to be quiet right now, okay?"

I nod.

"Good. Now stay here and stay hidden." She takes her necklace off and wraps it around my neck. "This will help." The bead I spent hours playing with every evening is torn off the chain that now wraps around me. "Just stay quiet, baby."

I let silent tears fall as she leaves me in the dark all alone. But a small crack in the door is just large enough for me to see through.

Mommy and Daddy fight against the men, but the men's guns loosen from their sides and aim at my parents' heads.

"Remain still!" the front man shouts. "Where is she?"

"Please!" Mom begs, now on her knees with her hands pressed together in prayer. "Please just let us be!"

"Sorry, but we cannot let a danger like her risk the safety of our world."

One of the other men whispers in his ear and points to the closet I'm in.

He growls and looks to Mommy and Daddy. "Silence them."

Two loud shots echo across the room, and I watch Mommy and Daddy fall to the floor in puddles of dark crimson blood. I want to shout out, to scream at them to get up, but I can't. I promised Mommy I'd stay quiet.

The men walk straight to me and open the closet door.

I stay stock-still, swallowing a whimper as they look straight at where I'm sitting.

Are they going to kill me?

"It's empty!" the leader growls. "It's fucking empty!"

"What?" The man that whispered before barrels past the leader to look for himself. "That's . . ."

"Let's go! Someone's probably taken her. Some friends, maybe. Let's regroup with HQ."

A hot sweat of fear shoots me awake from a nightmare I can't quite place; I was in a place I barely recognized, surrounded by people I didn't know, and they were all dying. Everyone around me was dying. Could this be a memory? Or just a random dream? It was much more real than the other nightmare fragments.

I try to forget about it and go back to sleep, but as the minutes tick by and my mind stays as wide awake as ever, I realize I need to know.

Nine will know. Plus, his rooms are only down the hall. I get out of bed, throw on a thin nightgown, and tiptoe down the hall. I have no idea what the time is or if he'll even be awake.

Maybe waking him is a bad idea.

What if he'll be angry with me?

It must be exhausting mentally babysitting me all the time. Maybe I'll try to give him more of a break from it in the future. But right now, though, I really need answers. Can I dream of a past I can't remember? Who are those people? Are they my . . . family?

Nine's rooms are only a few meters away, and I soon find myself in front of a slightly ajar door with a small amount of light creeping through. A familiar pair of voices are talking beyond the door, and I know it's rude to eavesdrop, but I'm ashamed to say their conversation intrigues me.

"You can't complain about that! You're not the one living her every fantasy and dirty thought, bro."

A few small moans follow, along with Dea's response. "But . . . she is just so . . ."

"Yeah," Nine sighs. "She is, isn't she?" They shuffle around a bit (well, I assume that's what they're doing) and resettle before Nine says, "I can help."

"That is why I am here, lover."

Lover? Right, they have something going on. I already know that. Dea's voice sounds so husky, like he and Nine are. . .

Oh! I turn to walk away, realizing I've eavesdropped on the wrong kind of conversation.

Come in.

Wait, what?

Come in and join us.

But . . .

I can hear your mind wondering. Want to see what we're doing?

Do I? Will that be okay? My mind says yes before I can stop it and say something more appropriate. But that would be rude.

Then I invite you in to come and see.

Will that make anything weird between us? Maybe just a peek . . .

I open the door farther and am thankful Nine's hinges are well-oiled. I intend to just have a quick peek out of curiosity (he did say it's okay) and leave, but what I see has me frozen to the spot.

Dea stands by the edge of the bed, eyes closed and head rolled back, his feet on the floor, and kneeling in front his legs is a head of bright red hair—Nine's hair—moving up and down on Dea's cock.

Nine chuckles in my mind, clearly amused by my stooped curiosity that has my feet firmly fixed to the spot.

Dea fists Nine's hair and commands, "Harder."

Nine says nothing; he just picks up the pace, using his hand to massage the base of Dea's cock to the same rhythm his mouth has set.

Dea stands the entire time, his knees buckling now and then, his usual galaxy eyes glowing shots of gold as he opens them. He starts gently moaning as Nine seems to change the pace to something else he likes.

I need to leave. This is private between the two of them. But, fuck me, it's hot as hell, and my entire body wants to jump into the mix and see what happens. But I don't. I can't leave, my eyes darting between what Nine is doing and Dea's face of pleasure, but I can't join in, either.

I still don't want the whole casual sex thing, even as every inch of me cries out for attention.

Dea tries to say something, but Nine sucks harder, his cheeks hollowing out, and Dea instead lets out an audible moan that has my insides squeezing in pleasure.

"Nine," Dea growls as he grips Nine's hair tighter and meets his mouth's every stroke with a few thrusts of his hips. Every thrust is harder than the one before until he's fucking Nine's mouth so hard Nine's gone still to let Dea use him and take his pleasure.

I want to look away, to give them their moment of privacy, and I finally make my feet turn around when Nine interrupts my thoughts.

Keep watching.

But—

You'll miss the finale.

I've never heard Nine be so incorrigibly filthy-mouthed before—well, filthy-minded.

And, goddess dammit, I want to watch. No idea what that says about me as a person, but so long as I have permission, I refuse to feel guilty about it.

I turn back around as Dea cries out with his head tipping backwards and his hands keeping Nine's head firmly in place.

Nine pulls away slightly with a wince, and if I didn't know any better, I would say he's giving me a better view. I watch Nine swallow every last drop of Dea's release and give me a cock-filled smile afterward.

My head lifts from Nine's face to Dea's galaxy-filled eyes once more, and, shit, they're staring right at me. I've been totally caught in the act. I have no idea if Nine told him I'm watching.

Nope. But he's fine. Promise.

Well, that's good news. Kind of. I mean, I'm still kinda peeping.

I don't know what to say, and every time I try to open my mouth to let any kind of defensible words come out, my voice dries up. Shit. My legs take me out of there as fast as they can before I say something stupid.

What was I thinking?

I just watched Nine sucking Dea's cock and chose to stay. "Grrr," I grumble to myself. Connie's gonna get a laugh out of this on Friday when she asks me all about my week.

I roll my eyes in exasperation as I climb back into bed, the essence of my previous nightmare having all but fled my mind as I lie there in a mess of sexual frustration while the image of Nine's lips wrapping around Dea's cock refuses to leave my mind.

I leap out of bed with a frustrated groan and run a bath,

hoping it will help relax my body into sleep and make me forget about Nine and Dea—fat chance of that.

Once the tub is full, I dip my toes in and edge the rest of my body into the bubbly water, sighing in relief once I sit up to my neck in the warmth.

Dea's eyes were like shining gold when he . . .

Stop thinking about that! Think of something else instead. Like that romance I was reading the other day: they sure were perfect for each other.

A bit like Nine and Dea in a way; they're perfect for each other, too.

For fuck's sake.

The memory of Dea's comment about some alone time flitters across my mind, and maybe he's right. Even Nine said I have a sex-filled mind, and he can read everyone's minds. If I want to continue working with this damn team, I need to take care of all this pent-up frustration and need.

Lowering my hand down my stomach, I take a deep breath and let the memory of earlier play over and over like a stuck record as my fingers brush the outside of my core, teasing the entrance until I'm a mess of need. I thrust one finger, then two inside, hooking them slightly and finding that perfect spot as I continue thrusting.

My breaths come quicker as I spread my legs wider and graze my clit with the heel of my hand, causing a small moan to escape my lips.

Before I know it, my imagination slips out of my control, and I'm imagining myself on that bed in Dea's place, with Nine's tongue working me into a frenzy that matches the speed of my own hand. Imagining Dea joining in is what pushes me over the edge, though, and I'm suddenly thankful for the size of this house.

I can't stifle the cry that slips out before I sink my head under the water and feel every muscle in my body switch off as I rise to the surface and lie there for a moment in a pool of unworried bliss.

Chapter Twenty

The next day is beyond awkward. I do my usual yoga routine at dawn and then sit down to breakfast with everyone. Connie immediately knows something's up, as Nine, Dea, and I keep exchanging awkward glances and returning to our breakfasts in silence.

Every time I glance over at them, all I can picture is them together on Nine's bed, and I get the feeling my memories are making Nine uncomfortable, as he looks more and more frustrated as breakfast goes on. He even grumbles something under his breath in a true, pretty accurate mimic of Arrie's usual nonsense attitude.

I can't stay there a moment longer in the awkward silence. "I'm gonna be in the library."

"We will be continuing from where we left off yesterday," Dea announces to my back.

It takes me a moment to realize he meant with training, not my midnight escapade. Fucking great. I'm gonna spend another evening bloodthirsty and turned all the way up. Ugh.

I thought some time to myself would fix all this pent-up need, but I was wrong. All it did was fuel the flame.

The library invites me in with its usual airs and graces of knowledgeable silence, a state I find myself mimicking every time something gets a little difficult. Fiction for a few hours, I think. Research can wait. I go in search of a new book down the various aisles and corridors of towering shelves. Maybe a romance? I flick my finger across a few titles and pick out one that sounds interesting: THE DRAGON SHIFTERS OF ANCIENT GREECE.

The nearest reading nook is a few corners away (I have most mapped out by this point), and I settle in and quickly devour page after page, and before I know it, I hear voices interrupting the character's badass battle with the evil dragon hunter asshole. I consider putting my book down and trying to find the intruders, but fuck 'em. Let them find me for a change. I have a climactic ending to finish.

It only takes a few more pages before Dea's whizzing form rushes by, and I catch a brief glimpse of galaxy eyes as he rushes past. He slows, and I hear him turn back around and come to a stop.

"What delectable book are you reading today?"

I hold up the cover as I continue to read, not bothering to respond. He can fucking wait a minute.

"Hmmm . . . You seem to have a thing for dragons, don't you?"

I nod, turning the next page.

Dea chuckles and sits on the bright orange pouf next to mine, leaning his arm over my shoulder to read with me.

I don't bother slowing down for him, though, I just keep reading, wanting to know if the characters inevitably beat the villain and finally mate for life in the end. Will he take her as his dragon bride after all?

"You read some utter drivel, Angel," Dea mutters close to my ear. "Mating does not really exist."

Again, I don't answer. I just keep on reading.

"Okay!" Dea steals the book from my hands, stashes it spine-up on the nearest small bookshelf, and grabs my hands. "You are ignoring me."

"Nope. Just trying to read."

"Oh, so you not saying a single word to either of us the entire morning has nothing to do with your little perverted escapade last night?"

That familiar, charming confidence is back, and I know Dea isn't going to let this go.

"I'm more concerned about other things right now. Like winning a magical war with next to no magic."

"That is why you are reading fiction rather than studying?" He tugs on my arm, and I sigh, letting him guide me into standing. "I know you read when you want to escape. Quit trying to escape this."

"Escape what?" I look up at him, mere inches from his face, and give my best stony exterior.

He sighs. "This conversation." He grips the tops of my arms. "Neither Nine nor I care that you were watching. Okay? It just took me by surprise. You are rather . . . innocent." He blushes at the comment, clearly feeling a little awkward.

I can't help it—I let out a giggle. "So Nine doesn't tell you all of my thoughts, then. That's nice to know."

"Nine does not tell anyone the private thoughts of another. Well, he does if it is important." Dea waves the comment off, as if to say it doesn't matter, and continues. "Look. Just quit feeling embarrassed and come to training?"

"Fine. But you should know that Nine asked me to watch.

I wasn't being some kind of weird pervert." Well, to begin with I was, but Dea doesn't need to know that. "I was invited."

Dea stands still as I turn and head toward the training room. Realizing he isn't following, I look back. "What?"

"He . . . He really invited you?"

"Yup." I smirk, knowing I have one up on Dea and am using it to be as confident as possible in the moment. I grab his elbow, link my arm through his, and drag him along with me in silence.

The training room is warmer today, and I realize Nine is placing some logs in the burning fireplace, heating the room.

I am gonna fucking boil alive in here.

Nine?

Yes?

I'm sorry I've been ignoring you.

I sheepishly look to the ground, arm still locked around Dea's. But, as Nine turns, he's smiling his happy smile.

It's okay, Sweetie. I was just giving you space. Last night was fun. We should do it again sometime.

Blushing, I get the feeling that Nine is more confident when speaking telepathically than vocally, like it somehow makes him feel more comfortable; in a way, I kind of understand. It's a private connection between the two of us.

"We need you to fight with your Vampire strength," Dea interrupts. "So we wanted you to feed, then take on Arrie in hand-to-hand combat." Dea doesn't even flinch as he says that; he just stands there all stoic and shit, looking like a lit candle by those sparkling flames in the otherwise boringly dull room.

For fuck's sake. This is going to be impossible. Even more so once someone bleeds. I remember the feeling of tension and heat radiating from my core yesterday, and I'm equally as terrified as I am eager to repeat the experience. On the one hand, being a . . . you know, thing, is weird, and it feels awkwardly intimate when feeding, but it's also desirable in a way normal food just isn't.

"Do not be scared," Dea says as he wraps me in his arms from behind. "We are both right here. We can give you anything you need to help ease the process."

Damn him. The fucker. He knows very well what I want when feeding, but I'm just not prepared to give it. Not yet. Color me old-fashioned, but I'm just not ready. That doesn't mean his words don't set a new flame alight in my body, making my nipples harden and my thighs clench.

I pull out of his embrace and turn to face him. "Fine. But if you're stuck in bed for a few days recovering, you ain't fucking complaining about it. This was your idea."

Dea smirks. "Deal."

I'll be right here to help.

Thank you. "So, how do we . . ."

I look nervously at Dea, who smiles gently and offers me his wrist.

Guess I'll need my fangs out for this one. It doesn't take much focus; all I have to do is concentrate on the memory of his blood from yesterday, and I can feel that familiar tickle and ache in my gums that signals the extrusion of my fangs.

I catch myself, shocked for a moment there. My fangs? How ridiculous my life has become. Though, you never know, my life may have been just as insane before.

But the moment doesn't last long, as that familiar hunger that comes as an almost-comical side effect explodes through my body, forcing my foot forward and causing my neck to crane toward Dea's offered wrist.

Dea still smiles at me, but it's a little weaker this time, and

I can see the nerves settle across his eyes. He's also worried about this, but he's doing it anyway.

Yeah, because he's a fucking idiot.

Dea, Arrie, and I will always offer to help with this; any one of us will willingly feed you to keep you strong and healthy. You're family.

I do not miss the exclusion of Connie in that sentence, or the small amount of warmth I get from Nine's surety that Arrie would participate despite his obvious disdain toward me.

Dea's wrist rests in the palm of my hand, and my fangs inch forward, itching to sink in and taste him once more. But if I do, will I stop? Will that black hole my mind always goes to become more permanent? I'd be lying if I said I'm not scared. This is it, though. There's no going back after this. But it doesn't matter because I can't go back to being human; I haven't been human since the moment I woke up in this house, and that isn't going to change just because of this. I am a Vampire—or at least part Vampire—and this is my new normal.

With that last internal pep talk, and the slight reminder that Nine is there at the edge of my mind ready to help, I sink my fangs into Dea's wrist and draw a few mouthfuls before pausing to savor the taste. This isn't just a drop, where I can taste the honey and metallic scent that pervades my senses and tries to lure me in; this is like my every need is being met. From all things physical to mental to emotional, I'm sated. Completely and utterly whole.

After the initial bliss, my mind returns to my body as I swallow another mouthful of Dea's blood, and the fire that has been a small blaze since my perverted escapade (as Dea politely put it) last night, is now a roaring inferno, setting every crevice of my being on fire. The thin tank top I chose to wear today is doing nothing to hide my hardened nipples—neither is the thin lacy bra, I might add—and I can feel every raw need pulsing through my entire body.

I need this man. In so many ways.

Before I know what I'm doing, I shove Dea back against the wall, pinning him in place, and look up at his face. His eyes are a slight haze, as though he's enjoying this, too, and I'm all too aware of his every muscle that tenses, every artery that echoes a gentle rhythm in my ears, and the feel of his erection against my body.

I want it all. His blood. His body. His soul. I want to devour every part of him.

Wait . . . what? Sudden awareness lights up my mind like a fairground. I don't want to devour him at all. That's just the bloodlust.

You need to stop feeding now, Sweetie.

Huh?

I blanch and tear myself away from Dea's wrist, not even realizing I was still latched on. Still drinking his . . . blood. Oh no! I nearly . . . I was just . . .

Shhhh. It's okay. Dea's fine.

I look up at my willing victim (because, let's be honest, he was prey for a minute there) and watch as the desire slowly fades from him.

One minute, Dea looks like he wants to yank me back against him and for me to drain him dry, and the next, awareness hits him like a freight train as he stumbles forward on shaky legs.

My arms go out to steady him, and Nine and I slowly sit him on the floor. All Dea says, though, is, "Time to fight Arrie."

Seriously? That's what he's thinking about right now?

"I will be all right in a few minutes." He looks up at the doorway. "All right, Arrie. Now it is your turn."

Arrie? He's been there the whole time? How much has he seen?

Everything.

Oh. Well, shit. He's sure to hate me even more now.

Arrie steps forward, a heated, angry glare on his face, and gets himself into the center of the room. "Fangs out, Vampire senses on." He cracks his knuckles. "Time to train."

I nod, trying to focus on my senses and the newfound strength coursing through me. Just like with the fangs earlier, it's instinctual, and my fangs descend easily. I'm not sure how strong I am right now, or how fast, but I am eager to find out. But I really don't want to hurt another teammate today.

Throwing a look over at Dea, whose color has returned to his cheeks and looks a little less weak, I grimace.

"Ready?" Arrie grumbles.

"Yes."

Arrie brings his arms up to his middle, protecting his vital organs that I can hear thrumming away, and closes his eyes briefly. Upon reopening them, his gaze is different; his eyes take on a more focused, battle-ready color. It's a little hard to describe, but this is not a man you fight against willingly.

I speed forward and raise a fist, hoping to get a right hook in before he's prepared to defend, but he jumps back, and I fall to the floor on two balanced feet.

Vampire senses rule.

I'm a little weightless so try using that to my advantage by spinning around Arrie and kicking him in the back. I catch him with my toe, but he mostly dodges.

So close.

Is he gonna fight back?

Just as the thought crosses my mind, Arrie spins on his heel and throws me to the floor. He has me pinned, his hands on my forearms and his knees on my legs. Pain radiates from his weight on my pressure points, but it isn't enough to cripple me; I can still move.

Arrie pierces me with his battlemode-hazed eyes, and I should be scared—this man (if you can even call him that) is far stronger than me, even after my feeding, and has the ability to magically figure out the best strategy for winning any fight—but I am not. Color me stupid, but I find his ability fascinating. He plays on my inability and unskilled body in terms of fighting, knowing I can outrun him if it comes to it.

Also, his battlemode is supposed to be an all-encompassing thing, and supposedly he struggles to come out of it until he's killed his opponent. So why can I still move?

He doesn't kill us in his battlemode.

Ah, okay. That makes sense. Guess it would be pointless anyway, because there isn't a strategy that can kill us in battle, so the two likely cancel each other out.

But, still, he's going easy on me in a mindset that's plagued him for years—centuries. I bet he doesn't go easy on the others. So why me?

"Arrie?"

I lose all pretense of this fight (we can go again in a moment); right now, I want to figure out why I can still move.

I wriggle my wrists free from his grip and grab his shoulders as his palms slam down on the floor. He groans under his breath before whispering, "Feed from me next time."

"Huh?"

"Do not hurt my family." He climbs off of me and walks to Dea, placing a hand on each shoulder. "You okay, dude?"

Dea wobbles from his now-standing position, and I fight back a gasp. He's hurt, isn't he? I did that? Me?

I can't . . .

Worry creeps its way through my mind, and although I can hear Nine's soothing words in my head, I can't actually hear them above my own anxiety.

Dea collapses to the floor, pale from blood loss, and Arrie catches him just before his head hits the concrete. "I'll take him to his room."

I can't breathe. I try hard to inhale and gather up oxygen, but I just can't. Air. I need air.

My feet run from the room before I can do anything else or warn Nine, who's halfway to reaching me when I zoom out of there at Vampire speed, leaving a windtrail in my wake.

I'm not really sure where I'm going, I just need some air. I run down the stairs, my feet finding the kitchen, where Connie sits reading some magical newspaper, and I exit through the back door and sprint into the forest. I don't stop until I reach a clearing in the middle that has Arrie's scent dotted around, teasing my Vampire senses and making me hungry in a way that makes me crave blood instead of food.

"Argh!" I cry out in frustration.

I don't want comfort right now, and I'm pretty sure that's why I came here, because Arrie's scent reminds me of something I can never have.

Family? Nine's a bigger idiot than me. I can't have a family here; even among the Horsemen of the fucking Apocalypse, I'm a freak. I just want to be normal!

A memory rushes across my mind.

Smoke pours from my hands in a simple backyard as I scream at a familiar man. "I just want to be normal!"

He looks at me with pity, understanding, and his blond hair and handsome features school my attitude as he scowls. "But you are not."

Tears stain my face as I sob, not really sure if it's the past's or present's fault, but in that moment, it all molds into the same pile of crap my life's become and seems to always have been.

My mind comes back to the present, and I find myself crouching in a ball in the middle of the forest clearing I've run to. I can't wallow in regret like this; it isn't like my life will change and I can wake up human tomorrow. But the memory of Dea collapsing replays itself over and over in my mind, like a stupid broken song that I can't quite jam to but keep playing anyway.

Arrie's face. He really hates me. If not before, then he definitely does now. I'll never fit in here, and part of me really doesn't want to stay in a house full of people I put in danger. Not to mention all the stupid dynamics that I've completely ruined just by being myself.

"Arrghh!"

I jump to my feet, frustration curling my hands into fists, and begin pacing in a circle around the clearing. I need to think myself out of this. Somehow. But no matter how many circles I think around, I'm stuck, because the world needs me; no matter what I'm doing to the four people I've come to call friends, the ten billion people on Earth are about to head into a war only I can stop (supposedly).

"Looks like I have to stay." I need their training, no matter what it puts us all through, no matter how torturous it might be.

As great as it is to come to some kind of conclusion about my life, the conclusion itself frustrates me beyond belief. I need to do something. Something to let all this pent-up energy out. Between the frustration and the blood I drank, it's like my anger has a fire fueling it.

I stand in front of a tree and do the first thing that comes naturally to my regret-addled mind. I punch it.

Yeah, I know. It's stupid. Even for me. But you know what? It helps. And since my skin heals as fast as I punch, it seems like a good stress reliever.

Left. Right. Left. Right. The skin on my knuckles breaks again and again, and eventually blood stains my hands, but nothing. No thoughts stop the anger from taking control.

Dea could have been seriously hurt.

Left. Right.

If he were human, I would have killed him.

Left. Right.

I'm breaking this team apart.

Left. Right.

I'll never belong anywhere.

Left. Right.

Who am I?

Left. Right.

It continues this way for an hour, until the sun starts to set, lighting pieces of the sky I can see through the trees in a beautiful pink blush. I must have been playing over that memory and drowning in my sorrows and guilt all afternoon.

That is so not like me.

But . . . who is that man in the memory?

What was that smoke?

Was I not human in my mortal life?

That question is enough to throw all the day's infuriating events out the window and force me back inside the house.

Connie, Nine, and Arrie sit around the kitchen table

eating various types of giant sandwiches, and they all look at my bloodied hands with shock and sadness in their eyes, but it's Connie who breaks the silence.

"Hon—"

I hold up a hand and shake my head. "Tell me when Dea wakes up."

She nods, and I grab the sandwich waiting for me and leave, working my way toward the scent of age-old knowledge and musty pages that I can smell, even from down here.

Chapter Twenty-One

Nothing. A big fat nothing. That's what I find when I ask my Seeing Stone about black smoky magic. There's no record in this library about that type of magic. Either I was someone insanely special with a unique type of magic when I was human (if I even was), or this is another one of those stupid times when the library is purposefully hiding things from me or not stocking them so I can't learn important pieces of info on my own.

Either way, it's frustrating as hell.

My hands are bleeding slightly—seems my Vampire healing, which speeds up even my Horseman healing, has started to wear off—but I leave them be. I want to be reminded of the reason for the pain. Dea's in his room somewhere, unconscious, because I nearly drained him dry. He looked so damn pale—

Nope. Stop thinking about that. It's not helping. You need to work on control, find out who the fuck you are, and fix this stupid magical war.

My sandwich lies untouched on the desk. Honestly, I only took it because Nine or Connie would have bothered me for hours if I didn't. But now, after a few hours of nothing-research, my stomach grumbles, and I take a bite.

It's made of some kind of meat, but I didn't bother to ask what it was in my foul mood, and it tastes damn amazing. It's salty, smoky, and melds well with the fluffy white bread and butter surrounding it.

"That is a pleasing sound," a familiar, overly flirty voice says. "Seems you like bacon. Not that I have ever met someone who does not."

Dea.

"Bacon? Ohmigod, of course. I used to eat this at a particular café in Akihabara; they served the most amazing dusted tea with their fucking rainbow cupcakes."

"Rainbow cupcakes? You have lived quite the colorful life, Angel."

"Hilarious." I roll my eyes to the floor, trying my hardest not to look at him.

"Angel . . ." Dea walks up to me and sinks to kneel beside my desk chair. "You know it was not your . . ." He notices my hands and sighs. "Fault." He grabs my hands and takes them in his, using his green-glowing healing magic to clear up the last of the cuts.

"Dea . . . I . . ." I don't even know what to say. What do you say to someone you drank dry in a Vampire-feeding frenzy? "I'm sorry."

He shakes his head with a smile. "Arrie should not have said anything to you. I knew the risks. I knew you were not likely to control your feeding this early."

"Then, why——?"

"Because I wanted you strong and using the magic

available to you. You are a half Vampire, Angel. You need to feed. It will make you the Horseman Fate intended."

That phrase reminds me of Nine's eerie words of wisdom the other day: You must become the person the world needs to you be.

Is that who the word needs? A blood-sucking Vampire?

"I just . . ." I sigh. "I'm sorry." Tears threaten to break the banks of my tenuous hold, and I bat them away. "I just don't want to hurt any of you, or break up the team, or let the world down, or never discover who I am—"

"You have a lot on your plate right now. That is okay. You should get some sleep, and tomorrow we will go to Earth to start seeing what the problems are."

"Earth? Really?" That perks me up. Finally. Going back to Earth.

Dea chuckles. "Yes. So get some rest."

I should tell him about the flashback. "Er . . . Dea?"

"Yes, Angel?"

"I had a flashback while in the forest."

He looks at me with raised eyebrows.

"I-I-I . . ."

"Take a deep breath."

Heeding his advice, I take a deep breath and force the words out of my mouth at a louder-than-normal volume. "I wasn't human!"

"Wh-what?"

"I wasn't human. In the flashback, I was using the Angel magic just like in the kitchen. I was screaming at some man that I just wanted to be normal, and it leaked out of my body."

"You . . . You what?" He looks genuinely taken aback. "You were an Angel-descended Witch in your mortal life? That . . . that is not possible."

"Why not?"

"Because the last of them were destroyed twenty years ago."

The next morning, we're all dressed and eating breakfast in the kitchen together as though nothing went wrong yesterday. They avoid talking about it. Arrie doesn't speak or look at me, and Nine's back to helpfully flirting. All in all, a pretty standard morning for the Horseman of Magic.

Dea fills them in on the flashback, saving me the job, and Nine could not be more excited by the magical possibilities.

But there's something they're not telling me. Something they're keeping quiet about. I can see it all in the silent looks they give each other, the occasional heated mental conversation between Nine and Dea, and the way Connie's constantly smiling sweetly at me. It's driving me nuts.

"Enough!" I slam my spoon down on the table—bending it in the process—and get everyone's attention. "Spit it out!"

"Are we that easy to read?" Nine asks sarcastically.

"Yes."

Connie's the one who comes forward with the answer, though. "You need to feed before leaving."

The spoon I try to pick back up clatters to the table. "No. No way. Forget it. You can take my Witch magic or nothing." I fold my arms over my chest and shake my head.

"Then nothing," Dea whispers through clenched teeth, then sighs. "You need to move past this, Angel. You are a half Vampire. You are at your fullest when you feed regularly."

"Half Vampire means I don't need to feed."

"Fucking christ," Arrie says in the loudest voice I've ever heard him use, and even then, it's barely above normal volume.

He picks up the knife he was using to cut the bread with and slices his palm. Blood drips onto the table in a steady stream that makes my gums tingle and my teeth ache as that familiar hunger returns.

Connie gasps and turns around, and I can't help but be a little hurt. She's clearly gone through something involving Vampires, and I should try to help her past that—the moment I can fully control myself because I have to fight every instinct not to rip Arrie's throat out right now.

Arrie grabs a glass and holds his squeezed palm up to the rim, letting the blood steadily fill the glass. He has to make a few more cuts, but he eventually fills the glass to the rim as I watch every drop land in my new favorite glass.

"Here." He slides the glass across the table and holds his hand, waiting for the last cut to heal.

But I don't care about that—he's a Horseman, he'll heal in a moment—all I care about is the delicious smoky, metallic scent wafting from that glass. It smells different from Dea's blood, which is like smoky lavendar, and that fact alone has me curious enough to drink it.

I tip the glass up to my lips and take a sip, trying not to bang my fangs on the side of the glass (yes, I'm aware of how odd an issue that is to have). When Nine notices my struggle, he hands me a straw from goddess knows where, and I down the entire glass in one, not even noticing my surroundings.

In that moment, I don't care that Connie's terrified of me, that Arrie looks at me with equal measures of disgust and fascination, that Nine probably thinks I'm some kind of strange science experiment he can probe whenever he wants. All I care about is the taste of foresty goodness lapping along my tongue asI swallow every drop.

Once the glass is empty and the straw is making that

weird, empty-cup sucking sound, I frown. I want more. Looking up at Arrie, I can almost see the artery in his neck pulsing, and I can definitely hear the beat of his heart if I concentrate. Right now, it's faster than it should be.

Is he scared?

My fangs snap back in an instant and my hand grabs the glass to go and wash it—thoroughly.

"Thank you," I say to Arrie once I sit back down and tap Connie to turn back around. I give her a sweet, understanding smile, hoping one day she'll open up enough to talk to me about it. I take a deep breath, wanting nothing more than to just be my normal self for the moment. "So," I say as I turn to Dea, "where are going? How are we getting there? Do we split up? What exactly are we—?"

Dea's laughter fills the air. "It has been a while since one of us had our first mission. You are staying with me and Nine, and we will be taking the Witches and Vampires, while Connie and Arrie will handle the Shifters and Fae."

"Handle?" That doesn't sound good.

Nine smiles at me. "We're going to talk to the leaders of each community, generally sniff around, and be a group of nosy shits. See what's going on. That kind of thing." He looks up at me. "Oh, and ask around about your seal."

I nod, understanding finally settling in. "Sounds good. Let's go." I stand up quicker than lightning but stop. "I can't believe this question hasn't occurred to me sooner, but how do we get to Earth?"

This time Arrie laughs a deep, belly-filled laugh that escapes his throat, and the sound surprises me so much I jump and nearly fall flat on my ass, but Nine catches me last minute.

"Thanks."

"You'll see, Sweetie."

We leave out the front door a few minutes later, after packing all the weapons we need (I'm carrying more knives than I know how to handle and a few sealed bottles of blood Dea prepared earlier), and head down the trail into town.

The town is only thirty minutes away, and it's awesome to get there in that time instead of the hour it took previously due to my injuries.

It's just as I remember, a combination of Victorian England and modern-day science magic. It's beautiful in a way I can't really describe, as though the best bits of Earth got together and called a truce to coexist peacefully. It's just . . . nice.

I breathe in the fresh air of people, shops, and flowers as we walk toward a tall building in what looks like the center of town. Inscribed on the front is a sign that reads: TOWN HALL. So we're getting to Earth through the town hall?

I hear Nine chuckle next to me, and I have a funny feeling he's keeping a closer mind's eye on my thoughts after yesterday. It's a little invasive, but I'm kinda used to it by now (since I think so loudly anyway), and besides, it's nice to know he cares enough to keep an eye out.

I don't think the old me really had that, at least not fully. I'm not sure how I know, but I just do. I briefly wonder who was in my life, and my mind latches onto the memory from yesterday, of me wielding black, smoky magic and shouting at some random guy that I wanted to be normal.

Even though I can be anything I want now, and can probably change my mind every fifty or so years, I still want that. To be normal. Human.

You might not be able to be human, but you could live out a human-spanned life as normally as you wished. You're not trapped here with us, you know. If you wanted to spend a few decades on Earth without us, you can.

But after we've dealt with this.

Yes, sorry, but the world does need saving.

And you'll rightfully have to call on me anytime a crisis that needs my attention comes along. I'll still be a Horseman, Nine. That won't change.

Secretly, or at least I hope I manage to keep it a secret, the very thought of spending time semi-permanently away from the team is a painful notion. I need them. Maybe that won't always be the case, but for now, I need people who understand what it's like to be me.

We walk through various hallways and past a whole host of office doors with all sorts of names and positions written on their respective plaques, until we reach a door at the end labeled: EARTH PORTAL.

"Portal magic?" But that's—

"Not around anymore, yes. We know. But this was created the same time as this realm, which was when we were born, so it was back in a different time," Nine explains.

There's going to be a lot of Nine explaining my questions today, isn't there?

Probably.

That was rhetorical, Nine.

He chuckles before opening the shiny black doors and clearly takes immense pleasure in watching my jaw drop at the sight beyond.

It's a room full of trees and brightly glowing flowers. From tall pines to small, glowing blue fairyroots, this place is like a snippet of the fairy garden back at the team's house—or how I imagine it looks at night.

I would love to capture it in some kind of painting or image.

We all enter, and Nine takes it upon himself to explain how the portal works. "It's a combination of Witch and Fae magic that takes your magical energy and distributes it on Earth. It's actually really clever. Portal magic doesn't exist on Earth because there isn't a Fae alive today who can use it."

"Hmmm. So, hypothetically, if I could open up my hypothetical Fae powers, I could hypothetically create something like this by combining my magic?"

Nine grows a wide smile and nods excitedly. "Exactly."

Arrie rolls his eyes. "C'mon nerds. Let's get going."

I look around, not really sure where to stand.

"Over there." Nine points to a section in the center with five chairs. "Seems the portal has already adjusted to your presence."

He gets lost in thought for a moment, and I catch myself wondering what it would be like to see the inside of his mind, see how his thoughts work, how his process happens when figuring things out. How much knowledge must he have, being two thousand years old?

"Oh god, we really do have two nerds to deal with now." Connie smiles, pulls me by the arm, and drags me to one of the chairs before sitting in the one on my right.

Nine plonks himself down on my left, and Dea and Arrie take the remaining two.

"Now wha—?"

My question is cut off by the sudden feeling of losing every part of myself to a weightless void of space, my body barely hanging onto its own limbs as I crash down into a random place full of scents and sounds I don't recognize.

"Wh-where are we?"

"Denver, Colorado, US."

Looking around, I notice we're in a sort of office-looking

room surrounded by the same type of fairy garden as the portal on the other side. But on this side, there're tables and chairs dotting the foliage and doors on the side of the perimeter wall.

Dea gets up first, followed by the rest, but my stomach feels like it's going to fall out of my body, and I swear that my breakfast is going to come back up.

Nine senses my predicament with an amused expression, but Arrie just grunts and walks toward the door.

"A little heads up next time, please."

"Sorry." Connie winces once she's noticed me half huddled over in my seat. "Let me help."

Dea wanders off somewhere to do goddess knows what, while Nine and Connie help me to my feet. Arrie's already exited the room, but I have no patience right now to deal with him.

"Here," Dea says, handing me something in his hand. "Eat this."

Eat? Like, now?

Seeing my confused face, Dea explains, "It is a ginger biscuit. Helps with nausea." He points to a desk by the main entrance in the distance. "They hand them out free over there."

I blush, feeling a little cared for with all the attention he seems to pay my needs. Between Dea taking care of my physical needs, Nine taking care of my mental and emotional wellbeing, and Connie helping to lighten things, they're my personal balance right now.

That makes Nine smile wider than I've ever seen, and that's saying something, because his neutral facial expression is smiling. Or at least, I assume it is; he never does anything else unless he's puzzling something out, and even then, he looks happily confused. Like he enjoys being as confused as other people are frustrated.

I nibble on the gingersnap for a moment, refraining from correcting Dea's comment about it being a biscuit (he obviously learned his English in England, or maybe he is originally from England?) But really, if you have a ginger snap in America, it's a fucking gingersnap. It would be a biscuit if it's something from the UK. Right? Maybe? You know what, I feel like I've gone off on a tangent here, and I should be focused on something else.

Nine doubles over in laughter. "Oh god, Sweetie. I can't wait for you to bring that up with Dea!" He can't control his laughter and has trouble breathing for a moment, wiping his eyes from the tears that spill. Then he corrects himself and dusts off his black jacket as he strides toward the door, the rest of us following on his heels.

"Bring what up?" Dea asks.

"Oh, nothing." Nine skips forward with a sly grin in the best mood I've ever seen him in.

Connie links her arm around mine and whispers, "Nine loves Earth."

"Ah. That explains his child-in-a-candy-shop attitude, then." Though part of me wonders if it's also due to my earlier thought.

"Uh-huh." She winks, and we follow the guys out the front door and onto Earth.

We step into an empty parking lot. I guess not many people use the portal, at least not regularly enough to need a permanent car here.

Nine fills me in with his usual fact-of-the-month voice. "Most people only use the portal for business, but none as frequently as us."

"Does the portal only open to here?"

"Yes," Dea says on a sigh. "It is a little annoying, actually. Takes ages to get anywhere, and I cannot tell you the stress of moving a horse across the ocean, even magical ones."

"You take the horses through that monstrosity of a mode of transportation?" I gesture back to the portal building, which I have decided to put on the top of a new list in my mind: places I want to spend as little time in as possible. So far, it only consists of two places. The portal buildings and alone with Arrie.

"Yup," Nine adds. "But only Dea really needs to on a regular basis. We rarely need them these days."

I look confusedly at Connie, who explains, "We only use them in battle, but Dea uses his when dealing with dying soul issues."

"Right, Horseman of Death. Almost forgot." It's hard to think of Dea as the Horseman of Death; he's just so . . . normal.

Right? I keep saying he needs to act the part more.

I internally chuckle. Are you going to stay in my mind the entire time we're here?

Sorry, he cringes. *But Dea asked me to. Your first mission, your first time here on Earth with not many memories, and yesterday . . . We just feel it would be best to know if anything upsets you.*

Right, because I'm a powerful Vampire Witch with untapped power and can probably level a country if I have a bad mood swing. Remind me not to spend time around other people when on my period.

Do we still get periods? Cause it would be a great perk if we fucking don't.

You do. Sorry.

Nine doesn't say anything else on the matter and gestures to Connie as if to say this is an ask-the-female kind of question.

Men. I roll my eyes. It's nice to know immortal men are just the same as the rest, though. It's also nice to know that I can start making those internal comments as my non-conscious memories of my Earth life settle in.

I'm looking forward to this.

Arrie waits for us at the road-side entrance to the parking lot with his usual scowl beside two amazing cars. Aperta 9000Xs. One is white, one is black, and I swear I nearly stop in my tracks. They run on a combination of magic fuel and leyline power, meaning they can travel off leylines if need be. They're top of the line, only released in the last year or so (I think), and the most ridiculously expensive vehicle I've ever seen in my life.

Nine, tell me I get to drive one of those?

Haha. They're Arrie's. Sorry, Sweetie.

Fuck my life. Well, I have all of eternity, I will get my hands on one of those bad boys one day, even if I have to send Arrie into a mini-vacation of unconsciousness to do so. The ass cannot have all the toys and not share.

But you can ride up front with me if you like?

I can?

Yeah. Ours is the white one.

"Shotgun!" I run up to the white car's front passenger door and refuse to move, my hands on my hips as I bob up and down on the spot. I'm so ready to ride one of these fucking cars.

Connie and Dea laugh while Nine silently smiles. Arrie, however, looks conflicted, as though seeing my love of his cars confuses him. Wait, am I breaking down some kind of barrier here?

Let me roll with this a sec.

"So, Arrie, how fast can they go?" I just look at him

expectantly, a little giddy with excitement.

"Up to 900 mph with the G-Zone safety function engaged."

"And . . . how fast can we go today without getting a speeding ticket? Wait, can we get speeding tickets? Do we even have ID chips?"

Arrie briefly smiles before covering it with his signature scowl. "I'm sure Nine will take you however fast you want to go, Killer." The way he says killer is . . . different to usual. Usually it's with a scowl, but this time it's almost endearing, and, dare I say it, even a little flirty.

But Fate must have a different kind of shit power-up item installed into my cosmic karma-meter because Arrie then looks me up and down with disgust and then huffs, turning and throwing a set of keys at Nine before storming off.

What the hell?

You know what, that was progress. I don't get what his fucking deal is, but that . . . that was the closest thing to a conversation I've ever had with the guy. So he likes cars. I add that little snippet of info to another list I've started: conversation starters for talking to Arrie.

I buckle up and sit eagerly in the front seat as I watch everything Nine does, analyzing his every button press and manual set-up process. One day, I'll be in that seat. Arrie will have to kill me to stop me (you know, figuratively speaking).

When Nine gets the engine going (almost silent, by the way), I squeal in excitement, genuinely happy for the first time in days. This is the best distraction ever. Doing shit like this forever? Sign me up!

As I said when I first learned about being the Fifth Horseman, there are pros to this; it's about time I start living some.

Nine drives onto the nearest highway just off the road the portal building's on, and shoves us into a steady 100 mph drive up the highway, following closely behind Arrie and Connie.

I'm giddy with excitement in this fucking car. It's awesome. Like, way more awesome than pepperoni pizza, and that's saying something.

"More awesome than your library?"

"Ummmm . . . no. But definitely a close second."

We drive for a couple of hours up the highway before taking an exit for a small town somewhere here in Colorado and finding ourselves navigating the annoying leylines of the small town that barely has more than a car's width of road in most of the main streets.

At the end of the main road, however, is a small cottage-like that looks out of place amongst the regular houses lined up beside it. But that's the exact place we stop in front of, right behind the black car that holds Arrie and Connie.

Dea gets out and grabs my door. "Welcome to our Colorado base, Angel."

I step out, thanking him like a lady should, trying to refrain from thinking of myself as a lady and totally spoiling the moment with a snorted laugh. "How many bases do you have on Earth?"

Dea answers. "Too many to list, but one in each state here in the US. Since most of the magical community's headquarters are here."

Nine interrupts. "Well, the Vampire and human division's HQs are here. Along with quite a few Shifter colonies. And they're the ones we deal with most. The Shifter's HQ is in Tokyo, the Fae's is in Paris, and the Witches's is in South Africa."

"South Africa? That's a bit of an odd place to have a HQ."

"Yeah," Nine adds with a sigh. "But the Witches move theirs to wherever they're least likely to be found."

I nod. Makes sense. Clever Witches.

The front door is a simple storm door with the usual white-painted wood behind. It's so old-fashioned. It's kinda cute in a way. The windows even have shutters, just like in those old movies. I catch myself stifling a giggle, not wanting to insult anyone. Keeping each base updated without the use of a magical house must be a nightmare.

The inside is so normal that, for a moment, I'm pretty taken aback. It's a standard four-bed house, with a lounge, kitchen-diner, and a bathroom. Damn. A regular family could live here.

We are a family, Nine reminds me.

If you guys are your definition of regular, I've got some bad news.

Fair point, he said through a laugh.

"I'll order some food in," Connie says. "Hon, preference?"

"Er . . . I haven't tried Indian yet?"

"Indian it is."

I give her a smile before she walks off into the kitchen to order some food, watching her ass all the way through that door in those tight black jeans. Sighing, I sit on the couch, watching as the guys give me a weird look.

"What? Those are some killer jeans, and trust me, she knows it."

"Damn straight I do!" Connie calls from the kitchen. I even hear her smack her own ass as though confirming that fact.

Right, Conquest hearing. Oops. I shake the worry from

my mind, determined not to let anything get in the way of this awesome road trip.

Mission, not road trip.

Shut up, Nine. We're not missioning until tomorrow. For now, it's a road trip.

"Right," Dea says once Connie returns and we're all sitting on various pieces of matching floral furniture. He pulls a bag from his shoulder I didn't realize he wore and digs through it. "Standard equipment." He hands each of us a stun gun, some kind of purple crystal, and a regular pistol. "Angel, that crystal is vital. Do not lose it."

"What is it?"

Nine, who's sitting next to me on the rose-patterned couch, rests a hand in his usual place on my knee. "They're teleporters. If we're in danger, they can teleport us back to *Sheruta* instantly."

"But why not just use those rather than the goddess awful portal?"

"They're expensive and difficult to make and take a high Fae Lord to create."

Riiight. Makes sense. Hopefully, if I one day master my powers in all four supe types, I might be able to create them for the team. That would be useful.

"How do I use it?"

Dea looks at me and smiles. Clearly, I'm asking the right question. "Smash it on the ground at your feet and think of home."

"Really? That's the most cliché magical thing ever."

"We know." Dea settles into the armchair. "Do you understand everything else? Have any more questions?"

"Yup and nope."

"Good."

Not long after that, dinner arrives, and I gorge myself on various curries, stealing a bit of everyone's order (including Arrie's, much to his annoyance), and finding that spicy food is soooo good. Then again, we haven't come across anything I don't like yet. Except tomatoes. Yuck!

"You really like food, hey, Angel?"

"Seems so." I look to the ground, suddenly reminded of why I can't really answer that question. "Wonder if anyone will know me at the Witches's HQ?"

"Still can't believe you weren't human," Connie says.

"Me neither," Nine adds.

Dea, ever the conversation-interrupter, interrupts. "Angel, you will have to share with someone tonight. We only have four bedrooms here."

I look briefly at Connie before realizing that probably isn't a good idea right now. "It's okay, I'll just take the couch. We're only here one night."

"If you are sure? Nine and I can always share, if you want to take my room?"

My mind flies back to the time when I caught Dea in Nine's room, and I can't help the ache that burns between my thighs, causing me to shift on the couch. "Ermmm, it's okay. Thanks, though."

Really? Is that memory ever not going to come to mind?

Probably not.

If I knew it would make you this happy, I would have invited you in days ago.

I barely knew you. It's weird now, Nine, much less a week ago.

We all sit chatting, with me interrupting now and then to ask a random question about something I either didn't know or have forgotten, while finishing up dinner.

I really like medium-level heat, but anything more than that and I find the spice overpowering, so I mainly stick to my own food, occasionally pinching things from Nine's plate, too. I fucking love samosas, as it turns out, and practically eat half the bag, leaving the rest to the others.

Everyone slowly heads to bed, but I have to wait until they all go upstairs to hit the hay, since I'm crashing on the couch. Eventually, just me, Nine, and Dea, are left, and it can't bemore awkward.

"So, Con's likely going to overhear this—sorry—but I just wanted to put it out there," Nine starts. He fiddles with the hem of his shirt while his eyes never leave his lap. I've never seen him look so nervous. "I'm sorry I didn't ask your permission for her to watch the other night, Dea. And I'm sorry that you made you feel awkward, Sweetie."

Both Dea and I look at each other and give sheepish smiles. Nine's clearly been worrying over it. Sometimes, it can be easy to forget that only he can read our minds, not the other way around. He has feelings and stuff, too.

Fuck, how bad is that to forget?

"It's okay, Nine." I rest my hand on his knee. "I shouldn't have stayed in the first place." I look briefly at Dea. "Sorry."

I can feel my cheeks burning and just hope none of the others' eyesight is as good as mine in the dark.

Dea sits on my other side, sandwiching me between them. "Do not be sorry. I . . . liked it. Well, I like the memory of it, since I did not know at the time."

We all laugh a little.

"Me too," Nine adds, now lifting his face to meet our eyes.

I don't know what to say to that. I enjoyed myself that night, but if I admit that out loud . . . I don't want to give them the wrong impression.

Say it out loud, Sweetie. It's important.

Sighing, I acquiesce. "I enjoyed it, too. But I don't want to give you guys the wrong impression. I really don't like the idea of casual sex. I'm sorry." I shake my head slightly, staring at my hands fiddling with the hem of my vest tee as though it's suddenly the most important thing in the room.

Dea puts his hand on my shoulder and whispers in my ear, "That is okay. I have an entire lifetime to persuade you otherwise." He winks at me, and I just know he's going to spend the next couple of centuries torturing me.

"For now," Nine adds, "feel free to watch anytime you want." They both stand, wink at me, and walk up the stairs in perfect unison, leaving me dumbfounded and stunned silent.

Chapter Twenty-Two

The next morning, we split up and head our separate ways at the nearest airport. Connie and Arrie are on their way to Paris to meet with the Fae Council. Apparently, they called ahead, and apparently, they know we exist—well, they know the others exist. I'm still trying to stay in the closet (for now). We, on the other hand, are on our way to New Orleans—Vampire central and home of the Vampire Royal Council. Sounds like fun.

Honestly, the thought of dealing with Vampires right now is less than thrilling, but I do get to ride shotgun with Nine again, so bonus! Everything's a little more serious than it was yesterday, given we have actual work to do, but I'm still excited. I'm part Vampire, after all. Maybe we'll learn more about me while there. Or maybe they'll rip my head from my shoulders and I'll have to somehow grow it back. Sounds painful.

"Dea?"

"Mmm?" He's half napping in the backseat, but I have a

nagging question.

"Why don't you drive?"

I feel him looking at me from behind and then hear him sigh. "Since humans cannot see me unless I stay corporeal for them, driving long distances is tough; when we get pulled over, they do not see the driver unless I focus. I cannot go corporeal for more than a few hours at a time, and it is draining."

"So," Nine chimes in, "I drive on missions."

"And when you're here on your own?"

"I bring my horse and we can travel at my usual speed everywhere while invisible to everyone. Only ocean travel is annoying."

Our flight is only an hour, since Fae magic is used to buffer the engines, but it's still an hour I have to fill with something other than the million questions running through my brain. I fear if I'm left to my own mind right now, I'll go insane.

You're going to be fine, Sweetie.

You're sure?

Absolutely. Firstly, we can't die. Secondly, we can crystal out of there if needed. Thirdly, you're with us, and we've dealt with these idiots for centuries.

Goddess, he's right. I need to get a grip. Everything will be fine. I breathe a sigh of relief as I repeat that over and over again until my mind eases.

I can do this.

Dea promised to go over the plan once we land and get to the motel (apparently, no safe house in New Orleans because the Vampires won't allow it), so, until then, I just have to sit tight.

"Here," Nine says and hands me a plasmascreen. "Do research, read a book, play some games, go online . . .

Whatever. Just please distract yourself and try to relax."

He grimaces at me, and I realize he's also getting frustrated with my internal thoughts; they're probably screaming at this point, and he's been told to stay in-tune with them. Poor Nine.

I take the plasmascreen and open an app that lets me download books. Searching for something romantic, I download the first thing that promises a lot of romantic suspense. Anything to get me engrossed at this point.

Not dragons this time, but werewolves. Honestly, I like reading other types of fiction, but nothing melts my mind more than fantasy romance, no matter how unrealistic or stupid it may be to other people.

An hour later, Nine taps me on my shoulder, pulling me out of the book. "Time to go."

"We're here?"

He nods and grabs Dea, who's fallen asleep on his other side. We leave the plane, grab our luggage, and hail a cab, and arrive outside a small, rundown motel not an hour later.

"Really?" This place looks like I might get infected just from standing in the parking lot. "This place?"

"We like to keep a low profile on Earth." Nine grimaces but tries to smile. "That's why we stay in regular houses and rundown motels."

Makes sense, but I don't really understand why they prefer to stay under the radar in the first place. Guess that's a question I'll have to ask later. For now, we're trying to get two rooms from the stingy man manning the front desk.

"I've only got one. Sorry, dude."

"C'mon," Nine urges. "You must have something available?"

"Look, it's one or nothing. Take it or leave it."

Dea stays behind us, letting Nine take the lead, and I

assume this guy is human because he never looks Dea's way once, and Dea is someone you don't just ignore. He makes a whole room turn toward him like he's the bright, shiny new kid.

I grab Nine's arm and turn to the man. "One room will be fine. Thank you." I snatch the key dangling from the man and hand the signing pen over to Nine.

I don't really know what name to sign, so I just let him handle it. He uses a fake name anyway (which makes sense), so I guess it doesn't matter.

I bow slightly before leaving toward our assigned room. The room is at the farthest point from the desk, at the other end of the motel, and has a single double bed, a dingy sofa I assume no one wants to sleep on given the mold creeping up the sides, and a small, pretty unsanitary bathroom attached.

Sorry. It's just for a few nights.

It's fine. I'm a grown adult, Nine. I can handle sharing a bed for a night.

But even just the thought of us all snuggling up in that bed has me quickly moving to place my bag down on the floor to remove the building tension between my legs.

It's going to be a long night.

"Right," Dea says as he sits on the edge of the bed. "Tomorrow, we have a meeting with the Vampire Royal Council. In that meeting, I am going to do the talking. Angel, I need you to remain silent, as though you are just someone working with us for the time being." I nod my understanding. "Nine, I need you relaying messages between us so the Vampire Council cannot throw curveballs at us." Nine also nods. "We are going to ask them how they are doing, have a general catch-up, and drink tea. We are not interrogating them or doing anything to piss them off. Clear?" He looks straight at us, as if daring us to challenge him.

"Clear," I say.

"Clear."

"Angel, no matter what happens in there, please be careful. They are going to be drinking blood and offering you humans to feed from. Just so you are aware."

Wow, I could be really dangerous in that room. I'm likely more powerful than most of the Vampires individually, but I'm hoping that'll go unnoticed given that only half of my powers are vampiric.

This is gonna to be a pain.

"But tonight," Dea continues, "we are going to a party."

"A party?" I didn't pack party clothes. What the hell?

"Seems," Nine says with a sigh, "we'll need to go shopping first." He flicks his head toward me while looking at Dea, who gives an immediate smile.

We head out to a nearby shopping mall, and Nine escorts me through a few shops to find a party-style dress, but nothing's really popping out. Dea trails behind us, mostly staying out of people's way so they don't bump in to an invisible him. He stays completely invisible at this point, not even letting himself be semi-translucent to supes. Why is that? Dea's been a little more restrained here on Earth than back at the house, so maybe it's best not to mention anything.

I've already walked in on them in a rather compromising situation, I don't also need to go poking around in their private thoughts.

"Nothing's sticking out at you?" Nine asks as he holds up a black dress in a silent question.

"No, not really. Everything's just so . . . meh." I shrug.

The real issue is that I know this is Vamp central, and now I am a Vampire, I don't know what to wear around other

Vampires. Is it expected of me to dress a little more provocatively to fit in with the usual slutty attire of Vampire kind? Is there any kind of Vampire dress code I should be aware of?

Nine doesn't answer any of my questions—he's probably leaving me to my private thoughts on the matter, given that this is one of those situations where I need to make my mind up for myself.

I growl under my breath in frustration. "Do I need to fit in with the other Vamps tonight?" I look at Dea, then quickly to the ground, remembering that staring at a fixed point no one else can see looks rather stupid.

Dea stops and looks at me for a moment with a curious smile. "You just need to be yourself tonight. Tomorrow might be a different story, but tonight, we are just scanning the area, getting into conversations with random supes—preferably Vampires—and seeing where the community's opinions lie."

"Okay. Okay." I can do that. All I need for that is a dress and an attitude that speaks open and chatty.

Nine grabs my arm, gestures to Dea to follow us, and leads us to a small boutique a few blocks over. "This might have something more you."

A little bell chimes in the fresh, rose-smelling store, and we're greeted by a young woman in a short yet flowing pink dress with blonde and pink-highlighted hair. Her smile seems genuine as she waves. "Welcome to Cathy's. Anything you need, just gimme a shout." She can't have been older than mid-twenties as she turns around and continues furiously tapping away at the cashier's plasmascreen on the desk.

"Thank you."

I stop to peruse the store briefly; it's small but looks beautifully laid out with lots of large mirrors and well-styled decor. It has a range of bright colorful clothing that instantly catches my eye, and I find my feet pandering to the nearest rack, which seems to hold a range of cropped and shortened tees.

"You can buy anything you like, Angel. You can always bring it home with us."

I nod, my eyes still focusing on the cropped tee they unharmoniously landed on moments ago. It's short, stops a couple inches under the boobs, and is a deep red with black slashes plastering through it. My current dark, confused mood likes its equally dark presence, and I find myself grabbing it by the hanger and handing it to Nine.

"I wanna try some things on."

He nods and hops away, seemingly excited that he's picked out a store I like.

We both spend around an hour picking out various items of clothing, holding them against my body, and selecting the best ones to be tried on.

The changing room is a single block with heavy, dusted violet curtains. "Wait out here." I open the curtains to find a larger-than-average changing room dotted with mirrors, a stool in the corner, and various hooks.

Oh, and Nine? Stay out of my head while I'm getting changed.

Haha. Okay.

I can practically hear him winking, and I have to repress a laugh. It's easy to flirt with Nine, especially with the telepathy making it private. But with the others, it's always more nerve-wracking; Dea makes me stumble over sentences I would otherwise speak perfectly while Connie makes me feel like a teenager again. It's all like walking on lava, trying to hop onto the right stones before you drown. And that thirty seconds of flirting with Arrie in the parking lot? Well, I don't even know what to make of that.

The first item is a potential dress for tonight, and I have to admit it looks rather flattering. Okay, it makes my boobs look fucking epic. But that's still flattering, right?

Stepping out of the changing room, Dea smiles and nods his head (which is pretty good for him), and Nine makes a motion with his finger, asking me to twirl.

"Looks good, but I've got my eye on a different one for the winner."

He isn't usually a shopping kind of guy, but since Dea can't use all of his energy on being visible right now with tonight looming on our calendar's horizon, I guess Nine's taking over shopping duty.

I return to the changing room, hoping to get a better reaction out of some of the others. Four dresses later, we have a potential winner, with a pile four-high of nopes.

This is the last one, and it's another black dress, but this one has a light-pink glow to the sparkles that light up the entire thing. I have to say, it matches my long, light-pink hair perfectly. But looking in the mirror behind me, I realize why this is the one Nine has his hopes on—the back is open and has a draped effect right down to my middle. My lion tattoo, which is a mixture of pink, blue, and violet, is on show, and I'm suddenly reminded of how it glowed in the dark under most club lights. My front neckline tattoo is hidden, but it doesn't matter.

"This one. Definitely this one," I say from behind the curtains. I swing it open and jump out, eagerly awaiting their reactions.

Nine smiles, obviously happy, while Dea stares for a moment and asks me to turn around. A couple of low whistles follow.

"I did not know you had such an amazing tattoo, Angel?"

"Oh, really?"

"I have seen the skull on your front, but this is . . . Wow."

"It glows under the typical lights clubs use."

"Damn, Sweetie." *Can't wait to see.*

"So, this one it is, then?" I ask.

"Yes," they both say in unison.

I go back into the changing room and sift through the rest of the non-dress pile, trying things on, showing some to the guys, some not, and by the time I'm done, I have a pile of about ten items I want.

Guilt races through my mind when we step up to the cashier, but I shake my head. Dea said last time we went shopping that it's okay if I spend some money. But, really, I want my own funds. I bet the others have their own money and don't rely on Dea.

I'll show you how we make money when we get home.

Okay. Thank you.

I genuinely mean it, too. I really hate scrounging.

I am just finishing up my hair and makeup in the bathroom mirror when I hear the guys chatting from the bedroom. We've gone back to the grubby motel to chill, which seems to have lightened Dea's mood, and I've spent the last hour showering and getting ready.

"She's doing great in training, but I really want to know if she'll have the other pillars of power as well."

"I am sure it will come with time, Nine. Just give her time."

Nine hushes to a whisper, probably hoping I can't hear, but Vamp hearing and whatnot. "We might not have time, bro."

I hear Dea whisper something back but can't make it out, so I shake my head and look in the mirror one final time before declaring myself pretty enough to party with Vampires—and I have to admit, I scrub up pretty well for someone who barely has an identity.

The bathroom door clicks shut behind me as I walk out, and I face the guys as they look the other way. "Ahhhmmm," I cough, trying to get their attention. "I'm ready to go."

I avoid their gazes when they look at me with stunned smiles, especially Nine's, and push the memory of their conversation to the back of my mind. Do not want to think about that right now.

Dea steps forward, grabs my hand, and raises it to his lips. "You look beautiful, Angel."

"Mmm, I have to agree. That dress really was made for you." Nine reaches for something in his back pocket. "One more thing." He hands me one of the sealed bottles of blood. "Drink up."

I look at them both with annoyance, but their stony faces remain insistent. Fucking damn it. I chug it down in one, trying to ignore the coldness of the blood and how it makes it taste stale and dry. "Ugh."

Dea grabs my right arm while Nine grabs my left, and they escort me out of the shitty motel and to the nearest, busiest club they can find.

I have the room key stashed in my bra, but the guys have everything else. I'm not even armed tonight, which seems a little stupid to me.

You have magic, remember.

Right. I don't need a weapon.

That is the fact I remind myself of as we walk through the

main door, past a few security guards, and into what I can only describe as a club of debauchery and insanity. There are supes everywhere, including a few Shifters in animal form (there's a panther curled up on a sofa in the corner a few feet from the door); Vampires are dancing and seducing all kinds of people on the dancefloor, from supernaturals to humans; and every few feet stands a topless dancer on top a small podium. There's an upper floor you can see from the ground, where runway-like floors crisscross and hold more topless dancers, but this time dancing with the public.

But the most obvious part of the club? The Vampires feeding in the darkened corners of the large space. I can see in the dark, but the others can't, so it's blindingly obvious when one male Vampire in particular has a party of three human women dancing around him in the far corner beside a main stage as he alternates feeding from each one.

As much as I hate it, I can smell the blood permeating the air, and the only reason my fangs don't come out is because Nine made me feed before leaving.

Thank fuck.

You're welcome. Got another bottle in my pocket if needed. Or you can, you know, go be a Vampire.

He gestures to the club with a wink, but I know he can't see in the dark, so he looks at me confused when I scowl at the joke.

I send him a mental picture of the Vampire frenzies going on all around us, including all the dark, hidden places, and he visibly recoils.

I . . . err . . . sorry.

It's okay.

I get the feeling this place is supposed to just look like a hot human-supe club. That's why Nine can't see all the feeding.

"We should blend in, have a few drinks, and go dance." Dea makes himself visible as he says this, and I can see the strain on his face the moment he does. He eventually rids his face of the signs of his discomfort and smiles, but it's clear he's more comfortable in his invisible form. "Basically, let's have fun."

He sounds almost modern as he says that, and I almost laugh at the attempt but manage to keep it hidden. Not from Nine, though, who sends me a mental laugh while remaining externally stoic somehow.

I turn to take another look at the club, and as I do, Nine and Dea gasp.

"Angel . . . your tattoo is glowing!"

"I did say." I show them my full back and hope like hell it looks as cool in real life as it does in my memories.

It does. Nine throws what he's seeing into my head, and the image of a glowing lion greets my mind.

Wow, it really does look cool.

"Well," Dea says, "Con will definitely want to see that in the dark." He winks and leaves, heading toward the stage.

Nine and I, on the other hand, go to the bar.

What you want to drink?

"A dusted vodka soda, please."

He raises an eyebrow at me in question, and I just shrug. It's an instinctual answer, and something I know I liked from when I was mortal. Haven't really had time to try alcohol yet, what with all the training. Connie said dust doesn't have as large of an effect on us anyway, so I'm hoping it just make's me happier (goddess knows I can use the pick-me up).

We'll spend some time getting you drunk and trying all the alcohol you want some day. It takes a lot to get us drunk anyway, so we should be able to look the part all night here.

That sounds oddly inviting and . . . fun.

We can be fun. He frowns at me in mock hurt, but I just laugh.

Our drinks are poured quickly once Nine orders them from a cute Fae bartender with pink hair like mine but short. The Fae winks at me as he hands mine over, and I turn to see Nine staring at him with the same appreciative glance.

"Like what you see, Nine?" I say, mimicking his mockery of Connie from last week.

He looks at me and smiles, eying me from head to toe. "Definitely."

Wait, is he talking about me or the bartender? I don't want to embarrass myself by asking, so I laugh and tell him to stop being so cliché.

"I'm going to go this way." I point to the area near the back where the most Vampire activity is, thinking I can probably get one or two to chat if I flash my fangs.

"Okay. I'll go the other way and we'll chat later."

I walk away with my drink in hand, but, just as I get a few feet, Nine says, *I was talking about you, Sweetie.*

Oh. Thank you.

He's probably laughing at my stupidity, but I don't have the time to ponder over it as I weave through the left-hand side of the dancefloor and attempt to fit in somewhere.

My drink still in hand, I start dancing with a woman who comes over and offers a smile; but she's human, so I need to find a way of ditching her and moving on. Honestly, I need a little more alcohol before I really get into this.

I dance for a while, only really bumping into humans and Shifters, but I eventually come across a Vampire seducing a female human. Please let me be able to say hi without getting my head ripped off.

Least it'll grow back.

I sidle on up, hoping to dance with them, but his fierce blue eyes stare at me as his fangs drop in warning. I raise my free hand in surrender, trying to show I'm not there to steal his . . . meal (ugh, what a crass way of putting it), and he relaxes a little.

I drop my fangs in defense anyway, just in case, and see the human woman smile in fascination. She grabs my hand, and I let her pull me forward. She's pretty, but she has nothing on Connie and isn't really my type (not that I know what my type was before), but I act interested for the sake of getting closer to the other Vampire.

Just one conversation, that's all. We both dance with her—him from behind and me in front—and she laps up the attention in sultry looks and giggles. I take a deep breath and step a little closer, pressing my body to hers.

God, this stuff is easy with Connie, Dea, and Nine; heck, even Arrie is easier to enjoy than this. But I'm not here to enjoy myself, I'm here to gain general opinions and intel. But I don't even know how to start a conversation, given that I know next to nothing about the current goings-on in the community. I really should have looked up some general news articles on the plane.

Live and learn.

Is he going to be in my head with little insults all fucking night?

Probably. This Vamp I'm talking to is a little boring, so thought I could probably hold two convos at once.

All right for some.

You're not talking right now.

Not with words, no.

And, to prove my point, I run my hand up the woman's shoulder and along her neck, lifting her hair out of the way of her pulse as I drag a nail alongside the gentle thrum. Her face lights up, and the other Vampire meets my eyes. I give him a smile, hoping it's at least slightly sexy.

Damn. You make one hot Vampire, Sweetie.

The other Vampire lands a hand on her other side and mimicks my movement.

She shudders in front of me, and whispers, "Do Vamps share?"

I don't know how to answer that. Do they? Instead, I look to the other Vampire in question and just hope it's a personal choice.

"Sometimes," he answers in a French accent. Seems he's a quiet one, which doesn't really bode well for me. "If we like the other Vampire enough."

"Well?" she asks, looking me in the eyes.

"I've only just met the guy, sorry."

She looks a little disappointed, and I go to walk away, but the guy grabs my wrist and flings me back around. "Doesn't mean I don't like you enough to share. You're new, aren't you?"

I just nod, and he shakes his head in laughter.

"You're doing fucking well for a newbie."

So, he's a talker . . . when you can get him talking. Time to keep him going.

"Yeah?" I giggle at his compliment, trying to act a little flirty. "Well, I've had a good mentor."

"It's nice when the person who turns you actually stays to show you the ropes, ain't it? But it's not common, unfortunately."

"Really?"

He shakes his head and resumes dancing. I don't actually plan to share this woman with him since I don't want to feed on anyone at all, but if I can hold a conversation while dancing, that might work enough to grab some useful intel. And I can use this newbie Vamp angle.

"He's been great, but it's nice to chat to others. Get to know the real community."

"God, it's been a while since I've been in your shoes."

The woman seems content to dance with us, not really contributing to the conversation, and I get the feeling she just wants to be fed from—probably a hoster (humans who enjoy being fed on by Vampires on a regular basis).

"Is it rude to ask a Vampire's age?"

"A little, but I'll answer. I'm 142."

I do a double take. He's how fucking old? I'm dancing with someone six times my age!

Really? Because Dea and I are over two thousand years old, and I distinctly remember the thought of you wanting to fuck him multiple times over the last few weeks. If age gaps are a problem for you, I've got some bad news.

I internally laugh at that. He has a valid point.

But you seem so . . young.

Hardy ha. Get back to flirting information out of that Vamp.

Yes, sir!

Not my kink, but you might have some luck with Dea there.

Ohmigod, shut the fuck up!

He, thank fuck, stays silent.

"I didn't realize we lived quite *that* long."

"You don't seem to know much for someone who has a mentor."

"Oh"—I scramble for an answer—"he passed away recently, so I've only had a bit of time to adjust."

"Oh, my condolences. Well, if you have any questions, I'd be delighted to answer."

"Really?"

"Sure."

The woman in front of me ups her dancing game by running a hand up my front and cupping my boob. I let her. This conversation has real promise, and for some unknown, beyond the depth of my thinking, reason, being touched by someone feels so good. Okay, so it's probably because I'm so pent up from all the non-interactive flirting with the team; so, shoot me, I like the attention. I'm only hu—

A Horseman of the Apocalypse.

I roll my eyes and dance a little more with the woman, not wanting to lose the only reason I have a connection to the Vamp standing behind her. She grabs my waist and pulls me flush against her, pressing her lips to my neck.

It gives me a small shudder of surprise, and my head lilts to the side, giving her greater access. The Vampire in front of me, however, has his eyes on us like a lust-filled prize and reaches down to press his lips to mine.

Shit. I don't want to kiss him. I pull away slightly, hoping it won't deter him too much.

"Lesbian?"

Oh. Oooo. "Yeah. Sorry."

He shakes his hand in the air as if to say no worries, and I feel kinda bad for him.

You're playing the lesbian card. Really? That poor guy.

I ignore Nine, hoping he'll go away.

"Still up for sharing?" I ask through nervously chattering teeth, and I think he might've noticed my nerves.

"Sure." He smiles. This guy actually seems kinda friendly. Not sure what I was expecting, but this isn't it.

"Soooo, what's the latest gossip in the Vamp community I've just joined? Any surprising lovers? Shock horror deaths? Who killed their husband in blind blood rage? You know, the good stuff."

I hope that's subtle and comes across all gossip-y, but I doubt it.

We need to work on my social interrogation skills, Nine.

Yup. I've put it on my mental list for training.

But, luckily for me, Mr. Nice Vampire decides to answer anyway. "Well, there's the usual stuff: the SC limiting our blood supplies, making these places more popular." He gestures to the club. "I hear one of the royal princes pissed off the SC recently after they killed someone, and it's causing a bit of turmoil between the SC and the Vampires."

Oh really . . . ? "How did he piss them off?"

"According to the rumors, he went behind the Royal Council's back and submitted a formal complaint about the misuse of their Hunter Society."

The Hunter Society: the Supernatural Council's way of bringing in criminal rogue supes. Basically, they're a human group of bounty hunters for supernaturals.

"What? That's insane!" I have very little idea of the magnitude of the info here, so I'm just playing along.

"I know. He's a fucking idiot. But he's actually a pretty decent guy. Partied with him a few times."

"Partying with a Vampire prince? Damn. Sounds . . ." Like a fucking nightmare. "Intriguing."

He shakes his head. "God, you girls are all the same. Even when you're not into men you find royalty alluring." He rolls his eyes and laughs a little.

"A Vampire prince?" the woman says.

"Vampires have a whole royal family, with three princes

total," Mr. Nice Vampire answers. "One of whom is a little bit of a partier, but he can be a bit hot-headed."

"I've never met a prince before," the woman says.

"Me neither," I respond.

We both laugh, and I find myself having fun. Well, what do you know?

"Hey." The guy grabs our hands. "After we've had some more fun, I'll tell you where you can party with him." He gestures to a free sofa in a dark corner behind us—one used for feeding, going by the general scent coming from that direction.

Shit. I don't actually want to follow through with this. But finding this prince will be helpful. He'll know more about the problems between the SC and the Vampires.

Nine?

Yeah?

Keep an eye on me.

The Vampire pull us toward the sofa, and we all sit down, the woman in between us Vampires. This is it. I'm actually doing this. Here's to hoping I don't kill her.

You sure about this?

Nope.

I'll help.

Thank you.

I place my arm on her thigh, trying to be as gentle as possible, and my other arm slides around her shoulders as I move her hair away from her neck.

"So," she says, "you said I could party with the prince?" She looks pleadingly at the other Vampire.

"I'll give you the address of the party afterward."

She nods, and I have no choice but to go along with it if I also want the address. She looks at me and smiles. "Bite me."

My fangs descend, and I find myself naturally drawn to her neck, where I can hear the blood rushing through her.

She lets out a small moan as the other Vampire bites her other side, and she grabs my hand on her thigh and tries moving it up, but I don't let her.

I run my tongue along her neck, eliciting another shudder from her, and sink my teeth in, drawing a few mouthfuls of blood that I quickly swallow, trying not to taste it. Just like when feeding from Dea, I want more than just blood, and I can feel that familiar ache pooling low. My hand on her thigh slips my control, and she finally manages to pull it higher, where I meet his hand fiddling under the hem of her dress.

The feeling isn't as strong with her, though, I notice, and the blood doesn't taste anything like Dea's or Arrie's; in fact, it isn't that pleasing except to satiate the hunger that comes with being a Vampire. But still, I want more.

"Angel," a voice beside me says, and a hand gently lands on my shoulder. "Stop. The other guy has stopped."

I gasp, pulling away instantly, the need to stay in character and get that address tearing to the forefront of my mind.

Dea sits on the sofa's arm, invisible again, and looks at me with a pained expression. He looks a little jealous, if I'm honest, but that's stupid. The Horseman of Death is not jealous of me.

Realizing I'm staring at someone no one else can see, I turn back around, and find the other Vampire smiling at me gently.

"You really are doing great for a newbie."

"Thanks." I smile a genuine smile. Because, although I may have lied about my magical status, I'm still, technically, a new Vampire, and it is kinda hard.

He turns to the human woman and gives her a

handkerchief from his pocket. "It's the house at the end of Addler Street," he whispers into her ear, then turns to me. "Name's Ryan. It's nice to meet you." He turns and leaves in a rush of Vampire speed.

I let Dea guide me off the sofa as my mind dazes off a little. Why is drinking Dea's blood so much more attractive? Why does it taste sweeter?

Nine stands a few feet away, and I grab his hand, steadying myself. "You did well, Sweetie. We can check that address out after tomorrow's meeting."

"We should head back for now," Dea says. "Regroup our information and get some sleep."

I let the guys guide me out of the club and back to the motel.

Chapter Twenty-Three

We decided to share the double bed last night after we got back and crashed—all fully clothed—so this morning, as I lie in the middle of two sexy as hell men (how has this even happened?), I don't bother moving right away. Because, let's be honest, who wouldn't lap this shit up? Nine's fast asleep on my right, his arm wrapping tight around my waist, so for once, he can't hear my thoughts. Dea's curled up asleep on my left with his chin on my shoulder.

These two men have woven their way into my life more than I can even say, and lying here with them, even though it isn't sexual, just feels so . . . right. It feels like home. I mean, Connie being here would make it one hundred percent perfect, but it doesn't take away from this moment.

I can feel Dea's gentle breaths tickling my shoulder and chest as Nine's arm swings low over my stomach, gripping my hip lightly; between that, the blood yesterday, and the memory of my midnight escapade running through my mind on repeat, I've practically had my thighs shifting gently all morning, and I can feel how wet this is all making me. If it wasn't for sharing this small room in a skanky motel, I could fix the unbearable ache between my legs, but, alas, I'm going to have to suffer until we return to *Sheruta*.

Or you could just ask nicely.

"Nine," I gasp under my breath. "How long have you been awake?"

Long enough to know the awkward predicament you're in.

His hand wraps tighter around my hip before loosening and traveling lower.

"Nine . . ." But rather than the sharp tone I was going for, it comes out as a breathy moan, and I lose all credibility that this isn't affecting me.

"Yes?"

His hand continues to press lower until he's no more than an inch from my clit, and I hold my breath, waiting for him to move lower and touch me everywhere I've dreamed of. "I—"

"Fuck, you two are killing me," Dea complains, his cussing taking me by surprise.

"Dea!"

How long has he been awake?

Longer than me.

What?

Nine laughs, and I groan in frustration, causing them both to shift closer and align their bodies flush against mine.

Dea's hand trails up my stomach, drawing light patterns that send sparks to my core, and are just about to dip under my pajama top when my mind remembers why I haven't slept with either of them.

"Guys, I can't do this."

The moment snaps as they both stop and look at me.

Dea looks confused but stops his hand from going any

higher. He also doesn't remove it from my body entirely. "Explain it to us, Angel."

"I . . ." Goddess, I really don't want to have this discussion, but being open and honest, like they've been from day one, is how they seem to run the team, and that's important. So, pulling my big girl pants on, I take a deep breath and force the words out. "I want more than you're prepared to give." My voice comes out as a frail squeak, and it surprises even me. "And, if we go there, I won't . . ." I exhale my held breath, unsure how to finish the sentence.

"You won't what?" Nine asks. He's purposefully not reading my mind right now, or he's asking out loud so that everyone can have the conversation together. Either way, I'm grateful.

"I won't be okay with that. It'll hurt me." Maybe that's silly of me, but the thought of them sleeping with me and then just sleeping with anyone else outside of the team makes my chest feel like it's going to implode.

They both stop breathing as they look at me, and I get the feeling they're having a conversation without me. I won't lie and say it doesn't bother me, but they already have some kind of relationship, and I can't expect to just barge in on that.

The silence that follows my admission drowns me in wave after wave of guilt, confusion, and terror, so much so that I try wriggling under the covers to hide my flushed face, but they both hold me in place.

Dea speaks up first. "We do not want to hurt you, Angel. We just know how much you need to release this tension, especially since you started feeding. Vampires usually feed and have sex together, or at least keep up a healthy diet of both."

"And we also know, as do you, the growing tension between

the three of us. We just thought we could help." Nine sounds actually hurt, his voice a little broken, and I'm beginning to see a real problem in the future if one of us doesn't cave.

Me not sleeping with them, given that this is their normal, hurts them, but them not being committed will hurt me. Goddess, this is such a fucking mess. I don't even care about them being with just me (I can't break the team apart like that), so long as they're committed to the entire team.

Nine looks at me with surprise, choking slightly in shock. "You'd really be into that?"

"Be into what?" Dea's out of the loop, and for once, it's bothering him.

Ha, serves him fucking right!

I shake my head when Nine looks at me expectantly, not wanting to say the words out loud, so he does for me. "She was thinking about a polyamorous relationship between the entire team. Freedom within but no sex outside of."

Dea looks at me with a smile touching the corners of his lips. "We have never considered that before, but it still poses the same issue. What happens if we all fall out?"

With that question, I'm done with the conversation and wriggle out from between them and off the bed, speeding into the shower.

I don't understand. I know duty comes first, and above all else, Earth must be protected from itself, but that doesn't mean they don't get to fucking live. They deserve to live and love. Just like anybody else. It's clear Nine and Dea love each other, but they won't do anything about it. And for what? The fear that something could go wrong? That's utter horseshit. What if nothing goes wrong?

I run that frustration under the hot water, knowing we have to meet with the Royal Vampire Council soon, and watch as the water washes it all away. Here, I can just be. No expectations to be someone specific, no blood making me crazy, no hot as hell Horsemen making me irrational with need I have no business feeling. Just me. And whoever that is, she is standing right here.

The Vampire Royal Council is housed in a giant, modern office building a twenty-minute drive from the motel we're staying in. I'm not sure what I was expecting—maybe something more underground and castle-like—but this isn't it.

The entrance is guarded by at least a dozen guards, all of whom are armed Vampires. I shudder at the thought of needing to make a quick getaway through them.

They'd need an army to stop us, and even then, they'd still likely lose.

It occurrs to me in that moment that I've never really seen any of the team fight. I have no idea how powerful they are. Not really.

Dea makes himself visible, and the guards blink in shock for a moment before some blond-haired woman dressed in a tight skirt suit and clippy heals and with perfectly polished nails walks out. "Death. Famine." She looks to Dea and Nine in turn. "Please, follow me."

They both nod, and I follow.

Nine? What kind of story do we tell them about me?

That you're a newly turned Vampire we rescued and have taken under our wing. No one's gonna try to go through us to get to you.

Are you sure?

Yes.

We walk through the halls, and the deeper we go, the fewer windows and less open space there is, until we end up outside a large set of ornate double doors with gilded silver inset into the intricate pattern of roses.

"The Vampire Royal Council is waiting for you inside." The secretary—I assume she's a secretary, she never introduced herself otherwise—walks away, and I listen as her clippy heals fade into the distance.

"Remember your story, Angel. And just as a warning, these meetings can be tense and boring and last hours."

"Also," Nine adds, "there will be live feeding and normal Vampire oddities ongoing, remember."

That has me stopping in my tracks. "But doesn't the SC outlaw all live feeding? Why would the Vampire Council break the law?"

Both Nine and Dea look at me with raised eyebrows, but it's Nine who answers in his usual fact-giving tone. "Vampires don't like the Supernatural Council and have always flaunted their rule breaking whenever possible."

Dea opens the doors, and I just hope my question hasn't been heard through those doors. But, boy, am I disappointed, because beyond these doors is a room full of plush velvet sofas with various Vampires and hosters lounging around, and every Vampire in the room is looking right at me with a menacing growl. If I wasn't secretly a Horseman of the Apocalypse and didn't have a teleportation crystal in my back pocket, I would have peed myself a little.

They're an intimidating bunch, I'll give them that. But the number of old Vampires and high-ranking officials just feeding on humans in the presence of guests bothers me. It just doesn't seem right. And, no matter how hard I try, I can't completely wipe the disgust off my face, though I wheedle it down to a grimace.

It's the best they're fucking getting, they'll just have to deal with it.

We sit on a sofa at the front, facing the whole room so we can address everyone. Well, so the guys can address everyone; I'm simply observing today.

Nine, any princes here?

If you're thinking about the one mentioned last night, then no. There are a couple, though. The pink-shirted, camp-looking one on the sofa closest is Prince Villané, and the dark, imposing one at the back trying to hide unsuccessfully in the shadows is Prince Phillipe. He's next in line for the throne.

Hmmm. Interesting. You'd think they would have someone with more presence next in line.

Lineage is based on strength.

Oh. So he's the strongest? Interesting.

"Death. Famine. It is good to see you again." An imposing man with a white beard and half-moon glasses approaches our sofa and holds out his hand to shake.

Nine gets up and shakes his hand, but Dea remains seated.

"Who, may I ask, is your friend?" The man gestures to me.

Nine, sitting back down and placing a hand on my knee, says, "This is Sarah. She's a newly turned Vampire we saved from a troubling situation a few months ago and have taken her under our wing since."

"That is saddening to hear, Famine. I apologize for the Council not being able to protect every newly turned Vampire." He falls back into a seat with all the grace of a Vampire.

Nine nods. *That's the king.*

Fuck me, he looks so . . . normal.

"No one expects you to be able to take care of every one of your kind; no Council can do that," Nine says.

Seems Dea's going to sit this one out, which I find

perplexing given he's the most well-spoken of the Horsemen. But I trust they know what they're doing.

"You called a meeting with us, Horsemen. Why?" A lady from the front sitting with Prince Villané stood.

"Nothing ominous. We're just checking in on all the councils. Things have been a little tense recently, and we are just looking to undertake a general assessment of things."

She nods and sits back down, seemingly satisfied with the answer.

"You expect us to believe that?" another Vampire at the back stands and spits out. His fists clench, and he puts one foot in front of the other; clearly, he doesn't like us.

This time, Dea raises a hand with a stoic expression on his face. His hand glows green, like it does when he heals someone, and the Vampire screams in pain as he falls to his knees. His screams pierce the air as every Vampire in the room, including me, flinches. Dea lowers his hand, and the screaming stops. "Yes," he grinds out.

"V-Very well. I apologize." The man sits back down.

Nine stands back up, ready to talk once more. "We understand the animosity between the Vampires and the Supernatural Council has been somewhat increasing of late, and we were wondering if you could explain why?" He sits back down, clearly following their 'you must stand to speak' rule, as though they were a bunch of children in a school classroom.

The king stands once more, stepping forward. "It is true, I'm afraid. They keep restricting our blood supplies, which is causing problems when trying to control the amount of live feeding. The SC have long since overlooked the live feeding, so long as we don't slaughter an entire species or kill anyone important. But since the supplies have been restricted, there are many Vampires choosing to ignore the live feeding restrictions we place on our own kind."

Well, what did the SC expect? The Vampires just to willingly starve?

"Blood supplies have always been up and down over the years since the Supernatural Council was formed. That is nothing new," Nine responds. "So why the problem now?"

Jumping straight to the issue at heart, I see.

They're not that political here. Vampires value openness in the modern world, since it's illegal and frowned upon to live feed without permission from the hoster. Feeding is their entire world, after all. It's created a more open atmosphere than we've ever seen among Vampire kind. The Witches, on the other hand, are an entirely different matter. We'll have to be more tactful with them.

I would have thought the Vampires would have been the problematic ones. But if the only issue is blood, then that's just one problem for an entire race, rather than the potential for multiple problems, like I expected.

"If you could negotiate with the SC for less restricted blood supplies, we could sort this whole mess out without hindrance."

"We'll take that under advisement. Thank you for your openness, Your Majesty."

The king nods and sits, avoiding answering Nine's actual question, I notice.

Dea stands, and everyone in the room ceases all kinds of small conversations that may have been ongoing. "There is the matter of succession. Since Vampires live a long life, we take the succession of the Vampire throne seriously. It is only once in a century you gain a new king, after all."

The king stands, nodding his understanding.

"We understand Prince Phillipe is next in line. Is everything prepared and ready for that?"

The room visibly bristles. Seems Prince Phillipe is not liked among the council. I can see the king trying to avoid answering Dea's question, but one scowl from the Horseman of Death and he caves.

"There are many who do not believe he would make a good king. He is a strong and good leader but not well liked. Not here on the Council, and not among the Vampire population."

"I see," Dea says and sits back down.

Nine stands. "That could pose a problem. If you're already having issues controlling the population through a blood restriction, won't having an unfavorable king make things harder?"

The king nods, his eyes falling to the floor.

Nine sits, clearly not having anything left to say.

Prince Phillipe in the shadows, though, simply smiles. He's also aware of this situation, but his eyes are not fixed on Dea or Nine, they're fixed on me. He steps out of the shadows, and everyone turns to look at him. "I have a question for your friend. Sarah, is it?"

I nod, standing to follow protocol. I purposefully place my hands behind my back to hide their trembling.

"Although we have always worked alongside the Four Horsemen—their power far exceeds our own—your king is the person you answer to. You are loyal to us, not them." Shit. This is going to be a problem, isn't it? "So, why do you sit over there? On their side?"

Their side? So he has a grudge against the Horsemen? Ballsy stance to have.

"They were good to me. I was ill for weeks after my poor treatment at the hands of the person who turned me. I will always be grateful to them."

"Yes, and being indebted to them is something I understand. Yet Famine over there has his hand placed on your knee as though he owns you. Does he own you, Sarah?"

"Own me? I'm sorry, I wasn't aware anyone owned me." Venom laces my voice as I try to calm the rising wave of anger.

Careful. We need to save face here. We can't lose their support. He is the next king. We need him on our side so he'll listen to us, especially if war is coming. And Dea already pissed him off once a few decades ago, please don't make it worse now.

What did Dea do, fuck his Vampire bride or some shit?

Nine doesn't say anything.

I turn to him in surprise, looking at Dea with an accusatory expression. Fucking really?

Yell at him later.

Right. The Vampire prince. "Nobody owns me," I say as I return to Prince Phillipe. "I am a woman of the twenty-second century. I am not a pet, or a tool, or a thing to be used. I recognize my Vampire Royal Council, as they are my own kind, but I am, and will always be, indebted to the Horsemen."

"I see." He steps back into the shadows at that, but he continues to watch any and all interaction between me and Nine the entire time.

"One more thing," Nine stands and says. "We heard a rumor about one of the princes aggravating the SC. Is that true?"

"Yes," the king says, though he doesn't stand this time, since he has his fangs deep in the neck of a human girl on his lap. He pulls his fangs away momentarily to further clarify. "We are currently in the process of dealing with it."

"If you value your blood supplies as much as you say you

do, I would advise you not to piss them off any further. Save face, Your Majesty. You'll need it for the future."

Nine walks away after that, and Dea and I follow, not really knowing what to do other than complete his dramatic exit.

"Well," I say once we get outside, "that was . . . underwhelming."

"Yes, I did say they were a little boring. Sorry, Sweetie."

Dea walks beside me and places an arm around my waist, causing me to flinch. "Sorry," he says as he takes his arm back.

"No, it's okay."

What's going on?

I've never seen Dea use his power like that. It was a little scary. I'm a half Vampire, remember. They are kinda my kind.

No, they're not. You can relate to them, which is probably Fate's point, but we don't have a kind. We're the Horsemen of the Apocalypse. We're our own kind altogether.

Nine leaves me with that little pearl of wisdom, as he so often does, and walks ahead, linking his arm through Dea's as I follow behind them in thoughtful silence.

I wear the same dress as last night to tonight's party, and as we walk up the stairs to the mansion with solid stone pillars and verandas and the whole I-have-more-money-than-sense look, I regret that choice.

What if someone sees me in the same dress? Will they think that's gross?

Seriously, the world is on the brink of war, and that's what you're worried about? Goddess, get it together, I mentally chastise myself.

My internal voice sounds distinctly like Nine's, but I just shake off the worried feeling and continue up the beautifully kept front yard.

Seems you don't need me anymore, if you're mentally chastising yourself in my voice.

I ignore that comment, because I'm not really sure what to say. He's right, it is weird. But, honestly, I don't really want to dwell on it right now. I'm oddly looking forward to the party beyond those doors, but I know we have work to do and that I can't really enjoy it.

When we get home, we'll go out properly. Sheruta has some great party life.

Really? Never really pegged it as the partying kind of place.

We've only taken you to the upper-class kind of areas. There's an entire shopping mall, a nightlife district, a supernatural zoo, and everything. It's really grown over the years.

Fuck me, there's a mall? And you never bothered to take me?

Nine laughs. *Sorry, Sweetie. I will next time. Promise.*

That sounds an awful lot like a date, so I cut off the conversation and head inside, arm linking through Dea's despite him not being visible to others this evening. He used up the last of his visibility for the boring Council meeting. Seems a little unfair on him if I'm being honest, missing the good stuff and remaining visible for the boring shit. I kinda feel bad for the guy.

"I'm going to stay with you tonight, Angel. So you and Nine can split up like yesterday."

"Okay."

There are three floors to this monstrous party: two dancefloors with different types of music, a relaxation area with minimal music, and a Vampire den. I stay away from the latter. Not repeating yesterday. One risky feeding session is enough for me. Well, figuratively speaking, of course.

There's also a pool party out back with the best swimming pool I've ever seen. It has lots of sections interconnecting with mini-waterfall style latches. It's actually quite pretty, and someone has clearly put a lot of time and effort into designing it.

"So," Dea starts, "where would you like to go first?" Nine already wandered off somewhere on the second floor, and I'm left with an invisible Dea, both of us trying to work our way around the first-floor dancefloor.

"Dancing, I guess. Best place to meet people, right?"

"That it is, Angel."

I walk us to the main dancefloor in what looks like a half-ballroom, half-lounge, with lots of gold and red drapes dangling around, making the whole place seem fancier than the actual party, which is closer to a frat house than an actual ball.

Dea dances behind me, being careful not to touch me, as I dance in the center with a few women in front of me. We've formed a sort of semi-circle and are all just having the normal kind of fun. None are Vampires, and I hope I don't come across as one in this moment, as I really don't want any hosters hanging around me. Just a nice, normal evening. I'm not quite as pale as a normal Vampire, nor am I as graceful on my feet, so unless my fangs are out, I probably just look like a pale-ish human (or supernatural, if you can distinguish us from humans).

"You know," Dea says from behind me, "this is not information gathering."

I resist the urge to respond, since that will look weird, but seriously want to give him a good solid right hook. Can I not just have a half hour to myself? Since coming to New Orleans, I've fed from a human to gain information, been kissed by a random Vampire I don't know, sat in the world's most dangerous room, had my loyalties questioned, had to keep up a lie about who I am, and am now fishing for information about a Vampire prince I couldn't care less about. Just thirty minutes really doesn't seem that much to ask for.

But fuck it, I can't be asked to deal with Dea grumbling behind me all night. If I didn't know any better, I would say he's channeling his inner-Arrie. Grumpy as shit. So I move along to find a few Vampires to chat to.

I try dancing toward lots of Vampires, but none of them give me the time of day, and it's frustrating. "They seem a little more ageist than the guy last night."

"Welcome to normal Vampires, Angel."

I sigh, deciding to find Nine and reconvene for a different strategy. We just have to try to find this Vampire prince.

"Do you know what Vampire prince we're looking for?"

"No. I just knew the two from yesterday would not have done something so stupid."

"Well then, let's hope this one's the only one that's here."

"Hmmm. Let's." Dea grabs my wrist but leaves it by my side so as not to look weird, and walks me up the stairs toward where Nine headed earlier. "Let's go and find Nine."

"That's what I was doing," I grumble.

"What has you all grumpy this evening?"

"Ugh." I don't bother answering him. I'm simply frustrated—with everything. With my growing feelings for a group of people who will never feel the same way back, with the brewing war caused by stupid people doing stupid shit, and with not being able to actually use all of my supposedly perfect powers.

Everything about my current situation is pissing me off, and, as much as I'm trying to not let it show, it seems to be affecting my ability to do my job.

Searching through crowds of people on the second floor, scouring various dancefloors, seating areas, and crowds of people on the edges of each room, we eventually find Nine with his arms around two Vampires with bouncy blond hair, wearing next to nothing as they're clad in bikinis way too small for them. He laughs and smiles at their every flash of fang.

Dea stops in his tracks for half a second before continuing toward him, which is the only indication I get that it bothers him. He smiles as he approaches, though, and Nine catches his eye briefly as something unusual passes between them.

"Hey!" I say in a way too cheery smile as I walk on up. "Fancy seeing you here . . ."

"Sarah, I didn't know you'd be here tonight." He smiles as he releases one of the blondes on his arm to grab my hand and pull me in, tightening me around his waist in a warm hug. "It's so good to see you."

What are you doing up here? Dea says you're having problems?

Ugh. Vampires are avoiding me like the plague. Like, seriously, they're ageist as fuck in here.

I see. Let's tag team then.

I nod, pulling away from him and sidling backward to grab each blonde by the arm, feigning being human (hopefully) by whooshing my hair back and exposing my neck.

Bingo. They each wrap an arm around my waist, still including Nine in our little circle, and zone in on my neck.

"You know 'im?" one of them asks as she nods to Nine.

"Yeah, we go way back!" I give her a raised eyebrow,

hoping to convey exactly how close we are, and she gives me a questioning look.

"Really? That's so cute!" She flashes a fang at me, and it takes everything in me not to return the threat. I could blow her to the Pacific Ocean if I really wanted to.

Nine seems to sense what's going on, even as I try hard to block any active thoughts from leaking, and steps out of the blonde's arms and guides me away from them.

What was that?

I don't answer, but Dea gives me a sad look of understanding and also remains silent. And in that moment, I'm certain: Dea's in love with Nine.

I try hard to keep that thought to myself, but it seems to come out of my mind loud and clear, because Nine stops in his tracks and throws me an angry look.

Sorry. Didn't mean that to be so loud.

It's fine, he snaps.

He schools his features as we arrive at the nearest dancefloor, hoping to once again find this stupid, elusive prince.

Dea joins us, and although we all have smiles and dance with a bunch of humans and Vampires, and even a few Shifters, we can all feel the tension. None of us looks each other in the eye, and we all stay well away from touching each other.

"You looking for Prince?" a foreign-accented voice sounds from behind me.

I turn around to a pair of golden eyes (a Shifter) resting a few feet above my eye level. He's a big guy, probably some kind of wolf or bear Shifter, with black-and-white-peppered hair, a graying beard, and a fallen expression.

"What of it?" I'm done with pleasantries for this evening.

I just want to grab the nearest cab and head to the Witches's Coven so we can be one step closer to returning to *Sheruta*.

"Follow." He turns and walks off the dancefloor.

I eye both Nine and Dea, who shrug and nod. Guess we're following Mr. Weirdo. We follow him down the stairs, across the first floor, and out the front door. The grand front yard looms in front of us, having since been lit up by various fairy lights dotted around.

"Where are we going?" I ask Mr. Weirdo.

"To Prince."

Okaaay. He could also be leading us into a trap. And, honestly, that seems more likely.

Stay alert. It's a trap. But he doesn't know who's laying it. He's just a hired man.

Right.

Dea says to use your air magic and your Vampire strength and speed in any kind of fight, but try to avoid any armed opponents; we'll take care of them.

And how exactly do you plan on doing that?

Dea has his sword on him, and I have my pistols.

Where the fuck are you hiding them? And why am I not armed?!

Quit complaining. Pay attention.

He sounds stressed, and I get the feeling it isn't because of the current situation.

Nine . . . I—

Not now. Later.

Okay.

We continue to follow Mr. Weirdo around the corner of an otherwise silent part of the front yard that's hidden from view. Only a Vampire would be able to see here (which could pose a problem for us).

We're just on the other side of the mansion when I hear footsteps. "Stay where you are, Horseman!"

We all stop, but Dea and Nine don't look worried. I gather a ball of air in each palm, readying for a fight.

"What do you want?" Nine asks in the emotionless tone he uses when trying to hide how he really feels. He's nervous, and that doesn't bode well.

"Nothing but your heads."

Dea yells at us both, "Now!"

We leap into action, and I suddenly realize that Nine can also see in the dark because he can see through the minds of the other Vampires. Dea, on the other hand, can't, so I stay near him, just in case. He's invisible, so no one even knows he's here, but still.

There're eight Vampires in front of us, all carrying some kind of weapon, and a few lurking behind bushes surrounding us.

You take those, I'll take these.

You sure?

Just do it.

Okay.

I leave Nine to it and leap into action toward the nearest bush. It's a small, low-to-the-ground thing with a few thorny roses sticking out, and the guy crouching behind it is trying not to be seen, but his bright blue hair gives him away. I use my air magic to send a gust his way, knocking him to the ground.

He flies to the floor, his head smacking against the ground—not hard enough to knock him out, since it's grassy, but enough to make him a little dizzy as he stumbles to his feet.

"Who the fuck are you?"

"No one." I send another gust of air, which this time, sends him to the concrete, and watch as his head splatters on the ground, knocking him unconscious (or killing him, but I'm trying not to think about that).

I hear a few screams from the direction of the other side of the fight, and I see Dea backing Nine up as he sends three Vampires to the ground in wailing agony.

So that move doesn't kill them, it just incapacitates them.

I move along, using the same method on a further three hiding Vampires, sending each one flying to the concrete, where they hit their heads hard enough to knock them unconscious. Or kill them.

I crouch on the grass, trying to discretely look around for other Vampires, but seem satisfied there are none left. Nine and Dea still have two opponents left, so I run toward them.

"Angel, look out!"

A loud thump hits my head from behind, and I stumble to the ground. Dea and Nine react almost instantly, but they're pulled back by their own opponents, who have them pinned to the wall in seconds as they use the distraction to their advantage.

I can feel blood dripping down the side of my face, and my vision is a little hazy, but I manage to make it to my feet, only swaying slightly.

Have. To. Save. Them.

Thoughts are barely coherent at this point, and I fear we might be about to lose to a small group of Vampires all because I missed someone.

For fuck's sake.

But just as a hand wraps around my throat, a loud gunshot goes off, and the hand loosens enough for me to stumble out of its grasp.

"Shit. Fuck. Shit," I mumble to myself.

Someone moves from the shadows beyond with a gun in hand, and I half run, half stumble toward Nine and Dea to try to help them escape so we can run.

But the gun sends off another two rounds, and the Vampires holding them to the wall collapse to the ground.

The shooter, however, runs forward, and the shock of blond hair and blue eyes has my memory doing twists and somersaults, but my mind is too foggy right now. I can't pinpoint the memory enough to relive it.

"Little hunter? You . . . you're a-a-alive?"

Nine and Dea stand beside me, Dea holding me up.

"Famine. And is that you, Death? But, hunter, what are you doing here? And how are you alive?"

I realize, after a moment of confusion, that he's referring to me. "You . . . know me?"

He laughs. "Of course I know you. I gave you a heads-up about being on the SC's hit list nine months ago. But . . . you died. They had a funeral and everything."

The SC killed me? I was . . . assassinated?

"But you were with the Horsemen all along?" He looks genuinely perplexed.

"Thank you for saving us, Prince Lucien. It truly has been a help," Dea says.

"Well, I could hardly let my own kind kill two of the Four Horsemen, could I?"

It's Nine's turn to laugh this time, and he puts an arm around my shoulders as he does so. "Sweetie, this is Prince Lucien. And I get the feeling he's the prince we've been looking for."

"Indeed I am."

"And Prince Lucien, this is Sarah. A recently turned

Vampire we saved from a difficult situation."

"V-V-Vampire? So you're a hybrid?"

"You know what I was?"

He nods, not really sure of himself. "An Angel-descended Witch, yes. It was I who accidently let it slip to the SC."

Dea looks at Nine quickly, grabs us both, and speeds us out of there faster than any Vampire could manage to keep up with.

Chapter Twenty-Four

Dea holds me and Nine on either foot, holding us in place with an arm around our waists, and races us back to our motel faster than I think possible. But even as the world speeds by us, I can feel the anger boiling beneath.

What was he thinking? That was my chance at answers!

As the motel comes into view, Dea puts us down in front of our door, letting us catch our breaths, and in my case, curb the nausea currently threatening to bring up what little I've eaten in the last few days.

Once inside and the door firmly shut behind us, Nine steps back, giving me a look of concern as I face Dea with a look of what I hope is scathing fury.

"What. The. Fuck. Was. That?"

Dea looks at me and steps forward, reaching his hand out to touch me, but I bat it away with some force, causing it to swing and slap his side.

"The more we talked with Prince Lucien, the more issues we were creating."

"That . . ." I take a deep breath, trying not to explode every ounce of frustration I've gathered over the last forty-eight hours toward Dea. But, ultimately, I fail. I push him so hard he flies across the room and lands inside the exterior wall.

He winces as he steps out, stretching his limbs.

"That was my chance at fucking answers, Dea! Why would you do that? You absolute, motherfucking piece of shit!"

My fangs have descended in my rage, and I'm pretty sure my eyes are now bloodshot red as I can feel them pulsing.

"Sweetie, maybe you shou—"

I hold up a hand to Nine, really not wanting to yell at him, and take my eyes off of the Horseman of Death. "I need answers. He is the only person I have met over the last few weeks who knew me before I was this . . . thing!" I gesture to myself.

"Angel, I—"

"Don't even think of calling me that." I turn away and pace the room, trying to vent some of my anger. "I can't even look at you right now. You took away the only chance I've ever had of getting answers." Facing the wall so I don't have to look at either of them, I whisper, "How could you?" The tears finally fall, and I let them, hoping they'll stress the seriousness of Dea's actions.

"If I had let that conversation continue, our mission to keep your true identity hidden until we are one hundred percent sure of what Horseman you are and who broke your seal would have been compromised in an instant."

"I don't have an identity to keep secret."

I storm out of the motel's door, slam it shut behind me, and stride down the path of rooms, aiming to just get anywhere away from them.

Don't go too far. It's not safe now.

Goddammit, Nine's right. So instead of finding the nearest bar and getting flat-out blind-drunk, I settle on punching a hole through the nearest vending machine and grabbing as much caffeine and sugar as possible. At least this way I won't be as tired by the time I'm finished. And if the manager has an issue with that, Dea can fucking pay for it.

I sit on a wall in the parking lot, downing cans of liquid energy and packets of sugar, causing my body to need to expel the overdose. I could Vamp-speed around the parking lot, but I think it might attract too much attention, so I settle on pacing. Something that's becoming a bit of a habit.

How could he? I need answers, and part of me wants to run right back to that party, find Lucien, and ask him. But instead, I'm walking in a dingy parking lot following the orders of a fucking a-hole!

I've never actually been angry at any of the team before (other than my frustration at Arrie, but that doesn't count), and it doesn't feel good. We shouldn't be at odds with each other. But why did he do it?

To protect me? I don't need protecting.

To protect Earth? Maybe everyone should do a better job of getting along, rather than expecting us to clean up their petty messes.

You're right. They should. But it is our job, nonetheless, and whether they deserve our help isn't the point. Earth is ours to protect. Even if that isn't what Fate intended, that's what it's become.

But what's the point? I don't want to live forever, protecting Earth, if I can't even live. I want my memories back. I want to know who I am.

By this point, I've stopped pacing and sink to the ground

against the wall. The tears won't stop flowing, and I can feel the start of a breakdown oncoming, so I wrap my arms around myself and focus on breathing.

In, out.

In, out.

I don't want to breakdown like I did in the forest the other day and cause the team more problems.

Ugh. Why do I even care at this point?

Because you're an amazing person.

No, I'm not. I'm a stupid little nobody who can't even use the powers granted to her by Fate, for fuck's sake. I don't even have a name!

Then pick one.

Huh?

We picked our names afresh, and they all correspond to our Horseman type. So, pick one for yourself.

I don't want to. I want my actual name.

Nine doesn't respond, so I let him be.

I don't want a new name or a new life (though I did get one). Maybe one day I'll like that, but I would like to know who I was before moving on and becoming someone else. I want to close the door on my old life first. What if I left someone behind? What if I caused the war?

I lay on the concrete path for a while, staring up at the pollution-filled night sky, trying to name as many constellations as I can. I manage five before giving up and walking to the motel for some sleep. Besides, we still have Witches to see; any excuse to get out of this damn city. I can always come back and ask Prince Lucien questions later. But I'm still mad as fuck.

I take my time walking back and manage a few laps around the block first, hoping that isn't too far for Nine's telepathy to reach. If it is, they don't bother coming to find me, which I assume they would if Nine can't reach me. The door to the motel is open slightly when I arrive, I assume to let me in since I didn't take a room key, and I lock it behind me as I enter.

The bedroom is empty, but I hear the shower running and murmurs coming from the bathroom. They're showering together?

Sitting on the edge of the bed, I place my head in my hands. They're really having sex while I'm having an internal crisis? But I can't be angry—I've drowned all of my anger in candy and caffeine—so I kick back and lay on the bed, assuming they'll likely be respectful since Nine will know I'm here.

You know, part of me doesn't want to be. I can hear the smirk in his voice. *But since Dea feels guilty and doesn't want to cause you more mental anguish, yes, we'll be respectful, as you so politely put it.*

Then be respectful to him, too, and stop talking to me while you're fucking your boyfriend.

He's not my boyfriend.

I don't answer that. I try to keep my mind on something else so as not to accidentally respond, and I succeed when I start doing some yoga on the dirty floor. Not my first choice of places to relax, but it'll have to do.

I manage multiple positions and flowing changes with an empty mind before curiosity gets the better of me, and, damn it, I have to actually resist not walking into the bathroom.

What is wrong with me? When did I become such a pervert?

When you realized you wanted to be where Dea is now. Nine sends me a mental image of Dea bent over, hands splayed against the bathroom tiles as the shower pours down his back.

I try to shake the image free, but Nine keeps it there.

Seriously, Nine, stop it.

That didn't sound all that convincing.

Ugh. You're impossible. What do you want?

Well, I know you're attracted to both of us, as you frequently refer to us as being 'hot as hell,' so I want you to indulge. To live. And I will continue trying to push past that barrier of yours until I succeed. Or until you stop finding us attractive.

Well, that last one is not likely to happen within the next couple of centuries, so I refocus on my yoga routine and ignore the blazing heat threatening to engulf me.

But, as I continue blocking him out, Nine ups game. He does something I didn't know he could do: show me what he's seeing. Not just a still image, but like a personal, live movie. And honestly, I would complain, but it's the coolest power I've ever seen.

It's like I can see everything from Nine's point of view, including their new position, with Dea on his knees sucking Nine's cock.

Am I going to be privy to all of your sex life?

Just the stuff you'll enjoy.

The personal movie is silent, but my Vampire hearing is pretty good—I was just trying not to use it until now.

"Is she watching?" Dea asks.

He knows? Well, that makes me feel a little better than last time, at least.

"Yes," Nine says on a moan. "She's listening, too."

"Really?"

"Vamp hearing."

"Hmmm. Angel, I am sorry for earlier. Let me make it up to you."

With my own personal porno? That's ~~fun~~ . . . extreme.

Extreme was not the word your mind came up with first.

Shut up and enjoy the bloody blowjob Dea is so expertly giving you. I would not watch and continue to do my yoga routine to block you out, but that doesn't seem to be an option you're letting me choose.

This one was Dea's idea, actually.

Really?

"Yes," Dea says. "I want to make it up to you. And technically, you are not having sex with either of us."

Well, that's just . . . cheating. Works. That works is what it that does. Does it make things weird? Probably. But it means I'm not connecting to them, right? That I won't fall into a relationship with two people who have no interest in being in one? But still, I can indulge slightly. I mentally chastise them for not allowing themselves to love because they're afraid, but I'm doing the same thing.

I lay on the bed, having forgone my attempts at yoga, and focus on watching my own personal pornographic movie, trying to forget about the weirdness of what I'm actually doing.

Maybe I'm not ready for casual sex, but that doesn't mean I can't join in, right? I can't mentally send anything to Dea, but Nine can.

What are you planning, Sweetie?

You'll see.

I conjure up the first image, the memory of my kiss with Connie, thinking to start it off light.

Send what you're seeing to Dea.

I hope to convey everything I'm feeling in the moment, but it's hard to do while watching them, so I try a different tactic and send them the memory of the last time I watched them.

"Fuck, Angel. That is how you saw us?"

Dea picks up his pace slightly, and I hear Nine cave under his skills, his breathing becoming heavier. "Dea, fuck me."

Dea releases Nine's cock and spins him around, bending him over into the same position he was in not ten minutes ago.

I don't have anything else to send them, but the fact that my nipples have pebbled and my clit is throbbing for any kind of attention makes it very hard not to touch myself.

Do it.

You'd be into that? Watching me?

You can't really judge about watching people, Sweetie.

He has a point. A really annoying but good point. But I don't want to masturbate to their ridiculously hot fucking, as that feels too much like connecting, but I do get a better idea.

Instead, I send them the memory of my alone time in the bath, hoping it'll be a good contributor.

And it works! Dea speeds up his pace as Nine's fingers try clenching onto a solid surface but slip under the wet tiles.

Nine yells in pleasure, throwing his aim of being respectful out the window. *One of these days, Sweetie, you'll be in here with us. And it'll be because you begged to join in.*

In your dreams.

"Angel," Dea moans as he thrusts harder into Nine, his fingers digging into Nine's hips hard enough to leave bruises.

Send us that last memory again.

I do as asked, lapping up the attention and the fact that they find me as hot as I find them. My core's burning by this point, and I need some kind of release, so I shove all my worries to the back of my mind and slide my hand lower to my clit, hoping that Nine can see and equally hoping he can't.

I hear Nine and Dea's releases as I see them, Dea's grip

on Nine's hips growing hard enough to bite into his skin.

Moving my hand faster, I chase my own release as Nine shuts down the movie and I'm left with nothing but the sweet memory. I never thought in a million years I would find watching two men as hot I do, but I'm past the point of caring as my orgasm crashes over me, and I have to stifle my own cries by biting my lip.

"Damn, Angel," Dea says from the doorway. "I wanted to be the one to make you look like that."

Technically, they are the ones to make me look like this, if you think about it, but I don't give him the satisfaction of saying that thought out loud. By the time I look up at the pair of them walking out of the bathroom in towels, a confident smirk has settled across Dea's face, and Nine just winks at me.

The fucker betrayed me.

I'm not mad, I'm far too high in post-orgasmic bliss for that. Instead, I roll over and get under the duvet, not even bothering to change into my pajamas, and fall asleep the moment my head hits the pillow.

CHAPTER TWENTY-FIVE

The next morning, I wake in a surprisingly good mood (well, it's not all that surprising, but it's welcome) and pack for South Africa. I didn't bring much with me, so I just shove all my things into my backpack and wait for the guys to finish.

"For a couple of guys, you take ages to pack."

"I have weapons to pack," Dea says as he carefully places a variety of guns, swords, and daggers into a suitcase specially designed for weapons. "And you did not pack that much."

I shrug. "Figured we could get anything we needed on the go. It's only recon." I snack on a giant fluffy pretzel Nine brought back from his breakfast trip a half hour ago, and it's one of the most delicious desserts I've ever eaten. The sugar, the cinnamon . . . Fuck me, it's honestly making my stomach grumble.

"True for most things," he says. "But our weapons are ours, and we hate losing them. Nine spends a while designing them for us."

I look to Nine with raised eyebrows. "You design

weapons?"

"I design a lot of things, mostly magical things."

I can picture him in a lab somewhere in one of those white lab coats, designing all kinds of fun and weird shit with all kinds of magic they've picked up on over the years. "I'll make you some daggers soon."

He's a little preoccupied trying to fold his clothes in that little precise way of his to really hold a conversation, so I let him be and wait patiently for them both to be done.

"Call us a taxi if you are bored," Dea suggests.

"I'm not bored, just shocked I was packed and ready to go before you guys."

Dea rolls his eyes and looks at the phone on his nightstand and then at me, as if he's giving me an order. Well, I guess he kinda is.

Sighing, I grab it and dial the local cab number we've been using since arriving in the city. And in thirty minutes, we're off to the airport once again, heading to South Africa.

Fourteen hours on a flight with Nine and Dea is torture. If they aren't purposefully pissing me off, they're snoring, invading my personal space, or generally being a couple of fuckwits. Getting off that plane and into open space cannot come soon enough, and when it does, I bound down the hallways of the airport, listening to Nine's and Dea's laughter in the distance as they watch me twirl my arms around just because I can and shout at the top of my lungs because I no longer have to be considerate to all of the people stuck in a small enclosed space hundreds of miles in the air with me.

I do not like flying, it turns out, but apparently no one does. It's a universally accepted hatred for everyone, unless you can afford your own jet, which sounds like it would come in real handy for the team. I make a mental note to bring it up with them later.

Grabbing the guys' bags from security, I wonder how Dea gets all those weapons through airport security.

We have a free legal pass given to us by the SC.

So they do like you?

Like is a bit strong. They tolerate us.

We manage to get out of the airport without too much hassle and hail a cab from the front entrance. "So," I ask as I get in the back with Nine, "where are we going?"

"To Howick Falls, please," Nine says to the driver.

Dea sits between us, completely invisible to the driver, and remains silent.

Dea says to hide your Vampire nature here. Be a Witch. One of the benefits of having both types of powers is that you can fit in with both communities, but Witches famously hate Vampires.

What should I expect of this place? Of the Witches?

They're . . . unusual but generally kind and humbling to most. Unfortunately, we're not most. They can be a bit hostile toward us. We're a little worried they'll know what you are straight away, since some of their clan are seers.

Seers?

People who can look into the future and heavily examine their surroundings. They often experience time in a less linear way. They also always know who we are, even when disguised.

Oh, shit. What if they do suspect?

Hopefully, they'll keep quiet.

I don't answer him after that, thinking that hopes are not something to base a plan around.

It takes hours to get to our destination, and the stifling silence all three of us have fallen into is suffocating. I can't stop thinking about last night, and not in a good way.

Are things weird now? They don't seem weird, but maybe everyone's putting on a brave face?

Goddess, they totally watched me come from the bathroom doorway; that is so beyond my nice, pretty line in the sand.

You ever make a massive mistake you can't take back, and then are left to steam in a pool of regret for days until you finally manage to mentally calm down? Well, this is like that, but I'll never calm down from this—and I'm immortal, so that's a long regret.

Okay, yes, they're both hot and insanely attractive, and I like them both. I'm not ashamed to admit that. But honestly, it's more than that. Without them both there to help over the last few weeks, I wouldn't be okay right now. Between Dea's guidance and Nine's assistance in almost everything, I'm slowly becoming the Horseman of Magic, a member of the team that maybe one day I'll consider family. And last night has put a giant wrench in that.

Dea has his head back and his eyes closed, so I assume he's asleep, but Nine has his head in his hands and his thinking expression on; that doesn't seem promising.

Nine's . . . sweet and caring and flirty in a way that's just fun. He's never made me feel awkward or strange (maybe a little embarrassed from time to time, but since he can read my mind, he knows exactly when it's too much). I love the way his face scrunches in concentration when he's figuring out some kind of puzzle, and the way he's nearly always touching Dea when they're in the same room together. Even now, Dea's hand is on Nine's leg. They try to hide it, but I know they entwine their legs under the dinner table, take every opportunity to sit next to each other, and probably spend more nights together than apart. Nine's a mind-reader (literally), so he must know how Dea really feels, and yet he's always considerate and has never backed away because of it.

And the fact that I can list all that after only a few weeks with these guys scares the shit out of me. How in the world will I manage centuries without falling . . . ? I don't want to say the words, not where Nine can hear them.

Fuck.

Last night was such a mistake. What was I thinking?

Both of you, shut the fuck up! You're giving me a headache. He audibly groans from his seat as he rubs his temples, and both Dea and I lift our heads to look at him. *You're both thinking too loudly. If I knew last night would cause you both so much fucking anguish, I would never have followed through.*

Sorry.

Hearing Nine shout with a frown on his perfect face puts me in my place rather quickly. It's such a surprise I sit up straighter in my seat and pull out the plasmascreen I used to read on the flight and delve into a book so quickly, I hope no more thoughts leak from my mind. But just before opening the book and settling down, I ask myself one last question.

Why is Dea so worried?

CHAPTER TWENTY-SIX

When we arrive at what looks like the end of a well-worn path just before a field, I get out, cross the field in an instant of Vampire speed, and look out over the clifftop. The view takes my breath away; for hundreds of miles, all you can see is the expanse of country as the waterfall rushes below, thrumming against my ears in a way that blocks out my worries. Greens and browns paint the scenery before me in a wash of color you'd never find in the city, and I find myself staring at the expanse of nature in a trance of awe and admiration. The Witches have chosen a beautiful location for their coven.

I can really do some good yoga here.

I pivot back around, realize I've probably taken way too long staring at the world, and find Nine and Dea gazing at me with gentle smiles.

"Beautiful, is it not?" Dea steps forward and grabs my hand. "Let me show you the rest of what the Witches call home."

Nine looks at us with a curious expression and grabs my

other hand, dragging us away from the cliff's edge and toward a path I didn't notice earlier that must lead to the bottom of the valley below, next to the waterfall's base.

Dea carries most of the bags, which I think is stupid given that I'm stronger than them both, but I let him have his chivalrous moment; I'll smash that stupid chivalry later, but right now, I'm still a little awed by my surroundings.

Sure, *Sheruta* is amazing, and this still has nothing on the team's home, but that doesn't take away from the beauty currently surrounding me. It's all just so . . . peaceful.

It's because you're a Witch. Eventually, you'll be able to use earth magic, and being in places like this helps earth Witches feel more grounded.

Curious, I try swaying some trees and shrubs without using my air magic, but they either remain stationary or flutter in a fake breeze I accidentally let slip. I keep trying as we descend the narrow path, but by the time we've gotten to the bottom, I'm well and truly frustrated. Again.

"Looks like I'm an air Witch for the time being."

"Indeed," Dea says. "And as much I hate forcing people to hide who they are, you are going to have to not let your Vampire magic slip while here. That would really put a wrench in our plans of trying to talk to them."

I sigh, knowing he's right but hating the idea of struggling through the next few days. They should have sent the others here, for fuck's sake.

"You'll be useful when trying to connect with them. They've always been difficult to work with, trying to stay out of the world's issues as much as possible."

"When they finally find out what you really are," Dea adds, "it will be easier to deal with them. They will finally have a Horseman they can relate to. Even with your Horseman magic, you were once a Witch."

"That would be great, if I could remember being one."

They both still hold my hands, and Nine begins stroking his thumb across my fingers. "It'll come to you in time."

"I'm not sure that's what I want anymore."

They both stop walking, and Dea puts the bags down and turns toward me. "Why not?"

I put my head to the ground and yank my hands out of their grip. "I don't wanna talk about it." I pick up the bags in one hand and descend the last few hundred meters to the base of the waterfall.

In truth, the more I learn about who I was, the more horrified I become. And, honestly, what's the point? No one cares enough to let me find out anyway.

I wait for them at the bottom, hoping they'll just meet me there and go on pretending like I'm not mentally falling apart.

No luck.

Dea steps up next to my perch on a rock and places a hand on my shoulder. "Talk to us, Angel."

"No."

Nine stands below us with a grimace. "She doesn't want to talk to us because she thinks we don't care about her finding answers. So, she's trying to block out caring about it, too, thinking that's what's best for the team."

Dea blows out a frustrated breath.

I'm being difficult, I know that, but I don't care. I could have gotten answers from Prince Lucien, but that isn't important enough to them to stop and consider how we could have gotten them without causing too much damage to my cover.

Dea grabs the top of my arm with a growl and yanks me to my feet, forcing me to face him. "For someone so good at reading the inner workings of this team, you are incredibly stupid." He takes a deep breath, as though he's trying hard not to explode in anger at me, and I recoil slightly from his tightening touch. "We do care. Not only because we care about you, but because without you knowing everything about yourself and becoming the Horseman you are meant to be, we cannot fix this war."

I don't know what to say to that, so I remove myself from his grasp and turn around to jump off my rocky perch.

"Arghh! You are the most infuriating person on this fucking planet, Angel." Dea grabs the back of my t-shirt, pulls me toward him, and throws me into the lake below.

The waterfall thrashes me around, battering my limbs in a tangle of mush, but a few powerful kicks have me breaking the surface, gasping for air as I try hard to stay afloat in the tumbling current.

Dea's in the water in front of me, a stony expression on his perfect face. "Sorry." He helps me swim to the edge and pulls me out.

"Now that you've had your tantrum, can I go back to sulking, so we can meet the Witches?"

He sighs in exasperation and storms off.

"Come on, Sweetie," Nine says and follows Dea along a treacherous rocky path toward the waterfall.

"Where are we . . . ?"

Dea falls behind the corner's edge of the waterfall and disappears beyond.

Nine smiles at my inner shock. "They really do have a beautiful home here. You'll like it." He grabs one of the bags, so I can better balance with only one in each hand, and jumps off the last rock to a little ledge just beside the thrumming water.

He probably won't hear me if I speak, so I don't bother,

but I can hear him just fine given my Vamp hearing; I just have to focus on separating the sounds.

"That's kinda how Connie's hearing works. Or how she controls it, rather. Otherwise, it gets a bit much and gives her a headache. So she zones in on things and blocks out the rest."

At the sound of Connie's name, a pang of longing throbs through me. I really hope we get back in time for our sleepover in a few days. We have so much to catch up on.

I love your feelings for Con. I know you won't talk about it, especially not right now when you're still mad at us, but I just wanted to say that you two are great together.

I can feel my face blush hard, and I have a hard time forming any kind of sentence, so I settle on not saying anything, verbally or mentally.

When we work our way behind the waterfall and into a massive cavern, we meet Dea, who gives me a pained look but smiles nonetheless. He really is trying, bless him.

He's mostly hurt you don't trust us, but he's also a little annoyed last night didn't make up for it.

I blush again, but this time I have an answer.

I'm not some sex-starved idiot like you find in books. I'm not going to get laid and then everything be okay again.

I know that. So does he. But he was hoping, that's all.

Why are you telling me this?

Because he asked me to.

Wow. You're like a telepathic intermediary. That must fucking suck.

A little. But I'd do anything for the team. Even act the mediator for petty tantrums.

My tantrum is not petty.

No. But his is.

I laugh at that, and Dea turns around to face us in a scowl, obviously aware of what we were talking about. "Don't worry, Death," I say, annunciating his title, "all in good fun."

"If you are going to sulk, stop having fun about it."

I can't really argue with that logic, but his grumpy, childlike face is really funny. I didn't realize the Horseman of Death could throw tantrums.

He's good at it, too. Beaten only by Arrie.

Ugh. The thought of dealing with an Arrie-Dea tantrum has me recoiling in emotional horror.

It's not pretty.

We're standing in the cavern—not really anything special—when I hear the sound of thumping feet in the background.

"Heads up," I say, catching Dea and Nine off guard.

They each grab a weapon out of their bags.

I form balls of air in each palm, ready for anything.

"Death, Famine," a male voice echoes around the cavern. "State your business."

It's Dea who does the talking this time, and I notice he doesn't drop his sword. "We are checking in on all the larger magical communities for an in-person update. We request to speak to the full Coven. We would have called ahead, but staying in touch with your kind has proven difficult."

"For good reason." The owner of the deep male voice steps out from the shadows I didn't bother looking in earlier, and I recoil.

He has on satin and leather pants but is otherwise topless, and patterned in the marks of a whip all over his body are scars inches thick. Even across his face. "I'm afraid you may have to wait a while; the full Coven is not present at the moment."

"Then, if it is okay, we will wait." Dea drops his sword

and picks up the weapons bag. "If you would prefer, we can wait in a hotel somewhere nearby."

"That won't be necessary. Follow me." He disappears back into the shadows, but this time I focus enough to notice a tunnel.

Dea and Nine look at me, and I nod, letting them know it's all right to follow. Neither of them can see in the dark, it seems.

Dea can if he's not using his powers to be visible.

Being visible is a real vice for him, and I hate it. Maybe we can find a way to use my Witch magic to create some kind of charm.

We follow the man, me taking the lead as I use my Vampire sight to see where he goes. I hope that won't make them suspicious of me and they don't think too hard about it.

Walking down dark cave tunnels, I wonder where we're heading, but as we get deeper into the cave, it becomes more and more habitable as signs of life start forming, from moss and plants to glowing mushrooms and fairylights lighting the way.

A giant light blinds me from up ahead, and I have to hold back my gasp of surprise as the set of tunnels we've spent the past half-hour walking down opens into a large cavern with a skylight pouring daylight down onto one of the best sights I've ever seen: a hidden world.

Trees, houses, small pockets of buildings, ponds and fountains are all mapped with semi-natural pathways crisscrossing the entire cavern. Lots of doors line the edges, and I bet they probably lead to more caverns like this one.

They use their elemental magic together as one whole unit to create homes like this. They've been doing it for centuries to stay hidden from the human world.

They use their elemental magic to create this? That is. . . incredible.

Chapter Twenty-Seven

We're staying in an elaborate hut—which I know sounds insulting, but it's actually rather charming. It's a small two-bed apartment-like thing that sprouts straight out of the ground and looks like it's been carved directly into the cave itself. Knowing this whole place is created using elemental Witch magic, I assume this is all via using earth magic. And I'll be damned if I'm not jealous right now.

I can do this? Well, I can do this when I can access my earth magic.

This is so fucking cool! Think of all the houses I can make when—

"I know this is like a Witch's wet dream, but we really need to make a plan about how to handle the Coven." Nine sits with his feet on the coffee table, lounging on the couch that looks like some kind of moss-covered log in the shape of a couch. He has a smirk on that pretty face of his, and I have the distinct urge to wipe it right off.

I sit on the chair handily placed in front of the couch and

lean my head on my hands, half-sulking, half-interested in their plan. "Why do we even need a plan? You just walked rightinto the Vampire Royal Council?"

"This is not the Vampire Royal Council." Dea paces the small lounge, occasionally bumping into corners of furniture but refraining from the usual cursing I would be doing if I stubbed my toe that hard.

"Okay . . ." Color me curious. "What kind of plan do you have in mind?"

"Well, for starters, we can't reveal your true nature," Nine says. "That would be devastating. The only thing they would think is that you're a hybrid, and they usually execute any they come across."

I laugh lightly, but Nine's face deadpanns. I sit up a little straighter. "Wait, you're serious?"

He nods. "And even if we were to tell the Coven what you truly are, they would either not believe us or just add you to the hostility they already show us. So that's not helpful either."

"Also," Dea adds, "we want to tell all the community heads at once, so no one can argue over favoritism, and it would be best if we waited until you gained your Fae and Shifter powers, so if they ask for a demonstration, you will be able to acquiesce."

"Right, show monkey. Got it."

Dea rolls his eyes, a movement that seems very me, and I have to resist the urge to smile at him. Damn him. Even when I'm mad at him he's sexy.

Nine smiles in that flirty way of his, not needing to say anything else for me to know he picked up on that.

Of course he did. Why does he always pick up on the dirty thoughts?

Because those are the ones you shout the loudest, alongside the emotional ones, of course.

Sure. Because that's obvious.

"What do we need from these people?" I ask, trying to get this little meeting on track.

"Information," Dea says.

"Honest information," I correct. "They could lie."

"Right. Nine has to physically invade someone's mind to read it. It is only ours he can read so freely. And the Coven usually use charms to protect against telepathic attack, lest it give their location away."

"So, you read the Vampires' minds, then?"

"Everyone but the king. He also has telepathic powers, and we can block other people out." My momentary look of panic has Nine smiling again. "He can't read our minds, of course."

"Of course." Actually, that doesn't make any sense.

"It is because we are not actually alive," Dea supplies in answer. "Plus, most powers work better against people weaker than them."

There's so much about how magic at this level works. It's really simple when considering it from a human perspective, but from a Horseman perspective, it's really fucking complicated.

You have an immortal lifetime to figure it all out.

No. I don't. I have until Earth destroys itself.

Nine's smile pales as my attention turns back to Dea, who's still pacing. "We need to manipulate them into talking about the SC, their relationship with the Vampires, and their continued closeting." He sighs. "And your seal."

"Okay. I think I can handle the closeting," I say.

Dea raises a single eyebrow.

"I'm a Witch who knows nothing about how her Coven

works. I can just ask."

Nine nods. "Should work. But the other two will require some effort on our part."

"I hate politics," Dea grumbles. He heads to a mini-fridge and grabs a can of beer, pops the cap, and downs a large mouthful as he falls beside Nine.

"I know." Nine places a hand on his knee, and I internally giggle at my correct assessment from earlier. "But we can do this. We always do."

"There has never been a magical war before. This is new territory, even for us."

I didn't think about that, and hearing him say it has my heart rate racing. They're right, this isn't normal. If we push these people in the wrong direction, we could kickstart this war.

Fate chose me for a reason, and I honestly have no fucking idea what that reason is, but surely this is part of it. Otherwise, why pick me so early? Why not wait until the war has already begun, like with the rest of the team?

"How long are they gonna take, d'you reckon?" The thought of sitting here stewing in my nervousness has my knees shaking and my hands sweating.

"No idea, but that is a good question." Dea stands and paces again, this time not bumping into any furniture. "We should get some rest. Then we can take Angel on a tour of this place."

That helps ease some of my concerns, but not all. At least I won't be stewing in nerves the entire time. Maybe they can help me take my mind off things.

I shake that idea out of my mind before it can even fully form, lest it go in a hot, sexy direction that I have no place desiring.

"I'm taking the room on the right." I point in the general direction of the bedroom I scouted earlier and grab my bag and head that way.

"Guess we're sharing, bro," Nine says in a tone that can't hide the suggestion if he tried.

The next morning consists of a breakfast of fresh fruit, meats, and bread, and I have to admit, the freshness has me thankful. I really want to eat a bit better. I mean, I'm immortal, and I can't really die from heart disease or anything, but that doesn't mean it doesn't matter. Plus, I want to look good. The rest of the team look fucking godlike all the time.

"Ready for your tour today?" Nine asks, clearly trying to break my thoughts away from their self-depreciating hole.

I appreciate it.

"Sure," I try to push out in a cheery tone, but even I notice it's a little lack-lustre than usual. "Let's go."

I'm excited to see how the world down here works, but I'm super fucking nervous about everything else.

"I am going to stay here and try to hurry this along." Dea turns away from the table and takes his plate of food into their bedroom.

I heard nothing from them last night, and can only assume they were back to being respectful, or they were as tired from traveling as I was. I can't decide if I'm relieved or disappointed by that, but either way, I try not to think about it while in the vicinity of Nine, as I don't want to have that discussion.

Nine and I leave the house at dawn and walk around the town, popping into shops and watching children playing, but my lack of enthusiasm does not go unnoticed.

You okay?

No. I'm not. But I'm trying to forget about it.

That does not seem to be working.

You think? Look, I know you don't see it this way, but I am a part of these people, just like I am with the Vampires, and it would be nice if at least one magical community likes me.

I'm sorry. I hope so, too, but it's unlikely to be the Witches. They really hate us.

Why?

He hesitates, and I get the feeling I'm not going to like his answer.

We tried to force them to come out with the rest of the magical community, and they didn't receive our meddling well.

You think?

I know. It was their decision to make, but having this unbalance of power is as dangerous as we thought it would be. There's more Fae, Vampire, and Shifter magic in the world now, and so very little Witch magic. I'm not certain, but I bet it's causing all kinds of trouble for them.

Did you support the outing of the magical community?

Yes. As did Connie, but Dea didn't think it was such a good idea. Arrie didn't really have an opinion. He hates politics. Tries to stay out of it.

Bet Connie's having fun with him. Then I remember that Arrie and Connie frequently sleep together, like Dea and Nine, and have to backtrack my own thoughts.

You know we can talk about anything, right? Even that.

I don't want to talk about me and Connie. Not that there is a me and Connie, of course. Argh, you know what I mean.

Nine laughs, and the few people around us stare like we're crazy.

I understand.

We stop outside what looks like a park for the children, and I stand and watch. A group of five children, all under the age of six by the looks of things, play on the grass, throwing balls of air at each other and shouting and face-planting the grass—all the while laughing. The parents stand off to the side, chatting and occasionally shouting at the kids to be careful.

It seems so . . . normal.

I'm never going to have this, am I? It hits me like a truck. Immortality takes away my chance to be a parent, have a real family, worry about money and my career. The tears roll down my cheeks before I can attempt to stop them, and I turn on my feet and look straight at Nine, who's staring at me with an expression I don't recognize. Maybe pity? But it seems more solemn than that.

Familiarity.

He wraps an arm through mine, and I let him guide me away as the tears continue to fall in a hiccupping mess.

As much as I want to live and try life—and I have all the time in the world to do just that—immortality also takes away other aspects of a mortal life I didn't realize I wanted until the option was taken away. A family—a real one—is something I can never have.

I unwrap myself from Nine and sit on a nearby bench, just letting myself be for a moment.

I don't know who I am, what kind of powers I will have, how to stop this stupid upcoming war, or how to be in this new world, and it's all so overwhelming.

Was it like this for all of you?

No. We were clueless together, and although it took a while, we worked together. We had our memories; we knew who we were. That changed over the centuries, and some things were hard, but we changed and evolved together.

Why me?

Likely because you were the most powerful supernatural on the planet at the time.

It's my turn to laugh. You're serious? That's insane.

An Angel-descended Witch is nothing to scoff at. You could literally bring death to anyone you touched if you so wished. And we're pretty sure you were the last of your kind.

Wiping away the tears, I get up. "Can we just head back? I kinda want to rest for a bit."

"Sure thing." Nine grabs my arm once more, and we head back, our tour not even extending beyond the hour.

When we enter the house, Dea's sprawled on the couch, staring up at the ceiling, and sits up faster than someone caught stealing a porn magazine. "Why are you back so early . . . ?" He trails off as he looks at me, probably noticing the puffy eyes and tearstains left on my cheeks. "What is wrong, Angel?" He stands up and heads over to me, wrapping his arms around my waist and pulling me into a hug.

"Nothing." I unwrap myself from his arms and head back into my assigned room, hoping to just wait out the Coven and potentially pull myself together before they arrive.

Chapter Twenty-Eight

No such luck. It takes three days for the Coven members to convene, and in those three days, I read five books while locked in my bedroom, only coming out to eat, use the bathroom and go on the occasional walk. I even do my daily yoga routine in the bedroom.

Both guys have tried to talk to me, but I've blasted music in my ears from an earstrip I found in Nine's bag and borrowed. Okay, I stole it. But I'll give it back when I get my own.

I haven't figured out how I feel about anything, and quite frankly, I can't be fucking bothered. They're just going to have to deal with my bad mood for a bit. Maybe I'm coming on my period? It's not like I know what my cycle is, but it's been a few weeks . . . Do immortal periods occur monthly? Or are they less regular given we live longer? Because that would be some good news—

A knock at the bedroom door startles me out of my train of thought, but I don't bother answering, hoping whichever

Horseman it is will go away after trying to coax out a conversation.

Again, no such luck. "Angel, the Coven is meeting in an hour."

I sigh. Can nothing go my way?

"I'll be there in a moment."

I get out of the pajamas I've stuck myself in for three days and get washed and dressed into a formal dress that's very not me, but Nine bought it me for this specific occasion, so I can't really avoid it. Apparently, formalities are a thing around here.

In the lounge beyond, a place I haven't ventured to in the last three days, Nine and Dea sit on the couch, each with a beer in hand, watching something on the plasmascreen—it's an oddly human sight that has me doing a double take.

I shake the surprise out of my system.

"Where? How long will this take?"

Nine and Dea look up at me, probably both surprised that one of the first things I say to them in three days is work-related.

Dea's the one who answers after turning back to the plasmascreen. "A chamber just off of this one. No idea. Hopefully as little time as possible."

You need to be calm in there. I'm being serious.

"Okay."

I sit on the armchair next to the couch and continue reading with the earphones in until we have to leave.

The chamber in question is exactly that: a chamber. I'm expecting something more grandiose, but it really is just a giant, excavated room with a hand-carved six-pointed star stretching across the floor. At the head of each point sits an elderly lady on a simple wooden chair, each wearing old-fashioned robes from the stone age, and each wearing a scowl on their face at the sight of us.

Each point represents a different type of Witch magic: fire, water, earth, air, charm, and seer.

Three chairs line the wall closest to us, and we sit in them, with me in the middle.

"Death, Famine," a Witch at one of the points says, "what is it you require the full Coven for?"

Dea handles this straight from the start, which does nothing to calm my nerves. "We are checking in on each of the four main communities and trying to get a feel for the current atmosphere of the magical community, given the rising tensions of late."

Another elderly lady snorts. "Shouldn't you already know the state of the magical community, Death? You are, after all, the reason it exists."

Okay. Now I understand what Nine and Dea tried to tell me. They openly hate us. I was expecting some kind of undercurrent or social decorum.

"Nothing like a little visit to all the councils to gain good first-hand experience of the problems. We want to explore everyone's viewpoint before taking any kind of action."

"I'm sorry," I interrupt. Nine and Dea give me scathing look, but I ignore them. "May I know why you're holed up in a cave in the first place?"

The Witch at the top point, sitting directly in front of us, stands and crawls over to us. "Who, my dear, are you?" She gives me a gentle smile, and it makes my nerves sit even further on edge.

She's the lead seer of the Witch community.

"Sorry. Of course. My name is Heidi. I'm an air Witch. The Horsemen took me in after a rough start to life. They just wanted me here to help smooth this conversation out."

She inclines her head. "So you're an air Witch?"

"Yes." Didn't I just say that?

"Well," she starts as she sits back down, "we remain in hiding out of choice. We do not feel comfortable letting the world know of our magic, lest they exploit it."

"Or start burning us on modern-day stakes," the Witch from earlier adds.

"So, you don't think we've moved past that by now? I mean, look at the other magical communities, they're all out of the closet and doing well."

"If by well you mean on the brink of a human-versus-magic war, then sure."

Dea steps in. "Human versus magic? What do you mean?" She remains silent, and it clearly annoys Dea, who schools his features quickly enough that not many notice his frustration. Except me. "Please. This is important, or we would not here."

She looks to the other Coven heads, who all nod, and she continues. "The Supernatural Council, as you know, is human-supernatural run, and they've been using hunters to bring in and arrest rogue supes for some time now. Those arrested are never seen again. We believe, as do many other groups, that they're being executed."

Nine recoils in horror. "Why?"

The seer stands once more and speaks. "Because that is what I have seen, Famine. I myself had that vision, and we have been trying to find more information. But mostly we've been staying out of it."

"The number of Witches arrested has been less than ten in the last hundred years, so it doesn't concern us."

They're staying out of it despite other magical beings being executed? That's sick.

That's Witches for you.

But they've seen it, unlike other members of the magical community, who are only guessing.

"This bothers you, young Witch." It wasn't a question.

The horror is written all over my face.

"No. Everything is fine."

"You cannot lie to a seer, child. Please, explain."

"I . . . I can't believe you'd sit back and watch the magical community be tormented by humans when you have the power to help."

"Only Witch problems concern us. We cannot be held accountable for other races."

"But we're all magical beings. We all exist together. Shouldn't we fight together, too? If it comes to that?"

She smiles. "I admire your comradery, young one, but it simply isn't possible."

"Because you're scared. Of being outed to the world. Right? You're leaving them to die because you're scared."

Sweetie . . . Nine warns in my head.

Instead of listening to him, I stand. My fists clench. "I know what it's like to be scared of being yourself. You're worried people will shun you, that they'll never understand who you are." My mind goes to Connie and how she'll probably fear me, on some level, for all eternity. "But that shouldn't stop you from being yourselves anyway. Is living in hiding really living?"

"Stop your foolishness!" Two of the Coven members stand in abject horror. "You're being ridiculous. We don't live in some fantasy world. We can't come out and hold hands with humans while we magically cross the rainbow together."

"That wasn't—"

"Who are you really?" the seer asks. She remains seated

this time, but eyes me with curiosity.

"An air Witch, ma'am."

"No. I feel the presence of air in your soul, but I also feel the presence of fire, water, and earth, as well as the potential for harnessing seer and charm magic. You're not a normal Witch, are you?"

The other Witches look on in surprise as gasps fill the room.

She didn't mention the Vampire part, so keep it quiet.

What am I supposed to say?

That you're a Witch.

"I've only managed to harness air magic. I'm sorry if that answer disappoints you."

She contemplates me for a while before smiling and returning to her seat. "No, young one. That is fine."

The Witches murmur amongst themselves while we wait for them finish.

You would have done well among the Fae. They forbid you from lying in their court, and it's a real pain. You just managed to answer truthfully without giving away what you are.

It's a gift. I hate lying.

Nine rolls his eyes at me while I give him a smile, and he smiles for the first time since we arrived here. I didn't realize just how much my mood was affecting him; he can't escape me here.

I'm sorry. I'll spend some time alone when we get back, so you can have a break from my mind.

It's okay. It's not usually an issue, I just have to actively be in your mind while on this trip. Dea's orders.

Is he the leader?

Yes.

Why?

Because he saved the world when we were first born. We helped, but it was he who opened the sealed gate into the next world so supernatural souls could pass and magic would once again be a safe practice.

Oh. I see.

Impressed, aren't you?

Maybe a little.

He's incredibly powerful. I would be surprised if you weren't impressed. He's certainly reaped the benefits from that fame along the years.

"Is there anything else you wanted to discuss?" one of the Witches asks.

Dea stands this time, clearly getting to the meat of the reason we're here. "What is your current relationship with the Vampires?"

They all recoil at the word Vampire, and I'm left questioning where his tact had gone.

They seem to be less frustrating than usual. He's just going with it for now.

"As hostile as ever. Why those vile, evil cretins still walk the earth is beyond me."

It's my turn to recoil, feeling a little personally attacked. But, really, after the last few days, all I'm feeling is fed up, and if I let that fester too much, it'll turn into anger, and that will let my fangs slip, and we don't want that. So I try to remain upset about it.

"They're unnatural, and they love Witch blood and often hunt us down."

Dea nods and sits back down. "Thank you for the honest answer."

They're an awful lot like the Vamps. They wouldn't appreciate that observation, though, so I keep quiet.

"We're quite tired, Horsemen, Heidi, so if you wouldn't

mind, we'd like to go to bed. Unless there's something else?"

Dea asks the question I've been waiting for. "I have another question, but I need your secrecy. It has become an important matter for us, and we will not take kindly to anyone using this information against us."

The seer Witch walks forward to meet him. "What is it, old one?"

"Have any of you heard anything about a Horseman's seal?"

The seer's eyes stretch wide. "You've lost one?"

Dea looks her straight in the eyes and lies. "No, of course not. We are tracking down a rumor is all."

"I see."

I get the feeling she does indeed see—all the way past Dea's lie and to the truth.

"I'm afraid none of us have heard anything about any of your seals." She takes a deep breath before returning to her seat. "Anything else?"

Dea and Nine shake their heads, but I stand up. Taking a deep breath, I ask, "Why do you not like the Supernatural Council? Other than the prosecution of supes?" My gaze drops to the floor, hoping they notice the sign of respect and not bite my head off.

"They support the Vampires. Even supply them blood. It's sickening."

"So, you hate them just because they try to keep peace between supes and humans?"

"Do not be ridiculous, child. Peace is but a farce."

"There's been no war and nothing but peace for two hundred years since they outed themselves—I'd call that peace. No matter how tentative."

"Then you're as childish as you look."

"I am not childish. You're the ones practically letting the SC murder innocent people just because you're afraid; you're not even bothering to make peace with other species because of a centuries-old spite. So, tell me, who are the childish ones?"

Stop speaking.

I seal my lips, realizing how angry I let myself get at their non-action.

"You are no Witch if you do not see the danger and horror of the Vampires," the seer says.

"I. Am. A. Witch." Of all the things I've been through this past month, that much is clear. I can feel my frustration over everything boiling over, my rage seeping into the top of a pot of bubbling fury. "And, as a Witch, I would like to openly practice magic and be a part of the new world."

"You are forbidden from ever doing so, as per the rules of our world."

"Yes," I say between gritted teeth. "I am aware. And it pisses me off more than I can say. I'm not allowed to openly be myself because of you!"

Nine places a hand on my shoulder, but I shrug it off. "This isn't going to go well," I hear him mutter to Dea, who agrees.

"Hold your tongue, child!"

"I am not a child!"

Air rushes around me, and it takes everything in me to keep my fangs fully retracted. Instead, my anger turns into a mini-tornado, sending the seer and the angry Witch (who I can only assume is the head fire Witch) flying across the room.

Gasps of audible horror echo across the chamber.

"Arrest them!"

Well done.

Can we not just leave?

No. We like to work with the councils, not against them.

For fuck's sake. I hold my hands up in surrender, despite the burning desire to rip out the throat of the Witch who binds my hands using a pair of magicuffs.

The air Witch. How fucking fitting.

Chapter Twenty-Nine

It can hardly be called a prison, really. A hole in the ground is more accurate, slightly larger than the lounge of the guest house we've been staying in previously, with shackles attaching us to the mud-caked walls. They think they can hold the Horsemen of the Apocalypse with simple iron shackles? Are they that dense?

"No, these are spelled. You could try breaking out of them, but it will simply drain your magic," Nine informs me with a hint of irritation.

I guess I've given him the right to be pissed off at me. I did land us in here.

"Not why I'm pissed at you."

"Huh?"

"I'm pissed at you because, despite the shitstorm you've caused here, you're still upset over something you can't change. And that is still the one thing on your mind right now."

Dea slumps against the wall, arms above his shoulders,

eyes closed. He doesn't seem to want to be a part of this conversation.

"Dea's not part of this conversation because he doesn't know what upset you the other day."

I look up at him, shocked.

"I don't tell the team what's on anyone's mind, ever. Not unless I really have to."

Somehow, having Nine angry at me rather than Dea is something I don't like. When it's just Dea, I can brush it aside because he's done something genuinely wrong (no matter how logical the choice might have been at the time); but with this, it's all on me. I fucked up. I let my anger get the best of me in a sensitive environment.

"I want a normal life," I mutter, hoping he'll hear me.

"I know——" Nine starts.

"I wasn't talking to you." I turn my face toward Dea, who opens his eyes. "I was crying because I realized that I would never have a normal life. A family, with a husband and children. I never thought I wanted that until the choice was taken away."

He nods, not saying anything. But eventually, he sighs. "We get it, Angel. Believe us, we understand." He blinks and scoots closer. "You may not be able to live a completely normal life, but you are not bound to the team. Maybe solve this war first, but you are allowed to live anywhere, with anyone. We are not holding you captive."

"Wait . . . But I thought——"

"What?" Dea asks. "That we would force you to stay?" The indignation in his tone can't be more evident. "No. We would never do that. We might occasionally pop in and ask for your help with something, since you will always be a Horseman and have that duty on your shoulders, but you are free to live your immortal life however you see fit."

"But . . . that's not . . ." That's not what I want.

Then what do you want?

I . . . It doesn't matter.

We have a fair amount of time before we can find a way to escape using Dea's tentative command of language. You might as well tell me.

It's fucking stupid. And lame. And you'll just cringe or laugh. Probably both.

"I would like to be a part of this conversation, please," Dea says calmly from where he sits.

I sigh. "That isn't what I want. Nine asked me what I wanted then, and I said it doesn't matter. He then said we have a lot of time to kill, so we might as well chat about it. But I don't want to chat about it. You'll both find it stupid. Even I think it's stupid."

"We would never find your pain stupid, Angel."

"You say that now."

"We won't," Nine reiterates.

"I want some kind of a family with all of you." Okay? There, I said it.

And now I've said it, I can't stop the rest from tumbling out.

I just want sex, I don't want some kind of weird relationship where I'm the only not getting sex, I want . . . I don't even fucking know! But damn it, I can't say it out loud. But I don't want it with anyone else! I . . . I can't explain it. I haven't been with you all very long, and I'm not in love with you all or anything, but I just . . . I want the chance, the option. I want the freedom to feel without having to hold myself back."

"She wants all of us to be the kind of family Arrie wanted us to be in the early years."

"Huh? Arrie wanted . . . ?"

"Yes," Dea said over a sigh. "He was the only one who, like you, thought it was stupid to not let each other be in love with any member of the team."

"The rest of us saw reason."

"We cannot give you that, Angel. I am sorry."

They both look to the floor, tears brim, and this is honestly the last fucking place I want to cry about not being able to be in love with any of them, despite how hard I seem to be falling for three out of four of them.

"I knew that saving the world would come at a price, but I didn't know it would cause this much heartache." And the tears fall.

We spend three days holed up in this prison, and I conclude that I'm just a really shitty teammate. Really, what I want is to be able to let myself fall in love without holding myself back. I like them, I do, but I don't know if I quite love them. Yet. But I really want that future possibility, the one where my new feelings for Connie, Nine, and Dea are allowed to grow. Instead, I have no choice but to taper them down (if that's at all possible).

And I have three days to spew over this nonsense while Nine listens to all of my thoughts, which I'm sure I'm shouting despite trying to whisper, and I can't stop myself from crying, either. It's torture. I'm crying because of them, and they're both in the same room, listening to my awkward tears as I try to cry as silently as possible.

It's pathetic. Even I know I'm crying over something pathetic. A love I don't even yet feel. I guess I'm mourning the loss of a possible future, rather than something I already have. I can't stay living with them all, knowing they're right there and I can't let myself have any of them. I could try being just friends. But really, when is that ever possible?

"This is all my fault," Nine says. "I'm so sorry." That has my ears perking up. "I should never have let Dea's plan continue the other night in that motel. I knew your true feelings and hopes for the future. He didn't. I'm sorry."

"Stop being so fucking stupid."

He looks my way.

"You're not responsible for my happiness, Nine. None of the team is. This is just the way my life is right now. I have centuries to get over it. I'm sure I'll fucking manage."

Dea sighs. "When we get home, Angel, I want to talk to you about this. Somewhere private."

Nine doesn't say anything, but the message is clear: somewhere Nine can't hear.

"Let them go!" a familiar voice in the background shouts. "Or I'll shoot you all, you fucking Coven-driven crazies."

Connie. A really pissed off Connie.

"Great," Nine mutters. "Another emotionally driven female come to make everything worse."

"I heard that, you ungrateful ass-pig!" Connie shouts from a distance.

"Good. Then maybe you'll stop attacking the Witches and try to debate our release instead. While remaining on their good side."

"If you wanted a . . . Oof . . ." I hear her fall to the floor in a scuffle. "Politician, you should have me swap places with Dea. I barely managed to chat to the Fae without spilling all our fucking secrets."

Dea looks at me in question, and I repeat what she said.

"Look, Con. Now isn't the time for this. Just get us out of here."

I hear a set of rumbling footsteps coming our way, and Arrie suddenly appears, yanking the gated doorway (did I mention it's made of six-inch steel?) out of the hole and then breaks Dea's chains with a single hand.

"Damn, Arrie! You've been holding out on me." I can't help it, he's stupidly strong. Even with my Vampire strength, I couldn't break those spelled cuffs.

He smiles at me but quickly shakes his head in a normal scowl. "Easier to break when you're not trapped in them, Killer."

"Ugh, could you not call me that? Especially where other, less than liking of me, people can hear."

"Do you want me to help you escape or not, Killer?" He emphasizes the nickname, drawing out every fucking letter.

"Fine! But hurry the fuck up. I'm hungry. It's been a really shitty mission."

Connie bounds toward the opening, looking shocked at the surroundings. "What happened here?"

Dea stands up, then helps Nine to his feet and looks hard at me. "Ask her."

I sheepishly look to the ground, but Connie lifts my chin, looking me dead in the eyes. "What did you do, hon?"

"I may have air-blasted the seer and fire Witch Coven members into a wall," I mumble.

She tries to hold back her smile, but she ultimately fails. "That's more like it. Maybe a bit of fear will help them listen."

"Ugh. Women," Dea groans. "Let's just get out of here, shall we?"

"But don't we need to make peace first?" I question as we run out of the prison cells and into the shadows of the main cave town.

"Well, ideally, yes, but you pretty much ruined all chances of that when you attacked the single most important Witch in the entire international community." At my questioning look, he says, "The seer."

Oh. "So, they're unlikely to forgive me after that, 'ey?"

"They are more likely to remove your head from your body."

"That's a bit fucking grim."

"They're a bunch of Witches completely removed from modern society, what did you expect? Flowers and chocolates?"

Nine's attitude is really starting to piss me off. I already have to deal with one Arrie, I don't need two in my life.

We run around the outskirts of the main cave town, everyone with their weapons drawn—Connie even hands me a couple of daggers (mine are back at the house we're staying in)—as we try to sneak to the exit without attracting too much attention. We nearly make it, too, but then we round a corner and have an army of Witches standing in front of us with menacing scowls on their faces that could rival Arrie's.

Fuck. "Now what?"

Connie smiles, and Arrie grimaces.

"Arrie," Dea says. "Your turn."

I look confused, but I watch as Arrie steps forward, his gaze having fallen into a gray-slate color I recognize.

"Dea, go invisible and take out the fire-throwers at the back; Nine, stay with Killer, try to stay out of this; Connie, you and I will go in frontline style."

"Okay," we all say in unison.

We rush out, but Nine grabs my arm just as my foot steps forward to help Connie avoid an oncoming ball of compact earth.

"Nope," he says. "Arrie's instructions are absolute in battle. We follow him, or we usually spend weeks in recovery from decapitated limbs or some other horror."

"Okay," I say meekly as I watch Arrie and Connie go to

work. They move together, working as a single entity to dispatch enemies two each at a time. They don't have to communicate, they just know how to act.

Connie pulls two arrows from her quiver and fires them in rapid succession, felling the guy with a mini-tornado about to rampage through Dea's general area and some woman with a ball of water about to suffocate Arrie. She dashes to her next target and takes them down with solid punches to the shoulder, resulting in resounding cracks that echo enough to make me wince.

Arrie is his usual self, spinning and cutting down anyone in his way. That doesn't surprise me at all. He's the Horseman of War, after all. But it does not fail to impress. He ducks, spins, pivots, and leaps at all the right moments, never taking a scratch, let alone a real hit. No one touches him, and he looks just as beautiful as he did before the battle started.

The difference? His victims are dead. Connie and Dea's were just down for the count or knocked unconscious. I shiver at that thought but don't mention it out loud, knowing how much Arrie tortures himself over it.

"Okay, Nine, Angel, come along," Dea says once they've taken down the army of twenty or so Witches in less than five minutes. "Time to leave."

We're leaving and heading back out of the cave system when it dawns on me. "I've just screwed everything up, haven't I?"

No one answers, but that's answer enough.

Fuck.

Chapter Thirty

We go back to *Sheruta* two days later, and I couldn't be more pissed off with myself and the world if I was actually trying. Nine, Dea, and I aren't speaking, which has become painfully obvious to the rest of the team on the trip back; and believe it or not, the person I feel most comfortable with right now is Arrie. (Yeah, I'm just as shocked as you.) But between Nine and Dea's anger, and Connie's weirdness ever since the whole Vampire thing, Arrie is the only one treating me like usual, and it's comforting.

So when we're all sitting around for breakfast the next morning, I ask Arrie what he's doing that day.

He just stares at me like I've lost my mind as the rest of the team choke on their fried eggs and bacon.

"Blowing off some steam in the woods, then probably tending to the horses. Why?"

"Mind if I join?"

"Err, sure." He huffs as he puts his face back into his breakfast, but I just smile. It's nice to have some sense of normality in my world of team turmoil.

The rest of them continue to stare at me.

"What?" I ask, exasperation filling my voice. "Am I not allowed to speak to any of you anymore?"

"It's fine, just not what we were expecting," Nine says. His leg is wrapped around Dea's under the table, despite the others not noticing, but the small gesture nearly brings a smile to my face. Nearly.

"I'll see you out there, then. Maybe we could start some of that physical training you were planning before we left?"

"Okay," he says.

I make myself my fifth cup of coffee that morning, filling this one with pixie dust to give my magic an extra boost—I'm likely going to need it against Arrie—and then head to my room to get changed.

Dressed in yoga pants, a sports bra, and a loose tank, armed with daggers, dust-boosted magic, and blood-fueled Vampire strength, I head to the clearing in the woods as prepared as I can be.

Arrie is running through some kind of weird dance-yoga combo thing when I approach.

Not wanting to disturb him, I sit cross-legged at the edge of the circle, nursing my sixth cup of coffee as I watch him gracefully move from one pose to another; some moves are fluid like a dance, never staying in one place for even a breath, but others he holds and focuses on his breathing. He's even doing some of my regular yoga poses, and I briefly wonder where he got them from.

"Stretch and warm up." His low, gruff voice reaches my Vampire-fueled hearing.

Placing my mug down on the nearest fallen log, I do as instructed.

"If you came to chat about your feelings, that's not—"

"I wanted to join you today so I didn't have to talk to anyone at all."

Arrie nods, seeming to understand what I want from him. Whether he'll give it to me is another question altogether. I've done enough reading between my time sulking with the Witches and the last few days locked in my library. This is my change of atmosphere.

Arrie stands in the middle of the clearing, arms resting by his sides, not holding any kind of pose for the time being. Once I meet him in the middle, he says, "Copy."

I nod. Placing my left arm in a warrior pose, I follow his yoga-dance routine for a half hour, getting a light sheen of sweat on my skin from some of the more difficult poses. Arrie, on the other hand, doesn't break a sweat. But I guess he has two thousand years on me.

"You favor daggers?"

"I can use them best with my air magic."

I love this particular aspect of Arrie. He isn't a talker, and right now, that is perfect.

"Okay. For now, we'll start with hand-to-hand combat until you've experimented with more weapons. Con will probably have you master a few over the years."

"Right." I strip off my daggers and throw them to the side, returning into a basic defense stance.

"Good. Always protect your middle and head. It's a bitch to heal."

I nod.

"Defend." He comes at me with a few basic jabs, the third knocking me flat on my ass. "Defend," he says again. And once again, he comes at me with more jabs.

I try to block them but don't really know how. "How do I

best block a jab?"

"With your clenched hand and arm meeting the punch."

Another nod, and we are back at it, with me blocking a few but mostly getting knocked on my ass. It doesn't deter me.

Arrie never bothers to help me up, and I don't complain at the forming bruises that aren't healing with their usual gusto.

We go at it for a few hours, me learning a few different ways to block a jab while Arrie remains as impassive and stoic as ever while giving basic instructions when I ask questions, until we're both a little breathless and ready for a break.

"Here," Arrie says as he passes me an empty glass. He slides a blade over his wrist and bleeds into it for a few minutes until it's full.

"Thanks."

There's no straw waiting for me out here, so I struggle to not spill any down my front, but eventually down every last drop. Arrie, however, seems to find my struggle amusing and has to hold back a laugh the entire time.

"Bring a straw next time." I roll my eyes and place the glass next to my empty coffee mug. I don't need a longer break after having fed, which, when I look at Arrie, is obviously the point, as he doesn't need a moment longer either.

We continue training basic blocks for basic types of hand-to-hand combat all morning and well into the afternoon until Arrie calls it a day and goes to tend to the horses.

"You coming with?" he asks.

I hesitate. I don't want to overstay my welcome here, and bonding with Arrie really isn't the purpose. "Nah. Thanks." I wave and walk away, heading back to the kitchen to make myself a salad.

"Training with Arrie to avoid us?" Nine's voice penetrates

my peace the moment I walk into the kitchen.

"I'm not avoiding anyone, Nine. Just getting some training in and trying to be the best Horseman of Magic I can possibly be. It is why I exist."

Nine sighs and puts the newspaper down on the table. "Not my question."

"Best answer you'll get right now."

"Why is your mind blocked off to me?"

That takes me by surprise. "Wha . . . What?"

"Your mind. I can't read it now. Not even when I go probing."

"Good." I continue making my chicken salad and put a lid on the leftovers before popping them in the fridge while continuing to ignore him.

"Play with me tonight?"

I stop dead in my tracks as I raise an eyebrow at him.

"I don't need to read your mind to know what you thought I meant, but that isn't what I meant. Play some of my new magic gaming systems with me? Tonight."

"Er . . . I don't think—"

"Ugh! Fine. I won't force you to hang out with me." He raises his hands in defeat and storms out of the room.

"Fine!" I call. I can't stand to see him miserable because of me. It's quickly become my Achilles heel, and I'm starting to hate its effect.

"Nine pm. My room," he shouts back down the stairs with a smug smile.

"Date with Nine?" Connie's insinuating voice echoes from the kitchen door that leads to the garden.

How long has she been there?

"Er . . . A date might be pushing it."

"Fair enough. This Friday, girl time. Still on? Since you're back to talking to us now."

Ugh. "Sure." I try for a smile, but it comes out as more of a grimace.

"Look, hon, we need to keep talking through things. Especially now we're a team."

"I know." I sink against the kitchen counter behind me in defeat. She's right, it's just hard to think of myself as part of the team. I don't know where I fit anymore. Not that I really had a place before the mission.

Connie places a warm hand on my bare shoulder, and I give her a genuine smile. She's trying, and I can't ignore that.

Maybe I can work it out with all of them.

Dea chooses that moment to walk in, forcing a grumbling moan to escape my lips.

Well, maybe not all of them. I'm still pissed at Dea for denying me answers. And I don't think I'll get over that soon.

Connie must feel the tension in the room rise, because she quietly leaves us alone and heads upstairs, probably to her room so she doesn't have to overhear the inevitable argument.

Dea sits at the kitchen table and picks up the newspaper Nine left. "Have something to say?" he asks once I stand staring at him for a good solid minute.

"No." I turn to leave, but Dea is at my side, grabbing my wrist.

"Come with me." He runs into the garden, and I sprint at top speed to keep up. Eventually, we stop on top of the hill created for my *Shinto* shrine. "May I?" he asks as he stands in its entrance, gesturing to the rug and cushions beyond.

I nod, not really even sure why he's asking.

"Please sit, Angel."

That nickname has some of the anger daring to leave my tense body, and I hate that he has that kind of effect on me.

All of the team do—even Arrie in his own way.

"I wanted to chat about what you said—what Nine said that you said—when we were in the Witches's prison."

I look to the floor, not ready for this conversation. I can feel the heat blushing my cheeks, and I want nothing more than to run away and hide from the embarrassment of this moment.

"Do not do that. Not with me. You have no reason to be embarrassed. You want something that is so natural to want. Eventually, it might become something you have to explore."

I give him a questioning look, not fully understanding.

"Just because we are immortal does not mean we are an exception to normal, sentient needs and desires. Like the desire for love. Or to have a family."

"Please, I can't . . ." I hiccup, feeling the tears breech their usual bloody wall. I spent weeks here barely crying over a thing, and this one damn thing I can't seem to stop crying about.

"I know it is hard, Angel. I know what it is like to love and not be able to actually be in love."

"You're talking about Nine, right?"

He nods. "He knows. I am sure of it."

"He does."

"But we both know nothing can come of it. It is harder for me since I rarely sleep with people outside of the team. Meaning my more intimate affairs are with the same few people. I bet Arrie has the same issue."

And I guess that would make it more likely to fall in love with someone. "You could just not have sex, you know. It's not a requirement for living."

Dea chuckles. "Sometimes, I forget how innocent you are. I will ask you that again in ten years' time and see if your answer remains the same."

Fair enough. I have no idea if I had any kind of relationship when I was alive, and I don't now, so I have no idea what abstinence is like.

"I know why you made your choice, Dea. I do. And I understand it. I just don't agree with it. It's not right to cut yourself off from love just because you have a duty to the world. You are still allowed to live. You are still allowed a life."

He stares at me, as though that notion has never been said to him before. Perhaps it hasn't. But either way, there really is nothing left to say.

"I am not sure if this will make things harder for you, but you should know, I would have loved the chance be in love with Nine openly and pursue something with you, too. Having a relationship with you both while maintaining the team and our current relationships would have been beautiful. I have not had the pleasure of dating, falling in love, or courtship for some time."

That insinuates he has done so before. I throw him a questioning look, but he just says, "A story for another time, Angel."

I get up and run back to my room as fast as I can, shutting the door behind me.

He would have liked to dated me? Maybe even fall in love, if that's how it went down? Damn. He was right. That does make things harder. Because now I know that my feelings are spot on, and he's trying as hard as I am to keep it together.

He's just had more practice than me.

Chapter Thirty-One

Tonight is going to be awkward as hell, isn't it? I ask myself as I get dressed in some basic pajama shorts and a tank, ready for my friend-only date with Nine.

What's he expecting? Me to just roll over and forget that his stubborn, idiotic self is hurting Dea, and potentially me, too, if I can sort through my feelings enough to decide whether I like him in that way.

Here's to hoping that mental block Nine was talking about earlier is still there, because otherwise, I can't promise my conversation with Dea will remain private. It's all that's running through my head. I still can't actually believe he's into me. He . . . loves me?

No. That's not what he said. He said he would have liked the chance if it was something we could have. I didn't realize it until he said it, but it really isn't the happily ever that after I want (though, that would be nice); it's the dating, the awkward first kiss, the romance of it all. I want to feel the butterflies and know that they're being returned. I want a romance like the ones I read about, but you know, more realistic.

I want my own romance.

Nine o'clock is in five minutes, and I decide that being a few minutes early will look best (not that I care about how it all looks), so I leave my room and walk the few paces to Nine's rooms and knock on his door.

It opens slightly, and Nine yells, "Come on in. I'll be right there!"

It's weird to hear him yelling. I'm so used to him talking to me in my mind.

His room is the same as the last time I was here: a massive four-poster bed with black drapes, a reading corner with a small bookshelf, and a corner full of various screens and gaming machines. I wonder which one we'll be playing today?

Nine comes out of the bathroom with damp hair, slacks hanging low on his waist with no top on, and from here I can see his nipple piercing glinting in the artificial light. Damn, he looks good just coming out of the shower. The few droplets of water that are left run down his shoulder and onto his abs, making my eyes travel lower as they stop at the waistband of the underwear poking out from his slacks.

"Enjoying the view, Sweetie?"

"Flirting out loud? Well I never," I say in my best Dea impression.

"It's been known to happen." He smirks that famous smile that always makes me melt and give into whatever it is he wants.

And, for a moment, I forget everything and go back to the old me, the me that never quite understood what it meant to be immortal. My smile quickly fades, not unnoticed by Nine, whose face also drops.

"So," I try for a distraction, "what are we playing?"

"Well, I've been trying to hook up older systems to newer

power sources, so we could play some retro games that were cool back in the day, and I finally managed to get it working."

He walks over to the corner of computers and screens and turns on a series of thelining the desk. His hand pats the other chair as he holds out a controller for me. "Come, sit."

I sit and take the controller, forcing my eyes to one of two screens turned on in front of me rather than the very topless Nine on my left.

"We're gonna play some of the most successful games of the 20th and 21st centuries."

"Really?" I ask, a little sceptical. "Aren't they a little . . . old-fashioned?"

He raises an eyebrow at me. "I don't know if you've noticed, but I'm pretty old."

Smiling and holding back a laugh, I manage to not laugh at his age as we start with something called MORTAL COMBAT on a controller I have no idea how to use. I eventually manage to get the hang of it, and we spend a few hours hopping from game to game, spending longer on the ones I enjoy the most. But at some point in the night, when I've forgotten all about the awkwardness, something in my mind latches onto a previous memory.

"Nine?"

"Mmm?"

"Could we perhaps create a charm that could control Dea's visibility better? You know, something that holds the magic and turns him visible rather than using his own stores of magic?"

Nine pauses the game we're playing and looks at me with raised eyebrows.

"I was just thinking about how much it holds him back when on Earth," I explain. "But with my Witch powers being able to most likely use charm magic, I could probably help create a charm that channels a Horseman power and works on one of you, right?"

Nine looks shocked, taken aback, and nearly falls off the chair. "Oh my god." He chokes on nothing, and I have to ask the house for a glass of water lest I lose Nine for a few minutes while he chokes to death. (You know, kind of.) "You're right," he says between gulpfuls. "That could work. But you'd need to master charm magic first."

I grimace at his words, unsure if I even can. I still can't master more than air magic, so it's likely I won't be able to, but you never know. Maybe? "I want to try."

Nine nods, a smile taking hold of his face.

"For Dea."

Nine looks at me with a curious smile, and the memory of my earlier conversation with Dea runs through my mind. Can Nine see it? I'm not sure if I want him to.

Yes. I could see that.

I wince. "He asked me not to show you. But I don't know how to do that."

You can't.

"Really?"

He nods and goes eerily silent. Pensive, almost. Looking over, I see him brush a tear from his left eye and try to act normal, but, clearly, he's hurting.

I put the controller down and turn to face him. "Come here." I open my arms and stand, pulling him into a hug. "It's okay."

Nine's tears grow heavier as I hold him in my arms, and he cries for a while in silence. I just continue to hug him, not saying anything—not really needing to—and let him just be himself for a bit. Not someone who constantly rebukes his love's affections for the benefit of the world, not someone who barely holds it together after sex knowing they can't actually be together, and certainly not someone who cries over the fact centuries later.

"I-I'm sorry." Nine sniffs.

"Stop being stupid. Everyone's allowed to cry."

"You don't help. Your emotions are so raw."

I wince. Sorry.

He sighs. "That's not fair of me. You're just a normal person, Sweetie, and we're really not."

I can't help but laugh at that. He thinks I'm normal?

"You're more normal than us. I can promise you that."

Sighing, I pluck up the courage to bring it up. Goddess help me if this ruins all the progress we've made. "I'm only going to say this once, and then we can go back to not talking about it. But you know you guys can change your minds, right? You don't have to continue with an agreement you made two thousand years ago. Things change. People change. Situations are allowed to change, too."

I stop talking after that, knowing it isn't something he's open to, and I really don't want to continue to bleed over those wounds. Lest I make them worse.

Nine nods and turns back the game. "Bet I can beat you with just a knife."

"Against dual pistols, a semi-automatic, and a rocketlauncher? You're fucking insane."

And that's how the night goes. It feels good. Really good to be normal and not have to think of magical communities and war and other shit I honestly couldn't give a shit about right now.

At the end of the night, when I'm walking toward the door ready to head to bed, Nine reaches out and grabs my hand. "I . . ." He takes a deep breath. "Stay the night."

This has me pausing and staring at him intently. "The night?"

He nods. *We don't have to do anything. Just . . . stay with me.* He looks so lost, as though he no longer knows what to do with his life, and the puffy rims of his eyes tell me he probably didn't stop crying while we were playing.

How can I leave him like this?

I nod. "I am already in my pajamas."

He smiles in relief and yanks me into his arms, inhaling the smell of ny coconut shampoo as he crushes me against his rigid, still-naked torso and wraps his arms tight around my body. I try hard not to think about it, I really do, but even though I know he needs me emotionally, I still have to tamper my stupid, not-helpful thoughts back.

"C'mon," he says as he drags me to bed. "It's late. Your training continues in the morning."

"Ughhh," I groan, causing him to laugh.

I let him drag me to his bed, where we lay underneath the red sheets next to each other, his legs curling around mine, and his arm wrapping around my waist as I wait for him to fall asleep. And, just as promised, we do nothing but cuddle. When he's halfway to the land of sleep, I place a gentle kiss to his forehead, hoping he won't notice, and close my own eyes.

Fat chance of that, Sweetie.

Chapter Thirty-Two

I can't believe I slept in Nine's bed last night. The fact that nothing happened makes it infinitely worse; that means it was an emotional thing, the exact type of bonding I'm trying to avoid. I'm starting to understand their no-love rule—doesn't mean I agree with it, though. Nine simply smiles at me in the morning and gets dressed, heading to his computer as I head to my morning yoga.

Halfway through my hour of attempting to relax, I give up. No matter what I do, I can't get my night with Nine out of my head. The more time I spend with the team, the deeper I fall. As if my body is working in tandem with my mind, I fall out of my handstand at that thought.

"Shit." I'm really falling in love with them, aren't I?

But honestly, what can I really do about it? I spent days trying to ignore them, just living with them because I have nowhere else to go; but even if I want to live elsewhere, I still need their help. I'm not trained enough to save Earth right now.

I give up trying to be peaceful and head to breakfast early, deciding I'll make everyone some toast in order to stay preoccupied. I have a full morning of research ahead of me before a whole afternoon with Nine and Dea, where Nine will be able to sense my every thought (since that stupid block has apparently come down), and where Dea will inevitably feed me to do more Vamp and Witch training.

"Making breakfast, hon?"

Connie joins me as I am trying to create as many slices of toast as possible and place all the condiments on the table, fully removing those pesky thoughts from my mind.

"Finished yoga early. Thought I'd help for a change. Think I can handle some toast." Just as I say that, I smell the start of burning bread from under the grill. "Fuck!" I yank it out and realize I caught them just in time. I sigh in relief.

"Uh-huh. Totally able to make toast," Connie says around a laugh before joining me at the table and starting on breakfast.

Nine, I mentally called out. Breakfast's ready.

Five minutes later, the guys are all accounted for and eating with us.

"So," Dea starts, "I have a plan to put by you all."

We all perk up, curious.

"We have received a number of complaints from the Vampire community as well, given that we had to defend ourselves against their ilk." He looks to Connie. "And what happened at the Fae Court? We have a letter from them saying they would be happy to dance with the team when we are free to do so?"

Connie blanches at his words and turns a dark shade of red. "Sorry, Dea. But we wanted information, and they weren't willing to give it, so I bargained them for it. One night of dancing with them—the whole team—and they gave us everything we needed to know. I'm still wrapping up the report."

Dea sighs. "Fine. At least one of the four pillar communities went okay. The Shifters seem to have a wealth of information for us. And the Vampire Council went well, it was afterward that fell apart."

"What happened at the Shifter and Fae councils?" I ask.

"We usually do a massive meeting following recon once all reports are in," Nine informs me.

Avoiding his gaze entirely, I say, "Okay."

"Ugh," Connie complains. "Are you two still not talking, even after your date?"

My cheeks flame bright red, and she just gives me a knowing smile.

"What date?" Arrie asks, suddenly and randomly interested in the complicated dynamic that has become my love life. Or lack thereof.

"It wasn't a date," I correct. "We just hung out while playing some old video games. Nothing untoward."

"So, you staying the night in his bed classifies as 'not a date' then?" Connie asks. And I swear, she's about to be kicked to the curb, Vampire style.

Nine looks to Dea, who looks at me with a bit of hurt, but eventually smiles. I can't tell what he's thinking, but Nine can, and he looks confused and then happy. Which doesn't make any sense to me.

Is he okay?

He thought we'd slept together, I corrected him, and now he thinks he's one step closer to having that poly-romance shit between the three of us you were thinking about the other night.

He wants that?

You and him both, apparently. I can almost hear the sigh of exasperation in his voice.

I look over at Dea and smile, realizing I may have someone on my side if I can play my cards right. Wait, what am I thinking? I can't manipulate them into a relationship. For starters, I don't think I can actually do that; they're much wiser than me. And secondly, I don't want to.

Stop stressing. It'll be interesting to see how think you can manage that. Game on.

Nine throws me a flirtatious look, and I have a feeling that bargaining him into any kind of exclusive relationship will involve sex.

"Er, guys?" Connie interrupts our weird, three-way conversation. "I asked if you'd slept together?" She looks at me and points to Nine with a flushed, flirty look in her eyes.

"Oh, no. No, not at all. Just a harmless sleepover between friends," I stammer, embarrassment flooding my features.

She looks a bit disappointed at that, as though she wanted me to sleep with Nine.

Well, it is Friday, I'll ask her about it tonight.

Arrie's back to being silent, as though he likes to observe conversations more than be a part of them. It's uniquely him in a way. Kinda cute.

I clear my throat to get everyone's attention. "Anyway. Dea, what was your plan?"

"Ah, yes! I think we should publically announce Angel to the magical community."

Connie drops her slice of toast and looks shocke.

Arrie growls in protest. Like, legit, he actually growls. "Why?" he squeezes out between clenched teeth.

"Because everyone is curious and angry with us. Besides, we need to know where her seal is, and for that, we need to draw out the person behind this. We can pacify the councils all year long, but she would not have been summoned if that were all that was required. We could manage that alone."

Arrie seems pacified with that answer and continues eating.

"I think we should host a ball," Dea says.

Connie's face could not be more child-in-a-candy-store-like if I placed a dead Vampire's head in her lap. She lights up like a child at Christmas. "When? What theme? Ohhh, what do we get to wear? Wait . . ." She holds up both hands, pausing by taking a deep breath. "Why?"

Nine chips in with the obvious explanation. "So we can tell everyone at the same time."

"Could draw out the person who broke her seal, too. That way, we might actually have some leads on the things going on behind the community's senseless bickering without causing ourselves to be the sole opposition in this war."

"You think someone's pulling the strings?" I bite into my toast, genuinely curious as to his thoughts.

"Yes. It seems odd that the SC are being so restrictive to supes all of a sudden. They have always been at odds with the magical community, but the blood supplies are below the minimum necessity. They would only do that if they wanted to cause trouble."

Nine rests a hand on my knee, a familiar gesture that sends heat straight to my core; I forgot how much I like his gentle touch while purposefully avoiding it over the last week. "And the Witches knew more than they were letting on, too. They're hiding something."

I nod. "What about the Shifters? You said we got some good info?" I look to Connie.

She swallows her last bite of food and stares down at Nine's hand on my knee and smiled. "Yeah, but honestly, it's a little complicated. Can we chat about it over dinner, once I've finished that report?"

"Sure," Dea and I say together, causing me to blush. "Sorry."

He shakes his head, not appearing too bothered, but I notice the frown underneath the facsimile of a smile. "Right," he says, shaking his head slightly. "Con, finish that report. Nine and Arrie, get the guest list together and send out invitations and do the planning nonsense Con usually handles. I want the ball as soon as possible. This cannot wait any longer. Angel, you are with me. More training. Let us see if we cannot unlock more of those powers of yours."

Everyone clears the dishes away and resets the dining table like we're on a mission, then heads off in their own direction. Arrie doesn't look too happy to be on party duty, and the thought of him doing invitations is almost laughable, but otherwise, it seems like a solid plan.

Dea and I head to my training room in the meantime, and I seriously hope he has a plan in place, because I'm clueless as to how to unlock these so-called powers.

"So," Dea asks the moment we're alone in the training room and has clicked the door shut behind him, not wasting a second of time. "What really happened with Nine last night?" He raises an eyebrow in accusation, but I know Nine's told him we didn't sleep together, so that playfulness I see on his face is probably genuine.

That doesn't mean I want to talk about last night, though. I look to the floor. It isn't because I'm embarrassed, it's because I'm not sure if Nine wants Dea to know. "I . . . Please ask Nine. I'm not sure if I should tell you."

"Huh?" He looks confused all of a sudden.

"Well, it's not embarrassing for me. But it might be for

Nine." Does Nine care about other people knowing he cried over Dea? Especially Dea himself?

Dea looks at me with his arms crossed over his chest expectantly as he leans against one of the concrete walls. "Tell me."

I sigh. We're going to get nothing done if I don't spill it, and they tell each other everything anyway, so Dea will find out at some point. "Nine wanted to smooth things over between us, so he had me help him test some retro gaming consoles he got hooked up to a new magical energy system. Everything was going fine until he saw our conversation in my mind when I accidentally thought about it."

Dea flinches.

"I'm sorry. I couldn't help it. He would have found out eventually. And it—"

Dea places his hands on my shoulders. "It is okay, Angel. Just go on."

"It made him cry, Dea. Like, proper, full-on sobbing."

He pulls away from me, nearly tripping over himself. "He . . . what?"

"You both feel the same way. It's hard to watch. We both played games all night to distract ourselves from this"—I gesture between us—"but he continued to silently cry all night. I stayed with him last night because he needed a friend."

"I-I-I . . ." Dea stutters. I've rendered him speechless—a state I haven't seen him in before. "I have not seen Nine cry in some time."

Ugh! That's it. "All right, both of you meet me in the library this evening at nine." I've fucking had it with them.

Nine! I mentally yell as loud as possible.

Fucking ow, Sweetie.

Sorry. I wince. Meet me in the library tonight at nine.

Okaaay. May I ask why?

No.

"Sure. But why?" Dea asks.

"Goddess," I moan as I run my hands down my face in frustration. "You're as bad as Nine. I'm not dealing with your emotional issues a moment longer. I'm fed up of being stuck in the middle of you two. I'm going to play Nine's role of mediator while you two have an actual conversation about this."

Dea looks at me in surprise, gets himself up off the wall and saunters over, wrapping me in a bone-crushing hug—or it would have been bone-crushing if he were stronger than me. "I am positive you will not manage to change anything, Angel, but thank you anyway. And you would love to be stuck between the two of us, our time in the motel taught me that little fact." He grabs my ass in one hand and flattens me against him, causing me to feel every rippling muscle under those low-hanging jeans.

I let out a small whimper, his words lighting up every nerve across my body in anticipatory need. "Dea," I moan, intending to tell him off but causing him to run a hand up my side and cup my breast over top of my vest. "Please . . ." Goddess, I hate how needy I sound.

"Yes?" he asks as he runs a harsh thumb over my nipple. How has my choice to wear a thin bra this morning suddenly become my main problem?

"Please st-st-stop."

He leans down and tucks a loose strand of hair behind my ear, leaving his lips brushing the edges of my ear. "You sure that is what you want, Angel?"

I nod, not trusting my voice. "Please."

He sighs and gives in. "Okay. I will leave you be." He lets

me go, and I stumble backward, my knees barely keeping me upright as I struggle to grab something—anything—for purchase and find Dea's waiting arm. "For now."

"Tr-tr-training," I stammer out.

"Right." He rearranges himself in those sexy-as-fuck loose jeans and shakes his head. "I want to see if we can unlock those potential Fae and Shifter abilities before the ball."

"You're really banking on that, aren't you?"

He shrugs, clearly not wanting to put any extra pressure on me, but the message is clear: if we want to pacify the magical community and show them that I'm a part of all of them, I need to show off every ability to some degree or another.

"Okay," I say. "Explain to me how Fae powers work."

He raises his eyebrows, as though shocked I don't know much about them.

He's wrong, of course, I know all about them.

"Yeah, yeah, yeah. I know how they work. Just repeat the basics to me for a minute."

"Well, unlike Witches, who can use the small amounts of magic in the air, Fae need direct access to local leylines on a regular basis. This does, however, mean they can use greater amounts of power. A leyline runs straight through town and under the house; it's what powers the house's magic. We think."

"Okay, so I should have a fully topped-up power by now. So that's not the problem. How do Fae learn their magic?"

"When they are young, their parents teach them spells, but they have always been able to use magic, once exposed to the leylines, in small ways. Like moving objects, for example."

He closes his eyes for a moment and exhales a deep breath.

Before my eyes, Dea's appearance changes. His skin glows and his cheeks hollow, but the most startling change is the black feathery wings that now reach from one wall to the other.

Dea plucks a feather with a wince before inhaling another deep breath and changing back to his normal form.

"What . . . What was that?"

"My Angel of Death form."

I wince without meaning to.

Dea hands me the feather and changes the subject. "Make it move without Witch magic."

I wince again, unsure if I can actually do this. "But . . . how?"

"I do not know. None of us has ever had to study magic like this before. But I think it might be easier if the thing you are trying to move is connected to one of the Horsemen."

"Great," I mumble.

I hold the feather in my left hand while raising my right and trying to focus on the feather and getting it to move. But all I manage is blowing it out of my hand with a gust of air.

"Ugh."

"Try again," he says as he hands it to me.

Okay, Horseman of Magic, you can damn well do this. The team are counting on you.

I try again, this time not raising my hand so I don't blow it away, but nothing happens. Nothing. I feel no tingling magic brushing along my arms like I do with Witch magic, nor do I get that exhilarating rush like when I go Vamp-mode.

Dea sighs. "This might take some time. I have asked Nine to search in everyone's library to see if there are any Fae Magic Starter Guides or something."

"Like Fae Magic for Dummies. Cause that would be brill

right now."

We both laugh slightly, but it's tight and restrained, both of us understanding how crucial it is to show equal powers at the party.

"Wait," I say, "does that mean Arrie is left on party duty on his own?"

Dea stands there for a moment and thinks about it. "Yes. But Con is joining him once she is done with her report."

I nod, checking back in on my feather and trying again.

Nothing. Fucking nada.

It's starting to grate on my every nerve that I can't just manage something. Even a small lift of one of the feather's veins. Anything!

"Still nothing?" I hear Arrie's grumbling from the doorway.

Great. Just great. That's all I need. "Fucking obviously."

Arrie holds up his hands in defense, one of which is carrying a binder full of paperwork. "I'm going to finish my work at the desk in here. If that's all right? I might be able to help. And this is fucking boring as shit."

Dea chuckles under his breath slightly, and I just raise my eyebrows.

"Sure, come on in. Let's all stay to watch the freak show of the Horseman of Magic with no fucking magic!" I stomp my foot a little harder than intended and crack the concrete, but I don't care.

"Being angry ain't gonna help, Killer."

"And since when have you cared about being helpful?"

"Since this war is as much ours as it is yours. So stop being a judgmental prick and start focusing."

Gah! He's right, and that pisses me off more than I can say. Arrie, Horseman of War, resident pain my ass, is fucking right.

I take a deep breath and wait for Arrie to sit at the desk before focusing on the feather once again. Still nothing, but at least Arrie has stopped moaning at me.

"You know," he starts. Too late, he's about to start again, isn't he? "If you wanted to learn Fae magic, you should have come with us on Earth. Would have helped more."

"You know what would help? You being quiet unless you have something useful to say."

Arrie grumbles something under his breath, but I relax when a sudden thought comes to mind: he's being more talkative since our little flirting session with the cars and then our training session.

Maybe he's warming up to me? Or maybe he just realizes that I'm stuck with them and is trying to be neutral.

"It was a useful suggestion. You should go see the Fae."

"No time for that," Dea responds. "Nine planned the ball for three days' time."

I stop all of my concentration, drop my feather, and stare at him. "Three days?" I shriek. "Three days? Are you fucking nuts?"

"Calm down, Ange—"

"Don't tell me when to be calm. You've given me three days?" I cough, choking on the realization. "Even if I manage to use both Fae and Shifter magic, I have no hope of controlling either enough to present to the magical communities on cue."

"Killer—"

"Shut. The. Fuck. Up. I don't need your stupid comments and arrogant grumblings right now. Because, just like Connie, I have supernatural hearing and can hear all of your mean words!"

"But, Kille—"

"What part of—?"

Sudden tingles spread over my body in a way I haven't experienced before. It's itchy, not like the beautiful tingles I feel when using Witch magic.

"What the—?"

And then comes the instant of pain. It's like every cell in my body has a knife slicing it into a million microscopic pieces, like a fire spreading throughout the entire inside of my body, but I don't scream because as soon as it starts, it's over.

My head feels light, and my vision is a little dusty. The dizziness lasts a few moments, but the nausea settling in my stomach lasts for a fair few minutes more before I throw up my breakfast on the concrete floor.

When I lift my head to look around, Dea and Arrie stand together, looking at me like I'm some kind of amazing freak of nature. "Angel . . . You changed."

"Yeah," Arrie says, "you're a . . ."

"A what?" I ask, but jump when I hear the masculinity of my voice. Looking down at my body, I'm suddenly naked, but that isn't the most shocking part. My boobs have vanished, I suddenly have abs, and is that a . . . ?

"WHY DO I HAVE A PENIS?!"

Chapter Thirty-Three

Connie and Nine rush into the training room and stand alongside the others, both looking confused.

"Who is that?" Connie asks, pointing at me.

"Sweetie?" Nine asks. "Is that you?"

"What?" Connie steps forward. "No way. That's . . . impossible. Nine, that's . . ."

"Insane?" Arrie supplies.

"Oh my fucking god!" Nine exclaims. "That's how your powers work."

Everyone looks baffled, including me most likely, because I have no idea what he's talking about.

"Don't you all see?" Nine looks at us with a wide smile. "You can't mix Witch and Fae magic in a single person, or Shifter and Vampire magic. They don't even create hybrids. But you could if that person had two forms. Like Dea's Angel of Death form. It's Sweetie, but it's a different body."

"I'm a . . . a guy?" I can't help it—tears burst from my eyes. "But . . . I don't want this!" My knees sink to the ground, followed by the rest of my body. "I'm already weird and strange, I don't need this. As if I didn't have enough of a non-identity before, now I don't even have a static fucking gender—sex. Argh! I don't even know!" I stand up, brushing myself off, and stamp my foot—this time not breaking the floor. "I can't do this anymore."

I don't want to live a life this confusing. I'm not straight, or gay, or anything; I'm attracted to more than one person, possibly falling in love with them; I have all four types of magical abilities from each pillar community, meaning I'll never have a home; and now I have two genders or sexes or whatever. What the fuck is wrong with Fate?

I just . . .

I'm not sure if I want to continue living like this. If immortality is going to be this hard, then what's the point? But even if I wanted to end it all, I couldn't. Because no one knows where my seal is.

"For fuck's sake."

The tears have vanished, as have my emotions, and with it, my body tingles all over, flitting into another moment of pain. But this time, I don't change back into my female self. I grow fur, go down on all fours, and change into . . . a panther. I think?

I try to ask, but it comes out as a roar.

"Yes, Sweetie, you're a panther. Interesting choice of shift."

I didn't choose this!

"No Shifter does."

Another tingle-defining shift, and this time I grow feathers. A bird? Am I a bird now?

"More like a fucking falcon. That's kinda badass, Sweetie."

Great, even my Shifter side is uncertain. This fucking

blows.

"Try to turn back into your male form."

If I knew how to do that, I would be back to my female self by now, Nine!

"Okay, okay. No need to snap."

Seriously? If there was ever an excuse for yelling, it was when I literally grew a dick!

That has Nine laughing, but everyone else just looks confused. Nine waves a hand at them, as if to say it doesn't matter. "I know. But I wanted to see if your male form can use Fae magic?"

Oh. That's actually a good idea. I focus on my body, think about what little of my male form I can remember, and quickly shift back—minimal pain this time.

"Okay," I say, still shocked at my voice. "Could I have some clothes, please? In whatever size I currently am now?"

The house does its gentle rumbling thing, and a pile of neatly folded clothes appear on the desk on top of Arrie's paperwork.

I pick up the underwear, jeans, and t-shirt, followed by the socks and sneakers. At least dressing as a man—male, guy?—isn't going to be too hard. But I honestly have no idea how I am supposed to put my new penis in these pants. Is there some kind of man protocol I don't know about?

Goddess, the things I didn't think to ask as a woman.

Nine laughs again but doesn't answer out loud, thank goddess. *However is most comfortable.* "Our internal conversations are about to get a whole lot more interesting."

"Oh my goddess, how do guys pee?" I ask out loud, feeling the comings of my third mental spiral in as many minutes.

"In a toilet," Arrie grumbles.

"If you suddenly grew a vagina, would you know the ins

and outs of bathroom etiquette?"

He shuts up at that, hopefully mentally thinking I'm right.

I try to air-blast the feather that fell on the floor earlier into my palms, but it doesn't move. Right. No Witch magic in this form. Goddess, that's gonna take some getting used to. I bend and pick it up by hand.

Trying the same exercise from earlier, the feather floats a couple of inches above my hand, and the team claps, clearly impressed.

I, on the other hand, am not impressed. Not in the fucking slightest. Not caring that I'm still in my male form, I ask the house for a mop and bucket, clean up my vomit (not something I recommend doing by the way—totally gross), and leave.

"Where are you going, Angel?"

"To bed!"

And that's exactly what I do. I snuggle up in my duvet and blankets, ignoring the world and everything in it for the entire afternoon. No one comes out of the library—that I know of—but someone does come to light the fire for me. Sleep takes me for one of the best naps I can remember, and I wake to all four of the Horsemen sitting in various chairs they've pulled from the library and scattered around my bedroom.

"Afternoon, Angel," Dea says from a chair on the left of my bedside.

Talk about déjà vu.

I don't answer. Instead, I look down, feel my body, and sigh. "Seems I can keep this form indefinitely."

"Yes, it would seem that way." Nine bellows the fire a bit, helping to coax the flames into a larger fire after they died down during my nap. *By the way, since your body is a Fae form, just remember that Fae forms are supposed to attract people to you.*

I groan at that. "Great."

"What did you tell her now, Nine?" Connie complains. "She's already got a lot to deal with."

"Just reminding her of the allure of the Fae."

Arrie snorts. "As if you need help with making that aspect of your life more complicated."

"Ugh, tell me about it." Am I casually chatting to Arrie about my not-quite love-life right now? Goddess, this day is crazy. "So," I start, "any chance any of you know how the fuck I change back? Call me crazy, but I love my boobs."

That has everyone laughing, but eventually, a solemn, tense air settles around us, and I get the feeling I'm not going to like their answer.

"No," Nine answers. "How did you shift into this body in the first place?"

"Arrie pissed her off," Dea supplies.

Everyone's eyes turn to Arrie, as if expecting him to make me angry.

"Well?" Connie asks.

Arrie sighs and folds his arms. "I'm not a dick on purpose. I can't just do it on cue."

Despite everything, laughter fills my chest and spills out of my mouth. "Great, Arrie." I look him straight in the eyes. "Give me back my boobs."

Nine snorts from behind me as Dea and Connie stifle laughs. They can laugh it up all they want, but I'm pretty sure I have an erection right now, and I have no idea what to do about it. I want my usual problems back.

That's it. That's what does for Nine. He falls off his chair laughing, his hand holding his splitting sides for dear life. "Oh . . . my . . . god. These are the stupidest thoughts I have ever had to deal with in my life."

"What? I don't know how to be a guy!"

It'll go away on its own. Luckily, you're still clothed under there.

"I feel so out of the loop here," Connie grumbles.

I shake my head at Nine, begging him not to the let the others know my little predicament.

Nine sighs, hopefully sticking to his no-telling rule. "It's nothing important."

Connie pouts. "No, but it sounded funny."

"Arrie!" I yell. "Please piss me off. I really want to go back to my previous self."

"I told you, I can't," he growls.

"So, you be an asshole every time I don't need it, but the one random moment I need you to step up, you won't?" I growl. "You are such a fucking dick!"

The frustration wells inside me, bubbling and boiling. Ohhh, maybe this'll change me back? My hands clench into fists as I ball the sheets under the duvet and focus on how unhelpful Arrie's being. But as frustrated as I get, I don't tingle, and I can still feel my male body betraying any sense of decency I have left.

"All right," I say eventually. "Everyone out. I'm gonna have a shower, look in the mirror to see the damage, and get changed." I sigh. "What's the time?"

"Four," Connie answers. "Still doing girls' night?"

I raise my brows at her. "Really?"

She stumbles over herself and looks uncertain and maybe a little embarrassed. "Riiiight. We might need to change the name. Still hanging out tonight?"

"Sure," I sigh. Might be a good distraction. "Can we stay here tonight, instead?"

Connie nods, a smile taking hold of her features and lighting up her beautiful, flawless face. I enjoy making her smile.

Nine coughs, breaking us out of our trance. "We'll leave you be, Sweetie." He gets up and gestures for everyone else to do the same.

"Why did you all stay in the first place?"

Nine looks at me and blushes. "To make sure you were okay."

Oh, he probably heard my less-than-happy thoughts from earlier. I hope he didn't share them with the team.

No, I didn't. But . . . please be okay.

The airy seriousness in his mental voice stops my heart for a moment. He's worried about me, so he got the team to stay while I napped off my frustration.

Damn him, that's amazingly sweet and caring.

After everyone leaves, I have the unfortunate job of getting acquainted with my new form in the bathroom. The crysal-inbued flooring glows at me, as though the house is trying to give me some encouragement. The mirror across the room grimaces at me in all its reflective glory, and I sigh. Time to see the damage.

I edge closer to the mirror, eyes squeezing shut, until I reach the sink's rim and grip tight. Deep breaths. Deep breaths.

My eyes peek open, but I snap them shut again at the first sight of my reflection. Short blond hair. I have blond hair. A Japanese woman—man, male—with blond hair. How unusual.

Another peek, and I stare in horrorified amazement, taking it all in. Chisled jawline, no facial hair, ash-blond hair, and I'm taller by like five or six inches. A little more musclar, but mostly I'm slim, slimmer than Dea. I lean in close until my breath fogs up the glass and smile. My eyes are the same brilliant shade of purple, and, looking into them, it's like I haven't changed. I can see my soul in those eyes. The fear of having to save the world, the confusion over my love of four people, my hatred of magical predujice . . . It's like I can see it all staring back at me.

I'm still me.

I think.

Peeing as a guy is not fun, let me tell you, and I'm so afraid of touching my penis (goddess, that's an insane thing to say) that I spend my entire shower avoiding it, until it's time to wash and I can't avoid it anymore. At least my new penis has stopped being so hard by this point; Nine was right, it does go away on its own.

It's like a newly wrapped and unwanted Christmas present.

Nine's going to spend the next few months in stitches of laughter being inside my mind while I get used to my shifting.

By the time six pm comes around, I'm showered, dressed, and ready for a night of fun with Connie. She'll want to know all about the two moments with Nine and Dea, what my tantrum was about, and how I feel about my new . . . . form. It's going to be a long night.

"Can I come in?" Connie asks from the open doorway, where she holds a dress bag in her arms.

I nod. "What's that?"

I lounge in the corner where I've set up a tray of peppermint tea and ask the house for some fancy types of cakes I have yet to try.

Gesturing to the seat in front of me, I put some music on as she shuts the door and sits down in front of me. "So," she starts and gestures to my body, "this might not be the best time to give this to you, but I bought you something while in Tokyo."

"Really?" I blink in confusion.

"Yeah." She hands over the bag. "Since you're Japanese, I thought you might like it."

I stand and unzip the bag, pulling out what is the most beautiful *kimono* I have ever seen. It's a dark, dusted-pink, buttons up all the way to the neck, and has long sleeves that puff out at the forearm section. It wraps around the middle and hangs down to what I think might be my mid-thigh at the front, and passing my knees at the back is a cream drape with a light pink and gold hem.

"Wow!"

"It matches your other hair perfectly." She wraps her arms around me from behind. "Thought you might want to wear it to the ball. But I'm not sure if you'll want to now."

"I'll find a way," I say as I turn around in her arms and wrap her in an embrace I hope lets her know how grateful I am.

She rests her head on my chest and breathes me in.

I don't want to break away, but I find myself managing it nonetheless.

Sitting back down in the corner, Connie gestures to me. "Fluidity, huh?"

"Ugh. Yup. Just another puzzle piece to add to the mess that has become my life."

She raises her eyebrows. "Gonna fill me in on everything that's happened since we last chatted. These are supposed to be about gossip and hanging out, after all. Male or female, you're still my friend."

"Well," I start, getting ready to launch into an update on the weird three-way relationship I've found myself in, "things got a little . . . interesting between me, Dea, and Nine."

"I figured as much. I overheard your chat at the safe house

on Earth. So, have you slept with them yet?" She bounces slightly in her seat, eager for the juicy gossip.

"No."

She frowns and is about to ask why, but she cuts herself off. She knows why.

"But . . . we've done . . . stuff."

"OMG. Tell me everything!"

So I do. I tell her about the time Nine asked me to watch them in his room, then about the time I nearly slept with them the morning in the motel, then about the stupidly hot not-quite-sex we had the next day.

"Damn! You're really holding out, aren't you? But seriously, I've never slept with any of the team together, just individually, so this is like the hottest piece of team gossip I've had in centuries."

"Really?"

"I know it's weird, but it always feels a little strange to me."

I shrug. It isn't really any of my business.

"Doesn't mean I haven't slept with two guys at once, just not any of these guys."

"Right . . ." That makes more sense. "So, what about Arrie?"

Connie smiles a knowing smile. "He's . . . a tough one. He prefers to just sleep with me. But he's dabbled outside of that, too."

Why is that? Does he love her?

The cake is soooo good. I can't stop eating it, and I find that I prefer different things in my male form, which is interesting. For example, coffee isn't as decadent in this form.

"Connie?"

"Yeah?"

"I . . ." I really want to chat about the whole not having a family thing. But I'm not sure I want to bring it up. I can feel the sting of tears threatening to break the banks.

"What is it?" She puts her teacup down and shuffles next to me, putting a hand on my shoulder.

Taking a deep breath, I exhale and tell her all about what's been wrong over the last week, including the moment in the Witches's coven.

"That is quite a lot of emotions. You've had a tough week, huh?"

I sniff, and I can feel the tears threatening to break the banks. Shit! I can't cry in this form. Can I? I've never seen the guys cry before—other than Nine that one time, I guess. Won't that look ridiculous, though? Oh, goddesses. "Understatement."

Connie sits on my lap and smiles up at me. "Don't do that." She places a gentle hand on my cheek. "Don't hold back tears because you're worried over how it'll look. You're allowed to cry, no matter your anatomy. Your sex or gender does not change that."

She's right. Of course she's right.

I shake my head and laugh, letting a few tears spill over. "It's just so hard, you know?"

"Well, no, I don't know. But I can only imagine how confused you must be right now." She kisses me so softly I barely feel it, but it's enough to send a warm tingle dancing across my body. "You know, just because your form has changed does not mean you have. You're still a woman."

"Huh?" I looked confusedly at her. "How in the world is this"—I gesture to myself—"a woman?"

"Firstly," she says, tapping me on the nose, "you are a person, not an it, this, or a that." She takes a deep breath and reaches both arms around my neck. "And secondly, gender is not the same thing as sex, you know. They're totally different things."

"So, I'm trans?" Does that even apply here?

Connie leans in and whispers, "I think you need to stop trying so hard to fit in when you are so obviously meant to stand out."

The tears start up again, but this time I let them fall, knowing that this amazing, beautiful woman in front of me is not going to judge. "But I don't want to stand out." I sniffle. "I just want to be like you guys."

She chuckles as she tucks a piece of my blond hair behind my ear. "We're not so great. Just look at Arrie. You really wanna be like him?"

We both laugh for a minute before she gets up and moves back to the other chair. "You know," she starts, "all you have to do is tell us what you want from us, and we'll comply." She looks at me with concern, as though she isn't sure how I'll take that statement.

It's a bit of a loaded sentence.

"I . . . I don't know what person this makes me." I take a deep breath and wipe the tears from my face. "I still don't remember much from my mortal life, I don't understand my sexuality—if I even have one—and now I don't even have a static form."

"But you're still you, even if you don't know who that is yet."

I shake my head. I don't get it. How can she say that? Everyone else can conform, even if that isn't their at-birth assigned identity. But I physically can't do that. Does this make me less of a woman?

I might still be me, but I'm not sure who that is anymore.

"Oh," Connie says, "and regarding the having children thing. I don't know what to say about it, really. I've never had children because I don't want them—I think it would make things complicated—but that doesn't mean you don't have to. I mean, if you wanted to start a family by having a baby with or without the team, you're free to do so." She falters, finger halting mid-air. "Assuming you can." She gestures to my body, and I suddenly get what she means.

Can I have a baby when I can change sex? "How can I still be a woman if I can't even have a baby anymore? Isn't that one of our greatest purposes?"

Connie sighs and puts her cup of tea down. "So elderly women aren't women? What about children? Are they less of a woman just because they can't have babies? What about people without reproductive organs?" Connie looks at me with stern daggers in her green eyes. "We're more than just baby-making chambers, you know!"

I flinched. "Sorry, I didn't mean to offend your choices." Sighing, I pick up my cup of tea and take a sip. "But . . . I want . . ."

"A mortal life?"

I nod.

"I know. It took us some time to adjust, too."

"Really?"

"Yeah. Arrie took it the hardest. But you'll have to ask him about that." She turns the music up and jumps me to my feet. "Enough serious talk for now. I want to see that hunk of a male form you have hidden under that t-shirt. C'mon! Off with the shirt!"

"W-W-W-What?"

"Oh, c'mon . . . I'm curious."

"You saw me butt naked just a few hours ago."

"Yeah, but I wasn't paying attention then. I want to revel in the fact that I get to drool over a Fae body whenever I want. Well, whenever you're not looking." She winks at me.

"You're just like Nine," I groan.

"We're the most openly flirtatious, yes. Now. Off with it!" She grabs the hem of my t-shirt.

"Okay. Okay. Okay." I laugh. It's just a t-shirt. She isn't asking me to strip naked or anything. I yank it over my head and lean against the wall, trying to hide my embarrassment from Connie, who just stands there and stares.

She traces a hand over the ripples of my slight abs that I don't fully understand how I even have and sighs. "Damn. Nine was right. It is alluring."

"You've never seen a naked Fae before?"

She nods. "Yes, but . . . It's just that our magic is always more potent. I would refrain from being naked in this form around anyone other than the team. Dea might break necks." She stifles a laugh before she tears herself away from me.

I pull my t-shirt back on and put the TV on, hoping we can catch some movies. "What you wanna watch?"

"Ohhh, we could binge a new show: SHIFTERS IN SHIFT. It's supposed to be good."

Connie lays on my bed, and I grab extra blankets from the ottoman, ask the house for some male pajamas, and change in the bathroom before settling down with her.

We snuggle, and it feels a little weird in this form, like the fact that maybe we're more than just friends is a little more obvious. But she doesn't seem worried, and honestly, I have bigger things to worry about. Like trying to shift back. So I try to relax and enjoy myself.

Chapter Thirty-Four

The next morning, I wake with my arm around Connie's waist and her curved back against my middle. I have no idea what time it is, but given that I have training for the next two-and-a-half days, I assume someone would have woken me if it's particularly late.

Connie stirs. "Mmmmm. Morning." She stretches, and her back straightens. "I like your male form. It's bigger and makes for a good big spoon." She's delirious with sleep, clearly, but I find it adorable nonetheless.

"Yeah? I like cuddling you like this, too." I wrap my arms tighter around her waist and give a gentle squeeze.

Connie stifles a laugh, and it takes me until she wriggles her ass against my groin to realize why. Fuck. I have to deal with morning guy problems now? What has my life become?

I groan and pull away. "Sorry."

She grabs my arm and yanks me back. "Don't be." Her ass wriggles some more, pushing back into me, and just the feel of it has my newly discovered cock twitching slightly.

"Ugh. Don't do that."

"Why? Like it?" She doesn't stop, and I have to admit that I don't want to pull away.

I groan in her ear, and she shudders from head to toe. But if I'm not ready to have sex with the team as a woman, I'm definitely not ready to have sex with them like this.

"Connie?" I ask as I pull away. "Does this change anything? You know . . . between us." I cough, trying to hide my embarrassment. "I mean, I know there's no us, but—"

Connie turns around, hooking a leg over my legs, and puts a finger to my lips. "No. Not at all. I like both your forms. Promise."

I kiss her finger in return, hoping it sends the right message.

"But I will admit, your male Fae form is hard to resist. But then, it's supposed to be. Fae struggled to breed with their own species, so over the years, their attractiveness grew in hopes to outbreed to other species. It worked. But the Fae can only do strong magic if they have two Fae parents."

"Really?"

She nods and wraps her arms around my waist, pressing her lips to my cheek. "Yup."

She's so warm, I find myself melting into her embrace.

Someone knocks on the door, and I grumble a little like Arrie. "What?"

"Angel, training really is important right now." Dea opens the door.

Neither Connie nor I bother to move. She's too warm, and I missed spending time with my . . . friend.

He takes one look at us and rolls his eyes. "Seriously? Did not take much to seduce you, did it?" He points daggers at Connie.

Connie blanches at his words and flies out of bed and across the room quicker than I can blink. "Dea! I have not slept with him—her—whatever." She looks at me apologetically, but I just shrug her off. "But we are good friends and enjoy spending time together. So . . ." She grabs him by the scruff of his shirt and throws him through the window, which shatters as he lands on the other side. "Fuck you."

Connie stands there looking furious. I don't bother to do anything—not even get out of bed. She has every right to be pissed off; he practically called her easy. Might as well have called her a whore.

Nine and Arrie rush in and take one look at the scene and just stand there. I can feel Nine looking through my mind, but I save him the trouble and send him the memory. He freezes, clearly surprised by Dea's words, but doesn't say anything.

I give him a questioning look.

Yeah, he's jealous.

Oh. That actually makes some sense. But I snuggled with them both and did more while on Earth. Maybe I should try to spend some more time with just Dea? I have spent some alone time with both Connie and Nine recently. I even did some training with Arrie (not an emotional thing, but still time spent alone).

"Dea," I call out as I get out of bed, ignoring my hard-on that was so obviously pitching a tent in my pajamas. "You should apologize to Connie, and then we can begin training." I walk toward the broken window and hesitate when I notice his blood, expecting a Vampire reaction, but get nothing.

Right, not a Vampire right now. That's actually kinda handy.

Dea stands up and looks sheepishly. "Sorry, Con. I did not

mean it." He climbs through the broken window and stands outside the entrance to the library.

I open the door for him, and he strolls on through.

"Could I maybe help with the party plans today, Arrie?"

Arrie nods and follows Dea into the library.

"Looks like everyone's working in your library today, Sweetie."

"Well," I say, "there's enough room. Besides, I think I'll need everyone's knowledge to help me learn how to shift back."

Nine nods and goes into the library. "I'll ask the house for a breakfast spread in the training room."

Connie and I are left standing in a breezy room in our pajamas, her face depicting a clearly pissed-off woman.

"Hey," I say as I wrap my arms around her shoulders. "He was just jealous of all the time I spent with Nine and you. He didn't mean it." I whisper into her ear, "I'm sorry."

She pulls away. "You really need to have that talk with them. This is getting out of hand." She smiles up at me, letting me know she isn't angry with me.

Right, I forgot about that yesterday. Oops.

I nod, hoping that changing back into my normal female self will make me feel better. We both get changed—myself in the bathroom and her in the bedroom—and head to the training room, where there's a table next to the desk with muffins, pancakes, maple syrup, bacon, and waffles spread out.

Connie stays a little temper-sensitive all morning, occasionally snapping at the rest of the guys when they ask something obvious or want to know if she's okay. The only person she is okay with is me, and I would be lying if I said it wasn't the cutest thing ever.

I, on the other hand, have spent the morning getting pissed off at everyone because I can't do fuck all to change back. Yesterday we were worried about me only being able to show off Witch and Vampire powers, but now I'm starting to have the opposite fear: what if I can only show off my Shifter and Fae abilities?

"Angel, stop getting so flustered and concentrate."

I growl at him. "Have you ever tried to relax, Dea? It's fucking impossible!"

"You seemed pretty relaxed this morning," Arrie comments in a huff.

I punch him in the arm as hard as I possibly can in this form—causing him to shift in his seat and me to cringe in pain as red marks begin forming on my knuckles—and go back to ignoring him.

Connie also grunts at him with glowering eyes. "Stop it."

Everyone's a little tense, and Nine seems to be suffering the most. He can leave if he wants, and I've told him multiple times to do so, but he seems adamant on staying.

I need to help you.

He looks at me with understanding eyes, and the mental anguish I see on his face tells me just how much being around all of us in bad moods is affecting him.

Don't worry about it.

But I do worry about it, and I continue to do so well into the afternoon, where I have still made no progress whatsoever.

"What did shifting feel like?" Nine asks.

"Like . . . a tingle all over, but a painful tingle, not like the kind I get when using Witch magic. And then it started to hurt so badly I nearly screamed, but it was over in under a second."

Dea steps forward, surprise etched on his face. "So it feels like a Shifter's shift, then?"

I think for a moment, trying to remember what it felt like when I first shifted into a panther, and nod. "Guess so. But that started to hurt less the more I shifted."

"It does. The more you practice, the easier it becomes." Dea holds up a hand and runs out of the room, pulling a phone from his pocket.

I raise an eyebrow at Nine, who tells me to wait.

A few minutes later, Dea comes back in with a smile on his face. "Tomorrow, a Shifter friend of mine will be coming to the house to help. Your shifting sounds like a form of actual shifting, or at least something similar. We cannot help because it is something we cannot do; our magic is different to yours."

I nod, understanding what he means. "So, until then?"

"We wait. But we might as well try to see if we can get some control of your Fae magic and produce something more than flying a feather."

Connie stands, then smiles to everyone. "We're done. Fuck yes. Ball's on Monday night. Japanese-themed, in celebration of our new Horseman, and everyone who knows about us is coming, and I've made it an open invitation to *Sheruta*. I've organized the caterers, bartenders, and an entire supply team for the decorating, all of whom will be arriving tomorrow to set up."

Dea smiles. "Great work. Pretty sure that is a record." He steps up to her and looks her straight in the eyes. "I am sorry, Con."

"I know, Dea. Just . . . promise me you'll all have that chat this evening."

He wraps his arms around her, embracing her much smaller frame as he plants a kiss on her cheek. "Okay."

The whole thing makes me grin, and Nine notices, a smile of his own creeping across his face.

You're all already more polyamorous than you realize. This should be easy.

You think?

Yup. I'm allowed to be who I want when I'm immortal, right?

Of course.

Then I have made my decision.

I'll try to get this team together in a way that none of them fears and all of them have wanted for centuries. It doesn't have to be forever, and when we're talking immortality, preferences and tastes are bound to change, but that doesn't mean everything has to vanish. So long as everyone's okay with us all changing and growing over time, including our love and sexualities, then it should be just fine.

Nine smiles at me, as though he's already committed to losing this battle.

I plan to be the Horseman of Magic, friend and girlfriend/boyfriend to the entire team, and I plan to romance them all into place.

All I need now is to make some devious plans.

Woman power for the win! Well, sort of.

Chapter Thirty-Five

Nine pm comes quicker than I would have liked, and my confidence from earlier has all but vanished; what if they're too scared? What if they don't like me the way I think they do? What if—?

Stop spiraling.

Looking to my left, I see Nine walking among the book stacks toward me, his red hair bouncing as he walks with an upbeat brisk to his step.

"Where's Dea?"

"Not far behind. Just wrapping something up with Arrie."

I didn't train physically today—we've been too worried about managing my shifting—but I'll start again tomorrow.

"Tell Arrie I'd like to resume training at dawn tomorrow?"

"Sure thing."

"Sorry," I wince. "Does it annoy you if I use your telepathy like that?"

He shrugs. "A little. But I'm used to it."

I shake my head. "You shouldn't have to be. I'll stop." I'll just get a phone and communicate that way. Phones are pretty old-fashioned nowadays, since Earth uses datachips to communicate, but we don't have those, otherwise we would be trackable by anyone, so we have to adjust.

"I'll make you one like ours. Should have done it already. Sorry."

"Cool. Thanks."

Dea walks up to us and sits on the couch to the right, one nestled in a reading corner I particularly like. "So you wanted to chat?"

I nod. "Sit," I order Nine. C'mon stern mindset. "Nine, please stay out of my head as much as possible. Dea, I need you both to listen and be honest."

I sigh. I'm not prepared for this.

"Watching you both is the most painful experience I've had since being here." They both blanch, clearly understanding my meaning. It's more painful than not knowing who I am, thinking I have no hope of a normal future. "I see the way you look at each other, the way you always touch under the kitchen table, the way Nine finds Dea's smile sexy as hell— which it is, by the way—and the way Dea finds Nine's nerding out adorable."

They both look at me, clearly uncomfortable, like they want to run.

But I shake my head. "Absolutely not. Neither one of you is leaving. I might not have my Vamp strength in this form, but Shifters are still pretty strong. Wanna test that theory?"

"Con and Arrie are both stronger than you in this form, by the way. Just a little tidbit of—"

"Shut up, Nine. Now's not the time."

I have to do this for them. They need to clear the air. "Even if, after this, you decide to go straight back to the way things were, that's totally fine. But lying to yourselves and each other isn't healthy, and you guys have the rest of time to be in pain, so that isn't really fair. Is it?"

Goddess, I feel like a mother hen.

"So?" I ask, expecting them to take it from here.

They both raise their eyebrows.

"You've never done this, have you?"

Nine shake his head. "Feelings aren't really the Horsemen's thing, Sweetie."

"Ugh! Oh my goddess, you both feel the same way. Trust me on that."

They both look at each other, and I can see the tears welling in Nine's eyes, though he chokes them back.

"Really?" Dea asks.

"I'm sorry," Nine says. "I've known how you feel for a while. And I knew that you wouldn't have that same surety as me."

Dea shakes his head. "That is nothing to apologize for. You are always surer of things than the rest of us. But staying silent . . . That is not okay. I have been thinking you just did not feel the same way."

Nine straightens at that. "What? How could you think that?"

I lean against a bookcase and listen. It isn't my job to talk for them. Just to be here and help.

Dea stands, hands balled into fists. "You rarely ever stay the night, you sleep with a lot of other people, and I am not telepathic, Nine!"

"We've been together for two millennia, Dea! You fuckin' moron. How could you not know that I'm in love with you?"

"Because you never said!"

"I shouldn't need to say it!"

"Maybe not to you, you always know. I do not!"

"Death. Famine!" This is my cue to step in. "Sit back down and talk like adults." Goddess, this feel a lot like mediating toddlers. You would think immortal beings over two thousand years old would understand emotions more.

Dea sits, but I notice a significant amount of tension between them, visibly represented by the entire person-sized space on the couch between them.

Ugh.

I take the seat between them and place a hand on both of their knees. "I can't stay in the middle of you anymore. I just can't. You both love each other, and you're displacing that onto me because it has nowhere else to go since you refuse to experience a regular emotion." They both go to speak at the same time, but I cut them off. "I know you're not ready for this, and I get that. I'm not asking you to be together exclusively or in any other way. I'm asking you to recognize each other's feelings, and maybe, someday, you'll find a way to be happy as a part of this team."

They both look at me in surprise, as though their happiness isn't even something they considered until this point.

"Your happiness matters just as much as the safety of Earth." I get up and leave, thinking I can probably hear them if things get out of hand anyway.

The next morning is a weird time for the team. Nine and Dea are smiling at each other, but both make no announcement that they're together, so I just assume they worked things out and are remaining in their no-love relationship they've got going on. And everyone at the table has noticed their good mood.

Goddess, this team is going to kill me. I'll die of emotional exhaustion before I ever manage to win the fucking war I was summoned by Fate to fix.

Dea tears his gaze away from Nine and looks at me. "My Shifter friend will be here at ten o'clock."

I nod and look to Arrie. "Training until then?"

Just as Arrie opens his mouth, Connie claps. "Can I join?" she asks.

I shoot a questioning gaze at Arrie, who nods—again, in silence. But I notice the smile underneath the stern frown.

"Yay!" Connie bounces in her seat and grabs my hand. "You're going to be exhausted by the time Arrie and I are done with you."

I don't think she intended that to be sexual, but that is exactly how I take it, and my blush clearly lets the whole fucking world know it.

"Oops," she says. "My bad." She winks and gets up, taking her plate to the sink to wash before she heads upstairs.

Nine laughs. "She's playing a game, too. Seems things will be interesting around here."

Nine doesn't look at me and instead focuses on his breakfast.

"Half hour. Woods," Arrie grumbles and gets up to follow Connie.

By the time I finish my breakfast, get changed into some workout clothes, and walk to the clearing in the woods, Arrie and Connie are already sparring.

Loud clangs meet my ears as they sprint at each other full-throttle, Arrie growling and Connie smiling. They whizz around the clearing, trying to draw some blood from the other, bouncing over rocks, flipping through the air, and I'm mesmerized by the sight in front of me.

If I'm ever that awesome, I'll have no problem impressing

anyone.

"Hey, hon!" Connie waves me over from where she stands, Arrie panting beside her. Connie doesn't even break a sweat, of course, her everlasting stamina being the reason she outlasts him.

"Hey!" We have three hours of training to go before I need to meet this Shifter who's supposed to help me with my shifting problem. "What's on the dossier today, Arrie?"

"More self-defense. After the ball, Con'll add in weapons training. But mastering your shifts is the priority for the moment."

I note his businesslike self is back the moment he starts talking to me. With Connie, he's effortlessly himself—he even smiles during their sparring match. But with me, he's his usual gruff self.

It's going to be a bitch bringing him on board, isn't it?

"Blocking various types of attacks today, not just the basics."

Connie steps up to me. "Show me what you got so far."

Her businesslike attitude matches Arrie's, and I have to admit, it has me feeling a little better about his mood.

I run through the basic blocks from the other day, Connie making some personal suggestions as Arrie attacks in a variety of jab combos. So far, so good. But as Arrie attacks in more advanced ways, I start taking more hits, bruises and broken bones healing fast, but not as fast as usual. Stupid lack of Vampire healing.

"I was thinking," Connie says as she attacks and gives Arrie a break. "We're going to have to split your physical training across both forms for you to stay in shape. You're taller in this form, meaning you'll need to adjust your attack and defense styles for each form. You should spend half of each of our sessions in each form."

Oh my fuck, I'm going to have to do two lots of yoga and exercise if I want to be fit and flexible in both forms, aren't I?

I groan as that realization hitt me, and Connie manages to get a lucky shot straight to my face, making me fall backward and land flat on my ass.

Arrie laughs, and I shoot him a dirty look. "Glad someone finds this amusing."

"Your drama is the most fun I've had watching in years, Killer."

I bristle at the comment and decide to put him in his place, Vampire strength or not. Anger forces its way through my usually perfect façade of any-emotion-other-than-anger mask. "You fucking asswipe." I swing a right hook to his face, but he blocks with ease. "My life is not a drama for your entertainment!" I try to take a jab at him, but he moves, and I stumble.

"Well, your attack needs some work. We'll work on that later."

"Argh! You. Are. The. Most. Infuriating. Person. In. The. World!" I launch myself at him and feel that familiar less-painful-than-last-time tingle reshape my body as I connect my paws with his shoulders, my panther form taking him down with ease.

I roar in his face, not stopping until the frustration is out of my system. Lifting my paws off his shoulders, I stride away and sit by Connie, not really sure how to turn back into a man.

She rests a hand on my head and scratches behind my ears. It feels . . . good. Kinda relaxing and tingly, but in a good way. I lean my head into her hand and purr, and she giggles and gives Arrie an I-told-you-so look.

But now what? How do I change back? How did I do it last time?

"Luckily," Connie says, "the Shifter is here."

Ah! Perfect timing.

Connie leads me out of Arrie's clearing, explaining that he doesn't like many people using his space, and to another part of the forest.

Nine, Dea, and a dark-skinned woman I don't recognize walk toward us. Dea's eyebrows raise in question when he sees me.

Pointing at me, Connie answers Nine's unasked question. "She's stuck, I think."

"Yup," Nine confirms. "She can't remember how to shift back."

The woman with them laughs and walks up to me. "I hear you are the new Horseman?"

I blanch at her words. They told her?

"Don't worry." She holds her hands up in surrender. "I'm sworn to secrecy. I'll be at the ball anyway."

I nod, my whiskers bouncing and tickling my face, causing me to sneeze.

Connie finds that hilarious. "Oh my fuck, that's so fucking cute!" I growl at her, and she holds up her hands in defense. "Sorry." But she remains smiling.

"Okay," the Shifter woman says. "Just think about your human form, visualizing the details, and want to shift back."

Sounds easy enough, and it is. In a matter of seconds, I'm a fully clothed male me standing next to Connie in the forest.

The Shifter holds out her hand to shake. "Name's Kally. I manage the Shifters here on *Sheruta*."

I shake her hand but remain unamused by her so far. She seems nice enough, but I've become wary of anyone not a member of the team. I haven't met many nice people so far.

"You have unlimited shifts?" she asks, looking a little dubious.

I shift back into my panther form using the same technique as before, and then move into a falcon, owl, horse, and bat with ease. Anything I can visualize, I seem to be able to shift into easily.

I shift back into my male body. "Shifting is the easiest power to manage so far. It's instinctive."

She smiles with wonder and awe in her eyes. "The only thing Shifters have to worry about is control. We shift under intense emotion."

"Makes sense. So, how do I turn back into a female?"

She looks at me confused. And one look at Nine and Dea tells me they haven't informed her.

"I have a male and female form. Male for Fae and Shifter magic, female for Witch and Vampire magic," I explain. "I turned into this"—I gesture to myself—"yesterday and haven't been able to shift back since. But I need to so I can demonstrate my powers at the ball."

She nods and cirles me, a hand scratching her shiny black hair in thought. "What makes you think I can help?"

Dea steps forward, gesturing toward me. "She explained it a lot like shifting in the young, so I thought you may be able to offer some insight."

"Okay. Explain it to me."

"It hurts, like every cell in my body is tingling with a fire I can't control, and it made me puke my guts up. Fucking sucked."

"Okaaay." She puts her hand on her chin in deep thought, and we all stand and stare at her. "It sounds like when a wolf cub first shifts. They're stuck like that until they get used to their wolf, then they naturally shift back and gain control over time. Usually happens around sixteen-to-eighteen."

"We don't have time," I remind her.

"I know. I know. Hmmmm." Another painful few moments pass before she turns around and says something that nearly knocks me on my ass. "Have you fully explored your male form yet?"

"Fully explored?" I look at her confused.

She means have you done everything you typically would as a man. Food, emotions, sleep . . . sex. Wolves usually shift after having sex for the first time, so long as they've experienced puberty and stuff.

"Oh. Ummm . . . no. But I'm not having sex with anyone. The magical communities can fucking suck it if they think I'm doing that just to pacify them."

Kally smiles. "Of course. Have you done everything else?"

I nod. "Think so."

"Okay, well then, we'll just have to keep working on your shift and hope it comes to you in time."

She spends the rest of the morning and the whole of the afternoon coaxing me through various shifting methods, none of which work. We find a few more cool animal forms (a few more birds, insects, and even a housecat) but no female me.

Arrie comes along at some point but remains silently observational for now. Thank fuck, because I don't think I can take his sarcasm right now.

Gah! This is so frustrating. How am I supposed to do anything to help this war if I can't even shift between my human forms?

Arrie chooses this moment to step up and annoy the shit out of me. I assume that's what he's going to do, as he has that usual scowl on his face he seems to save just for me. "Killer, come here." He pulls me to him and turns me around, away from the ears of everyone but Connie as I face away from everyone else and have my back to him.

"I used to be friends with Dea's old Shifter friend, too, and he once told me something about his young Shifter days."

This is the closest I have ever come to a normal, pleasant conversation with the man, and honestly, it's nice.

"He told me that, sometimes, when we're trapped in our emotions, Shifters tend to get stuck in their shifted form." He places his hands on my shoulders and kneads the tense muscles into relaxation.

I have to refrain from moaning out loud. This man knows how to give a good massage. Despite my extra height in this form, he still has a good few inches on me, and it reminds me just how sexy as hell this damn man is.

"I know you have a lot to be worried about right now, and I haven't made that any easier on you. But right now, you need to let all that go. Dea, Nine, and Connie are going to spend the rest of eternity being completely enamored by you." He sounds almost annoyed but also slightly amused. "And, eventually, you'll get what you want from them."

"And you?"

Arrie breathes a sigh of tension. "I don't know, Killer. But I'm trying."

I nod and feel the tension leave my body as he continues to massage my neck and shoulders. "But that's not the main issue . . ."

"Then what is?"

"I . . . I want a normal life, Arrie. Marriage, children, growing old, friends, getting so drunk I can barely walk in a straight line, and not having the world on my shoulders."

"You can have all of that. In time. We've had some great

years together of complete peace."

"Really?"

"I promise."

Some of the weight of my uncertain immortal future lifts from my shoulders, and with it, that painful tingle comes back, quickly turning into an inferno that inflames my entire body in a million pounds of pain. As I feel my body change back to female, the nausea comes with it, and I once again puke my guts up.

"Ugh," I say, wiping my mouth after. "I have to get that under control."

Looking down at my body, I notice I'm shorter, have curves, and . . . boobs! I grab them in excitement. "I have boobs again."

I spin and fling my arms around Arrie's shoulders and murmur, "Thank you," into his ear before letting go and skipping around the clearing, reveling in the fact that my boobs bounce when I jump.

Boobs! I have actual boobs! Goddess, I didn't know I would miss them so much.

You are really fond of your boobs, Sweetie.

Shut up. You would be, too.

Nine chuckles from his spot against a tree just behind Dea. I've noticed since being here that no one even looks curious when Nine laughs at something someone's thinking or when he appears a little strange as he jumps into mental conversations.

It's just the way I am. They've spent two thousand years living with this. You'll get used to it.

It's actually kinda sweet.

The faintest hint of a blush reddens his cheeks.

"That was great," Kally says, "but now we have to focus

on you being able to switch between the two at will. Hopefully, in time, you'll be able to do it mid-fight and with no side effects."

"I'm going to spend a lot of the afternoon throwing up, aren't I?"

They all stare at me with grimacing smiles, Arrie also holding in a laugh at my future pain. Fucking asshole.

And that's what I do: Arrie pisses me off enough to make me change forms while Nine calms me down enough to change me back. Back and forth we go as I vomit up every last scrap of food in my stomach until I'm retching bile every time.

"There has to be an easier way," Connie say. "We're not going to be there every time she needs to change form, and we're not always gonna have the time to anger or calm her enough to manage it."

Kally looks at me—currently in my male form—with a sort of painful wonder. "Did it take you all this long to manage your abilities?"

Nine flinches. "It took us years to manage them enough to do our jobs. We've just honed them perfectly over the years."

"Great." I wipe my mouth, trying in vain to rid myself of that acrid taste etched into the back of my throat. "I don't have years."

"Neither did we," Dea says, coming forth from the hours of silent observation. "The world went to hell while we mastered our skills."

"Things were different then," Nine says. "The world was already hell, we just needed time to fix it. Nothing got worse because of that. But if Sweetie takes too long, things will get worse, and I don't think any of us can live with that."

"Let's just keep going. The more I practice, the more it'll

sink in." I need to be useful. I need to help. I can't let the team down.

I stand on shaky legs, nearly tripping, but catch myself before I face-plant the forest floor.

"You can barely stand, hon. Let's get you som—"

"No!" I stand straighter, trying to look more confident than I feel. "I need to get this. We only have another day and a half."

"But—

"Just shut up, Connie!"

She flinches, and I instantly feel guilty. I didn't mean to snap, and the look on her face tells me I've made a mistake. She looks a little heartbroken before she takes a deep breath and replaces it with her usual resolve.

"Sorry," I breathe. "Just stressed."

"I know. It's okay."

I put that aside for now. I can always find some way of making it up to her later. This is my priority right now. Getting this right.

Taking a deep breath, I sit on the forest floor, away from the steaming pile of vomit I've managed to produce over the course of the afternoon, and inhale the familiar scents of those around me: Connie's mango shampoo, Arrie's tangy metallic scent mixed with whatever the hell amazing shit he uses as body wash, Nine's page-and-ink scent that never fails to excite me, and Dea's lavender, heavenly smell of home. I let them encompass me and ride my mind into peace.

I hear them trying to talk to me, but Nine hushes them, telling them to be silent while I concentrate.

I don't mind my male form so much, if I'm honest. I need more time with it, to get myself properly acquainted, but it seems useful; especially if I'm going to try to bring people together. But right now, I need to be in my female form because that way I can wear the amazing *kimono* Connie bought me from Japan (cos there's no way that'll fit on me now), and I can dance with the guys at the party, try to mingle with some of their friends, meet people of power and make face. I can do all that better in my female form. Right now, I need to be female.

I try to picture my own body in my mind, from my light pink hair that trails down to my waist, to my five-foot-six frame with small curves and clunky feet. If I picture my body enough, I can even produce fangs with the image, blood-red eyes, a pale complexion, with air magic streaming from both hands. That's me. Or part of me, at least. Half of who I am.

That's why I felt so . . . not myself before. Because that isn't me. I'm both male and female. I'm all: Witch, Vampire, Fae, and Shifter. It allows me to blend in with the world, become something of a glue that will hopefully allow them to celebrate their differences and similarities alike.

Goddess, I sound so whimsical, like some kind of soothsayer from one of my books. Although it's a cliché, it's true.

I don't want to win the war. I want to prevent it.

"You did it!" Someone exclaims from a distance.

Opening my eyes, I notice they aren't speaking from a distance, my mind is just far away. They're a few feet in front of me, bouncing around in their typical excited fashion. Connie.

"Reckon you could do that on cue at the ball?" Dea asks, ever the planned one of the team.

"I reckon I need more fucking practice, but yeah. Hopefully."

Nine looks at me with some kind of prideful smile on his

face.

I want to ask what it means, but Connie grabs my arms and yanks me to my feet. "C'mon!" she shouts. "Let's grab some food and have a movie night. All of us."

I look around at the people in the forest and have a sudden warm feeling I can't quite put a name to. I've only known them for a month, and two of them have spent that time confusing the hell out of me, while another has spent it trying their best to break my calm resolve (and succeeding on several occasions), but all four of them are amazing. Maybe one day I will call them family.

"You gonna join us, Kally?" Connie asks.

I totally forgot she was there. "Thank you," I say, stepping up to her. She has on a nice smile, and I think she might be the first non-team member I've met and actually like. "You saved the day today."

She laughs and shakes her hands. "Nah. You guys are the heroes, right? The rest of us just help when we can." She turns to look at Connie. "Thanks for the offer, but I'm gonna head on home. Got a few hungry wolves to feed before bed." She gives us all a little playful salute and heads back through the forest.

"Soooo." I thread my arm through Connie's. "What we watching?"

"Well, it's Arrie's turn to choose tonight."

I look over at him, and he shrugs. "I think Killer should choose. She's earned it." He strides off through the forest ahead of us.

I stop still. "Did he just . . . compliment me?" My head rushes in dizziness for a moment, but I steady myself and continue back to the house. "Goddess, the world's gone fucking topsy turvy." And now I'm starting to sound as English as Dea.

Fuck it all to hell.

Chapter Thirty-Six

I choose a Disney animated feature for the evening, a movie that speaks to some long-forgotten memory of mine. No one complains, and even Arrie seems to enjoy some of the jokes and singalongs. We all curl up on one of the larger corner sofas. I'm tucked in the corner between Nine and Connie, with Arrie lying across Connie's lap on my left and Dea in the crook of Nine's shoulder on my right.

Compared to the last time I was here with them all, when I cuddled with Nine and Dea and the others sat on a separate sofa, this feels more . . . right. More like home.

The final song comes on as the credits roll, and Nine and Connie burst into song and dance, leaping off the sofa and dancing around the floating platform, performing a terrible rendition of one of the movie's main songs.

"You'd think after two thousand years, you'd be able to sing better." I shrug and smirk at them, even as Connie throws a pillow at my face using her full strength (which hurts like a bitch, by the way). "Remind me not to piss you off. You could do some serious fucking damage to my face." I throw the pillow back to her.

"You'd just heal anyway!" she yells as she jumps off the platform and lands on the floor below without a scratch, leaving me momentarily speechless.

"You're a Vampire, Sweetie. You could probably jump that easier than her."

Really?

Putting it to the test, I jump off the side (not like I can die anyway) and land on my feet, not even feeling a tremor as my feet hit the floor.

"Nice jump." Connie puts her arm around my waist and pulls me away as the guys lower the platform and get off. "Next movie night's on Arrie, right?"

He rolls his eyes. "Fine. After the ball, I'll pick something." He walks off, probably heading to bed.

I have other ideas. "Connie, come with me."

Nine smiles at us as I grab her hand and drag her out of the theater and into the kitchen, where we head back outside. Night has fallen somewhere between dinner and the movie, but that isn't stopping me. I have an apology to give for snapping. It isn't her fault; she's just looking out for me.

I walk us over to a small clearing in the fairy garden and have her stand in front of me. "Ready?"

"For what?"

"For the world's best apology." I wave my hand in the air and lift us both a good twenty feet off the ground, above the trees of the forest and high enough to look at the whole of *Sheruta*.

Flying myself closer to her, I grab her from behind and wrap my arms around her waist. "C'mon, let's go exploring."

I fly us toward the town and over the fancy section Nine

and Dea took me to, and then above a more modern street with clubs and bars and various entertainment facilities. "What's in that direction?" I ask her as I nod ahead of us. In the far distance, I can see the coast, but the bit in between us and that has a large circular building.

"That's the mall."

"Mall? We have a fucking mall?" That's right, Nine promised to take me.

"Yup."

I grab her hand and whisk us through the air, reveling in her laughter as I twist us in corkscrew motions and fly us in circles toward the ground before flying us back up into the air last minute.

When we get closer, the mall looks ridiculous. It has at least ten stories and is lit up like a Christmas tree.

"Nine and Dea didn't take you here?"

"Nah. We couldn't walk very far because I was still healing."

"Dea doesn't like it, says it's too modern. He probably just wanted to avoid it."

"He doesn't seem to like public places. Probably because of the visibility thing."

Connie grabs my hand once more and pulls me toward her. I use the air to bring us closer together as she wraps her hands around my neck. "Wanna see the coast?" I nod, and she points to the edge of land ahead of us. "It's that way."

I fly us over there in less than a few minutes and land us straight on a pure-white sandy strip of coast that is as beautiful as the starry sky above us.

The moonlight reflecting off Connie's blond hair enraptures me for a brief moment, before I realize I'm staring.

She gives me a quizzical look.

What the hell. Might as well. "You really are beautiful," I murmur.

"Thank you," she says as she steps in front of me, our bodies pressing together as her arms wrap around my neck. "But so are you."

I blush and look away from her bright green eyes, not really knowing how to take a compliment from this woman.

She gently grabs my neck and forces my eyes back to hers. "You are beautiful. You shouldn't be ashamed of how you look."

"I'm not. Just . . . I now have two bodies to worry about; two sets of confidences to deal with."

"It's all the same. They're both you."

"I freaked out to begin with, but you're right. I kinda feel whole now. Like I've gained something I've been missing this entire time."

She smiles that perfect smile at me, flashing the dimple that makes her face adorable under the single light of the moon. We barely talk in whispers, being so close, but when she presses her lips to mine, I sigh in relief.

Kissing this woman feels so right, and I couldn't care less what people think. She's amazing, beautiful, powerful, and strong, and I'm lucky to have my interest in her returned.

She deepens the kiss, encouraging me to open my mouth by swiping her tongue across my lips, and then she delves deep, connecting our kiss and exploding my mind into stars. Her hand slides up my t-shirt to rest on my lower back, pressing me flush against her, and I find myself tiptoeing up to her, getting as close as possible to the Horseman of Conquest, someone I have come to call my friend.

Maybe a little more than a friend, but labels aren't really something I'm interested in right now.

As she raises her hand higher up my back and brings it round to the front, she grazes a thumb over my nipple.

I gasp against her lips before pulling away, breathless.

She looks at me a little disappointed but smiles. "Maybe next time."

The sudden memory of Nine's comment this morning brushes itself across my mind: *Looks like you're not the only one playing a game.*

Is she trying to get me into bed? Is that her end game?

I smile at the thought; although it isn't something I'm ready for, the feeling of being wanted—needed—floods my mind, and I find myself sighing in comfort. "We should head back," I whisper. "Got lots more training tomorrow. And I'm sure the party décor needs arranging."

She grabs my hand. "You're right. You need some sleep."

I raise us both into the air and fly us back to the house, where we land on the backyard porch and share another melting kiss goodnight before I head off to bed with another cup of coffee.

The next day is as frustrating as the last, as I spend it trying to speed up the process of shifting forms, but I have about as much luck as a leprechaun born on a Friday the thirteenth.

"One more time, Angel."

We're back in my training room this time, Arrie sitting just outside the open door with a book I don't recognize in a language I didn't even know existed. Nine is sitting at the desk, taking diligent notes while Dea coaches me through each shift. Arrie's taken to joining us recently and dragging me off for physical training every time I get too frustrated to continue. The balance is nice, but what would be nicer is managing an effortless shift.

"Dea, how do you do it?"

"Hmmm?" he asks, turning around from his examination of my weaponry contents. "Oh, you mean shift?"

I nod.

"Took me a while to get it right, but I just imagine my soul's power and let it fill me up, and I just shift."

"Right. Makes sense." And is completely useless to me. I don't have soul magic, so that won't work.

"Sorry, I know that is useless. That is why I have not bothered to tutor you based on my own shift."

"The party's tomorrow. This is as good as it's going to get, I'm afraid. Everyone's just gonna have to stare at me meditating for a solid five minutes before seeing anything." I cringe at the thought. Meditating in front of a crowd almost sounds like a paradox. How is that going to be relaxing? "Sorry."

Dea waves off my concern. "We will make do."

Nine stands. "Let's all have some dinner and get an early night. We'll all be needed by Connie's drill sergeant orders tomorrow, I'm sure," he groans.

I laugh, but they just look at me, deadly serious. Damn, she's going to be bossy tomorrow, isn't she?

Yup. Good luck. Though she'll likely be easier on you, given your date last night.

I roll my eyes. It wasn't a date, just an apology for snapping at her.

Uh-huh. Whatever you say. But it's been loudly playing on her mind all day.

This is what I get for apologizing? Nine's annoying commentary? But it's kinda normal by this point. It's a refreshing change from Dea's politeness and Arrie's silent, grumpy attitude. Though, since our moment in the forest, Arrie seems less grumpy with me. Maybe we've made progress?

That thought goes completely out the window when we're all sitting around the dining table—Nine teasing Connie and I about our not-date last night, Dea raising his eyebrows in that annoying way of his, and Arrie . . . Well, he just gets up and storms offce.

I get the feeling there's more to his feelings for Connie than I originally thought. They don't seem as close as Nine and Dea, but maybe I misjudged.

Dea sighs, Connie practically sinks into her chair, and Nine looks stoically at the table (probably trying to remain impassive).

Back to square one.

Chapter Thirty-Seven

The following morning, I wake up a bundle of nerves, but as I get downstairs, I realize the entire team have started preparing for the ball without me. My Vamp hearing leads me down a wide hallway (I can probably sprawl across its width twice lengthways) with a gilded arch at the end, leading into a vast open space with higharched ceilings, a window wall on one side leading to a fancy balcony, and walls painted in an intricate golden detail. It looks like something out of a fairy tale.

Dea and Nine wear gray aprons and hold feathers dusters, Arrie is helping a bunch of people I've never seen before put up decorations, and Connie is barking orders at the caterers on how and where to place all the food. All in all, it looks like everyone is busy.

"Sweetie," Nine calls, "Con wants to see you." He barely looks over his shoulder as he says it, but the moment he does, Dea turns around to give me a wave.

I run over to Coniie and watch as she carefully moves the

giant cake in the center of the table two inches to the left. "You wanted to see me?"

"Er, yeah. Could you help Arrie with the decs, please? Your air magic will make it much easier."

I look at her with raised eyebrows, but she doesn't even bother turning around to greet me, so she doesn't notice.

Arrie's working in one corner, layering pink and gold drapes along the ceiling edges and letting them hang in sweeping arcs halfway down the wall. He seems to be struggling on a ladder to reach each point, and I see him stumble.

"Here."

I wave my hand and air-lift him off the ladder so he can drape the fabric more effectively. After he's pinned that one into place on the wall, I set him down on his feet, where I watch him take a deep breath.

"Want me to handle this?"

Arrie frowns and hands over the next pink and gold drapes to be placed on the next section of wall.

I don't waste any time getting them pinned up, using my air magic to stick the pins, drape the drapes, and swing the arches. All in all, it's pretty easy. Arrie hands me all the material, tells me how low to hang each one by giving me a faraway point of view, and I do the heavy lifting (magically speaking). We're done in no time, and the almost-silent routine we have going on feels . . . peaceful.

"What's next?" I ask as I spin around to meet him.

He shrugs. "Ask Con." He spins around and heads her way, and I watch as he has the same kind of discussion I had with her, before marching back my way.

"She says we should take a walk into town and make sure the guild is sending over the correct number of staff for the event and that there are no problems."

"Could we not just call them?"

Arrie shrugs. "She said to go there in person."

"Right."

I go to grab my shoes from my room and then meet Arrie by the front door, and by the time I've come back down, he's dressed in jeans, a tight-fitting t-shirt that shows off his muscular form underneath, and boots.

"Ready?"

Everything is so simple with this man, and I love that. There's no guessing what he's thinking, no weird flirting that promises something I can't obtain, and no secrets or hidden thoughts. It's so . . . relaxing.

"So," Arrie says in what I can only assume is supposed to be suggestive, "you and Con went on a . . . date?"

Ah, so that is why he's acting all moody today.

"Yeah, about that . . ." I look at him, not really sure what to say. "I'm sorry." There, I said it.

He stops halfway down the trail we're walking and looks at me. "Why?"

I sigh, walking straight past him and continuing on our way. "I'm not really sure." He jogs to catch up, and we end up walking side by side. "I didn't realize you had feelings for her, and I'm sorry if that's upsetting you."

He laughs. Like, legit laughs. And I forot how magical it sounds. To make someone laugh who doesn't usually loosen up enough to feel humor is a challenge I can spend the rest of my life puzzling out and always be fulfilled when achieved.

"I don't have feelings for Con."

"But—"

He holds up a hand. "I'm just a little off-put by her interest in you. It's not normal for her."

"Oh?"

"She's usually a sex-only kind of girl, just like the rest of us. Kind of our thing. And it's weird to see her actually falling for someone. Especially someone on the team."

"Falling?" It's my turn to laugh. "Goddess, Arrie, she's not in love with me. Stop being so stupid."

I walk a little bit ahead, trying to hide my flushed cheeks, but he grabs my arm and pulls me back into step with him. "Maybe not right now, but she looks at you differently." He gruffs and goes back to silence.

She does?

I get the sense that he doesn't want to continue talking, which is fine by me, so we walk the rest of the half hour it takes to get to the *Sheruta* guild in the center of town in silence. Not the uncomfortable kind of silence one often finds themselves in and wonders how on earth they're going to navigate an attempt at conversation, but the amicable kind two people often find when comfortability succeeds mindless conversation. And while I love Nine's endless chatter and Dea's artful communication, the peace that comes with being in the presence of this silent man is something I haven't found in the other members of the team, and I find myself rather enjoying it.

Maybe we can be friends after all.

The center of town holds the guildhall, and just behind that sits the portal building; Arrie explains that the guildhall is how the Horsemen communicate with the residents here, both when looking for new workers around the house and when needing the assistance of the magical community. The guildhall is all stone and copper plating, looking like a fancy steampunk designer got all modern with the Victorian-esque natural look of the town and settled on some fancy in-between that I have to admit looks rather quirky.

The inside is everything you would expect of a guildhall in a realm you never thought existed: grand and fantasy-like. Its interior stone buttresses that reach to the arched glass ceiling are simply phenomenal in design and remind me of the kind of architecture you find in Europe in grand, medieval buildings; each one depicts a different scene with all kinds of magical creatures showing off their powers.

Various high desks dot the scene in front of me, each one labeled so you'd have no problem distinguishing one from the other, and the one Arrie stops in front of says COMMUNITY AFFAIRS on the golden plaque. The man sitting at that desk is small, smaller than I think I've ever seen before, and he wears a brown top hat with a floppy open top that would have me laughing if I didn't catch myself in time.

"Mr. Handser." Arrie speaks in the most dignified way I've ever heard from him. It barely even sounds like him. "Just checking in to make sure all thirty-eight workers are prepared and ready for this evening. It's an important event."

The small man waves a hand at Arrie and then holds up a finger telling him to wait while his eyes, that so far have not looked up from the papers he's signing, lift slightly and startle at the sight of us. "Ah, Arrie, sir. I do apologize."

"No apologies necessary." Arrie tips his head slightly in way of thanks and stands straight.

"I spoke to the team lead for this evening this morning, and he personally assured me all thirty-seven of them will be . . ." He pauses, just noticing his error. "Thirty-eight?"

Arrie nods his head once. "Yes, thirty-eight. That is what Connie said when I left."

"You're sure?"

I step a little closer. "Yes. Thirty-eight. Heard it myself, and I have good hearing, like Connie."

The man gives me a confused look, as if to say who are you, but then backtracks on whatever he was about to say and sits back down. "I've scheduled you thirty-seven workers, as I have on the paperwork you submitted three days ago."

Arrie sighs. "Please don't make me go back to Connie with that message."

"I'm sorry." He holds up his hands. "I can't do anything this late. But you could always take a look around town and see if anyone wants some paid work for this evening?"

Arrie grumbles but concedes, and we find ourselves taking a walk around the same area of town I came shopping in all those weeks ago. It almost seems like a lifetime ago. We knock on a few doors, but most people are so startled by Arrie they can't even think, let alone offer up their evening to help us out.

I sigh as we turn our back on the fifteenth closed door. "Let's take a break." I lead us to that café from last time and order two ice-cream cakes (they sound amazing) as we sit down in the window seat.

Arrie sighs over a cup of his usual pumpkin latte, and I breathe a sigh relief over my extra-large cup of coffee. We continue our silent afternoon in the usually pleasant fashion, but Arrie seems a little tenser than earlier.

"Something wrong?"

He grumbles but doesn't say anything.

"C'mon, you might as tell me. You know I'll just annoy you until you give in."

He sighs (again), but is that a hint of a smile I see breaching the corners of his mouth? "Do you not find my company . . . unpleasant?"

I balk. "What? No. Why?"

"Most people feel the need to fill silence with conversation, and you're usually so chatty with the others."

"I like the silence with you. There's no expectation to talk or even think much of anything. I can just be. It's peaceful." I blush as I say those last words.

Arrie places his cup back on the saucer. "You find me . . . peaceful?"

"Yeah, I guess I do."

He smiles and then laughs, and I get that familiar sense of self-satisfaction I always get when I make him laugh. "Sorry, but finding the Horseman of War peaceful is . . ."

"Ridiculous?"

He nods.

"Then maybe people don't know you as well as they should."

Arrie seems to relax after that, and I'm really hoping that today and yesterday means I'm getting on the guy's good side, and we can start working on being friends.

The ice cream cakes are amazing, as is the mutually comfortable silence that ensues while we devour them.

At the counter as I go to pay, Arrie by my side with the payment chip ready, a friendly face says, "Still stayin' with the Horsemen?"

It's the baker from before, the one who made all those scrummy cakes for me and Connie on our gaming night.

"Indeed."

"What brings you out 'ere rather than exploring their mansion? Bet you haven't seen all it has to offer yet."

Arrie hands over the payment as I laugh.

"Well, we need an extra worker for tonight's party, and we were sent on an errand run, so here we are." I gesture to the two of us.

"You really need more workers?"

I nod.

"Me nephew is lookin' for some extra work to help pay for 'is wedding. I could ask?"

I look at Arrie, who smiles reassuringly in a way that I assume isn't supposed to look like a grimace. "Sure. That'd be great, actually."

The baker winks in my direction and loads up his chip's communication device before heading out back. We move aside to make way for the rest of the queue when some assistant replaces the baker. A few minutes later, he comes back out with a smiling face. "He said he'd love to 'elp. The usual party stuff, I assume?"

He directs that last question at Arrie, who nods. "Five pm start. Late finish. Working with a team of thirty-seven others."

"He'll be there. And thank you."

"Always happy to help," I call as we turn around to leave.

"You have more friends here than I do, Killer." Arrie smiles at that.

I just shrug. "It pays to have a chat with people now and then, you know."

He grumbles, and we head back in silence, satisfied that we fixed a problem we now don't have to report back to Connie. That would have been terrifying.

Chapter Thirty-Eight

Turns out, Connie's hired us a hair and makeup stylist for the afternoon of getting ready so we can look our absolute best. The guys are doing their own thing, but this lady is extravagant to say the least. She's a Fae, so that's their way, but she's a little extra. And that's putting it nicely.

"Soooo, Connie, who's your little friend here?" she asks for the hundredth time. We keep trying to evade her question, because we a) don't know my name, and b) aren't supposed to discuss who I am.

Connie sighs, and I can see by the tense set of her shoulders that she's getting tired of this conversation. "She's just a new friend, Treeb. Now please drop it."

"A new friend you haven't taken your eyes off since I started doing her hair?" She raises her painted-on eyebrows up to her gold—literally the color of gold—hairline.

Connie smiles at that, clearly satisfied that this is a conversation she can at least navigate. She looks my way with questioning eyebrows, but I do and say nothing. "We're just friends."

Ah, so she's going with completely anonymous when it comes to telling people we're slightly more than . . . friends? Okay. I'm a little disappointed, but it's hard to ask the team to admit to themselves they want more out of their relationships, much less to others. This is probably just a standard line of answering for Connie.

"That's what you always say!" Treeb removes her hand from my hair and waves it in front of Connie's face.

"And that's what I'm going to continue saying." Connie sits on the edge of the bed, hair and makeup done but otherwise in her underwear. She wants us to show off our dresses together.

I'm just thankful I've managed to learn the whole shifting thing in time, otherwise I would be navigating a suit right now. Ugh.

A knock sounds at the door, a knock neither Connie nor I hear coming (which is the most surprising part), and I startle, causing Treeb to curse and yell at me to stay still.

Connie goes to answer it, saying, "The room is spelled to keep any and all sound out so I can sleep. Only Nine's telepathy can get through."

I go to nod, but one warning look from Treeb tells me I probably shouldn't if I value the current length of my hair. She held those scissors to Connie's hair with some force, and therefore, I don't let her anywhere near mine with them.

Dea comes in, not the least bit perturbed by Connie's underwear look (he's probably seen it all before; probably even taken it off a time or two), but stops dead when he sees me in a chair in nothing but my thin silk bathrobe. "Er," he stumbles, clearly not really sure what to say. "This is for you." He holds out a beautiful suit, and I sigh.

"I'm going like this, Dea." I roll my eyes.

"Yes, but when you change, you want to fit in, right?"

He's being cryptic, and Treeb clearly gets the not-supposed-to-know-anything message, as she blatantly ignores the conversation and continues working on my hair.

"I guess."

Connie grabs it from him and ushers him out of the room. "I'll make sure she looks great in both. Now get!" She shoves him a little harder than I would have expected, and he lands on his ass outside the bedroom door, where she slams the door in his face.

She hangs the suit on the back of the door, and I guess I will be navigating a suit after all. Fucking hell.

By the time Treeb's done and left and Connie and I have helped each other into our gowns, I have to change form and start the styling all over again.

Connie sighs exasperatedly. "God, you're lucky Fae look good anyway. Otherwise getting you ready for anything would take all bloody day."

She's applying some gel she stole from Nine to my hair, and I just let her get to work. We can't ask Treeb to do it without raising suspicion.

"Time for the suit." She grimaces, noticing how many golden buttons the front has. "This is gonna be a fucking nightmare, ain't it?"

"You're two thousand years old and you don't know how to put on a suit?"

"I know how." She folds her arms across her chest in defiance. "But I'm not the fluid Horseman here. I've never put one on myself."

"Good. Because I have no fucking clue."

She sighs and starts picking apart the suit, piece by piece, placing each section on me from the underwear up. Eventually, and after about half an hour of cursing and prodding, I'm ready to go.

"Change back and forth for me."

She steps back, and I focus on relaxing and changing my form, managing to turn back into my female-self with ease (well, with about five minutes of concentrating). As it turns out, my look from earlier has survived the shifting. Must shift into whatever look my other form had on previously.

"Good." Connie holds out her arm, and I tuck mine around hers as we head out of her room.

We descend the fancy stairs, where all three guys wait for us, and I manage to have my first fairy-tale ball moment as they all stare at us—me in particular—with open mouths. Even Arrie's eyes linger on my face without a scowl longer than usual, but it isn't long before he rips his gaze away and rests it on Connie's beautiful smile beside me.

Arrie whisks Connie off, muttering how beautiful she looks into her ear so no one can hear it—though I clearly can—and I'm left with Nine and Dea, who wait on either side of me when I get to the bottom of the stairs, both holding out their arms.

Dea wraps his left arm underneath my right while leaning in and whispering, "You look beautiful, Angel."

Nine, on the other hand, wraps his right arm underneath my left and mentally whispers, *You'll be turning heads tonight, Sweetie. Even Arrie stumbled at the sight of you.*

"He was probably stumbling at the sight of Connie, Nine. Trust me on that."

He gives me a look that says he's not believing a word out of my mouth. Dea, thankfully, stays out of the conversation, as he often does where Nine and I are concerned. It's nice that he gives us time to just be . . . friends. In fact, they're all pretty good at sharing time with each other. Guess practice makes perfect.

Nine and Dea are both dressed in suits that match them perfectly. Nine's wearing a dark brown suit with a red tie and an off-white shirt, while Dea is sporting a Victorian-style black suit that has a floral design in black silk covering its entirety, matched with a top hat, pocket watch chain, fancy black cane with a gold head, and a frilly vest-y neck thing that matches his pocket's hanky thing.

Goddess, this suit nonsense is ridiculous. But he looks very Dea-like, and only he can pull off a suit like that. Being around him, especially dressed like this, is like being around someone pulled straight out of a Victorian romance novel. It's all very swoon-worthy, and by the smug look on his face, he damn well knows it.

"What do you look like in yours?" Nine asks, a slight blush creeping across his cheeks.

"My suit?" I turn my head his way, making sure I understand the question.

"Yeah." He scratches his head in befuddlement and adjusts his suit jacket for the third time since walking down the hallway. He clearly hates wearing suits.

"You'll see later. I'm most likely going to be changing back and forth all damn evening. So, if you wanted to hang out with any particular version of me, just watch out for the magically sex-changing person in the room." I roll my eyes, trying not to let my sarcasm drown my voice.

While I'm comfortable in both forms—a comfortability that came surprisingly quickly—and I know the team have adjusted well so far, I have yet to see the general public's reaction. Historically speaking, the general populace are not ones to be well-adjusted to categorical things such as this.

"Try not to let it bother you, Angel. We like both your forms." He gestures to Nine when he says we and gives me a wink.

Ah, I see where he's going with that. I wonder which form they prefer? I mean, I can really use that to my advantage if I'm serious about bringing the team together.

That's just mean.

Using every tool at your disposal is not mean. It's just being clever. You use your telepathy to flirt with me all the time.

Fair point, he says in an amused tone.

We get to the archway that signals the entrance to the ballroom, and I pause. The room is full of people—not too full, just enough to make it look like a fancy ball without it being too crowded. Some make small talk on the fringes, some hide out in the shadowy corners the candle flames don't illuminate but my Vampire eyesight can identify, but most of the crowd are dancing. And not just any kind of dancing, but ballroom dancing.

I . . . er . . . don't think I can dance.

"It's okay. We didn't expect you to."

"What is the matter, Angel? You looked perturbed?" Dea spins me around to face him, and the sight of those galaxy eyes lit by the iridescent candles makes me take a gasp.

Nine comes up behind me and sandwiches me between them, and I'm acutely aware of a few people near the entrance watching us.

"I can't dance. I don't think. At least not like that."

Dea ponders for a moment. "Hmmm." He brings a hand to his chin in thought and leans in closer. "Then, I will just have to teach you."

"Wha—?"

But before I can finish the question, he whisks me away to the center of the dancefloor and stops. "Place your left hand on my shoulder and your right on my arm."

I do as instructed, hoping no one can hear us—well, no one but Nine and Connie.

He places a hand on the small of my back and another on my shoulder. "Just follow me and try not to step on my toes."

I restrain a laugh, but he smiles anyway. "For future reference, you guys should tell me when I need to do stuff like this, so I can practice and not make a fool of myself."

"Duly noted."

He moves us around in circles on the spot for a bit, before he moves to the center of the dancefloor, weaving in and out of other couples who apparently know exactly what they're doing, and I only step on his toes a few times. Mostly, I use my Vampire speed to keep up with his fancy footwork.

I don't take my eyes off of his, though, and by the time the music's changed, I find myself not wanting to let go of this beautiful man.

"Could we dance some more?"

"Of course." He smiles at me, and we continue in a different style of dance that suits the new song.

The music's being played by a group of fairies and Fae who each hold different types of instruments, switching them between songs so they can get the right texture. This one is more of a stringed song, and is being played by some violins, a harp, and cello, with a beautiful female singer at the front whose voice holds magic within her notes. Or, at least, it sounds that way. But I'm pretty sure no such magic exists.

Someone comes up behind me when we stop and coughs.

Turning around, I notice Nine holding out his arm. "May

I have this dance?"

"Of course." I look to Dea, who looks at us both and turns to walk away.

Nine watches him leave and says, "He's an amazing dancer. Not quite as good as Arrie, but he fits the mood more for these types of things."

"Wait. Hold up. Arrie can dance?"

"Sure." Nine smiles. "He even incorporates it into his morning workouts, I believe."

Oh, that's right. He did seem rather flowing and dancelike when I watched him that time. It'd be great to dance with him sometime.

He'd ask you if you ever let him.

"No, he won't. But that's okay." I take a deep breath and let Nine waltz me around the dancefloor, careful to avoid any of the other dancing pairs. "We've managed an amicable, working friendship, I think. That'll do for now."

"Friendship, 'ey?"

"I damn well hope so. At the least, he doesn't seem angry with me as much."

"Well, that's progress."

We continue to dance for a few more songs, and just like with Dea, the attractive man in front of me dazzles, but unlike with Dea, Nine knows it. He knows that I find the way the light bounces off his red hair to be enrapturing, and so he circles us more toward the candlelight, and he knows that I enjoy being pressed up against him in some of the closer sections, so he presses me flush at every chance he gets.

He knows exactly what I like about him, and it makes it hard not to fall into his every step and move, to become enthralled by his presence and send myself into a daze of lust and . . . feelings.

Just when I think the evening is going great, Dea steps up behind me and places a hand on my shoulder. "It is time, Angel."

I wince and step away from them both, nodding. It's time to show the world that the Fifth Horseman really exists. I can do this. Right? I mean, nothing bad is going to happen this night? No one's going to try to attack me for simply existing?

Dea takes me by the arm while Nine follows, and we head for the stage. Connie and Arrie join us moments later, and we send the musicians off the stage while Dea takes to the microphone. He's been visible for all of one hour, and he doesn't have much time left to enjoy it. The sooner we get this part over with, the sooner he can enjoy the party.

"Thank you for joining us here tonight," Dea announces.

Everyone turns toward us and crowds around the stage.

"You might be wondering why we gathered the heads of the magical and non-magical communities together in one place, especially since it has not been done in quite some time." Dea gestures to me, and I come to stand by his side, the rest of the team forming an arc behind us. "We have an important announcement to make."

Everyone's silent—even I hold my breath. But looking over the crowd, I can't recognize many faces, other than the ones I met on the mission and Kally from earlier in a bright orange dress that perfectly matches the color of her lips. I recognize most of the Vampire Royal Council, including the three princes I've met, and I recognize all the Witch's Coven, but I note that the seer is missing.

"Nine months ago, the team was made aware of a special someone who recently died. We would like to introduce you to the Fifth Horseman, the Horseman of Magic."

Everyone's stunned silent for a moment, but the whispers

and gasps erupt seconds later, and before we know it, everyone is shouting questions. The biggest being why did we lie to them all recently.

Dea hushes everyone and continues. "We apologize for lying on our recent travels, but we wanted to get a feel for things before people made the connection. Horsemen are only born when there is a need."

What few whispers there are die instantly.

"That is right. War is coming. A war requiring the Horsemen of the Apocalypse—all five of us—to fix. We have been keeping things steady for years, but for some reason, Fate decided we needed extra help."

"How do you know she's the Fifth Horseman?" someone from the crowd shouts. By the looks of his golden eyes, I would say he's a Shifter.

"That," Nine says as he grabs the microphone from Dea, "is why we waited to have this ball. We wanted to her to be able to show you her powers for herself."

Everyone nods their agreement, clearing seeing the logic, and I get the impression it's time for me to do my thing.

Dea and Nine step back, allowing me to take center stage. I don't want to give a speech, so I don't. Instead, I produce my first power: air magic. I can't access the rest of the elements yet, but I can still create a whirlwind that sends the room into darkness and start a mini-tornado above the crowd's heads.

The candles are quickly relit—I assume by some fire Witch—and I focus on the memory of blood and feeding to produce my fangs.

The audience gasps, and I know I look like a less-pale Vampire hybrid.

I sit on the floor, cross-legged as much as I can in this dress, and breathe. I hear the crowd growing restless as they wait for something to happen, and murmuring conversations start up a couple of minutes in. I want to yell at them to shut the hell up, but I know it won't help. What will help is changing form.

Eventually, after minutes of insufferable inner-peace finding, I feel the familiar tug of my magic changing my form. I don't vomit (thank the goddess), but I do revel in the gasps and audible what-the-hells from the audience.

Using Fae magic, I bring a few of the candles from the wall to me in midair and dance them above everybody's heads. I hope that's enough and that the lack of wind will distinguish it enough from my earlier magic. But it's the next display of powers that has them leaping back and shouting yells of surprise.

I first shift into a wolf, then my preferred form of a panther, then into a couple of birds I've mastered, and then into a few insects—of which, Nine gathers me into his palm to demonstrate I haven't just vanished into thin air.

Coming back into my male form—and then returning back to my female form—the questions begin.

"So, she's . . . he's one of us? All of us?"

"Do we refer to her and a she or a he?"

"She belongs nowhere, then?"

"Does she have an allegiance?"

Dea steps forward with the microphone once more. "Please, enough. We understand this is troubling. We understand that having someone who is clearly meant to balance you all is a threat to quite a few ways of life in this room." He takes a deep breath. "You know us. We would not threaten you or your way of life unnecessarily. We have served and helped you for two millennia. That has not changed."

A few heads nod, clearly agreeing with Dea, but a few

look disgruntled, angry almost, and it's those faces I try to memorize. Those are the people we have to worry about.

Chapter Thirty-Nine

Half an hour later, Dea takes me by the hand and leads me out of the ballroom and into the house—the part of the house guests can't enter. The team's home.

He takes a deep breath, and I can see the physical exertion being visible for so long has had on him: he's donned a light sheet of sweat on his forehead, and his skin is paler than usual.

"Dea?" He looks at me from his place on the kitchen chair. "You can go back to being invisible for a while here. Please, don't exert yourself."

He chuckles lightly. "Do not worry yourself over such an insignificant problem, Angel. I am fine."

"Don't be a fucking idiot. Just relax for a moment." I place a hand on his shoulder and squeeze hard enough it causes him to wince but light enough that I don't actually cause any serious pain. "Turn. It. Off."

He sighs. "Fine." Taking a deep breath, he exhales, and the color returns to his cheeks almost immediately, and his eyes sparkle brighter. "There."

I give a firm nod and remove my hand. "That's better." Taking the chair beside him, I place a hand on his knee. "You okay?"

"Just needed a moment."

Then why bring me?

It'll probably be best to give him his moment and remain silent, hoping he'll appreciate it as much as Arrie and I do.

"You were amazing this evening, Angel."

"Thank you."

"Are you enjoying yourself?"

"It's . . . amazing." I smile. "I never thought I'd be in a scenario like this."

"When all this is over"—he lowers his gaze to me—"I am going to show you the world, show you a life worth living forever. It is not all doom and gloom."

"That sounds nice. Can the others join us?"

He chuckles. "Yes, of course. If you would like."

"I would."

"Even Arrie?"

I sigh. "Assuming our current peace keeps up forever, then yes."

"Is he included in your so-called plan Nine mentioned?"

I wince. "He told you about that?"

Dea stays silent but grabs me by the hand and leads me through various hallways; clearly there isn't a destination, but we continue walking nonetheless.

"If I am honest, the thought has crossed my mind before. But I was not sure it would work." We stop outside my bedroom door, and he pins me where I stand with those wanderlust eyes and pushes me up against the door. "But everything is different now." His voice turns husky, and it makes me shiver in anticipation.

He has me locked between his two arms, palms spread out on the door beside my head.

"How?"

"Because we have you."

He leans closer, and I can't help but lean out to meet him halfway. His presence is overbearing, and his smoky lavender scent has my head spinning in various directions; logic is all but evaporating from my brain, leaving just the curiosity and building need for a man I've wanted for weeks but couldn't have.

His lips crash against mine, and I sigh in relief. All of my need and desire spilling over. But this isn't a quick or gentle kiss, this is Dea full of need and passion that I didn't realized he held for me unleashing all at once. He pins me to the door with his body, his hips trapping my lower torso to the wood behind me, and trails one hand down my waist, where he slips it behind to rest on the small of my back, and presses my body against his. His other hand rests behind my head, pulling my lips closer to his until we're a tangle of passion.

When he slips his tongue across my lower lip, tingling need shoots through my body. Dea takes advantage of the distraction and slides his tongue into my mouth to meet mine, and I can't help but buckle slightly, feeling weak at the knees. Dea catches me, of course, and pins me to the door once more.

I groan, making his hand in my hair grip tighter.

But I need more. I can feel his growing erection pressing into my lower stomach, and the hot need growing there matches my own. I need more. More of him. More of this. My thighs shift, trying to gain any kind of friction to release the growing tension.

Dea notices and lets out a small chuckle as we break for

air. But the spell doesn't break with it; instead, I grab his shirt and yank him forward, slamming my mouth against his once more and lifting my hands to tangle in his hair.

He groans into the kiss, causing my hands to travel under his shirt and trace all the lines of his muscles, gently raking my nails down his front to the hem of his pants.

His hands travel south to my ass, and before I know it, he's lifting me up against the door and wrapping my legs around his waist, my core lining up with that delicious heat of his.

"Dea," I warn, breaking the kiss suddenly.

He places a finger on my lips. "Shhhh. Relax. We are not going there today. Just enjoy the moment with me."

I nod. Honestly, I'm done holding back with this man. Everything about him draws me in, and he currently has me backed up against my bedroom door, legs wrapped around his middle as he holds my weight with a single hand on my ass, leaving the other free to roam. He well and truly has me pinned.

I can feel his cock pressing against my clit gently, not moving but creating a whirlwind of pressure I need to release lest I explode. I buck my hips against him, and he groans in response, pulling away from my face slightly as he looks at me in question.

"Dea . . . Please."

I've lost all sense of the plan, all sense of what I feel is wrong and right in that moment, and am driven by something far less logical.

My hips continue to grind against him, and I watch him struggle to retain control; what I wouldn't give to watch this man break that carefully mastered control, to watch him come undone by my hand.

He places needy kisses along my jaw and down my neck,

landing in a sensitive spot on the crook of my neck that has me moaning his name on a gasp of air.

"Dea . . ."

"Angel . . ." he gasps. "I want nothing more than to hear you moaning my name all night, but I know that is not what you want right now."

Lowering me to the floor and pulling away, he looks at me with pained restraint. I'm disappointed but thankful one of us is able to use our brains in a logical manner.

"I . . . I'm sorry." I look to the floor, embarrassment flooding my features. I can't believe I just did that.

Dea grabs my chin and lifts it to meet his eyes. "Do not apologize. You are amazing." He bores those galaxy eyes into mine, and I understand what he means; he wants me to know that he enjoyed himself, too.

He grabs my hand and leads me back to the party, where we quickly break apart and rejoin the fun.

I stand at the edge of the ballroom, Dea having vanished the moment we entered the first thrall of people, where I'm hidden in the shadows only few can see. I change into my male form as I watch the party—specifically, I watch Connie and Arrie dance the night away. I've never seen her smile so brightly, nor have I seen Arrie so relaxed. I have to wonder if it's Connie causing that reaction or the dancing. Maybe a bit of both?

"Hey, Sweetie. Watcha doing way out here?"

"Observing." I have a glass of champagne in hand, though I'm only drinking it because everyone else is—have to at least try to fit in.

Nine stands beside me and looks down my line of sight. "Ah. Observing Connie?"

"Observing them both, really. Not in a bad way, just in a

curious one."

"What's so curious about them that has you hiding in the dark to observe them?"

He grabs my champagne and downs it in one before leaving the glass on a server's tray that floats past, courtesy of Fae magic.

"Nothing I want to voice. Nothing to be concerned about."

"This about your plans for the future of the team by any chance?"

I look at him and have to quickly look away. "Maybe." I cough out the tension in my throat. "It's just a fantasy. But an entertaining one."

"I don't know. You have a way of just existing that's intoxicating. The way you think so freely about emotions and love is almost beautiful. You're also annoyingly stubborn. Don't peg it as a fantasy just yet."

That's saying a lot more than normal for Nine. He knows everyone's thoughts and feelings, usually before they know them themselves, so, if he thinks I stand a chance in the long run—of making myself and the team happy—then I have an honest chance.

"Besides," he continues, "I like the effect you're having on us."

I look at him confused, but he doesn't elaborate, and I get the feeling he's referring to his private conversation with Dea. I wonder what the damn hell they talked about after I left, but I don't want to ask and ruin anything, and if Nine wants me to know, he'll tell me.

"Let's get some air, shall we?" Nine takes my arm just like he did when I was in my female form and leads me through the edges of the crowd and out onto the balcony that leads to some stairs I didn't noticed before.

We descend with ease and enter a secluded section of the garden I've never been in. "Where are we?"

"It's just a cute, cut-off section of the garden. You can only get here through the ballroom."

"Ah, I see."

"There are more nooks and hiding places in this house than you'll be able to fully explore in the next hundred years, trust me."

"It's like a child's hide-and-seek dream."

He laughs and slips an arm around my waist. "That it would be."

I raise an eyebrow. "Never once had a child here? Not even a child of one of the cleaners or servants?"

"God, no. Children are . . . difficult."

Now it's my turn to laugh, and I stop us at a water fountain shaped like a pair of doves to do just that. "Seriously?" I wipe a tear from my eye. "You're the Horseman of Famine, and you're uncomfortable around children?" I can't stop laughing, and I kinda feel bad, but the scenario is ridiculous. "It's just so . . . You fight wars and basically run the world, but children are a step too far?"

Nine smiles, clearly finding my amusement funny. "They're just not something I have an awful lot of practice with."

He turns away from me slightly, and I get the feeling he's a little offended by my laughing, so I turn him back around and make him face me. "Is everything okay? Did I upset you? I'm sorry—"

He holds up a hand. "No. You didn't upset me. Sorry."

"Then, what—?"

He doesn't let me finish that question, as he leans forward

and presses the gentlest kiss to my lips, hard enough to leave a slight tingle that has me brushing my thumb over its shadow, but light enough that I would have barely felt it had I not known what he was doing.

Grabbing my arm once more, he continues walking us around the garden, past more fairy patches, glowing flowers, singing vines, and a few more fountains shaped like various pairs of mated birds, and I have to admit that this is turning into the perfect night.

Dancing with Dea, then Nine, showing off my powers was nerve-wracking, but making out with Dea was something else, and then watching Connie and Arrie having a good time and coming out here. It's all so . . .

Romantic?

"Yes."

"These things are supposed to feel like that. It was the main form of socializing for the upper classes at one point. Romances were made, flings were had . . . They were a thing of the time, I guess."

"Do you miss it?"

"The time?"

I nod.

"Yes and no. Time moves on, and each new era is more interesting than the last."

"It's something I'm looking forward to. Being able to see how the world evolves and moves." I snake my arm around his waist and move closer (a little more confident now I know for sure he likes this form, too). "There will be things that are hard"—my mind instantly goes to having no family and being alone for so long—"but just for this evening, I want to focus on the things I'm looking forward to. I'll deal with the rest later."

"You have all the time in the world, Sweetie." Nine shuffles on his feet and looks from me to the fountain. "Erm . . . sorry to change the subject, but how are your nightmares?"

I blanch and take a step back. "Ho-how . . . ?" He taps his head, as if to remind me he can read minds, and I sigh. "They're okay," I whisper. Now that I think about it, I haven't really had any since before we went to Earth. "They've stopped. For now." But I get the feeling they'll come back, and when they do, I'll have to deal with them.

"When they do," Nine says on a low whisper, "I can help."

I look at him with a puzzled expression, silently asking him how.

"I can enter people's dreams and help guide them through. Eventually, we might be able to pinpoint the problem and try to stop them altogether."

"Entering people's dreams?" That's . . . absurd. Out of all the things I've seen this team do, that is the most insane. Well, it's definitely up there.

Nine nods. "I don't often do it because it's so invasive, but I can if you ever need my help." He grabs my hand and looks me in the eyes. "Don't hide your problems because of some sense of duty to the world. I care." He gestures to the house, where the team are probably still dancing away. "We care."

I don't know what to say to that, so I just nod. Hoping to convey my gratitude with a kiss to the cheek rather than words.

Chapter Forty

"Well, well, well. Look who we have here," someone's deep baritone voice penetrates the darkness. Out of the corner of my eye, I see a trio of people dressed in fancy suits walking toward us—armed with magiguns (because of course).

Nine grabs my arm and pushes me behind him, causing me to roll my eyes. "Really?"

They're from that same Vampire clan that attacked us in New Orleans.

Wait, what? They are?

They descend a few feet to stand in front of us as more than a dozen other people—Vampires, I now realize—come out from the shadows.

How did I not see them?

I step out from behind Nine to stand at his side, wishing like hell I had some kind of weaponry in this bloody suit. If it's gonna restrict my movements, I should at least be able to kick some ass with a few throwing knives.

"What do you want?" Nine asks, going to step forward

once again and in front of me, but I stop him by yanking his arm backward.

"Her." The Vampire in front jerks his chin toward me. "Or him." Waving a hand in the air, he says, "Or whatever it wants to be called."

"It?" I ask, surprised I've been deemed less than human already. "I am not an *it*, you overgrown bat."

Nine snickers beside me, but his face remains serious. "Yeah," he says, "that's not happening."

I've alerted everyone else.

Good. Now be careful and move out of my way.

He raises an eyebrow at me but steps to the side just in time to avoid me shifting into a panther.

The Vampires balk but stand straight and face me. They're brave, I'll give them that. But bravery is often stupid.

I leap off the ground and swipe a paw at the leader's face, gouging an eye out in the process. We tumble to the ground, but he manages to get off a shot from his magigun in time to send me sprawling backward and crashing into Nine.

"Get off!" He shouts from beneath me.

When I move, he sucks in a deep breath of air and jumps to his feet in a quick jump.

Stay out of my line of sight.

Okay.

I stand behind him, with every Vampire in front, and he raises his hand in the air and mutters something under his breath I can't hear.

Every Vampire in front of us stops dead in their tracks, but the leader just looks at Nine and smiles. "Not gonna work, Famine. Sorry."

"What?" I hear him gasp. "Ho-how?"

The leader pulls out a silver leaf from his pocket and

crumbles it into dust to let it fly in the wind.

"For fuck's sake," Nine grumbles. "Should never had told them that."

"Silver Vine. Telepathy blocker," the leader answers as he looks at me, clearly responding to my confused face.

Telepathy blocker? Wow. That must really piss Nine off.

You have no fucking idea, Sweetie. I'm unarmed, you can't change back into your other form to use your air magic while under attack, and your Fae magic is too untrained to be useful.

Ah. We're fucking screwed, aren't we?

You'd think two of the Five Horsemen couldn't go down like this.

We're not going down, stop being ridiculous.

I shift into a falcon and swoop toward the back of the Vampires and claw out a few more eyes, hoping if they can't see, it'll give us some kind of advantage. The leader only has one eye now, and honestly, seeing the socket bleed all down his face is more satisfying than I expected.

Dea, Connie, and Arrie are on their way, so we just have to hold them off long enough. But where's Dea? Why hasn't he fazed here?

No idea. But it can't be good. He's not responding.

I grumble but shift back into human beside Nine, hoping for some kind of princess rescue from Connie. She'll slay these fuckers into pieces if they even try to mess with the team, and I'll laugh alongside her.

Damn. You two are dark.

We have seventeen Vampires in front of us, each of them armed with magiguns—although my last wound healed when I shifted—the leader only has one eye left, and a few of the others are blind, but otherwise, we're still where we started.

The leader steps forward, aiming his magigun straight at me. "This won't kill ya, but it will cause some damage.

Hopefully you'll come along quietly after."

The rest of the Vampires crowd around Nine, and between them all, they have him pinned against the fountain.

Fuck! Run!

But if I turn around now—in my non-Vampire speed form—I'll likely get shot.

I stand with my hands in the air for a few moments, trying to think of what to do. But, really, there's only one thing I can do. Fight.

I spread my arms wide and imagine my body turning into a bear. I've never tried it before, but desperate times and all that.

A roar escapes my lips as my body twists into its new form, and I have no time to check if I managed it because I have to jump out of the way of the Vampire's magigun, and I barrel into him from the side.

The Vampire goes sprawling with a twist but quickly gets back up again. Vampires are fast healers, and they're pretty strong, so it'll take a lot to bring this guy down. If I were in my other form, I could just blow him away or rip his throat out, but in this form, I'm limited to Shifter abilities.

I need to fucking work on my Fae powers when this all blows over. Would be great to know a few destructive spells right now.

"You fucking bitch!" the Vampire snarls. A few of his cronies step forward to try to help, but he holds his hand up. "Nah, I got this."

Raising his magigun once again, I shift into a bird and flit around his head, hoping to minimize my target size and stay on the move.

"C'mon, bitch. Fight like a man. Stop being a coward!"

Does he really think that'll work? The whole world can

call me a coward if it saves my life.

He takes a shot and clips my wing, sending me spiraling to the ground, but I shift back into a panther just in time. The wound heals almost instantly, and I leap onto the fucking asshole, hoping to do some damage with my claws.

"Taylor!" someone shouts from the distance. "Taylor!" A man leaps from the balcony and shifts midair into a panther, landing right beside me.

Who is he?

I can see Nine slumped on the fountain with blood trailing down his face. Nine! He looks unconscious, and likely has been for a few minutes, but that's ridiculous considering the rate at which we heal.

The new panther snarls and leaps at the Vampire, and I follow suit. He takes down that Vampire leader with a single swipe to the face, clawing his head clean off his shoulders.

Fuck me! I'm glad to have this guy on my side. His panther form is three times the size of mine, and right now, I'm glad for it.

I leap into the fray of the dozen or so Vampires guarding Nine and snarl, swipe, and claw at as many of them as I can. None of them go down, and I realize just how fucking untrained I am. But a few of them step back, leaving themselves open for the new panther to dispatch.

If Nine were armed, he could help.

As if my wish has been heard, Nine leaps to his feet and steals a magigun from one of the Vampires and takes out three in a row quicker than I can blink.

Damn. You're amazing.

Thank you, he winces. He slinks to the ground beside the fountain.

He's hurt.

Why aren't his wounds healing?

I shift back into human form and crouch beside him. "Nine?"

The other panther shifts into a man, and I concentrate enough to shift into my female form so I can at least try to help heal Nine with my semi-Vampire blood. I rip open my wrist and let it pool into his mouth, watching as it slides down his throat.

Please, please, please let this work.

Nothing happens.

"What isn't it working?"

"He's been shot with these bullets," the man says as he holds one up to the moonlight to it. "They're made with Silver Vine leaves. Toxic to Famine in particular. Seems this was planned."

I take a good look at the man's face as he holds up on of those bullets and recognize him, but I can't quite place where from.

What? I almost shriek but refrain.

"Taylor?"

Is he speaking to me?

"Who's Taylor?"

He looks at me with surprise. "You are."

My breath refuses to come out, but one more look at a struggling Nine and I know I have to take him to Dea. "C'mon," I say as I scoop Nine up and carry him bridal-style back into the ballroom.

I'm met with gasps and murmurs as I walk through the double doors, but nothing is more shocking than Connie, Dea, and Arrie stopping their dancing to turn around in shock.

"You've been dancing?" My outrage clearly takes them by

surprise. "We needed you!"

Arrie is the first to understand what's happened. "Everyone out! Go home!" His voice carries like nothing I've ever heard, booming across the doomed room.

Guests clear away in a hurry, leaving the ballroom empty except for us five and my mystery savior.

"What happened?" Dea asks as he takes in Nine's body slumped in my arms and tries to grab him from me. But I refuse to let go. "What. Happened?"

Eventually, I let his body go to Dea. "We were ambushed by the same Vampires from New Orleans. They're all dead in the garden."

Arrie raises an eyebrow at me in question.

"Not me. Him." I jerk a thumb back to the mystery savior and kneel beside Nine, who's now lying at Dea's feet.

Everyone looks up at the Shifter behind me and stands stock still.

Connie steps forward with an outstretched hand. "Mr. Compton. We are in your debt."

He shakes his head. "Anything for Taylor." He gestures to me, and everyone immediately shuts up.

I stand, really needing some answers from this guy. "You keep calling me that. You . . . knew me?"

"Very well." He grabs a glass of champagne from a floating tray nearby and comes back to join us. "You are Taylor Angelis. You are—were—last of the Angel-descended Witches. And my goddaughter."

I balk, my eyes going wide. "No."

Connie comes to rest a hand on my shoulder. "It's oka—"

"No!" I shrug her hand off my shoulder and walk up to this Mr. Compton guy. "Tell me everything." I grab him by the shirt collar and yank him to me. "Now."

He nods.

Dea's healing Nine as best he can while Connie stays by my side as I sink to the floor, needing to feel the stability of something solid.

He's about to tell me everything.

"Taylor Angelis, last of the Angel-descended Witches. You were born twenty-five years ago to your parents, who loved you dearly. Your powers grew stronger and stronger by the day, and before everyone knew it, you could kill with a single touch. Your parents were both Angel descendants, too, but they didn't possess your level of power. Unfortunately, word got out in the magical community, and the SC sent a hit out on you. But when the hunters came, they killed both your parents. You alone survived."

"How?"

The man looks to Dea, but Dea's so focused on Nine he isn't even listening to the story. "Your mother gave you an invisibility charm, one of very few in existence. It hid you until it was safe."

That grabs Dea's attention. He looks to me and then to Mr. Compton, and just shakes his head, uttering, "It's a small world."

"That was your charm, wasn't it?"

He nods and continues working on Nine. He needs a lot more healing than usual, and I can see it's taking a lot out of Dea, who's starting to sweat and go pale like earlier.

"I took you to a Witch community and set you up with some friends of mine. They looked after you, loved you."

"Why do I get the feeling there's more to this story?"

He grimaces. "You had a difficult start to life. You hated magic with a vengeance. You refused to use yours, despite the good it could do, and grew up a normal human, for all intents and purposes. But it didn't stay that way. One day you came to me with some news I didn't like. I didn't say anything back then, but now I wish I had."

"What aren't you saying? Just spit it out!" My hands ball into fists, shaking and clenching in the cooling air.

"Taylor . . . You were a hunter for the SC. The only supernatural in their employ."

I laugh, not really sure if I should be upset, infuriated, or if this is a joke. "There's no way I was a hunter. They take people to the SC for prosecution, often to be killed."

He nods.

"You're serious?"

He nods again, his eyes looking straight at mine.

No. It can't be . . . "I killed supernaturals—my own kind—for a living?"

Arrie grumbles something that sounds like, "Told you you were a killer."

I throw myself at him before anyone can stop me. I ball my fist and throw a right hook to his face, sending him flying across the room. "I am not a killer."

Connie takes one look at me and flinches, turning around. Ugh. Great. Between Nine's blood and the anger, my fangs have come out.

"Sweetie . . ."

"Nine!" I turn around and run to him. "Nine." I grab his hand, holding it to mine. "Are you okay?"

He nods and places a hand on my cheek. "Oh, Sweetie, what you were isn't relevant. None of us cares."

I flick my gaze toward Arrie, and he flinches and storms out of the room.

"Even him." Nine coughs as hesits up, and Dea holds his weight. "Promise."

I'm weak. I haven't fed in days, and the scent of Nine's blood is everywhere. No one's in the right shape to help me with that right now, so I take a shuddering breath and try to rein myself in, trying—in vain—to retract my fangs so I can turn back around and smile at Connie.

But it isn't enough. I've used lots of magic in the fight, and unlike when I first started using my powers, I'm now used to the extra power blood gives me. It has, without me realizing it, become my new norm.

"Fuck it," I mumble as I sprint to my rooms, away from everyone else, where I lock myself in my library, vowing to stay until I can be bothered to come out.

"Fuck!" I kick a stack of books and watch them fall to the ground in a splutter. "I was a hunter."

Ackowledgements

Hey readers! Thank you for making it this far and for being an important part of Magic's journey. If you enjoyed my book, please do consider leaving a review. Every one is like a golden nugget.

Writing this book has been a tough journey so far. I have to admit, handling a character so fluid has not been an easy feat. But it has been worth it to explore something so integral to our society and asking questions I wouldn't otherwise have thought to ask. Getting to know the genderfluid and transgender community has been an absolute blessing, and I thank you for being brave enough to openly exist, to answer my often sily questions, and for sharing your experiences with me. You have all been a part of this character's development.

When I first started writing this book, it was simply because I love the genre and wanted to write my own. It was fun playing with such a complex romance with so many moving parts. But it became something more than that pretty early on. I've never seen sexual fluidity in a book before, and that is something I wanted to change. So for that reason, I created a poly relationship between five characters who are all sexually fluid, with a central character whose sex (and eventually gender as the series continues) is also fluid.

I wanted to take the time to thank my writing buddies, who have had to deal with my incessant questions, to my friends and family, who have had to put up with my bubbly excitement for the last year and half, and to my husband, who has had to deal with the ups and downs of writing, editing, and publishing. It's never easy. But you all make it worth it.

About the Author

Freida Kilmari is a writer, editor, and author from south-west England, with a love of fantasy and romance. After graduating Plymouth University in 2017, she created her editing business and focused on her writing. This is the first fantasy romance she's released, and she hopes to release many more.

www.ingramcontent.com/pod-product-compliance
Lightning Source LLC
Chambersburg PA
CBHW011147190726
48288CB00010B/3205